THE GIRLS OF ENNISMORE

A sweeping heartrending saga

Ireland, 1900. Two girls meet. They are from vastly different worlds, but will be united in friendship through loves, losses and wars. It's the early years of the twentieth century, and Victoria Bell and Rosie Killeen are best friends. Growing up in rural Ireland's County Mayo, their friendship is forged against the glorious backdrop of Ennismore House. However, Victoria, born of the aristocracy, and Rosie, daughter of a local farmer, both find that the disparity of their class and the simmering social tension in Ireland will push their friendship to the brink...

THE GIRLS OF ENNISMORE

THE GIRLS OF ENNISMORE

by

Patricia Falvey

Magna Large Print Books
Long Preston, North Yorkshire,
BD23 4ND, England.

British Library Cataloguing in Publication Data.

A catalogue record of this book is
available from the British Library

ISBN 978-0-7505-4510-5

First published in e-book in Great Britain in 2016 by Corvus
an imprint of Atlantic Books Ltd.

Published in Large Print 2018 by arrangement with
Atlantic Books

Magna Large Print is an imprint of Library Magna Books Ltd.

Printed and bound in Great Britain by
T.J. (International) Ltd., Cornwall, PL28 8RW

For Aunt Nan

PART ONE

SCHOOLDAYS

1900–1910

CHAPTER 1

The sun was not yet up when eight-year-old Rosie Killeen pulled the door of her family cottage closed behind her and stood shivering in the morning chill. Usually she enjoyed venturing out alone in the early hours but this morning was different. Anxiously, she looked around for her friend – a young black and white collie with a bent ear. Only when he trotted up beside her and sniffed her hand did she begin to walk.

Taking a deep breath, she set off barefoot down over the shadowy fields, her new lace-up boots tucked securely under one arm. Cows peered over low stone walls, watching her with limpid curiosity. Broody hens warbled as they squatted on their eggs while an angry rooster, his morning call pre-empted, followed her for a time, pecking at her feet.

She slowed her pace as she neared the narrow, rutted road that separated the Killeen farm from the Ennis estate. The bravery she had felt when she boasted to her ma that she could make the journey alone was gone. Now she fought the urge to turn and race back up to the safety of her cottage and kneel beside her mother as she thrust a skillet of soda bread into the big turf fire. The urge passed and she walked across the road and up to the tall, wrought iron gate that guarded the estate. She stood looking up at it, clutching her boots even tighter under her arm and biting her lip. Squaring her shoulders, she pushed hard against it. As it creaked open she turned to her dog.

'Go home now, Rory, there's a good boy.'

The dog looked up at her with mournful eyes and began to whimper.

'You can't come where I'm going, Rory. You don't belong there.'

The gate opened on to a dark, twisting, tree-lined avenue and into a strange and terrifying world. Ghosts from stories she had heard around the family fireside leered at her from behind the gnarled beech trees – headless horsemen, howling hunting dogs, tortured souls rising from their graves. She hurried on, looking neither left nor right, her heart thumping in her chest.

As the avenue gave way to open pasture-land she slowed her pace, but still she did not dare raise her head. She heard the squelch of her toes on the damp grass beneath her, the gathering notes of birds preparing for their dawn chorus, and the faint squawks of wildfowl from the distant lake. The familiar sounds calmed her a little and she allowed herself to look up. There ahead of her, sitting on top of a gentle hill and surrounded by smooth green lawns, stood the 'Big House', its lime washed stone bathed pink in the pale dawn light.

She stopped. For all the stories she had heard from her family and neighbours about the 'Big House', she had not been prepared for its beauty. It rose three storeys above its basement, its lines square and clean, its tall windows equally spaced on either side of a massive, white-oak front door. It looked like something from a fairy tale. Rosie let go of her fear and allowed herself to imagine princesses inside singing fanciful songs and sipping tea from dainty china cups. Small waves of pleasure flowed through her as she stood, lost in her imagination.

Distant shouts startled her and she remembered why she had come. Reluctantly, she tore her eyes away from the house, stepped out of her imagination, and bent down to pull on her boots, carefully tying the laces. Straightening up, she tucked her black curls behind her ears and smoothed out her striped, cotton smock hoping no one would notice where Ma had carefully mended it. She took a deep breath and, remembering Ma's directions, hurried along the path and under the archway that led to the stables and courtyard. By the time she ducked in through the kitchen door at the rear of the house her sweet fantasies had evaporated.

The heat of the kitchen slammed into her like a fist, knocking her backwards. Fire roared in a massive black oven, on top of which steaming pots shuddered. The cook stood at a wooden table in the centre of the kitchen, shouting instructions at a young maid. A boy shovelled coal into the oven to keep the fire going. Maids and footmen rushed in and out fetching and carrying buckets and mops, dishes and linens. Gardeners hauled in baskets of vegetables, while a gamekeeper tossed a brace of dead fowl on the kitchen table. The girl watched them, fascinated.

'Who are *you?*' the cook shouted.

Rosie looked up in awe at the giant of a woman

15

with black hair and ruddy cheeks who frowned down at her.

'Rosie Killeen, miss.'

'Ah, you'd be Bridie's sister come to help out. How old are you?'

'Eight last month, miss.'

'Old enough, then. Well, don't be standing there like a spare dinner. Make yourself useful. Start peeling them spuds.'

Rosie swallowed hard. 'Yes, miss.'

At ten o'clock the butler came into the kitchen and clapped his hands. 'Everyone up to the front steps,' he shouted, 'Her majesty Queen Victoria is about to arrive. Come quickly, now. You know your places.'

The female servants smoothed their uniforms with red hands and arranged unruly hair under caps while the men dusted themselves down and stood erect. One by one they marched to the back stairs that led up into the main house. Rosie lined up behind them but the firm pressure of the butler's hand on her shoulder stopped her.

'You stay here,' he said.

Rosie's heart sank. She looked around her. There were no windows in the room or in the adjoining servants' hall. How was she going to see the Queen? After all, such a prospect was the reason she had come to help at the Big House. The moment her sister, Bridie, a housemaid there, had told her family about the Queen's visit and that extra help would be needed, Rosie had clapped her hands and jumped up and down.

'Can I go?' she had begged. 'Oh please, Bridie, I've never seen a queen before!'

16

Bridie had been about to say no, but Ma had interceded.

'Oh, let her go,' she said. 'Can't you see how excited she is?'

Now it looked as if she would not see the Queen after all. Fighting back tears, she looked around her. Surely there must be a window somewhere. Gathering her courage, she tiptoed out of the kitchen and into a long, dark corridor. Looking over her shoulder to make sure no one was about, she pushed open a door and found herself in the butler's quarters. Forgetting her fear, she rushed over to the small basement window and, pressing her face against it, peered out through the dusty panes.

From her vantage point, if she craned her neck enough, she could see the people assembled on the front steps of the house. A finely dressed man and woman she took to be Lord and Lady Ennis, the master and mistress of the Big House, standing together on the bottom steps. Crowded behind them were their guests, colourful as peacocks. Stretched across the bottom of the steps, to one side of their employers, were the servants arranged strictly in order of importance – the butler standing closest to the master, and the scullery maid the farthest away.

At the clatter of approaching carriages Rosie stood on tiptoe. Gravel hopped and skittered under its wheels as the first carriage, drawn by four glistening black horses and driven by a coachman in a top hat, halted in front of the house. Her eyes followed him as he climbed down, opened the door and extended his hand to help the female occupant alight. So *this* was Queen Victoria. Crest-fallen, Rosie drew back from the window. She had imagined the Queen would be a beautiful lady with a cloak of red and a golden crown. But instead, out of the carriage had stepped a fat, stern-looking old woman in a stiff black taffeta dress, and in place of a crown, an ugly lace cap. She was attended by an equally dour lady-in-waiting. Leaning on a walking stick, the old woman limped to the bottom of the steps where Lord and Lady Ennis, their guests and servants, greeted her.

Rosie was indignant. All this commotion over that oul' biddy? she thought. You'd think she was the Pope himself. She remembered Bridie telling their ma how the whole place was in an uproar over the visit and how everything had to be scrubbed and polished and the servants' uniforms immaculate as nuns' habits. She didn't understand it at all. Then she thought of the fourpence Bridie had promised her for today's work and she grinned, dimples punching her red cheeks. At least that would make up for her disappointment.

It was June 1900. Queen Victoria was making a rare visit to Ireland and had agreed to include a stop at Ennismore, which was the proper name for the Big House, in her itinerary. She was, however, only staying for lunch. Rosie counted at least six courses, all on different plates, sent up to the dining room in a contraption the servants called a 'dumb waiter'. How could anybody eat all that food in one sitting? That amount would have kept her family fed for a month. Only when the Queen took her leave at three o'clock did the cook collapse on a chair and bend over to rub her sore feet.

'Well, Her Majesty can't complain we sent her away hungry,' she sighed. 'From what the footmen said she scraped every last morsel off every plate.'

Anthony Walshe, who carried the lofty title of 'Head of Maintenance' but who was in truth an odd-jobs man, diminutive of stature and of uncertain age, cackled. 'Fair play to herself,' he said. 'She's not fretting over her figure like some in this house!'

Sadie Canavan, one of the maids, pushed her copper curls under her cap and raised the hem of her apron to mop the sweat off her face.

'So much for royalty,' she said. 'That oul' biddy had no manners at all. You should have seen the way she's after stuffing down the food. They say that fat son of hers, Bertie, is just as ignorant.'

When Rosie had carried out the last bucket of potato peelings and dumped them in the pigsty, she returned to the kitchen and looked around. Ever since she was old enough to understand she knew that one day she would have to go to work at the Big House, just as her sister Bridie had done a few years before. It was the lot of most Irish country girls to enter into domestic service at the nearest big house and to count herself grateful for the chance. Short of entering the convent, or obtaining a rare scholarship to secondary school, there was little choice. Rosie's ma had worked at Ennismore before she married, and *her* ma before her. A wave of nausea rose up inside her and she reached for a stool. She told herself that the convent would be a better choice any day than the likes of this.

'You can go now,' said the cook. 'No point sitting there on your arse.'

Rosie jumped off the stool and was about to run out of the kitchen when she remembered the fourpence Bridie had promised her for her day's work. She had thought Bridie might come down to the kitchen to pay her but there had been no sign of her. She looked up at the big woman who scowled down at her, and swallowed hard.

'Er, if you please, Mrs O'Leary, ma'am, me sister Bridie said I was to get fourpence for me wages, please, ma'am.'

She stepped back and waited for the eruption which would surely come.

Anthony Walshe and Sadie Canavan burst into laughter, but the cook's ruddy face turned crimson. 'Did ye ever hear such boldness?' she roared. 'Away with you now before I box the ears off you. You'll settle that matter up with Bridie.'

Certain now that she had overstepped her bounds, Rosie raced from the kitchen. The air outside was cool and fresh. She took several deep breaths and decided to take the long way home along the path beside the lake. Lough Conn was the largest lake in County Mayo and ran along the edge of the Ennis Estate property. When she was very young her granda used to take her out fishing in a small wooden rowing boat called a currach. He was dead now, and her da, a tenant farmer beholden to Lord Ennis, had little time for such outings. She stood at the lake's edge and looked out over its still blue waters to Mount Nephin, which rose smoky purple on the far shore, lost in her own thoughts.

A faint movement behind her made her turn. Standing a few yards away was a girl about her own age. She had long blonde hair tied with a pale blue ribbon that matched her beautiful dress. As Rosie stared at her she saw that the girl was crying. She marched up to her.

'What's wrong with you?' she said.

'My boat,' the girl whimpered. 'I let go of the string and it's sailed away and now I can't reach it.' She pointed to where a small object floated near the shore.

'Go in after it then,' said Rosie. 'Sure, I can see it from here.'

'I'm afraid of the water,' the girl whispered.

Rosie looked at her in astonishment. She'd never met anyone who was afraid of water. She and her brothers and sister swam in the local streams without a thought.

'Did nobody ever teach you how to swim?'

'Oh, what shall I do?' cried the girl. 'It was a birthday present from the Queen. Oh, Mama will be so angry.'

'Ah, for God's sake,' said Rosie, mimicking her ma's favourite expression.

Swiftly she pulled off her dress and boots and, clad only in her petticoat, waded into the water and swam a few strokes. She retrieved the boat and swam back to the shore. 'Here,' she said, handing it over to the girl.

The child looked at Rosie wide-eyed. 'What's your name?'

'Rosie Killeen. What's yours?'

'Victoria Bell. I'm named after the Queen. She gave me this for my birthday. It's today.'

'What age are you?' said Rosie.

'Seven.'

'I'm eight.'

Rosie studied the toy boat that the girl held. It was painted blue and white and was a perfect replica of an ocean liner, the sort of toy only a rich child would own. It dawned on Rosie then that the girl belonged to the Big House.

Both girls stood for a moment locked in each other's gaze. At last Rosie broke the spell.

'I have to be away now,' she said, and picking up her dress and boots she fled across the green lawns, down the twisting path, out through the estate gate, and back to the safety of her own farm.

Victoria Bell watched Rosie Killeen disappear into the distance. She hugged the toy boat to her chest, ignoring the damp patch it made on her dress. She wondered for a moment if the girl was a fairy like the ones in her story books, but she hoped she was real. Victoria had met very few girls her own age and Rosie Killeen was not like any of them. She doubted if she was like any other girl in the whole world. What other girl would be as fearless as to strip off her clothes without a care and dive fearlessly into the lake? Victoria was fascinated. She decided then and there that Rosie must become her friend.

'Please, Papa. Please!' she begged her father the next day as she walked with him in the garden. 'Why can't she be my friend? I have no one to play with. I'm so lonely.'

Victoria gazed up at Lord Ennis, widening her blue eyes in a practised manner that usually bore results. She knew that her papa had a soft spot for her that did not extend to her two older brothers. She had learned early how to use it to her benefit.

'Have you asked your mama?'

Victoria stiffened. The very thought of making such a request of her mama terrified her. She shook her head.

'No, Papa,' she whispered.

Lord Ennis nodded. 'I thought not.'

Victoria slipped her hand into his as they walked in silence back towards the house. Without understanding why, she instinctively knew what she asked for was risky. Such a request was far beyond begging for a new toy, or to be allowed to ride with Papa on one of his prize horses, or to stay up late to watch the guests dance at the annual Christmas ball at Ennismore. She loved her Papa dearly and was suddenly anxious that her request might cause trouble for him.

When they reached the front steps she squeezed his hand. 'Don't worry, Papa,' she said. 'It's all right if you have to say no.'

Her father smiled down at her, love brimming in his eyes.

That evening Victoria hid in the library, her eye pressed to a keyhole through which she could observe the family dining room. Normally she would not have dared take such a risk, but her encounter with Rosie Killeen had emboldened her. If Rosie could have been so brave as to dive into the lake, then she, Victoria, could certainly spy on her family. Her heart fluttered as she watched Papa lead her mother into the room, followed by her aunt and governess, Lady Louisa. She hoped against hope that her father would bring up her request and that he would prevail. After all, her mama, Lady Ennis, was in excellent form following Queen Victoria's visit, cheerful and jubilant, unlike her normally stern demeanour. Perhaps Papa might be able to take advantage of her rare good mood.

'A triumph if I may say so,' said Lady Althea Ennis as she sat down at the dining table, beaming at her husband and sister. 'I actually persuaded Her Majesty on one of her rare visits to Ireland to journey from Dublin to visit us here at Ennismore. I daresay no other hostess in Ireland could have achieved such a coup.'

Lady Louisa glared at her sister. 'You may call it a triumph, Thea, but I can hardly believe how you were willing to embarrass the family with your scandalous letter-writing campaign, not only to the Queen but to her closest associates, most of whom you did not even know. How could you have grovelled so? I'm sure we are all the laughing-stock of London.'

'Perhaps,' said Lady Ennis, 'but we *are* the envy of the Anglo-Irish aristocracy all over Ireland.'

Lord Ennis grunted. 'A triumph perhaps, Thea, but a very costly one.'

His wife waved her hand at him in frustration. 'Must you always reduce everything to money, Edward? It's so vulgar.'

'Vulgar or not, we cannot ignore reality, Thea. You know very well the estates are not bringing in the revenue we once enjoyed and–'

'Please, not at dinner,' interrupted Lady Ennis. 'Such topics bring on my headaches.'

24

Victoria watched nervously as Burke, the butler, and a footman served soup, followed by fish and meat courses. Her family ate in silence. Had Papa ruined Mama's mood by bringing up money? She sighed and focused on her father as if just by staring at him she could make him speak. Please, Papa, she pleaded silently, please say something soon.

Lord Ennis had once been a handsome man, rugged and bearded, an outdoorsman whose love of horses and hunting had endeared him to his fellows who flocked to Ennismore for weekend sport. Now, at fifty, his looks had begun to fade, his once lithe figure running to fat. His thick, dark hair had grown sparse and a slight paunch now pressed against his shirt buttons. Nonetheless, he retained the attractiveness of a man at ease with his place in society.

He pushed his empty plate away from him, signalled the footman to remove it and turned to his wife.

'So have you thought about my proposal, my dear?'

Victoria held her breath.

Lady Ennis put down her fork and frowned. 'It's absolutely out of the question, Edward. I cannot believe that you are contemplating such a thing.'

'Nonsense, Thea,' said Lord Ennis. 'Our Victoria has persuaded me that it is a splendid idea.' He looked up and smiled. 'She's been pestering me ever since she met the girl.'

His wife's plump bosom rose and fell in exasperation, causing the garnet pendant which rested upon it to sway precariously. 'How can you allow a common peasant girl to take lessons with our daughter?'

Victoria stifled a squeal. Rosie to share her lessons? Oh, this was so much more than she had hoped for. She squinted, trying to read her mother's expression.

'It's what Victoria wants,' said Lord Ennis.

'And is Victoria to have everything she wants? Is her every whim to be indulged no matter what the cost, while you scold me for every penny I spend?'

'This proposal will cost us nothing. Lady Louisa can as easily teach two girls as one.'

Lady Louisa scowled at her brother-in-law.

'And besides,' he went on, 'the girl is not exactly a peasant. I have made enquiries and her father is one of my most reliable tenant farmers. John Killeen is a splendid chap.'

A small cry escaped from Lady Ennis. 'Killeen. Don't we have a maid named Killeen?'

'The sister,' sniffed Lady Louisa.

Lady Ennis dropped the fork with which she was about to stab the fresh rhubarb tart the footman had set in front of her. 'Have you lost your mind, Edward? And what of Louisa? Surely you can't expect her to give lessons to the sister of one of our maids.'

Lord Ennis poured fresh cream on his tart and smiled at Lady Louisa. 'I'm sure Louisa will be happy to cooperate in whatever is best for our family, won't you, dearest sister?'

Lady Louisa glared back at him but said nothing.

'But, Edward...' began Lady Ennis.

Lord Ennis sighed and laid his fork down on the

26

table. 'No more, Thea,' he said in his rich, deep voice, honed from years of speechmaking in the House of Lords, 'my mind is made up. The child needs company her own age now that her brothers are away at school.' He leaned closer to his wife. 'I had hoped we might provide a sister for her, but that is hardly likely now, is it, my dear?'

Lady Ennis flushed. 'You know very well, Edward, that Victoria's birth nearly killed me,' she said, looking wounded.

'Not to mention what it did to your figure,' muttered Lady Louisa.

'Since she has no sisters close to her own age,' continued Lord Ennis, as if nothing was said, 'and since there is no girl of suitable age and class within miles, then this child – er, Rose, is it? – may serve as well as any.'

He leaned back in his chair and beckoned to the butler to bring him a brandy.

'Our Victoria is like a high spirited thoroughbred,' he began, ignoring the women's groans. 'She is dreamy and temperamental. I bed my thoroughbreds down with stout stable horses. The companionship calms them, and in time they perform at their best.'

'Victoria is not a horse,' snapped Lady Louisa.

Lord Ennis stood, signalling the end of dinner. 'I shall speak to John Killeen. I'm sure the chap will consider it a great honour. Have the girl join Victoria when the boys return to school for the autumn term.'

Victoria could not stop herself from clapping her hands. 'Oh, thank you, dear Papa,' she cried.

She raced out of the library and up the stairs to

her bedroom. She could hardly wait for the summer to be over.

Lady Ennis swept indignantly out of the dining room followed by her sister. Ten years her husband's junior, she still possessed a comely figure. Her excess pounds were cleverly encased in corsets and stays, while low necklines displayed her white bosom to great effect. Her gowns, though slightly out of fashion, were well cut and her dark blonde hair impeccably coiffed.

Entering the drawing room, she sat down on a pink, tufted velvet love seat, wincing as her bottom collided with its unyielding upholstered surface – she had chosen the new furniture for its style rather than comfort. She smoothed out her skirts and rang the bell to summon the butler.

As she waited for her tea she looked around the drawing room with a satisfied smile. Despite her husband's protests she had insisted on lifting this one room above the antiquated shabbiness of the rest of the house. After all, the drawing room was where Her Majesty would be received and first impressions were of the utmost importance. Now she took in the fresh wallpaper with its smart pale green and white trellis design, the freshly painted white mouldings and the blue velvet cane-backed chairs, all acquired within the last month. She frowned slightly as she peered at the mantel and fire surround. She had wanted marble but the excessive cost had obliged her to make do with cleverly painted wood that, from a distance, resembled marble. She had done her best to distract suspicious eyes by displaying her prized collection of Meissen porcelain on the mantelshelf.

Meanwhile, her sister, Lady Louisa, paced back and forth across the room.

'Oh, do sit down, Louisa,' snapped Lady Ennis, as Burke entered carrying a silver teapot followed by Sadie, the red-haired maid, bearing a tray of china cups and saucers. 'You are making me quite dizzy.'

Muttering to herself, Lady Louisa perched her bony frame primly on the edge of one of the new cane-backed chairs at a considerable distance from her sister. With her brown hair pulled back into a bun, her silk, high-collared dark grey dress, and her charmless demeanour, Lady Louisa Comstock was the epitome of the very role she fiercely resented – a governess. She had come to live with her sister after several 'Seasons' in London, during which she had failed to secure even one offer of marriage. True, she lacked her sister's attractiveness, and had no sense of humour, but her worst failing was her fatal inability to flatter men. Relegated now to her place as an unpaid member of the household staff, Louisa's prickly nature often expressed itself in open hostility.

The servants dismissed, Lady Ennis sipped her tea and turned to her sister.

'I hardly know where to begin,' she said. 'I have sacrificed so much for Edward all these years, and now this! It is really the last straw.'

'What would you know about sacrifice, Thea? You have a husband, a home, social status and security. I have none of those things.'

'Don't start, Louisa. It's your own fault. If only you had tried to be more pleasant to your suitors,

29

you would not be in your present predicament.'

Lady Louisa banged down her teacup, sending the saucer rattling. 'If you mean by refusing to debase myself in front of slobbering, drunken fools, then I plead guilty.'

'Don't exaggerate. A smile here, a little flattery there, it wouldn't have hurt you. It's unfortunate you did not choose to take your cues from me.'

A look of scorn spread across Lady Louisa's thin face. 'I think you did more than smile and flatter, dear sister. As I recall you went out of your way to malign any other girl in whom Edward showed an interest so that you could have him for yourself. You even made up a story which sent poor Charlotte Dowling scurrying off to the Continent to comfort her supposedly sick sister just to get her out of the way.'

Lady Ennis sniffed. 'I didn't make it up. It was merely a misunderstanding. It wasn't my fault if that silly Charlotte was gullible enough to believe it.' A shadow passed over her grey eyes. 'Anyway, look at where it all got me in the end, isolated here in this backwater in the west of Ireland with a husband who holds the purse strings in a death grip. If I'd known then what I know now – I had so many other suitors to choose from...'

'But you chose Edward, for better or worse.'

Lady Ennis gazed dreamily out the window. 'But he was so charming, Louisa. And he made Ireland sound so romantic. Imagine my shock when he brought me to this unfashionable old house surrounded by bogs and marshes!'

'You made your bed,' said Louisa, standing up.

'Yes. And I have lived stoically with the consequences. But this latest demand of Edward's is beyond my patience to bear.' She paused and stretched her mouth into a thin, unattractive line. 'I have been determined since Victoria was born that she shall have a better life than was afforded me. She will be brought up strictly and with the utmost care so that when she enters society her manners and demeanour will be flawless. If her looks fulfill their promise, she will become a beauty. She will have her pick of suitors, and I shall settle for no less than the well-to-do eldest son of an earl.'

She looked directly at her sister. 'What Edward is suggesting will ruin all my plans for Victoria, and I simply will not allow it.'

'I don't see that you have a choice.'

'I may not be able to stop that wretched peasant girl from entering this house for lessons but once lessons are over I shall forbid Victoria to have anything to do with her. Her corrupting influence will be limited to your classroom only and I expect you to make things so unbearable for the urchin that even her visits to the schoolroom will be short-lived. Do you understand me?'

Lady Louisa regarded her sister with pursed lips as if contemplating a sharp reply. Instead, she put her hand to her forehead. 'I must go and lie down. I have the most frightful headache. Please ring for that maid to bring me water.'

Without waiting for an answer, Lady Louisa withdrew from the drawing room leaving Lady Ennis staring after her, aghast at the fact that her sister had just dared to give her an order.

Bridie shot through the door of the Killeen cottage and came to a halt in front of Rosie. 'You conniving wee bitch,' she shouted, her rough, red hands resting on her thin hips.

'Bridie!' said Ma. 'How dare you speak to your sister like that?'

'But she is, Ma,' protested Bridie, tears of frustration clouding her pale, blue eyes. ''Twas her put the idea in the girl's head, and she did it all to spite me.'

Ma took Bridie's arm and marched her to a chair beside the kitchen table. 'Now sit down and tell us what this is all about.'

Bridie poured out what the maid, Sadie Canavan, had just told the servants about Lord Ennis's decision.

'Sadie said Lady Louisa told her it was Victoria's idea, but I think it was this one put her up to it.'

Rosie listened in horror. 'Why would I do that?' she said. 'I don't want to go up there. I like me own school, and me own friends.' She looked up at her mother, tears gathering in her eyes. 'I don't have to go, do I, Ma? I don't have to go if I don't want to?'

Mrs Killeen looked from her two tearful daughters to her husband who sat on an old settle bed beside the huge open hearth in which a turf fire burned.

'John?'

Rosie held her breath. Surely her da would never agree to such a thing. Ever since she could remember he had sided with her, protecting her from her brothers' taunts or her ma's scolding.

She had a sudden image of herself as a toddler, sitting tearfully on his knee while he took the broken pieces of a dinner plate she had dropped and slid them behind his chair.

'We'll hide them,' he'd whispered, 'so your ma won't find them. 'Twill be our secret.'

Of course Ma had found the pieces of the plate that same evening and looked at her husband quizzically.

'Arrah, sure it just slipped out of me hands, Mary,' he'd said, winking at Rosie.

Now she waited for him to rescue her again. His eyes met hers for an instant as he pulled slowly on his pipe, the white smoke encircling him. Then he bowed his head.

'If his lordship wants it,' he whispered, 'I don't know what choice we have in it, Roisin dubh.'

Her da always called her by her full name, Roisin, and added 'dubh' which he pronounced 'Ro-sheen dove'. He told her it was Irish for 'Dark Rosaleen' and was another name for Ireland. It had always pleased her when he called her that. With her black hair and hazel eyes, so dark they looked brown in certain lights, the name suited her. But this night it brought her no pleasure. She began to cry harder.

'Ah, for God's sake what do *you* have to cry about?' said Bridie. 'How d'you think it's going to be for me with you coming up there every day and me having to wait on you?' She turned to her mother. 'And the staff will be trying to get gossip out of me. I'll have no peace at all. And what if this one disgraces me? I could lose my job over the head of her.'

Ma went to stand beside Bridie and stroked her head. 'Och, 'twill be all right, love, you'll see. Rosie won't let you down.'

For the rest of that summer, Rosie tried to put thoughts of what lay ahead of her out of her mind. Every morning she collected the eggs from the chicken pens and brought them home where she helped Ma prepare breakfast. Her work over, she passed the long, bright days chasing after rabbits with her brothers, or swimming in the streams with children from the neighbouring farms. Often they ventured deep into the woods looking for caves or fairy forts. But at night, with all distractions gone, and after her family had gone to bed, she often stood gazing around the little cottage as if trying to memorize it. As she looked into the embers of the turf fire she was filled with a certain knowledge her life would never be the same.

All too soon, the summer drew to a close. The Killeen cottage roiled in preparations for the new school year – a fury of haircuts and squabbles over why the oldest brother always got the new boots and schoolbags, while the others had to make do with hand-me-downs. Rosie watched in silence and hoped against hope for a miracle. But it was not to be. Ma insisted that Rosie accompany her into the nearby town of Crossmolina to buy material for new dresses to wear up to the Big House. Normally Rosie would have been delighted at the prospect of shopping with her mother, but this time she followed Ma out the door like a prisoner going to her execution.

At Hopkins' Drapers Ma bought several yards of soft, cotton cloth, which Rosie knew they could barely afford, along with lace trimmings and matching buttons. For the next two nights, Ma stayed up late sewing two new dresses for Rosie, one blue and one grey, each with lace-trimmed collars, a sash that tied in the back, and big white buttons on the front.

'There,' said Ma with satisfaction, 'these should do ye for a while as long as ye keep them right. No running or rolling about on the grass now, or tearing them on fences.' She looked sternly at Rosie, who bowed her head.

The night before she was to go up to the Big House, Rosie lay in bed weeping quietly. How could her da have betrayed her so – taking the side of strangers over his own daughter? And why was her ma so delighted at the prospect of her daughter being educated with the girl from the Big House? What had she done to deserve having her life turned upside down? Why were they punishing her this way? As she drifted off to sleep she wished fervently that she had never set eyes on Victoria Bell.

CHAPTER 2

That same night, Victoria Bell was too excited to sleep. Rosie would be coming to start lessons with her the next day. What fun it was going to be having her new friend with her in the schoolroom! She had thanked her papa over and over for allowing Rosie to join her, throwing her arms around his neck and kissing his cheek every time she saw him.

'Now, now, Victoria,' Lord Ennis had said, gently pushing her away, 'this doesn't mean you can play all day. You and young Rose must apply yourselves to your lessons. I shall be receiving reports on your behaviour from Lady Louisa and if she has found you wanting I shall have to send Rose back to her farm.'

'Oh no, Papa,' Victoria had said in alarm, 'I'll be good, I promise.'

Lady Ennis, however, had a different, more unsettling message for her daughter.

'I have agreed to this arrangement because your father insisted,' she said, 'but it extends to the schoolroom only. You are forbidden to see or speak to that girl outside your lessons. I will not have her peasant influence corrupting you. Is that understood, Victoria?'

Victoria had nodded although she had not understood at all. She did not even know what the word 'corrupting' meant. All she knew was that for some reason her mama disliked Rosie even though she had never even met her.

By the next morning, as Victoria's excitement grew, all warnings were forgotten. She gulped down her breakfast in her haste to get to the schoolroom. She burst into the big, airless room that smelled musty as old rags and, seeing Rosie standing quietly by the far door, ran towards her, squealing in delight. She grabbed her by the hand and pulled her forward.

'Come and sit next to me, Rosie,' she said, pointing to two wooden school desks with matching

36

chairs that sat side by side.

In her exuberance, Victoria did not notice Rosie's pale face and bowed head. It had not even occurred to her that her new friend might not share her own excitement. She climbed onto her chair, smoothing out her pink cambric dress and white pinafore, and patted the empty chair beside her. Tentatively, Rosie slid on to it, pulled it up to the desk, and waited.

'Please settle down, Victoria.'

Lady Louisa, in a navy serge dress, stood erect beside a blackboard and easel, her face so grim it could have turned milk sour. When Victoria had settled in, she began pacing back and forth in front of the girls. She glared at Rosie.

'You will address me as "my lady".'

Rosie swallowed hard. 'Yes, my lady.'

'You will speak only when you are spoken to. If you have a question you may put up your hand, but if I ignore you then you will put it down again.'

'Yes,' murmured Rosie.

'Yes what?'

'Yes, my lady.'

'Now, as to your dress,' went on Lady Louisa sniffing through her long, thin nose, 'that will do, I suppose, but for goodness sake ask your mother to remove that awful sash. And ask her for a pinafore in case of spills or ink stains.'

Rosie's face turned crimson. 'Yes, my lady.'

Lady Louisa looked from Rosie to Victoria. 'There will be no giggling from either of you, and no mischief. You are here to learn, and it is my poor fortune to be the one to stuff some knowledge into your heads. You,' she said, nodding

37

towards Rosie, 'I suspect you've learned next to nothing in that school for urchins you have been attending in the village. Let me see just how deficient your education is.'

They spent the remainder of the morning on drills of spelling and arithmetic, a long ruler gripped in Lady Louisa's bony fingers as she pounded on the blackboard. She then handed each girl a book and instructed them to take turns reading aloud from it. Victoria's stomach churned. She hated reading aloud and was embarrassed that Rosie should hear how halting her delivery was. In her nervousness she stumbled even more than usual. When she finished she sat back in awe as Rosie raced smoothly through the paragraph without one mistake. She couldn't stop herself from clapping her hands when Rosie finished.

'Ooh, well done, Rosie!' she said.

'Quiet, Victoria,' said Lady Louisa.

Sadie served lunch at eleven o'clock. Rosie, who had had no appetite for breakfast earlier in the day, now devoured the tiny ham sandwiches in front of her while Victoria bit daintily into hers. Rosie swallowed her milk in gulps and slapped the empty glass down on the table with a sigh.

'Quiet, please,' snapped Lady Louisa as she left the room. 'I have a headache.'

'Sorry, ma'am, er, my lady,' said Rosie.

Victoria jumped up from the table and grabbed Rosie's hand. 'Let's go and see my toys.'

They were still in the schoolroom, she reasoned, so she was not breaking her mama's rules. She pulled Rosie towards the big cupboard in the corner of the room.

'Would you like to see my dolls?'

For the next half hour Victoria pulled out every doll from the cupboard, telling Rosie their names and when she had received them. She took down a box which contained all manner of doll's clothes – dresses and hats and scarves of the finest material. 'Come on, let's dress them up. Oh, it's so much fun to have someone to play with, Rosie.'

Rosie smiled for the first time that morning.

The nursery clock chimed noon and Lady Louisa returned.

Rosie whispered to Victoria, 'Can't we go outside for a minute? It's so stuffy in here.'

Victoria shook her head. 'It's not allowed,' she said.

Lady Louisa, having evidently recovered from her headache, rapped on the blackboard for attention. 'Now we will have some French conversation, shall we?' she announced. 'You may join in if you wish,' she added, looking at Rosie.

Rosie blushed and sank lower into her chair. Victoria, on the other hand, clapped her hands in delight. Now it was her turn to show off to Rosie. She prattled back and forth with Lady Louisa, grinning at Rosie when she finished. Seeing Rosie's worried face, Victoria leaned over to her.

'Don't worry, Rosie, I'll teach you French. And you can help me with my reading.'

There followed an hour of deportment and etiquette. Both girls giggled as they walked around the schoolroom, each balancing a book on her head.

When three o'clock struck, Rosie made for the back stairs. Victoria got up to follow her. Only the sharp clap of Lady Louisa's hands stopped them. 'I've never seen such appalling manners. Come back to your desks this minute and wait until I dismiss you. And you should know better, Victoria. Just wait until I tell your father.'

'Please don't, Aunt Louisa, or he will send Rosie away.'

'Then you will do well to remember your manners in the future. You may go only when I tell you, and quietly please. No running.'

Ignoring her command, Rosie got up and ran to the back door of the schoolroom, heading for the servants' stairs. Victoria, who did not dare move, called after her but she did not turn around. Victoria's face fell. Why was Rosie so anxious to leave? She didn't even say goodbye. Could it be that Rosie didn't like her? The thought had never even occurred to her. Lady Louisa finally dismissed her and she fought back tears as she walked over to the toy cupboard. Ignoring the pile of dolls that lay on the floor, she reached up and pulled out the blue and white toy boat that Rosie had rescued and cradled it against her.

Later that same evening, after the family dinner dishes were cleared and washed and the kitchen scrubbed, the household staff assembled in the servants' hall for their own evening meal. They sat at a long, well-worn, wooden table, the men on one side, the women on the other, arranged according to rank, with Mr Burke, butler, presiding at its head. On the table sat platters of leftover food. Tonight there were more leftovers than usual because Lord Ennis was suddenly called away to London and Lady Ennis and Lady Louisa had eaten little. The smell of roast beef, savoury sauces, and warm buttery bread mixed with the smells of bleach and cleaning fluids from the kitchen. Thelma, a big country girl and the youngest of the maids, served water, while Mr Burke solemnly poured wine into heavy glasses for himself, the housekeeper and the cook.

'Where is Miss Canavan?' Mr Burke enquired, noting the empty chair next to Immelda Fox, Lady Ennis's maid.

'Lady Louisa rang for her just as we were about to sit down,' said Mrs Murphy, housekeeper. 'Apparently she was not feeling well and wanted fresh water.'

''Tis no wonder. She had to put up with Rosie Killeen today as well as Miss Victoria. Sadie said the Rosie one already disgraced herself the way she gulped down the lunch like a starving goat.' Mrs O'Leary looked at Bridie who sat next to her. 'Did your ma teach her no manners at all?'

Bridie said nothing.

It was a warm night for September. Mrs O'Leary opened the top buttons of her blouse and fanned herself with her right hand. 'I'm roasted with the heat,' she sighed. 'Seaneen,' she said, nodding to the younger of the two footmen, 'would you ever go and open the kitchen door and let in some air?'

'I will, mum, but 'tis the horse dung ye'll be smelling if I do.'

Mrs O'Leary was a tall, big-boned woman who towered over the rest of the staff, except for Mr Burke. Her considerable bulk was anchored, however, by exceptionally small and dainty feet which

41

she pointed and twirled coquettishly as she sat sideways on her chair stretching her legs out before her.

'Arrah, whisht,' she said. 'Do as I say or I'll be after stripping this blouse off meself altogether and treating ye to a show ye won't soon forget.'

Thelma giggled as she refilled the water jug.

The servants' hall, which adjoined the kitchen, was a long, narrow, stone-floored room with a low ceiling and no exterior windows. The only window was the one on the inside wall that divided the servants' hall and Mr Burke's quarters, thus allowing the butler to observe the staff even as they took their leisure. Smoke from years of cooking in the adjacent kitchen had rendered the once whitewashed walls a dull, stony grey. The heat from the kitchen stove and the steam from boiling pots made the temperature almost unbearable, particularly on warm days.

Sean was right about the smell of horse dung. It wafted from the stables through the kitchen and into the servants' hall as soon as he opened the door. Mrs O'Leary rolled her eyes and took a gulp of wine.

'Let us say grace,' said Mr Burke, bowing his head.

Mr Burke was a member of the Church of Ireland, as were the Bell family. The rest of the servants were Catholic. So it was Church of Ireland prayers that were said before meals, Mr Burke intoning loudly, while the rest of the servants muttered along with their eyes closed.

Mr Burke had just begun the prayer when Sadie burst into the room, her curls bouncing

42

around her white cap. 'Sorry I'm late,' she said, 'herself was in a desperate temper.'

Mr Burke held up his hand and Sadie bowed her head and mumbled the prayer. Then she sat down between Immelda Fox and Bridie Killeen.

When he finished, Mr Burke cleared his throat and gave Sadie a stern look. 'You will show respect, Miss Canavan. You will not refer to Lady Louisa as "herself".'

A tall, skeletal man with the grim face of an undertaker, Mr Burke took seriously his obligation to attempt to civilize the often unruly servants.

'Aye, Mr Burke. But wait till I tell ye–'

'No gossip, Miss Canavan. You know the rules.'

But Sadie was undaunted. 'Herself, er Lady Louisa, says the Rosie one is as thick as a turnip and her manners are shocking. You should have seen the face of her. Red as a turkey cock she was.' She looked pointedly at Bridie. 'So what do you think of that now, Bridie?'

Bridie glared at her and shrugged.

An uncomfortable silence followed until Anthony Walshe slapped his small thigh and grinned. 'Well, more power to wee Rosie,' he said. 'On my oath, I wouldn't want to be the one facing that weasel of a governess every morning, I'll tell ye that.'

Brendan Lynch, the black-haired, older of the two footmen, allowed a scowl to mar his handsome face. ''Tis only using her they are, the way they do all of us. When they've finished with her they'll throw her out like a pile of oul' rubbish and what will she do then? Bloody gentry. They all deserve to burn in hell.'

'Don't be blaspheming, Brendan,' Immelda Fox said sharply.

Mr Burke stood up. 'Enough,' he shouted. 'There will be no more talk of the matter.'

Over the following months Rosie dragged herself up to the Big House each morning, dreading what new humiliations the day would bring. Lady Louisa went out of her way to find fault with her, missing no opportunity to criticize her brogue, or rough manners, or ignorance. Before, everyone had always said how clever Rosie was, but now she felt her confidence ebbing away as if she had contracted some rare sickness.

Victoria seemed unaware of her struggles. Rosie didn't blame her. How could a girl like her ever understand? She had been brought up in luxury, in a world that was safe and secure. Rosie wanted to hate her, but the girl was so kind and gentle that she couldn't. Besides, Victoria was so delighted to have her as a friend that she ran to her each morning and gave her such an eager hug it almost smothered her.

At home, Ma constantly reminded Rosie of her good fortune in being able to receive the same education as one of the gentry.

'I go down on me two knees every night, Rosie,' she said, 'and thank God for the blessings He has bestowed on us. It's no less a miracle than the sick being cured at Lourdes. Sure, there's not a girl in County Mayo who wouldn't jump at the chance you have. Amn't I right, John?'

John Killeen stared into the fire, avoiding his wife's eyes, and nodded.

Rosie supposed her mother was right. But that knowledge did little to ease the loneliness buried deep inside her. Every day as she crossed the road that divided her farm from the Ennis Estate she felt more and more as if she were entering a foreign land. She struggled to understand this feeling. Wasn't the grass the same on both sides of the road? Didn't the same sun shine from above, the same rain quench the earth, and the same flowers bloom? And yet each day it was as if she had crossed a chasm into another world where, for all its lushness, the land appeared artificial and constrained, like a child on its best behaviour – a place where no untamed grasses and flowers sprouted unbidden, no wild rabbits and foxes scurried and burrowed and bred babies, and no friendly dogs ran to meet you.

Eventually, Rosie realized that if she were to thrive in this strange world she must force herself to fit in, and to fit in she must try to understand it, and to understand it she must become like the people who lived in it. Thus she resolved to endure Lady Louisa's barbs while learning everything she could – not just from books, but the things that weren't in books, like how the gentry walked and talked and ate and dressed.

She continued to excel in reading, delighted with the new books that Lady Louisa introduced. Her French became passable, thanks to Victoria's coaching. She was allowed to take piano lessons from a tutor with Victoria and they enjoyed playing duets together. Her table manners improved, which was a subject of much ridicule from her brothers. She began to take more interest in her

45

appearance, insisting on ribbons to tie back her unruly black curls, and a clean pinafore every day which she washed and ironed herself. Even her diction changed. She picked up Victoria's inflections and ways of expression and her brogue softened.

Rosie herself was unaware of these changes, but her ma and her sister noted them and greeted them very differently.

'Our Rosie is turning into a proper lady,' said Ma one night.

Bridie snorted. 'I don't know who she thinks she is. I told you she'd get above herself. The next thing you know she'll be ashamed of the lot of us. She'll be too grand to set foot in this house.'

'Our Rosie would never forget her family,' said Ma.

Something seemed to snap in Bridie.

'Why's our Rosie being given chances I never got?' she asked. 'I've been a good girl all my life. Haven't I minded you and worked hard up at Ennismore? But *I'm* still only a parlourmaid, cleaning ashes out of the fireplaces every morning, and emptying slops and scrubbing floors. And there's no end in sight. Unless Immelda or Sadie get married or sacked there's no chance for me to move up at all. I'll be a skivvy for the rest of me life!'

Bridie paused for breath. There were tears in her eyes as she looked at her ma. 'But what do you care about my troubles? All you think about is Rosie. It's Rosie this, and Rosie that, and isn't it grand how pretty Rosie's getting, and what a great future Rosie will have. It makes me want to spit.'

Ma looked at her daughter's thin sallow face,

her narrow shoulders and her rough hands. She reached over and put her arms around her. 'I'm sorry, love. I know you have it hard. And your da and me's grateful to you for being such a good daughter. We couldn't ask for better. Now go on in to bed. I'll bring you a cup of warm milk. You'll feel better in the morning.'

The effect of Rosie's friendship on Victoria, though less obvious, was no less profound. She remained obedient to her mama's orders to confine her association with Rosie to the schoolroom. Victoria had always been an obedient child, although this had more to do with fear of her mama's displeasure than her natural inclinations. She strove every day to eke out the smallest of smiles or nods of approval from her mother, but rarely succeeded. If it were not for her papa's kindness she would have been a very lonely child.

Now that void was filled by her new friendship. Her concerns on the first day of school that Rosie did not want to be her friend had evaporated. During their daily lunch, when Aunt Louisa left the schoolroom to rest, Victoria peppered Rosie with questions.

'What is it like to live on a farm, Rosie? Did you ever milk a cow? How many servants do you have? What's it like to eat your meals with your family? What kind of food do you eat – is it the same as ours? Does your mama love you?'

Rosie had answered patiently and Victoria began to form a picture of her friend's world and to realize it was very different from her own. How she longed to live in the cottage that Rosie described

47

with a loud and loving family, and a mother who barely scolded her when she forgot her manners and who always kissed her goodnight.

'Mama, why must I behave like a lady all the time? Rosie doesn't have to.'

Lady Ennis gave her daughter a look of disapproval. She and the girl sat stiffly together in the nursery during one of her infrequent afternoon visits.

'Because you *are* a lady, Victoria, or at least you will be when you enter society.'

'But what if I don't want to enter society, Mama?'

'Nonsense, girl, you have no choice. You are the daughter of an earl. It is your duty.'

Victoria scowled. 'I don't like duty,' she said.

'Stop scowling, Victoria, it will spoil your looks. And it doesn't matter whether you like duty or not, you will do what is expected of you and that is the end of it.'

'But–'

'Enough, Victoria!'

Lady Ennis rose from her chair and stared down at her daughter.

'It's that dreadful girl putting thoughts in your head, isn't it? I warned your father this would happen.'

Victoria jumped to her feet, filled with alarm. 'Oh no, Mama, Rosie hasn't done anything. Really, she hasn't. These are my own thoughts from my own head.'

'Well, get rid of them.'

Her mama had swept out of the room, leaving a cold draught behind her. Victoria began to tremble. She had gone too far. What if Mama ordered Papa to make Rosie leave? She sensed that Rosie would be happy enough to go back to her own world, but she herself would not be able to bear life at Ennismore without her. Why had she said those things to Mama? She should have known it would displease her. She must be careful in the future. She could not risk Rosie being sent away. She made up her mind to keep such thoughts to herself. From now on she would be the perfect daughter her Mama expected.

Later that evening, Lady Ennis sat musing in front of her mirror while her maid, Immelda Fox, brushed out her hair. Without looking up she began to speak.

'Fox, I want you to keep an eye on my daughter.'

Immelda Fox had arrived at Ennismore from a convent several years before, having failed to become a nun. The staff had immediately regarded her with suspicion. Her black hair, intense grey eyes, snow-white skin that had never seen the sun and the way she noiselessly slipped in and out of rooms, added to their view of her as a mysterious, dark spectre. Everyone was shocked when Lady Ennis chose her to be her lady's maid. What they did not realize was that Lady Ennis had correctly judged that Immelda Fox would be the least likely of all the staff to carry tales. She trusted her implicitly.

The maid's eyes widened with curiosity.

'My lady?'

'I had a most disturbing conversation with her this afternoon. She exhibited a defiance I have never seen in her before. I am sure it's the influence of that … that girl!'

'You mean Rosie Killeen, madam? But surely Lady Louisa would be better suited than meself to watch her.'

'No, Fox. I fear my dear sister is not always candid with me about such matters. She sees the classroom as her domain. I had hoped by now she would have made things so unpleasant for the Killeen girl that she would have left of her own accord. But it appears that is not the case.'

Fox shrugged. 'These country girls would surprise you sometimes, my lady,' she said. 'They often have more fight in them than you would expect.'

'You will observe Victoria's movements outside the classroom. I want to know if she is defying me and spending time with that girl.'

'I will do me best, my lady.'

Immelda Fox finished brushing her mistress's hair and helped her into her nightdress. Her expression betrayed no emotion. It was only when she closed the door to Lady Ennis's room and descended the stairs that a smile crept across her thin, pale face.

CHAPTER 3

On 1 June 1906, the sixth anniversary of the arrival of Queen Victoria at Ennismore, Victoria Bell sat in the formal dining room for the first time with her family and guests. The occasion was her thirteenth birthday. They were about to begin dinner when a carriage drew up outside. Victoria jumped to her feet and ran to the window.

'It's Aunt Marianne!' she called.

Lady Marianne Bellefleur, Lord Ennis's sister, had an uncanny knack of knowing when the Bell family was giving a dinner party to which she had not been invited. It amused her greatly on these occasions to arrive unexpectedly, knowing that it would throw her sister-in-law into a sudden swoon over seating arrangements and the like, not to mention her panic that Lady Marianne's eccentric behaviour would shock her guests.

Now she swept into the dining room accompanied by Mr Shane Kearney, the young dandy whom she had taken under her patronage, and who was her constant escort. A tall, dark-haired woman with an exquisite figure and fashionable attire, Lady Marianne always commanded a room. Victoria grinned at her brother, Valentine, as she watched their mother arrange her face into a gracious smile. Valentine, older than Victoria by two years and with the same blond good looks, grinned back.

'Why, dear Marianne,' Lady Ennis said as she rose to greet the new guests, 'what an unexpected surprise.'

Lady Marianne nodded while Mr Kearney took Lady Ennis's hand in his and lavished a theatrical kiss upon it before she snatched it away.

'How could I miss such an auspicious occasion as my dear niece's thirteenth birthday?' said Lady Marianne, nodding towards Victoria. 'Look at you, my dear, so grown-up. Is she not

51

divine, Mr Kearney?'

'Worthy of an Ingres portrait,' said Mr Kearney, flipping back his dark locks with a pale, be-jewelled hand. 'I must illustrate her.'

It was a fine summer evening. The sun filtered in through a west-facing corner window, etching dancing leafy patterns on the small game table that sat beneath it. Flowering bushes brushed against the windows on all sides and the distant call of birds drifted in from the lake. Mr Burke and both liveried footmen stood at attention at the sideboard on which various dishes were placed on silver salvers.

Victoria looked around the table. Her mother eyed Sir Humphrey Higgins, a portly local merchant and hunting friend of Lord Ennis, with disgust as he stuffed huge quantities of food into his fleshy mouth, while Lady Louisa's gaze was fixed expectantly on Reverend Watson, the recently widowed local rector on whom Louisa, in apparent concern for her future once Victoria left the schoolroom, had set her sights.

Lord Ennis gesticulated towards the men. 'This Home Rule nonsense just won't die,' he declared in his full, deep voice. 'The legislation is to be brought before the Lords again, even though there are no votes for it. It is really becoming tiresome.'

'I don't know why the House of Lords are so against it, Papa. It is bound to pass eventually,' said his older son, Thomas, who bore an astonishing resemblance to his father in his youth.

Lord Ennis grew more agitated. 'Not if I can help it. Why on earth would we give Ireland its own parliament?'

'Their power would be limited.'

'For now, perhaps, but what if they want more? What if it leads to land reforms? Or worse, what if they push for full independence? What would become of us then? And as my heir it will be your battle to fight, Thomas. The landed Irish aristocracy is under siege as it is.'

Valentine, who fidgeted throughout the meal as though he had something on his mind, finally spoke up.

'Thomas is right, Papa. If it's delayed much longer, it could lead to violence. The native Irish might take up arms to achieve their independence.'

'That's enough of that sort of talk, Valentine!' said Lady Ennis.

'The boy may be right. There is indeed evidence of growing Irish nationalism, even among people of our class,' said Lady Marianne, evidently enjoying Lady Ennis's discomfort. 'Why, dear Lady Gregory from Galway and Mr Yeats, partners in the Abbey Theatre and both of the Protestant Ascendancy, are championing such a movement. And the young Butler sisters, girls from a very well thought of Protestant family, are causing talk all over Dublin because of their nationalist pursuits.'

Lady Marianne looked pointedly at Victoria. 'I am delighted to hear of young women like the Butlers charting their own course. You must do the same, my dear. Young ladies such as you are poised at the beginning of a new century to throw off all the old ways and march boldly into the future. It is what the French have always done.'

Lady Marianne was a fervent proponent of all

things French. She had never forgiven her forbears for changing their family name from Bellefleur to Bell during the Reformation when they abandoned their Catholicism and swore the required allegiance to the Church of Ireland in order to hold on to their lands. Lady Marianne had changed her name back to Bellefleur as a young woman, and had relished in it ever since.

'And of course we mustn't forget the famine,' put in Sir Humphrey, gulping down a heaped spoonful of bread pudding and eyeing Lady Marianne's conspicuous bosom. 'You landowners created a lot of resentment in your day, and the Irish have long memories.'

Victoria grew excited. Rosie had told her a lot about the history of Ireland. Now she was thrilled with the opportunity to join in the adult conversation. 'Rosie says her brothers talk about a united Ireland all the time. They don't think Home Rule goes far enough. And anyway, Rosie says we stole the land from them in the first place. I think they deserve to have it returned.'

Victoria sat back, pleased with herself, but her mother let out a gasp of horror. Lady Louisa pursed her lips while Valentine burst out laughing. Even Brendan Lynch, the elder of the two footmen, could not conceal a smile. Lady Marianne, who was fingering a threadbare spot on the linen tablecloth, looked up and smiled in triumph.

'You see, Edward?' said Lady Ennis, her face red as she turned to her husband. 'You see what has happened? I told you not to let that awful girl near our daughter, and now listen to her.'

She swung around to her sister. 'Louisa?'

54

'She didn't learn that in my classroom, I assure you.'

The tension broke when Burke entered bearing a pink, iced birthday cake ablaze with candles. Victoria smiled with pleasure. She closed her eyes and made a secret wish then blew out the candles.

'How lovely to be thirteen, and just entering young womanhood,' said Reverend Watson, looking from Victoria to Lady Louisa who, in turn, glared at her niece.

A sudden rain shower sent the footmen scurrying to close all the windows. Lord Ennis took his cue to stand up.

'Gentlemen, shall we repair to the library?'

The men, except for Mr Kearney, rose to follow him. Valentine leaned over and kissed Victoria on the cheek. 'Happy Birthday,' he said. 'I wish I could join you in the drawing room. This is bound to be boring. At least Papa's so caught up with Home Rule he won't be berating me about my school marks.'

'Are they bad?' whispered Victoria.

'Tragically so. I doubt if I shall be going back to Eton.'

Victoria was about to answer him when Brendan brushed past her carrying a tray.

'Happy Birthday, miss,' he whispered.

She swung around but he was gone. She stood for a moment, bemused.

'Victoria? This way please,' called Lady Ennis as she and Lady Louisa walked towards the drawing room, followed by Lady Marianne and Mr Kearney.

When they were seated and Mr Burke had

poured small sherries for each of them, including Victoria, Lady Ennis turned to her daughter.

'Now, my dear, it is not too early for us to begin planning your future. In three years' time you will be ready for your first Season. Isn't it exciting, Louisa? I never thought the time would come.'

'Nor did I,' muttered Lady Louisa.

'And the sooner we get you away from that peasant girl, the better,' continued Lady Ennis.

Victoria looked at her mother. 'Please, Mama, don't keep calling Rosie "that peasant girl". Rosie is my best friend. Surely we will attend the Season together.'

Lady Ennis gasped. 'Victoria! What absolute rubbish. The girl is not of our class, and never shall be. She was allowed to be your school companion only. And she should be grateful for all we have done for her. But when the time comes for you to be presented in society she must be dismissed.'

'But where will she go?' cried Victoria.

Lady Ennis shrugged. 'Back to the peasant cottage where she belongs. Really, Victoria, I thought you had more sense than to think she would be your companion for life.'

Victoria stared at Lady Ennis as if seeing her for the first time. How could she be so cruel? Didn't she understand how much she loved her friend – and needed her? Didn't she understand the guilt she felt every time she allowed her mother's criticism of Rosie to go undefended? A mixture of defiance and anger welled up in her. She stood up and faced her mother, blinking back tears.

'The only way I will go to the Season is if Rosie comes too!'

Lady Ennis laughed. 'As your maid, perhaps, Victoria.'

Lady Ennis's scorn fuelled Victoria's anger further. 'No, Mama. As my equal. And furthermore I will see Rosie whenever I want to. From now on I shall invite her on to this estate and into this house any time I wish, so you can tell Fox she can stop spying on me!'

'Bravo!' exclaimed Lady Marianne, ignoring the shocked faces of the other women. 'Is she not a warrior, Mr Kearney? Is she not a credit to her French heritage?'

Victoria, suddenly exhausted from her outburst, walked to the door, paused and turned around. 'Good night, Mama,' she said quietly, 'thank you for the lovely party. Good night, Aunt Louisa, Aunt Marianne.'

Lady Marianne followed her niece to the door, took her arm and squeezed it. 'I meant what I said,' she whispered. 'If you ever decide to run away and forge your own path you may come to me in Dublin. And tell your young friend Rose that she is also welcome.'

It was the summer of 1908 and Rosie and Victoria walked arm in arm in the walled garden that lay behind the house, strolling along the gravel paths that ran between the manicured boxwood hedges and around the ornamental flower beds which overflowed with red and yellow dahlias. In the year since Victoria had stood up to her mother about seeing Rosie outside the classroom the garden had become their favourite place to spend time.

It was also during that year that Rosie developed

a crush on Valentine. In the past she had seen him only occasionally, and from a distance. He had merely been Victoria's brother and she had not paid him much attention. He had not seemed to notice her either, often strolling past her and nodding absently, his hands thrust in his pockets and a faraway look on his face. She couldn't remember when it happened exactly – that moment when she felt her heart flutter slightly in her chest and her face grow warm at the sight of him. Even then, he still did not notice her. At first she was glad of his seeming indifference. It gave her leave to look at him freely, admiring his tall, slender figure, the way he moved like a stealthy cat, the delicate set of his jaw and the way the light played on his blond hair, rendering it dark as wet sand on some days, and pale as wheat on others. But in time she grew tired of being invisible. Why would he not look at her?

It was a question she wrestled with in the waning days of that first summer. When he departed for Dublin she hoped he would fade from her mind. But he did not. He occupied her thoughts at every turn, disturbing her sleep at night and ruining her concentration by day. She found herself tracing his name in her school note-books, taking loving care over the 'V', decorating it with flowers, often oblivious to Lady Louisa's harsh voice calling her to attention. She longed to share her feelings with Victoria, but a small voice chided her that Victoria would laugh. And at night a sharper voice warned her that she was reaching for something so far beyond her grasp that it could only end in unhappiness.

She tried hard to chase away all thoughts of him and almost succeeded until the week before Christmas when they almost walked smack into one another under the archway that led to the stables. Rosie had been in the kitchen bringing a message from Ma to Bridie, and Valentine was on his way to exercise his favourite horse. He wore jodhpurs and a tweed riding jacket and the wind tousled his hair.

'Excuse me,' muttered Rosie, stepping quickly aside.

He stopped and smiled at her. Such a beautiful smile, she thought, her heart leaping at the sight of him.

'Ah, Rosie,' he said, 'there you are. I was hoping to run into you.' He chuckled. 'Not literally, of course. Please forgive me, I was in a rush to give Phaedon his exercise. I missed him so much when I was in Dublin.'

Rosie nodded, incapable of words. He stood facing her, his blue eyes beaming with good nature and pleasure. A mild panic gripped her and she turned and fled back to the kitchen, her heart thudding against her ribs. She sensed him staring after her.

'Next time don't be in such a rush, Rosie,' he called.

Mercifully, he had only been home for a week. Rosie kept vigilant watch at all times, darting behind a tree or a wall when she saw him coming and, when she could not avoid him, simply bowing her head and rushing past him, muttering comments about being late for lessons. Of course, she knew that he knew lessons were suspended for the holidays. How foolish she felt, running away at the very sight of him. Hadn't she yearned for his attention all last summer? And now, when he was here, greeting her with a cheery smile, all she could do was hide. She didn't trust herself to speak to him for fear of betraying her feelings. What an eejit he must think her. If she went on this way, he was bound to lose any interest in her at all. And yet she could not help herself.

Now it was summer again, and she and Victoria walked companionably in the garden. When they reached the arched stone grotto they sat down on a bench, chatting and laughing in the sunshine.

'What are you two in such deep conversation about?'

Valentine strode up to them, smiling.

Rosie's face grew hot. Everything in her wanted to flee but she was trapped. He stood directly in front of her and she was forced to look up at him. He and Victoria could have been twins, she thought, except for the two year age difference – Valentine had just turned seventeen. Flustered, she jumped up from the bench.

'I should be going,' she said. 'Ma will be wondering where I am.'

'Then I shall walk with you,' said Valentine.

Rosie had no choice but to allow him to walk alongside her. When he closed the garden gate behind them, he took her elbow. She tried not to tremble, although there was nothing she could do about the blush that burned her face crimson. Now sixteen, she had grown tall – far taller than Victoria and almost the same height as Valentine. Her white skin was dusted with light freckles from her love of the sun, and while she was slender she was exceptionally strong. Her black curls were still untamed, no matter how often she forced them back with ribbons or stuffed them beneath bonnets. She had no idea of her beauty, awkward as she felt around Victoria's delicate grace.

'I promised myself I was not going to let you run away from me this time,' he said.

She blushed. 'I don't know what you're after talking about,' she said, setting her gaze straight ahead.

He said nothing, merely tightening his grip on her elbow as he led her on around to the front of Ennismore and across the expanse of green lawns, past a copse of beech trees, towards the wooded avenue that led from the estate.

'Victoria says you're going to be a banker,' Rosie said at last, for want of something to break the tension.

Valentine laughed. 'She's optimistic then. I don't think I'm any more cut out for banking than I was for the law. But Papa *will* keep trying to make a respectable man out of me.'

'Are you not respectable then?'

'Not in Papa's eyes. Thomas is the respectable one. He excelled at Eton and is doing well at Oxford, just as is expected of an oldest son. Thomas is not one to upset any apple carts.'

'And you are?'

'Oh, too many to count. It's a wonder I stayed at Eton so long. I was on probation most of the time. If Papa had not been in the House of Lords I would have been tossed out years ago. And as for my recent venture into the law,' he paused and sighed, 'I tried to tell Papa it would never work, but he refused to listen.'

Without thinking, Rosie bent to pick a buttercup which she twirled between her fingers as she walked. He was surprisingly easy to talk to, and she wondered why she had so often avoided him. She felt quite grown-up strolling with this handsome young man.

'So what will happen if you're not good at banking?' she asked.

They had reached the avenue which wound down towards the main gates of the estate. The trees formed an arch overhead, blocking the afternoon sun. Rosie had a delicious feeling that she and Valentine were the only people in the world. When they reached the gate he slowed down, and instead of opening it climbed up to sit on the top bar. She leaned casually against it.

It was a moment before he spoke and when he did his words were accompanied by a sigh. 'Heaven knows. You see, Rosie, I am a second son. Do you know what that means? When your father is an earl, I mean.'

Rosie shook her head.

'It means that I will not inherit Ennismore or the Ennis Estates, or the title of Earl of Ennis. That is Thomas's birthright and I bear him no ill will because of it. But it does make me sad that I will not be able to stay and work on the land. The reason I've failed at law and will likely fail at banking is that I cannot stand to be cooped up in small, dusty offices. I've tried so hard for Papa's sake to make a go of it, but my soul withers in such places. I need to be out in the fresh air where new life is pulsing all around me.' He paused to take a deep breath. 'Alas, as the second son I am expected to go into the law, finance or the Church.'

Rosie looked at him. 'But why do you have to do what is expected of you? Surely you have a right to choose your own future.'

He gave her a wan smile. 'Ah, but you are wrong, Rosie. When you are born into this life you give up that right. It's the price one pays for all this privilege.'

He laughed suddenly, but the sound rang hollow in Rosie's ears. 'So my remaining options are the army or to marry a wealthy heiress and contribute to the Bell family fortunes.'

'A rich wife wouldn't be too bad now,' said Rosie, trying to lighten the mood, 'as long as she wasn't too ugly.'

'I think I'd rather face a bayonet.'

They were silent for a while. Birds chattered in the trees and the leaves rustled in the soft breeze.

'It's lovely here,' said Valentine, as if speaking to himself. 'I hate to think of having to leave it someday. This is where I belong.'

'I know what you mean,' said Rosie, for the first time expressing her own fears aloud. 'I suppose I will have to leave it someday too, when Victoria goes off to Dublin and finds a husband.'

Valentine nodded. 'You and I are alike, Rosie. We neither of us will be allowed to stay at Ennismore.'

They stood in silence for a while. She sensed that he was as reluctant to leave as she was. They might have stood there forever had they not had to move aside to let the estate cattle-herder and his men enter. When the men had gone, Valentine took Rosie's hand. 'You see, you don't have to run from me, Rosie Killeen. I'm not an ogre, just a lost young man who craves your company.' Without warning he leaned forward and kissed her on the cheek then turned and walked back up the avenue towards the house.

Rosie walked the rest of the way home in a trance. She had actually talked to Valentine. He had taken her elbow and walked her all the way to the gate. He had taken her hand. And he had kissed her. She sighed, trying to remember every detail of the walk, his every movement, every expression, every word. As she neared her cottage, she tucked her sweet memories tightly inside her sixteen-year-old heart. Would her family see any change in her? Would they realize she was no longer a child, but a young woman on the verge of first love? Most likely they would not. She would be the same old Rosie to them. But to herself, she had crossed a threshold from which she would never return.

By early spring of 1910 Victoria's mind teemed with preparations for her first Season. In only a few months she would be seventeen and ready to depart for Dublin to be formally introduced into society. For two months she would attend a swirl of teas and outings and balls with other young people – all of them chaperoned, all of them hoping to make a profitable marriage.

Her papa had insisted that she must wait, even though her mama had wanted her to go the year before. Victoria welcomed the delay. Part of her was excited to go and part of her was terrified. But on a deeper level she was sad. She realized that once she left, her life would change for good. She wanted to hold on to her present world here at Ennismore with Rosie for as long as she could. She thought back to the secret wish she had made on her thirteenth birthday that she and Rosie would always be together. How foolish she had been.

Now she twirled around her bedroom wearing a blue chenille gown with silver beading. The gown seemed to float around her slender frame. Rosie sat on the bed stroking a pile of dresses which Victoria was trying on. They were stunning – colours and beading and material the likes of which neither girl could ever have imagined.

'Isn't it heavenly, Rosie? Have you ever seen anything like it?'

'You'll be the most beautiful girl there,' Rosie said. 'The boys will be tripping over themselves to get a dance with you.'

'Do you think so?' said Victoria blushing.

She turned to study herself in the mirror. As she did so she caught sight of Rosie's reflection over her shoulder. Her friend had bowed her head and appeared to be wiping away tears. Victoria was suddenly ashamed of herself. How could she not have noticed Rosie's distress? She went over and sat down beside her on the bed and put her arm around her shoulder.

'Forgive me, Rosie. I got carried away.'

Rosie nodded. 'Who could blame you?'

Victoria sighed. 'I still wish you could come with me. Remember all the times I insisted that you would? I wanted so much for it to be possible.'

Rosie looked up at her. 'We were both naive, Victoria. There was a time when I wanted to believe it too. I was as caught up as you were with the notion. What girl like me wouldn't want to go to fancy teas and outings to the seaside and grand balls?'

'I know. But I realize now how my insistence made it more painful for you. I was being selfish. I wanted you with me.' She paused and looked at Rosie. 'Ever since that first day when you dived into the lake and retrieved my little boat I've admired your bravery and I've wanted to be more like you. The truth is, I only feel brave when you are around.'

Rosie smiled. 'Ah now, that's not true. I wasn't there the time you stood up to your mother and insisted we should be friends outside the classroom and that you wouldn't go to the Season without me. And you did so in front of your aunts, too. I don't know if I would have had the courage.'

Victoria giggled. 'You should have seen their faces! They were stupefied with shock, although Aunt Marianne cheered out loud!' She paused. 'Of course, Mama knew I would go to the Season eventually – and by myself – she was content to wait for me to come to my senses. So I suppose giving in on us spending more time together, although it seemed like a concession at the time, was a good plan for her.'

The girls lapsed into silence for a moment, each lost in her own thoughts.

'What will you do, Rosie?' asked Victoria at last.

The question had nagged at her for some time. Her own future was already mapped out – attend the Season, find a suitable husband, and get married. She tried not to acknowledge the small twinge of resentment that rose up every time she thought about this, the real reason for going to Dublin. Instead, she concentrated on the flurry of exciting new adventures that awaited her – balls and outings and teas and a wonderful new wardrobe.

'I mean after I leave here,' she continued.

Rosie looked off in the distance. 'I truly don't know. My ma thinks I should have no trouble getting a position teaching or as a governess. She doesn't understand that without proper certification I wouldn't stand a chance at teaching. I might get taken on as a governess somewhere, but only if I get a glowing reference from Lady Louisa. And I doubt that will be forthcoming.'

'Have you asked her?'

'No, but I suppose I will have to. I don't hold out much hope though.'

'Maybe I can help persuade her.'

Rosie shook her head. 'I think that might make it worse.' She stood up. 'There's one thing I *do* know, Victoria, and that is I will never be a servant at Ennismore or anywhere else. No matter what else I have to do, I will not do that.'

Later, Victoria watched from the bedroom window as Rosie made her way across the lawns down towards the gates of Ennis Estate. Instead of her friend's usual confident walk, her shoulders were slumped and her head bowed. She tried to put herself in Rosie's place. But no matter how hard she tried she knew she could never understand what it would be like to be a farmer's daughter who was thrust into the world of the gentry and then abandoned. Tears filled her eyes as she watched Rosie's figure disappear and realized how much responsibility she bore for her friend's misfortune.

CHAPTER 4

As he had predicted, Valentine also failed at banking. He returned to Ennismore in late April 1910 and a cold formality settled upon the relationship between the young man and his father. As soon as he could, Valentine sought out Rosie's company.

'So you see, I have failed again,' he said, approaching her in the garden where she knelt cutting flowers. 'I am a worthless lout.'

Rosie detected the irony in his voice. 'No you're not,' she said.

Valentine shrugged. 'It's what Papa says, and I appear to be proving him right.' He looked at her. 'I tried my best, Rosie, I really did. And I might have stayed on but the bank ran into financial trouble. I was not the only clerk who was sacked. But still, in Father's eyes I am a failure.'

Rosie's heart ached for him, caught as he was between his heart's desire to stay and work the land and his duty to his family. And his father's disapproval must surely add to his pain.

'Our lessons ended early today,' she said, standing up and shaking the soil from her dress.

'Victoria claimed to have a headache so I am gathering some flowers to cheer her up. But I think the truth is she is bored and distracted. She and your mama will be away to Dublin in a month.'

'Yes, and Papa says that as I have nothing better to do I am to accompany them and serve as Victoria's escort,' said Valentine, his tone bitter.

Rosie felt a twinge of envy. How much she would have loved to ride to Dublin in a coach with Valentine at her side. She sat down on a nearby bench and laid the bunch of ox-eyed daisies beside her. Valentine joined her, his arm resting on the back of the bench and his long legs stretched out before him.

He smiled. 'And what of you, Roisin Dove? Would you welcome such a trip to Dublin to attend teas and balls and meet the boy of your dreams?'

Valentine had taken to calling her 'Roisin Dove', after she mentioned that this was her da's pet name for her. 'It means 'Dark Rosaleen,' she had told him, 'and 'tis another name for Ireland.'

'I suppose I would,' she said, in answer to his question. 'But where would I be getting fancy dresses and invitations to balls?'

She did not add that she had already met the boy of her dreams. Wasn't he sitting here beside her? As he turned away to gaze out at the horizon she stole a look at him, taking in his flaxen hair, the firm lines of his nose and jaw and his pale, well-groomed hands folded carelessly in his lap. He smelled of clean soap, with a faint hint of lavender. How different he was from the other boys she knew. Her red-faced and rugged brothers, whom

69

she loved dearly, were good and hardy souls but were a different breed altogether. And the young lads beyond in Crossmolina who leaned against shop windowsills, whistling after girls and asking for a kiss, struck her as oafish compared with Valentine's dignified manner. She wondered if she would ever have been attracted to one of them had she never set foot in Ennismore. She shuddered at the thought.

Surely there must be something about him that was not perfect, but she could think of nothing. As their relationship developed, the previous summer, she had witnessed his gentleness, like the time he had struggled to free a frightened calf that had caught its head in a barbed wire fence, all the while reassuring the animal with soft whispers. Perhaps her brothers would have done the same, she allowed, but how many of Valentine's gentry peers would have bothered? She loved his passion for the Ennis Estate – how he loved every blade of grass and every stone on it – and yet he did not begrudge his brother's right to it. She admired his loyalty, and knew that he would lay down his life for any one of his family. And underneath his polite exterior she sensed a rebel, just like herself. She sighed. They were kindred souls, Valentine and she, caught between duty and freedom. For all that, the small voice still whispered that he was not meant for her – that he was beyond her grasp. But she shut it out, putting her hands over her ears so she would not hear it. She must not listen, or her dreams would vanish.

Valentine turned towards her and took her hand. 'I would buy you all the dresses you wanted if I could, Rosie. But alas, like you, I am a pauper, except for what Papa begrudgingly doles out to me.'

Rosie nodded. She had no doubt of his sincerity. But what good were his words to her? A cloud of gloom had hovered over her for some weeks. She had tried to ignore it, but it kept returning. She did not want to think about the future. In a month from now Victoria would be gone and what would become of her? Even her request to Lady Louisa for a reference had been met with coldness.

'Isn't it enough that I stooped to teach you all these years, you ungrateful girl? How dare you demand more of me?'

Rosie had finally admitted the truth to herself. It was something much greater than missing the Season that plagued her. Rather, it was the reality that she could never now be satisfied with life as a tenant farmer's daughter. She had tasted the world of the gentry, and God help her, she wanted to be one of them.

She took her hand away and looked directly into Valentine's eyes.

'At least you have your choice of what to do with your life – even if it's not law or banking. You'll still have money. Surely there'll be plenty of other things that would suit you. 'Twill be your own fault if you let your so-called duty get in the way.'

She spoke more sharply than she had meant to and she regretted it at once. But he did not seem to take offence.

'You're right, Rosie. But alas, what would suit me would be to stay here and run the estate. I love this place more than I can say. I love the land, and the animals and the house itself.' He gazed out across the garden towards the lake and Mount Nephin. 'I love it in winter and in summer. I feel free here. I would waste away cooped up in a stuffy office in Dublin or London or elsewhere.'

'I love it here, too,' said Rosie.

They sat in silence for a while. Rosie thought how comfortable it was to sit with him and say nothing. They understood one another. The shock was that Valentine, the privileged son of the gentry, was lost just like herself.

'There you are.' Victoria walked towards them, waving her hand. 'I had a frightful headache, but it's gone now, thank goodness. What are you two talking about?'

'We've been speaking of many things, dear sister, of cabbages and kings, just like the Walrus and the Carpenter,' said Valentine referring to Lewis Carroll's poem.

'And why the sea is boiling hot; and whether pigs have wings,' laughed Victoria. 'I haven't thought of that poem in years.'

'But didn't they trick the poor oysters?' said Rosie. 'Sure they lured them into their world and then they devoured them.'

The day that Rosie was dreading finally arrived. It was 1 June 1910, ten years to the day from when she had first met Victoria. She had wakened early that morning and considered not going near Ennismore at all, but she knew Victoria would be hurt if she did not come. Besides, she did not want to betray her jealousy that Victoria was off to a new glittering life and she was to be left behind. It wasn't Victoria's fault, she told herself, neither of them had asked to be born into the lives they had. God was responsible for that.

Now, as she got out of bed and dressed herself in one of her old school dresses, shabby from wear, she prayed for God's help to get her through the day. When she approached Ennismore she saw the carriage outside. Brendan Lynch, the first footman, loaded two large trunks on to the back of it as the driver stood waiting in his black coat and top hat. As she approached, she saw Immelda Fox coming down the front steps carrying a small suitcase. Rosie assumed, as Lady Ennis's maid, Immelda must be accompanying them.

'Mama has leased a house in Merrion Square,' Victoria had said. 'Papa is very upset that she has spent the money to do so instead of staying with Aunt Marianne, but Mama says she will not have her interfering.' Victoria giggled. 'I think it would have been rather fun to have my aunt involved.'

Immelda approached Rosie and nodded.

'Fine day, thank God,' she said, setting down her bag. 'A grand day to travel, so.'

'Have you been to Dublin before?' asked Rosie, making nervous conversation.

'Me? Sure how would the likes of me ever get the chance to go to a place like Dublin?'

'Well, I just thought ... you know, Lady Ennis has travelled to Dublin many times.'

'Aye, well she did it without me. She used one of the Lady Marianne's maids. This time she wants me with her since she'll have her own house. And I'll be expected to do for Miss Victoria as well.'

Rosie detected a biting undertone in Immelda's voice.

'Ah, Rosie, there you are. I was so afraid you might not come to see me off.'

Victoria ran down the front steps of Ennismore, her arms outstretched. She looked radiant in a two-piece dove-grey travelling costume and matching hat. Her blonde hair was swept up and she looked quite grown-up. She's no longer a child, Rosie thought to herself. I suppose neither of us is.

'And why wouldn't I come?' said Rosie with a brightness she didn't feel. 'Isn't my best friend in the whole world going off on a great adventure?'

Victoria enfolded Rosie in a tight hug. 'Isn't it thrilling?' she said. 'I shall write to you every day, Rosie, and tell you all about my adventures. Oh, I can't wait.'

Victoria's happiness was contagious. Rosie smiled at her friend, and hugged her in return. 'Have a brilliant time, Victoria. And I want to hear all about it.' She paused. 'I'll miss you,' she whispered.

A cloud passed over Victoria's blue eyes. 'I'll miss you too, Rosie. I do wish you could come with me.'

Rosie nodded. 'And me.'

The girls stood, locked in each other's gaze.

'Victoria! Come along, say goodbye to your father and get in the carriage.'

Lady Ennis bustled down the steps followed by her husband and Lady Louisa. She swept past Rosie, ignoring her. At the bottom of the steps Victoria hugged her aunt and then her father, who wiped away a tear. Then she ran to the carriage and climbed in, helped by Brendan Lynch. As Rosie watched, she had an idle thought that he held on to Victoria's elbow for longer than was necessary, only letting go when a sullen-looking Immelda shoved him aside to climb in.

Valentine was the last to arrive. Rosie watched him as he ambled down the front steps, his long stride graceful and fluid. He bowed to his father who gave him a curt nod. When he approached Rosie he stopped and smiled.

'Wish me luck, Rosie,' he said. 'No doubt Papa's waiting for me to fail as an escort too.' Then he added in a whisper, 'I will be back as soon as I can.'

Rosie blushed and bowed her head. She said nothing.

The carriage kicked up dust and gravel as the horses cantered around the drive and out to the path that led to the main gate. Victoria leaned out of the window waving furiously. Rosie, Lord Ennis and Lady Louisa stood in silence waving back. Then Lord Ennis nodded at Rosie, took Lady Louisa's arm, and together they turned and went back up the steps and into Ennismore. The front door thudded shut behind them.

PART TWO

SEPARATION

1910–1912

CHAPTER 5

'No,' Rosie cried, sitting straight up in bed. 'No!'

Her ma rushed up to her bedroom. 'What on earth's wrong with you, child?' she said, holding a candle close to Rosie.

She touched her daughter's face. 'You've a terrible fever on you. Did you take sick?'

Rosie looked from her mother to the small window beside her bed and back again. She rubbed her eyes. 'Oh, Ma, I had an awful dream. I was running after Victoria's coach and when it stopped and the coachman turned around he had no head, and he tried to get me to go with him, and...'

'Ssh now, darlin'. Sure it was only a bad dream.'

'But what did it mean? Am I going to die?'

'Not at all,' said Ma. 'Sure we've all heard too many stories about headless horsemen and the like. 'Tis a wonder all of us haven't died of fright.' She pulled the quilt up over Rosie. 'Go back to sleep now, daughter, I'll sit with you for a while. You're just worried about young Victoria, that's all. And you're sad that she's gone away. That's all it is.'

'Aye, Ma. Goodnight.'

As things turned out it was not Rosie but Bridie who fell sick. Shortly after Victoria's departure to Dublin, she began to cough. The symptoms were mild at first, but one day she collapsed on the floor of the library in Ennismore. The other

79

maids brought her down to the servants' hall and gave her laudanum to bring her round. Mrs Murphy, the housekeeper, insisted Bridie go up to bed and rest. But the next day she was so weak she could hardly stand up. Brendan brought the cart around and drove her home to the Killeen cottage, where the doctor was sent for. He pronounced that she had a severe case of pneumonia and ordered a month of bed rest.

'The girl is worn out,' the doctor told her mother. 'She needs a rest, or she'll have no strength to fight this.'

'But I can't lose me job,' said Bridie. 'The whole house has to be cleaned top to bottom while Lady Ennis is away for the summer. They need me up there. And if I'm gone for too long there's plenty of girls in the village waiting to take my place.'

Bridie tried to climb out of bed, but the doctor and her mother restrained her. 'Pay heed to the doctor, Bridie,' said her ma, 'and follow his orders.'

'But what about me job?' said Bridie again. 'We need me wages.'

'Don't be worrying your head about that now, we'll be grand.'

Rosie listened from the doorway. While there was no love lost between herself and Bridie, she felt sorry for her sister all the same. It would be a terrible blow if she lost her job. She wasn't fit for anything else. She'd not even finished at the village school before she went to work as a maid. And she was going on twenty-five and no sign of her getting married.

Rosie hadn't realized how much her family depended on Bridie's wages. Hearing her ma's worried voice now, she knew that it was going to cause hardship. A small voice whispered in her head that it had nothing to do with her. She had been thinking of what she must do now that Victoria was gone. She couldn't stay at home forever without earning her keep. And she had no intention of ever setting foot in Ennismore again. She would have to go away, she decided. But where to? She had no money. She was well-educated, yes, but had no trade and without the money to take her to Dublin or even out of Ireland she was stuck here.

Rosie sighed. She'd hoped she would have longer to make a plan. She had thought she might speak to Valentine about things when he returned. But Bridie's illness had interfered. Annoyance filled her. If she didn't know better she'd have believed Bridie did this on purpose. Hadn't her sister been pestering her all the years since she had gone for lessons with Victoria? Hadn't she tried to make her life miserable at every turn? Well it wasn't fair. It just wasn't fair at all.

She slipped out the door of the cottage and breathed in the fresh air. Her old dog, Rory, limped up and began to walk alongside her. As she climbed the steep fields at the back of the cottage, tall grasses tapped against her bare legs and the wind tossed her hair. She felt cleansed and free as she walked, the cloying odours of Bridie's sickroom receding far below her. When she reached the large boulder where she had played as a child, she sat down on the grass and leaned against it, shading her eyes from the sun with her hand.

From here she could see Ennismore, with Lough Conn shining in the distance and Mount Nephin wrapped in wispy clouds, and beyond that the vast expanse of black bog that reached to the sea.

Her guilt grew by the day as she saw how the loss of Bridie's wages was affecting her family. At first Ma had insisted that nothing had changed, but small things began to reveal the truth. Her oldest brother was told there'd be no new boots or schoolbag this year, which meant there were not even hand-me-downs for the two younger ones. Da said he'd given up tobacco because he'd lost his taste for it; and eggs no longer appeared on the breakfast table.

'Porridge will have to do ye,' Ma had said. 'I can get a good price for the eggs in the village.'

The truth of their predicament had begun to loom large.

'What am I to do, Rory?' Rosie said to the dog as he lay panting on the grass beside her. 'I'd die rather than take Bridie's place up there. That's even if they would take me on. I'm sure I have few friends among the staff. And I won't go begging to them, either.'

She closed her eyes and inhaled the smells of the rugged grasses and riotous wildflowers that surrounded her. 'Please God, make Bridie better in the morning,' she whispered, blessing herself.

But Bridie was not better in the morning, or the next, or the next. It seemed the doctor was right – she would need a long rest to overcome the illness that had beset her. The oldest daughter of the Killeen family, called Nora, who was seldom

82

mentioned, had died of pneumonia when she was fifteen, and the spectre of her ghost came back to haunt the cottage. The family tiptoed about for fear of disturbing Bridie. Even Rosie's brothers spoke in whispers.

'I suppose it's time I was going up to the Big House to ask for Bridie's job,' said Rosie, when she could stand the guilt no longer.

Ma turned to her. 'Ah no, love,' she said. 'Sure the last place you belong is down on your knees scrubbing floors.'

'We need the money, Ma. And Bridie needs me to hold her place for her.'

In the end it was settled, and on the following Monday morning Rosie put on a pair of old boots and Bridie's uniform and left the cottage. She walked as if she were going to a funeral, dread mounting with her every step. She remembered the innocence of the first day she had approached the Big House, filled with childish fear mixed with wonder at what adventure awaited her. But no adventure awaited her now only drudgery at best, and humiliation at worst. She went around the back of the house to the kitchen door. Mrs O'Leary pulled her inside as soon as she saw her.

'Is it Bridie?' she said, her voice filled with alarm.

'No, Mrs O'Leary,' said Rosie. 'She's still very weak, but the doctor says with rest she should pull through.'

Mrs O'Leary blessed herself. 'Thanks be to God.'

'Mrs O'Leary,' said Rosie, 'I've come to take Bridie's place until she recovers. She's afraid she'll lose her job if she's away too long.'

The cook looked down at Rosie, her keen blue eyes travelling over the uniform and apron and down to the well-worn boots. She shook her head. 'Sure what do you know about housekeeping, Roisin? You've not dirtied your hands since the day the Queen herself came to Ennismore.'

Mrs O'Leary's tone was not unkind and Rosie took the opportunity to press her case. 'Please, Mrs O'Leary. I know I've no experience, but I'm a farmer's daughter, after all. I still clean out the chicken pens every morning and I milk the cows when I'm needed. And Ma says I'm a great hand at baking. Please give me a chance. I'll show you how hard I can work. Would you do it for Bridie's sake?'

Mrs O'Leary sighed and rocked back and forth on her tiny feet. 'If it was up to me, love, I'd give you the chance. But it's Mrs Murphy you'll have to convince. She's in charge of the maids. I can't promise you what she'll say, but if you're polite and tell her you're doing it for Bridie she might give in to you. She's very fond of Bridie.'

Mrs Murphy was harder to convince than she had expected. She told Rosie that she doubted if Mr Burke, the butler, would approve on the grounds that having her in a servant's position would upset the clear lines between staff and gentry.

'But Mrs O'Leary says it's you has final say over the housekeeping staff,' said Rosie, desperate to plead her case while showing Mrs Murphy respect.

A faint smile played on Mrs Murphy's lips. She paused before answering. It was only a few seconds, but it felt like a life time to Rosie. At last she said, 'I am a fair woman, Miss Killeen, and I know how much this means to your family and to Bridie. I shall give you a try for a week. I will tolerate no slacking. And you will not put yourself above any of the other servants. As the newest member of the staff you will take your lead from them. Is that understood?'

'Yes, Mrs Murphy! Thank you Mrs Murphy!'

Two hours later Rosie was down on her knees scrubbing the front steps of Ennismore. As she scrubbed, a torrent of feelings flooded through her. What would she do if Valentine were to come upon her in this state? What would he think of the cut of her in the apron and cap and old boots? What if Victoria came back before Bridie returned and found her friend transformed into a servant? After all she had said to her about never becoming a servant at Ennismore or anywhere else – well she wouldn't blame Victoria if she laughed in her face. With each thought she scrubbed harder until her hands were red and blistered.

It was agreed that Rosie would live in at Ennismore, with only Wednesday and Sunday afternoons off. She was not even allowed to run down to her own cottage when things were a bit slow, or sleep there the odd night. Bridie had earned that right because of the years she had served at the Big House. Rosie was to be afforded no such leniency. She was disappointed. She had hoped to escape from the place and sleep in her own bed some of the nights. But her work called for her to be up before dawn to clean the grates and light the fires – even in the summer months the old house was cold. And on top of it all, to Rosie's horror, she was to share a room with the red-haired maid, Sadie Canavan.

'Sure I can't believe my good luck,' said a smiling Sadie when she came into the bedroom and found Rosie lying under the thin covers of a narrow iron bed. 'If it isn't the likes of the high and mighty Miss Rosie Killeen herself come to grace me with her company? Who would ever have believed it?'

Rosie said nothing as Sadie kept up a stream of sarcasm. She was obviously delighted at Rosie's downfall. 'Just wait 'till I tell Lady Louisa. I'd say she'll be as shocked at the rest of us with this turn of events. But she always said you were just a jumped-up wee peasant girl. She never liked you.'

Rosie turned her back to Sadie and pretended to be asleep, determined to give her no satisfaction. When Sadie finally gave up and went to sleep, Rosie opened her eyes and sighed. How was she going to put up with this? Once more she silently cursed Bridie, and then blessed herself for the sin. She cursed Victoria for going off and leaving her, although she knew there was no choice. She cursed all the gentry that had ever been born. And lastly she cursed God for causing her to be born into poverty. When her anger subsided she slipped out of bed and knelt and asked the same God to forgive her for her wicked thoughts.

CHAPTER 6

The humiliation Rosie received at the hands of the servants was nothing to what she heaped onto herself. With every sweep of the broom, or rub of the cloth, or shovel of the ashes, she despised herself even more. The work was hard but she could have stood that if she'd been an ordinary tenant farmer's child who left the village school and went up to work at the Big House, just as Bridie had. But she was not just an ordinary tenant farmer's child – not any more. She had seen too much. She had enjoyed the touch of her fingers on dainty china cups, and the pleasure of French vowels rolling in her throat, and the fresh scent of laundered white linens. She had enjoyed the restful pleasures of walks in the walled garden, picnics beside the lake, and the exhilaration of riding the finest horses across the countryside.

Why should she not be angry with God for showing her a glimpse of this fine life and then thrusting her back into such drudgery? And she was! But she was even angrier with herself for having believed that such a life could one day be hers. Bridie was right all along – she had been a foolish girl to think that someone from her station could ever cross that line that separated the classes.

One evening at dinner in the servants' hall Sadie informed her that Valentine was due back any day. He had been away for several weeks in

Dublin visiting Thomas and escorting Victoria on outings. Rosie tried hard not to blush at the mention of his name but with no success. She realized that the servants had seen her walking with Valentine and drawn their own conclusions. A prickly heat covered her cheeks and throat as she bowed her head and tried to ignore all of the faces turned towards her.

'I wonder what he'll say when he sees you dressed up like a servant?' said Sadie.

'I *am* a servant,' muttered Rosie.

'Aye, so you are.'

The first footman, Brendan, regarded her thoughtfully.

'Now we'll find out whose side you're on,' he said.

'What do you mean? I'm on nobody's side.'

'You're either on the gentry's side, or you're on our side,' said Brendan.

Rosie fought back hot tears. She stood up. 'I don't know whose feckin' side I'm on,' she shouted at Brendan. 'I don't know where I belong. Are you satisfied now?' She drew a deep breath. 'May I go now, Mr Burke?'

Mr Burke nodded. 'I think that would be prudent, Miss Killeen. You appear overwrought. I have not heard such language from you before, and I do not wish to hear it again.'

'So much for her refined manners,' Rosie heard Sadie laugh as she rushed out of the room and up to bed.

As she tossed and turned she could not get Brendan's question out of her mind. She had never thought about things this way before –

servants on one side, gentry on the other. Was the separation of the classes as stark – and as simple – as that? She pondered the thought all night and by the time she crept into Valentine's bedroom the next morning to light the fire, she brought all her frustration with her. As she knelt over the hearth, her head echoed with memories of Brendan's question. He was right, she thought, I need to take a side.

'Rosie? Is that you? What are you doing here?'

She froze at the sound of Valentine's voice. It was customary at Ennismore to light the fires even in unoccupied rooms in order to keep the house warm. Regardless of the previous night's conversations she had not expected him to have already returned. She remained still, hoping that he might fall back to sleep. But instead she felt his hand on her shoulder.

'Rosie?'

She swung around. 'Go ahead, laugh!' she said. 'Everybody else is. Yes, it's me, Rosie, servant girl, skivvy, down on my knees lighting your fire.'

Valentine took a step back. 'I don't understand, Rosie. Why – why are you...?'

Rosie stood up and faced him squarely, dusting her hands on her apron.

'Bridie took sick and I had to take her place,' she said, her face upturned in defiance.

'Is she all right?' said Valentine flustered.

'The doctor says it will be a while.'

'But – was there no alternative? Surely it was not necessary for you to do *this?*'

He looked down in bewilderment at the bucket of ashes Rosie held and then back at her. His obvious shock fuelled her embarrassment. She was determined not to let him see it, although she could not stop her cheeks from burning.

'Hard work is nothing to be ashamed of. And no, there was no choice. Bridie needed me to keep her place for her, and my family needed the wages. We don't have pots of gold like some people.'

Still looking mystified, Valentine sat down on the bed and scratched his head. He wore his pyjamas, and his blond hair was tousled from sleep. Rosie thought he looked very young.

'Please,' he said, 'can you take a walk with me?'

'No. I've work to do.'

'Later, then? When you have completed your duties?'

'I've no time off 'till Wednesday afternoon.'

'I see. Well I shall meet you at the stables on Wednesday. Perhaps we can go riding.'

'And where would I be getting a horse? I'm not the gentry.'

'I can arrange for one,' he said quietly.

'Fair enough,' said Rosie.

They stared at each other for another moment, then gritting her teeth she stooped and reached under his bed to pull out the chamber pot.

'Please, Rosie,' he whispered, 'please leave that alone.'

At one o'clock on Wednesday afternoon Rosie stood near the stables waiting for him. She had wrestled with herself for several days as to whether or not she should go. She yearned to see him again – to pick up their friendship where they had left off before Victoria's departure. But she could hear the warning bells clanging in her head. She remembered Brendan's question: 'whose side are you on?' If she met Valentine, would she be choosing the gentry's side? She knew that would be a terrible mistake. Hadn't she begun to see her place clearly in the last few weeks? A voice deep inside told her she was setting herself up for trouble. She should turn away now and run to the safety of her cottage.

'There you are.'

It was too late. Valentine approached her. He looked so handsome with his warm smile and wide, blue eyes, that she felt all resolve melt. He carried some clothing over his arm.

'Here,' he said. 'I realized you would need a riding costume, so I brought one of Victoria's. I hope it will fit you.'

Rosie looked down at her grey maid's dress and white apron and blushed.

'I'm sure it will,' she said reaching for the clothes. 'Victoria used to lend me hers all the time.'

'Good,' said Valentine. 'Go and change and I'll see the groom about a horse for you.'

Rosie ran into one of the empty horse stalls to change. Her heart beat fast. She knew everyone would disapprove but at the moment she didn't care. She was going riding with Valentine and that was all that mattered.

The groom helped her up on her favourite gelding and tightened the stirrups. When she was young she had ridden her da's old farm horse without a saddle, her legs astride his thick back. She had encouraged Victoria to ride astride a horse as well, although Lord Ennis had put a stop to it. She smiled now, thinking back on it, ignoring the groom's questioning stare as she threw her leg across the saddle.

Valentine trotted up next to her on Phaedon, his fine, chestnut stallion. 'Let's go,' he said. 'Race you to the woods.'

They set out across the vast pasture that surrounded the house and made for the woods in the distance. Rosie was well able to keep up with him so he had no need to slow down for her. As she galloped, joy swept over her. She was free. She rode the gelding hard, jumping over fences and ditches as she raced across the fields, Valentine in hot pursuit. She had never ridden with such fierceness before, but now the faster she went the farther her troubles fell behind her. She was outrunning them, and the thought sped her on towards recklessness.

'Slow down, Rosie,' Valentine shouted from behind her.

Her gelding frothed with exertion and Rosie knew she should slow her pace, but she could not help herself. On she rode until at last her horse shuddered to a stop in front of a ditch and she almost somersaulted over his head. Valentine rode up beside her, breathing hard, and looking angry.

'That's no way to treat a horse and you know it. What's wrong with you?'

Rosie dismounted and looked at him sheepishly.

'You're right,' she said, 'but I couldn't seem to stop myself.' She stroked the panting horse's head. 'I'm sorry, Gideon,' she whispered.

Valentine dismounted and tied up both horses

to a nearby fence. He held his hand out to Rosie and she took it. 'Come on,' he said, 'let's walk to your favourite place.'

Rosie's favourite place was the fairy fort in the woods where she had played as a child. She had first shown it to Victoria and told her about the little people who lived below the ground and who should not be disturbed. Later, when Valentine rode out with them, Victoria had brought him there, and afterwards it became the best-loved destination of all three on summer rides. Rosie sat down on a flat rock beneath an oak tree and Valentine joined her. Sunlight pierced through the branches, throwing patterns on the forest floor. A stranger might have thought this a quiet place, but as a country girl Rosie had learned to listen to all the sounds around her. Birds sang and a light breeze whispered through the leaves, and rabbits scurried in the undergrowth. In the distance she could hear the seabirds calling from the lake. She was sure she could hear the fairies chattering below, but when she had mentioned this once to Valentine and Victoria they had shaken their heads and said they could hear nothing.

'Maybe you have to be Irish,' she had said.

'But I *am* Irish,' they had both answered in unison.

Now, as they sat together like old friends, Rosie leaned her head against Valentine's shoulder. She had never dared be this forward before, but she was exhausted after the ride, and in need of comfort. All the troubles she had tried to put in the past came flooding back. She sank down into helplessness.

'What am I to do, Valentine?' she said. 'What is to become of me?'

Valentine held her hand. 'It will be all right, Rosie,' he said. 'Your sister will be well soon, and Victoria will be back, and everything will be as it was.'

Rosie shook her head. 'No, it won't, Valentine. It will never be the same as before.'

Valentine sighed and said nothing.

'Even Victoria and I won't be friends in the same way,' she said, voicing a new dread that was welling in her. 'She has only written to me once, and even in her letter I could see how she is beginning to change.'

'She's busy, Rosie. You should have seen all the teas and parties I accompanied her to. And the summer is only half over. There are balls still to come, and a trip to London, and–'

'Sure I know all that,' put in Rosie. 'That's what I mean. Before, we shared every new adventure together. But now she's part of a new world that I know nothing about. We have nothing left in common.'

'Nonsense. You have your childhood friendship.'

'But we're no longer children,' said Rosie.

When they rode back into the stables, Brendan was waiting for them. Rosie was surprised to see him. Had he been spying on her? He gave her a pitying look as he helped her dismount.

'You're to see Mr Burke,' he said. He moved closer to her. 'The groom told him you had gone out riding with Master Valentine. I tried to tell Mr Burke the groom was mistaken, but he said others had seen yez as well.' He sighed. 'You know everybody here has eyes in the backs of their heads.'

'What does he want?' said Rosie.

Brendan shook his head. 'I think you know, Rosie girl.'

He was right, of course. She knew exactly what was coming. She and Valentine exchanged looks but said nothing. Rosie turned and followed Brendan to Mr Burke's quarters.

'It is not proper, Miss Killeen, not proper at all.' Mr Burke's expression was stern as he looked up at her from behind his desk. 'You must remember your place. You are no longer Miss Victoria's young companion with free run of the estate and access to her brothers. You are a servant in their house, and as such you shall act accordingly. In the future, you will not avail yourself of Mr Valentine's company, nor that of his brother, Thomas. You will speak only if a member of the Bell family addresses you first, and even then your head must be bowed and your answer short. Otherwise you are to make yourself invisible. Is that clear?'

Rosie could not bring herself to answer. Inside, resentment warred with her good sense. She wanted to lash out at him, to make him see the unfairness of his words, to make him understand. Instead, she clenched her fists and nodded.

CHAPTER 7

By August, Bridie's health had greatly improved. She was able to take walks outside without growing short of breath, and help Ma with the housekeeping. She was anxious to get back to her job at Ennismore but the doctor insisted she stay home for another fortnight.

'There's no rush, Bridie,' Ma said. 'Sure Rosie's doing a fine job up there, and she's been giving us part of her wages, just like you did. Let her stay on for another while so.'

Bridie scowled. 'She might get to liking it too much. Then where would I be?'

'No fear of that,' said Ma. 'I'd say she'll run as fast as she can out of there as soon as she gets the chance. She's a great girl to have stood it as long as she has.'

Bridie was not about to show her gratitude. 'She's getting paid for it, isn't she?'

Her wages were the one bright spot in Rosie's life. She had been able to put a little money aside since she began working. It was not enough to get her very far but it was a start. Apart from that, the drudgery and humiliation were as bad as ever. She had heeded Mr Burke's orders not to go near Valentine. She explained the situation to him the following morning as she lit the fire in his room.

'But that's ridiculous,' he said. 'How can he tell you what to do in your free time?'

'You're the one being ridiculous. You of all people should know how it is between your lot and the servants.' Rosie's tone was bitter.

'Our lot?'

'Yes, your lot.' Rosie could not hide her frustration. 'We're no more than furniture to you. We're not to be seen or heard. Think about how you treat the other servants. I'd bet you don't even know their names.'

Without realizing it, Rosie had begun to see the lot of a servant very clearly. In the past, when Bridie had told stories and complained, Rosie had paid little attention. But now that she was in that role herself she saw how miserable and restricted their lives were, and while she still had not accepted that she belonged in their world, a new understanding and compassion had replaced her former resentment.

'They don't matter to me. You do.' Valentine paused. 'At least we can meet here every day,' he said, 'where there's nobody to spy on us.'

'You don't give up, do you? For your information, Mr Burke has thought of that and starting tomorrow the young maid, Thelma, will be taking care of your room.'

'Who's she?' said Valentine.

Rosie would have laughed if she hadn't been so upset. Valentine had just proved the point she made to him about not knowing the servants.

'Goodbye, Valentine,' she said as she turned away to leave the room.

Without warning he grabbed her by the waist and swung her around. He leaned over and kissed her firmly on the mouth. She was so surprised she almost dropped the bucket of ashes she held. She pulled away abruptly.

'For God's sake, Valentine, what am I just after telling you?'

'You're not getting rid of me so easily, Rosie.'

As she climbed down the back stairs, Rosie experienced a confused mixture of elation and embarrassment. She had so often imagined what it would be like to have Valentine kiss her – but always it was in the garden in moonlight, or by the fairy fort in the woods – she never imagined it would be in his room with a bucket full of ashes in her hand. But he *had* kissed her.

'Ah, Valentine,' she said to herself, 'why d'you have to go and make things so hard?'

The week before Bridie was to come back to work, Lady Ennis and Victoria returned to Ennismore unexpectedly. It was not unlike Lady Ennis to do such a thing. According to the servants it was her way of keeping them all on their toes. It happened so suddenly that Rosie had no time to prepare herself for her first encounter with Victoria. She wedged herself in behind a curved stairway out of sight of the main hallway. From there she could see Mrs Murphy and Mr Burke almost knocking one another over to reach the front door. Immelda Fox entered first, looking no happier than the day she left. The Season had not done much to improve her temperament, Rosie thought. Next came Lady Ennis, shouting orders to everyone within earshot.

Then Victoria arrived. Rosie drew in a deep breath. She hardly recognized her friend. She appeared to have grown several inches, but that may have been because her carriage was so erect, or the feathers on her hat so tall, Rosie couldn't be sure. What she was sure of, even from this distance, was that the girl had changed. In fact, she was no longer a girl, but an elegant young lady. Rosie suddenly felt awkward and coarse. She flattened herself behind the stairs until Victoria had passed.

That evening, in the servants' hall, Sadie Canavan took centre stage with all the gossip.

'Lady Louisa is fit to be tied they're back so soon. She'd really enjoyed having the house to herself. There's no love lost between them two sisters, I'll tell you that.'

Mr Burke cleared his throat, but Sadie ignored him.

'And on top of that, she says Miss Victoria is not long for staying. It seems she wants to go to London to visit some of her new friends, and she needs a chaperone, and Lady Louisa is marked for the job. I almost feel sorry for her ladyship. Sure she has no life of her own at all.'

Mr Burke cleared his throat again, but before he could call Sadie to order she started up again, this time looking directly at Rosie.

'According to Lady Louisa, Victoria's new friends are of her own class – you know – the gentry. Oh, and she says she has to have her own maid now, and she must be addressed as Lady Victoria. I was afraid at first I'd have to do for her as well as me other work but thank God she's insisting on a maid of her own. It might be a good job for you, Rosie, now that Bridie's coming back.'

There was silence around the table. Mr Burke bowed to say grace. The others fixed their eyes on

Rosie as they murmured the prayer. Rosie turned scarlet. She felt sick to her stomach. Victoria's *maid?* Hadn't she been humiliated enough? She swallowed hard and forced herself to smile.

'I'm sure Miss Victoria would want a maid more experienced than me. Sure I'm just a plain country girl. She'll want someone who knows all the latest fashions and hairstyles. I'm sure she's already picked one in London.'

It took every ounce of courage Rosie had to stay and eat her dinner as if nothing had happened. She chewed her food, giving no trace of her anxiety. Brendan stared at her. She thought she saw pity in his eyes and the anger it caused saw her through until the meal finished. She did not rush from the table as she would normally do, knowing she would be the subject of their speculation. She would not give them the satisfaction.

Later, as she lay in bed ignoring Sadie's stream of chatter, she thought about Victoria. Would she be so insensitive as to ask her to become her maid? Would she not realize how much it would hurt her? But there again, by next week Bridie would be back and Rosie would be out of a job. No, she thought. No. Even if I was out on the bog starving for a crust of bread I would never subject myself to such shame.

'But it's a perfect plan, don't you see, Rosie?' Victoria said the next morning. 'We could still share each other's company, and our secrets, just like before.'

Rosie stood beside the fire and stared at her friend. She no longer knew this girl who sat across from her in the drawing room of Ennismore. Oh, she looked the same, all right, beautiful as always, more beautiful, in fact. Her blonde hair was coiled on the top of her head like ropes of honey and her blue eyes were clear as the lake that glittered beyond the window. But Rosie felt a distance between them that was never there before.

Victoria pressed on. 'I am delighted I thought of it. My friends and I intend to spend some time abroad. Just think what it will be like for us to see Paris and Rome together and...'

'I'm sorry,' said Rosie, looking down at her worn-out boots. 'I just can't do it. I'd think you could understand.'

'Explain it to me then.' Victoria's tone was impatient. 'Explain why you are refusing such a wonderful opportunity. Why are you being so ungrateful?'

Rosie turned away, fighting back tears. How could she explain to this girl who had been her closest friend the hurt and humiliation she was feeling? She searched for the right words but all the bottled up frustration tumbled out in spite of her. She felt like a child wrongly accused of some misdeed.

'I'm not being ungrateful. Don't you realize what you did to me? You stole me from my own family and brought me into your world and when I'd served my purpose you tossed me aside like an old dress,' she said, turning back to face Victoria. 'And now I belong nowhere. The servants despise me and so does your family, and your new friends will too.'

'But it wasn't like that, surely it wasn't,' protested Victoria, rising from her chair. 'We were happy together. We were friends.'

'We were never really friends. All that palaver about growing up together and finding husbands and living beside one another for the rest of our lives – it was all lies.'

Victoria sighed. 'Oh, Rosie, we were children,' she whispered, 'we delighted in fantasy. And we *were* friends. But things couldn't go on the same way forever. You must see that. We're from two different worlds and there's nothing either of us can do to change it.'

'I know,' Rosie said. 'But it tortures me, so it does.' She began to sob, rubbing her fists against her eyes in the way she had done as a child.

Victoria drew closer and took Rosie's hand. 'Don't cry. I'm sorry I asked you. I see now how humiliating it would have been for you. How could I have been so uncaring? Please forgive me.'

In the end it was Bridie who accepted the post as Victoria's maid.

'And to think this one here thought she was too good for it,' said Bridie to her mother.

'I didn't,' said Rosie.

'You did so,' said Bridie. 'I'd say you were hoping that Miss Victoria would ask you to go with her as her companion.'

'I wasn't,' lied Rosie blushing. In truth that was exactly what she had hoped. As it was, she was condemned to remain at Ennismore scrubbing floors in Bridie's place.

'Ah, come on, Rosie, sure everybody knows you thought you deserved better than the rest of us.'

Tears burned at Rosie's eyes. 'Ma, tell her to stop.'

Ma got up from her stool beside the fire and came over to put her arm around Rosie. 'Ah, now, leave her alone, Bridie. Sure you're after getting what you always wanted – to be a lady's maid in the Big House.'

Bridie smiled. 'Aye, indeed I am,' she said, 'and I've no intention of going back on me hands and knees after this. I'll be seeing the world, so I will. Paris and Rome and all them foreign places. Who knows what class of people I'll be meeting.'

Rosie had never seen Bridie so happy. She swallowed hard on the resentment that rose up in her. It was pleased for her sister she should be, not begrudging her good fortune. She excused herself, climbed up the ladder to her attic bedroom and got into bed without lighting the lamp. She could hear Bridie and her ma chattering downstairs. She looked out the small window. Not even the moon kept her company, hidden as it was behind a scrim of clouds. She was alone.

Throughout the autumn of 1910 an unforgiving rain poured down upon the land as if attempting to wash away the sins of history that still lingered there. The servants said it was the worst flooding they had ever endured. Anthony Walshe told stories of the ferocious storms that had visited Ireland long before any of them were born. 'Sure this weather's no calamity at all compared with them times,' he announced, waving his small arms about to emphasize his point.

But for Rosie, it *was* a calamity. The damp fog

pressed in around her like a prison from which there could be no escape. After Bridie left to accompany Victoria on her travels, it was agreed that she would stay on in Bridie's place as a housemaid. What else was she to do? She didn't have enough money saved to take her farther than the next town and besides her family needed her wages even more than before. A fox had killed several of Ma's best laying hens. Her ma had kept hens for as long as Rosie could remember. She often traded eggs in the village shops for goods the family needed. But now, with few eggs to trade, they needed money instead, and there wasn't enough of it.

The mood around the servants' dinner table turned sombre. Everyone missed Sadie Canavan's chatter. Lady Louisa had refused to go with Victoria as her chaperone unless she had her own maid. Lady Ennis had reluctantly agreed. And with Bridie gone as well there was not much craic at all. Anthony Walshe was unable to cheer them up with his usual banter and Brendan Lynch brooded more than usual, while Immelda Fox was even more sullen since her return from the Season. She spoke to no one except Brendan, and Rosie thought the two of them made a quare pair. The youngest maid, Thelma, a big, doughy country girl, blushed every time Sean, the younger footman, looked at her. Only Mrs O'Leary and young Sean showed much sign of life.

Rosie tried not to think about Valentine. It hurt too much. She had not seen him in months, and the word was he had gone to visit cousins in England, dispatched, she supposed, by his disappointed father. She had not even seen him to say goodbye. It hardly mattered anyway. Ever since her argument with Victoria, Rosie was determined to stamp out all the remaining fantasies in her head as fiercely as if stamping out flames.

She put her head down and concentrated on her work. Every month she was able to put a little more money aside. Soon, she told herself, she would have enough to get her to Dublin. She tried not to think about how leaving would mean abandoning her family. 'Let my brothers do their part,' she told herself, 'instead of talking about going to America. Why should it be left to me?' And, more importantly, she tried not to think about how leaving would mean abandoning her secret hope for a future with Valentine.

Bridie had written often throughout the months – colourful postcards with foreign stamps that Ma proudly displayed on the kitchen dresser.

'She's enjoying herself, so she is,' said Ma. 'And she says Miss Victoria is treating her very well. That girleen is a pure angel.'

Rosie often wondered why Victoria had chosen Bridie as her maid. It was obvious to everybody that Bridie had no skills in that area – a point Sadie Canavan was quick to make. Mrs O'Leary said that it stemmed from Miss Victoria's kindness – she knew Bridie had been ill and wanted to give her a holiday. Maybe the cook was right. Regardless, she supposed she should be grateful since Bridie's absence had given her the opportunity to continue working and save more money. She confessed to no one that some nights she lay in bed imagining what it would be like to be in

Bridie's place, seeing all those exotic places she'd written home about. Well, she had no one to blame but herself. It was her own pride that had prevented her.

Eventually a letter arrived from Bridie that shocked the Killeen household. She'd met a man in Dublin, she wrote, and she was staying there to get married. She would not be coming home.

CHAPTER 8

One day in early November of 1911, Lady Ennis swept into the servants' hall – a most unusual occurrence – just as the staff were about to begin their breakfast. They jumped to their feet, chairs scraping on the stone floor. She glanced around the room with a faint look of distaste and began to fan herself vigorously. She addressed her remarks to Mr Burke who appeared most distressed at her ladyship's sudden encroachment upon his realm.

'I have news of great importance,' her ladyship began, 'which is why I have made this unprecedented visit to your quarters so that you should all hear it directly from me. Next month Ennismore will be entertaining two most important guests and it is essential that every aspect of our hospitality be perfect.'

'Lord have mercy on us,' cried Mrs O'Leary, 'is it the King himself?'

Mr Burke turned pale at the cook's impertinence. 'Lady Ennis, please forgive...'

But Lady Ennis merely fluttered her fan at him and gave him an icy smile.

'No, not the King, Burke, but royalty nonetheless. American royalty. Mr Jules Hoffman, the American industrialist and a leader of New York Society, and his daughter, Miss Sofia Hoffman, are to be joining us for a month. I wish to show them the best that English hospitality has to offer. Nothing must be left to chance. Even the smallest detail must be attended to. I shall expect all of you to rise to the occasion. And Mrs Murphy,' she said turning to the housekeeper, 'you may bring on whatever extra staff you deem fit. No expense must be spared. That is all, good day.'

Mr Burke almost tripped running to escort her ladyship out of the room and up the well-trod wooden staircase to the main floor. When she had gone only the faint scent of gardenias lingered. The staff looked at each other.

'Well, that's us told then,' said Mrs O'Leary. 'English hospitality, my arse! 'Twill be good Irish cooking they'll get from me.'

Thelma gave her a bovine stare. 'I've never met an American, Mrs O. Are they like the rest of us, at all?'

'Sure, they all have horns on them,' put in Anthony, 'and they carry pitchforks, and they eat young girleens like you for their dinner.'

Thelma let out a squeal.

'Ah, stop codding the girl, Anthony,' said Mrs O'Leary.

'I'm sure they are very decent people,' said Mrs Murphy. 'We must do everything we can to make

107

their stay as pleasant and comfortable as possible. So enough of this silly talk and let's get down to business.'

Although the visit of an American heiress was a novelty to the servants of Ennismore, such an event had become familiar in great houses in England and Ireland. Like the Bell family, most of the gentry across Britain in the early twentieth century were finding themselves in unprecedented financial difficulties. Traditionally, the aristocrats viewed themselves as benign benefactors to those who lived on their vast estates, and the crops, livestock and tenant rents were considered sufficient revenue to cover estate expenses.

For their personal expenses such as holidays abroad, household refurbishments, gambling debts, keeping a mistress and the costs of 'keeping up with society', they turned to willing bankers who had not had the temerity to push too robustly for repayment of loans. Lord Ennis, like his peers, had inherited such attitudes from his predecessors, and while he was more prudent than his wife in financial affairs, nonetheless had not dwelled upon such matters.

However, as competition for grain and livestock from America slowly eroded incomes from their estates and as inheritance taxes began to rise, financial ruin loomed for many cash-poor landowners. Thus it had become more and more common for the landed aristocracy to turn their eyes west to the New World of America and its abundance of wealthy heiresses willing to swap their fortune for a title.

Lord and Lady Ennis, therefore, became

acutely aware that their older son, Thomas, must make a good and profitable marriage if Ennismore and the Ennis Estate were to survive intact. Thus Lady Ennis finally came to terms with the possibility, distasteful as it was to her, that she may have to accept an American daughter-in-law.

One such heiress was Miss Sofia Hoffman. The Bells' neighbours, the Marquess and Marchioness of Sligo, had sent word that the Hoffmans would be visiting them at their Westport estate in late autumn, and Lady Ennis had seized her opportunity.

They arrived in early December. An astute observer may well have drawn a comparison of this event with the prior arrival of royalty to Ennismore more than ten years before. Instead of carriages and coachmen in top hats, this royalty arrived in a fine motor car which glistened as brightly as the horses that had pulled Queen Victoria's carriage. The persistent rain had suddenly stopped and a shaft of sunlight emerged as if in greeting. On this occasion, instead of peering from a basement window, Rosie lined up on the front steps with the other servants. And one might conclude that when the American 'Queen' emerged, Rosie's reaction would have been very different than before.

Miss Sofia Hoffman would not have disappointed. She was taller than any woman yet seen at Ennismore. Her thick, black hair, olive skin and large dark eyes gave her the look of an exotic foreigner – a look she owed to her Italian mother and Jewish father. She wore a dress of red wool which followed the natural lines of her slim figure and fell scandalously short of her ankles. Her father, Mr Jules Hoffman, cut less of a dashing figure. He was shorter than his daughter by six inches, swarthy, full-bellied and mustachioed, but he carried himself with the confidence of a pugilist – inelegant but powerful.

Lady Ennis summoned all of her considerable breeding in welcoming her guests, bending stiffly to allow Mr Hoffman to plant a kiss on her cheek and extending her hand in formal greeting to his daughter. Lord Ennis, by contrast, welcomed them with loud enthusiasm – a practised mix of the country squire and politician. The servants bowed and curtsied, each of them storing their impressions of the visitors for discussion later below stairs.

That evening the family and visitors gathered in the library. It was an austere and formal room filled with leather and brocaded chairs in autumn hues of dark red and muted amber. A threadbare oriental rug covered the wooden floor and faded red velvet drapes held back by gold-fringed ties flanked the tall windows. Hunting and fishing trophies adorned the walls – a grinning fox head and a silver filigreed trout among them. A fire blazed in the grate, the flames softening the dim shadows of the dwindling afternoon light.

Miss Sofia Hoffman, just returned from a walk in the gardens, took all of this in at a glance before flopping down unceremoniously on a leather sofa. She bent over and unlaced her boots, slipping them off and pushing them to one side. She held her feet out and wiggled her toes with a sigh of pleasure.

'That's better,' she said, smiling around at the

assembled company whose eyes were fixed upon her. 'Burke, may I have a glass of sherry?'

Mr Burke turned in her direction. 'At once, ma'am.'

Lady Ennis could not hide her astonishment at the forward behaviour of this girl. Well-bred ladies waited to be asked if they wished for refreshment.

As the butler handed Sofia her drink, Thomas and Valentine Bell looked at each other and grinned. They had just arrived back from riding and were still in their riding clothes. They had not bothered to take time to change into their formal wear, so anxious were they to meet the guests, particularly Miss Sofia.

Sofia patted the sofa. 'You must be the Bell boys.' She laughed, her wide mouth more open than was proper and displaying a set of perfect, white teeth. 'Come and sit beside me.'

She grinned at her father who stood beside Lord Ennis at the fireplace, sipping his brandy. 'Bell boys, Papa, get it? Isn't that droll?'

Jules shook his head at his daughter and sighed. 'Don't be disrespectful, dear,' he said.

He turned to Lord Ennis. 'She's got such spirit, Edward. She was brought up in Chicago where manners are, shall we say, less formal than in New York. I have difficulty reining her in to suit New York society, and my dear late wife is no longer with us to temper her manners. I am hoping some of your English decorum will rub off on her.'

'Don't count on it, Papa,' laughed Sofia.

'Reminds me of my thoroughbreds,' said Lord Ennis. 'Their spirit is what sets them apart from mere nags. They just need to be handled in the right way – I recall thinking the same thing about Victoria when she was a child. I arranged for a young farm girl to take lessons with her and it settled her down nicely.'

Lady Ennis, who sat upright in her winged chair, cleared her throat, looked pointedly at her husband, and tapped her foot. She could barely disguise her horror as she regarded Sofia and her sons talking animatedly with one another. She glanced at her sister. Louisa was regarding their guest as if inspecting an alien specimen under glass.

Victoria, on the other hand, smiled in delight. She was fascinated by this girl not much older than herself who had swept into Ennismore like a fresh wind, cutting through the mustiness that had permeated the old house for centuries. Her voice was louder, her laugh heartier and her movements freer than that of any other woman who had set foot in this house before her. She paid no attention to the withering looks from Lady Ennis and Lady Louisa or Lord Ennis's arched eyebrow – in fact she seemed unaware of the wordless signals of disapproval that were universal among the gentry.

Jules Hoffman and Lord Ennis, unaware of Lady Ennis's growing distress, entered into a spirited discussion about the growing labour unrest both in Ireland and in America.

'There's a fellow called Larkin stirring up the workers in Dublin,' said Lord Ennis, signalling Burke for another drink. 'He's threatening to bring the city to a standstill with his blasted strikes. He's nothing but a rabble-rouser. And now his confounded sister, Delia, has organized a union for the female workers! As if we didn't have enough problems with this Home Rule nonsense. Now we have to deal with this.'

Jules Hoffman looked up at Lord Ennis, who was a good foot taller than he. 'Our labour problems at home go back far longer than yours, Edward,' he declared in a loud voice somewhat at odds with his height. 'We've seen our share of national strikes, while you English have been passing your time leisurely playing cricket. You have little experience dealing with the problems of the real world.'

Jules, ignoring the deepening crimson hue of his host's face, continued. 'And I wouldn't discount the female unions, if I were you. I am in the textile business, as you know, and we employ predominantly female workers. We were brought to our knees by the Shirtwaist Strike in New York in 1909 when nearly twenty thousand women walked out. Took us months to settle, but settle we had to. We cannot stand in the way of progress.'

Valentine had left Thomas alone with Sofia and joined the men at the fireplace.

'But it resulted in better working conditions for the women, and better wages,' Valentine said, paying no attention to his father's warning glare. 'But it didn't go far enough. I mean, look at the Triangle Shirtwaist fire that happened in your city just this year – over one hundred women and girls died in conditions that were abominable.'

Jules shook his head. 'Terrible tragedy, I agree. Unfortunately, not all of the factory owners took the lessons from the 1909 strike. Perhaps they will now.' He looked back up at Lord Ennis. 'Smart lad you have here, Edward. Unlike *your* generation, he seems up on what's going on in the world. And aware of the need to treat labour fairly.'

Valentine grinned, oblivious to his father's thunderous look. 'Thank you, sir.'

'Perhaps you might consider visiting us in New York soon, Valentine. We can use progressive young men like you.'

Valentine bowed. 'A kind invitation, sir, but I think your daughter may prefer a visit from my big brother.'

He looked over to where Thomas and Sofia were sitting, heads almost touching, lost in deep conversation.

Burke walked to the middle of the room and cleared his throat. 'Dinner is served,' he said.

'At last,' sighed Lady Ennis as she rose and led the company into the dining room.

The Hoffmans stayed for three weeks during which time Sofia's lack of concern for the gentry's strict rules of decorum was a frequent topic of discussion among the servants.

'She's a breath of fresh air, that girl,' smiled Mrs O'Leary.

Sadie Canavan nodded. 'Lady Louisa doesn't know what to make of her at all. But I hear Lady Ennis is fit to be tied. She can't wait to see the back of her.'

Young Thelma smiled dreamily. 'D'you think they'll get married? Master Thomas and Miss Sofia?'

Sadie chuckled. 'Wouldn't that be some craic? The shame of it would send her ladyship to her

114

bed for six months.'

''Twould be a shame of her own making, so,' said Mrs O'Leary. 'I'd say she should be over the moon with such a match. A lovely, down-to-earth girl for our Master Thomas would be the best thing could happen to her ladyship.'

'Not to mention the money she'll bring with her,' said Sadie.

Rosie did not join in the speculation. She liked Sofia well enough from what she had seen of her, and she was glad for Thomas, but in the end whatever they did would make no difference to her life. Her concern was Valentine. Sean, the younger footman, had mentioned Mr Hoffman's offer to bring Valentine to New York. He'd said no, according to Sean, but what if he thought it over? What if he did decide to go? She knew she had no claim on him but much as she'd tried to stamp out her feelings for him, the embers kept reigniting themselves.

On the day of the Hoffmans' departure for London where they were to spend Christmas with some American friends, Rosie watched Valentine wave goodbye to their coach. She'd had very little opportunity to see him since he'd returned with Thomas for the Hoffmans' visit. He'd been caught up in the activities Lord and Lady Ennis had arranged for their guests – riding, shooting, fishing and visiting various neighbours of importance. And Thelma continued to clean his room. As the coach departed he turned around so swiftly that Rosie had no chance to dodge out of the way before he caught her eye. He raised his hand and waved at her but all she could do was nod back at him. She stood frozen, even after Thomas had put his arm around Valentine's shoulder and led him inside the house. As he entered the front door, Valentine looked back at her and smiled.

She supposed that his smile should be enough for her, but her heart ached for more. She fought back tears as she edged her way around the house and back into the kitchen. If only there was someone she could confide in. But Ma was beside herself with worry over Bridie. In years past, the logical thing would have been to talk to Victoria. But she could hardly do that now. Ever since Victoria's return home from her travels they had encountered one another only rarely, and while Victoria was pleasant enough in her greetings, there was a distance between them wider than Lough Conn.

After the Hoffmans left, the servants had little time to relax. Christmas was almost upon them and even though no more guests were due it was expected that they should enter into the usual seasonal preparations. Lady Ennis was adamant that the standards be maintained. After all, some of their neighbours might drop in unexpectedly.

As it was, the only guests who did drop in un-expectedly were Lady Marianne Bellefleur and her companion, Mr Kearney. As usual, they arrived unannounced. It was Christmas Eve and the family and Reverend Watson, who had been invited as an afterthought, were about to sit down to dinner when a commotion came from the front hall. At first Lady Ennis jumped up in delight. They were to have more guests after all. But when her sister-in-law swept in her smile faded and she sank back down in her chair.

'Greetings of the season to you all,' Lady Marianne said, 'Mr Kearney and I are on our way to dear Lady Gregory's estate in Galway and thought what a fine idea it would be to pay you a surprise visit.' She paused and looked around the table.

'Oh dear, is this your only guest?' she continued, looking directly at Reverend Watson. 'I was hoping to meet your Americans.'

'They weren't *our* Americans,' said Lady Ennis, 'and they left for London last week.'

Lady Marianne and Mr Kearney took their seats at the table as the footmen rushed to set two more places. 'Well I heard the daughter was a wonderful example of New World society,' she said. 'Rumour has it she rides like a man, flouts rules and is most outspoken.'

'And she doesn't wear a corset,' put in Victoria, giggling.

Lady Ennis gave her daughter a withering look while Thomas winked at Valentine.

'There's apparently been a growing trend in women's fashion,' said Victoria, ignoring her mother, 'championed by Monsieur Poiret, the French designer. His goal is to free women from the confines of tight undergarments and allow them more freedom of movement.'

'Really, Victoria,' said her mother, 'this is not a fit conversation for the dining room – and especially not in front of our guest. Do forgive her, Reverend Watson.'

The vicar, who appeared to have been drinking in Victoria's every word, started and turned crimson. 'No forgiveness necessary, Lady Ennis,' he muttered. 'Just a young girl's enthusiasm boiling over. Charming, really.'

He tore his eyes away from Victoria, while Lady Louisa scowled.

Lady Marianne sipped her wine and addressed Thomas. 'Well, young man, and what did you think of Miss Hoffman? Would you and she make a good match?'

'Really, Marianne...' began Lady Ennis.

Thomas smiled. 'She's a capital girl, Aunt Marianne. So much more refreshing than the young ladies I am used to. I hope to visit her in London when I return to Oxford. She will be there until April. Then she and her papa are sailing home on the new ship, the *Titanic*.'

'Perhaps you will go with her,' said Lady Marianne. 'A chance to see the New World for yourself.' She looked from Thomas to Valentine. 'Perhaps you should both go.'

'Mr Hoffman was kind enough to invite Valentine,' said Lord Ennis, looking at his younger son. 'Perhaps it would be an opportunity to discover his path. Heaven knows, he's never found one here.'

There was silence for a moment until Lady Ennis spoke up.

'Really, Edward, we could not possibly let both of our sons travel on the same ship to America. What if something dreadful were to happen?'

'The *Titanic* will be quite safe,' said Thomas. 'It is said to be the finest ship ever built. But don't fret, Mama, neither Valentine nor I have committed to such a journey. Have we, brother?'

Valentine shook his head, avoiding his father's gaze.

But Lady Marianne was not finished. 'Oh, I'd wager after you visit Miss Hoffman again you will change your mind, Thomas.' She turned to her companion and rested her hand on his arm. 'Love is so unpredictable, isn't it, dear Mr Kearney?'

CHAPTER 9

By the day after Christmas, only Victoria and Valentine Bell and the servants remained at Ennismore. Lord and Lady Ennis and Lady Louisa had left for their annual visit to the Marquess of Sligo at his grand house in Westport and Thomas had repaired to London to visit the Hoffmans. Since they were only to be gone for a short time, and since the Marquess's household had an excess of servants, Lady Ennis had excused Immelda and Sadie from attending.

The servants heaved a collective sigh of relief. It was rare that they had the house to themselves with little work to be done. The Bell family seldom left the estate, except for a month each in Dublin and London in the summer, during which absence the servants were put to work cleaning the house from top to bottom, laundering all the linens, polishing every piece of silver, and washing the dozens of windows until everything sparkled. When Lady Ennis returned she inspected every inch of the house with an eagle eye, Mr Burke hovering behind her, grimly noting any instance of dissatisfaction.

Now, however, no such labour awaited them. Those who wished to go home and visit their families were allowed to do so, but very few did. The truth was that Ennismore was more comfortable than most of their own cottages, and the food better. Besides, this was the time when they could have a holiday celebration of their own and they all wanted to be part of it.

On New Year's Eve Mrs O'Leary served up a feast fit for royalty. The canny cook had, over several days, set aside provisions in amounts that would not be noticed by Lady Ennis. The servants' hall was decorated with holly wreaths, mistletoe and poinsettias, most of the plants relocated from the main salon above. The mood was light as everyone assembled around the big table. Mr Burke, as always, led the prayer for grace, and instead of the usual murmuring, the servants recited the words with great gusto. Wine was poured and they dived into roast leg of lamb, potatoes, carrots, greens and thick gravy. Everyone talked at once, all except for Immelda Fox who, as usual, said little.

'There's not a family of gentry in Ireland dining better than we are this night,' declared Mrs O'Leary, raising her glass.

Everyone nodded their agreement.

'And no better company to be found,' said Anthony Walshe.

Rosie smiled and nodded with the rest of the staff, but took little pleasure in the evening. Her mind was on Valentine and what changes the new year would bring.

Mrs O'Leary, grown melancholy from the effects of the wine, looked at young Sean. 'Ah, Seaneen, sure this may be the last holiday we'll ever share together. You may never come back to Ireland again.'

Sean patted her arm. 'Ah, sure I will, so, Mrs O. I'm going to America to make my fortune, but my heart will always be here.'

'I heard tell nobody ever comes back from there,' burst out Thelma, wide-eyed.

Sean smiled, his cheeks dimpling. 'And would you be missing me now, Thelma?'

Thelma turned scarlet and bowed her head.

'You make it sound like a death sentence, Thelma,' put in Brendan.

'Well, most of the time it is,' said Anthony, stretching himself as tall as his short frame would allow and affecting a solemn voice. 'Them that comes back are few and far between. It's been that way since the famine times.'

Silence fell upon the table as each person was lost in their own thoughts.

He's right, Rosie thought to herself, Sean probably won't come back, and neither will Valentine if he goes.

When the food was cleared away, the table was pushed back against the wall to make room for music and dancing. Anthony bent over and with effort lifted his accordion on to his lap. The instrument almost overwhelmed his tiny body. Brendan opened a battered, leather case and took out a fiddle which he laid gently against his shoulder. Sean took out his bodhran, a hand-held skin-faced drum which he played with two sticks and Mrs Murphy took a tin whistle out of her pocket.

Anthony led the musicians off with a fast-paced jig, followed by some traditional reels. Soon, feet were tapping and hands clapping. The house servants were joined by some of the groomsmen and gardeners and the noise rose to a crescendo that rocked the room. Rosie watched them with pleasure. It was as if the music freed them all from the constraints of a life of being neither heard nor seen in the Big House. Now they expressed themselves with a robust declaration of freedom.

When the jigs and reels stopped, Mrs Murphy took up her tin whistle. She played a slow, halting lament, and the room fell silent. She was a tall, slender woman, still in her prime. She had never been married – the title of 'Mrs' having been bestowed upon her as a sign of respect. Mr Burke watched her intently as her pale, delicate fingers moved up and down the whistle in an ancient pattern. When she finished there was riotous applause, Mr Burke clapping the loudest of all.

'Let's have another jig,' shouted Anthony, 'and a bit of a dance.'

He began to play 'The Haymakers' Jig', pushing the buttons on his accordion with nimble fingers, as the other musicians joined in. Mrs O'Leary jumped up, pulling young Thelma with her, and began to dance. Mrs O'Leary was unexpectedly light on her feet for a woman of her ample size, lifting her skirts to show off white dimpled knees. Young Thelma stumbled through the tune, her legs and arms jerking awkwardly, and her face blazing with embarrassment. Before long Sadie was up on her feet, dancing round the room with one of the gardeners, and Rosie accepted Sean's invitation to dance.

Then Anthony switched the pace to an old-time waltz called 'The Revenge for Skibbereen'. No one moved, transfixed as they were by the music. Rosie watched as Brendan stroked his fiddle as if stroking a lover. His normally stern features seemed to soften before her eyes until she no longer recognized him. At last, Mr Burke approached Mrs Murphy and bowed. She looked flustered, but rose and took his hand as he led her to the centre of the room and they began to dance. The others exchanged glances and smiled.

Immelda Fox sat in the corner observing the scene. She had never been one for dancing. There was no music in her home growing up and certainly none in the convent where she had lived before coming to Ennismore. Her mother was a brilliant singer, and Immelda had inherited her talent but her early life, growing up without a father, and with a mother perpetually atoning for some unknown sin, had not given her much to sing about. But Sadie had heard her singing to herself one night and had begun pestering the life out of her to sing next time there was a ceili below stairs.

'I think Immelda should give us a song,' Sadie declared now. 'She has a grand voice, so she does.'

The servants began to clap and encourage Immelda to get up. At first she resisted but Sadie would not let it go. At last she stood up, although she refused to move to the centre of the room, preferring to stay in the corner where she was.

123

She began to sing a love song called 'The Banks of My Old Lovely Lee,' softly at first, and then more loudly as Brendan's fiddle rose to accompany her. The servants sat in awed silence. Immelda's voice was pure as rain and carried a sadness that clutched at their hearts. When she had finished nobody moved. Immelda sat down, expressionless. Then Anthony let out a roar.

'Fair play to yourself, Immelda. Sure who knew you'd the voice of an angel? God himself has blessed you.'

'He has surely,' cried Mrs O'Leary, clapping her hands like mad.

The others joined in, clapping and shouting for more. But Immelda shook her head, though a ghost of a smile crossed her face.

There followed more music and dancing, and when the company was exhausted, they begged Anthony to tell a ghost story. Anthony was a seanachie, a teller of stories. So good were his renditions that he could make the hair stand up on the heads of his listeners, and cause children to hide behind their mothers. He had the look of a story-teller, too, with his small stature, merry blue eyes and silver hair.

'Arrah, sure you've heard them all before,' he said in his low, soft brogue, as he always did before he launched into his recitations.

Rosie took the opportunity to sneak out the kitchen door. She was desperate for some fresh air. As she walked away the sounds of the festivities followed her. She walked faster, trying to clear her mind. At last she sank down on a log and leaned against the wall of the Big House.

There was no moon and the stars were hidden. A velvet blackness surrounded her.

A sliver of light cut the darkness as the front door opened and she heard voices on the front steps. It was Valentine and Victoria. They had their backs to her as they walked a little way away from the house. She held her breath and shrank back closer to the wall.

'It's freezing out here,' said Victoria.

'I know, but I needed some fresh air.'

'Ssh, listen. The servants must be having a party. Oh, the music sounds so jolly. Perhaps we should join them, Valentine.'

'No. I hardly think we would be welcome. Let them have their night to themselves, God knows they deserve some time away from us.'

'I wonder if Rosie's with them.'

It was a while before Valentine answered.

'I expect she is. I imagine she's up dancing a reel with the rest of them.'

'I miss her, Valentine. I mean, I miss the way things used to be between us.'

Valentine did not answer.

'We used to be such close friends,' Victoria went on, 'we shared all our secrets. But now she'll have nothing to do with me. She avoids me at every turn. I just don't understand her. She tried to explain it all to me once when I asked her to be my maid.'

'You did *what?*'

'Well it seemed perfectly logical to me,' protested Victoria. 'It was a way we could be together, explore the Continent, and–'

'Oh, Victoria, how could you? Didn't you realize how much that would have humiliated her? Poor Rosie.'

'Well after she explained things, I understood her point. So I took her sister on instead. But I still don't know why she won't just talk to me like old times.'

Valentine sighed. 'Don't you see? She's caught in an impossible situation. She's a servant now, and servants are not allowed to mix with us – it would upset the whole order of things. Mr Burke even forbade her to clean my room because we went out riding together.' Valentine's tone had grown bitter. 'How I hate this society and all its rules.'

Victoria's teeth began to chatter. 'It's the way things are. There's not much we can do about it. C'mon, let's go in, I'm frozen.'

'You go. I need to stay out here for a while.'

The light disappeared as Victoria closed the door leaving Rosie surrounded again by darkness. She remained very still, hardly daring to breathe. A flicker of flame winked as Valentine lit a cigarette. Every impulse in her wanted to rush up to him and put her arms around him, tell him that she loved him, beg him not to leave for America. But she could not move. He walked past her, close enough that she could have reached out and touched him. Instead she shrank back as if hoping the wall might swallow her up.

Valentine began to whistle along with the music that flowed out from the kitchen through the basement windows. Immelda was singing another melancholy air – a tale of love and loss and heartbreak. Her voice keened like a mourner at a

126

funeral. A muffled sob escaped from Rosie's throat. Valentine stopped whistling.

'Who's there?' he called. 'Come out where I can see you.'

Rosie stayed very still. Perhaps he'd think the sound came from an animal. But Valentine walked directly towards her. 'Come out, please.'

Reluctantly, she gathered up her skirts and stood up. He struck a match and came closer.

'Rosie?' he breathed in recognition. 'Rosie, what on earth are you doing out here?'

Rosie turned away. She could not let him see the anguished state of her. 'I'm just out for some fresh air,' she said. 'Sure the heat of the kitchen would smother a pig.'

She tried to sound casual, but the words were like jagged glass in her throat and she could not stop herself from trembling.

Valentine reached for her arm and drew her out into the open. 'What's wrong, Rosie?'

'Nothing,' she said, 'I just needed air, that's all.'

'Walk with me.' It was a command.

'You know I can't be seen with you, Valentine. Mr Burke already warned me. I'll be sacked.'

Valentine ignored her. 'Walk with me,' he said again.

She let him lead her behind the house, across the back lawns, and through the gate that led into the garden. She stumbled in the blackness and his arm tightened around her waist. Their feet crunched on the gravel pathway. She knew every inch of this garden, even in the darkness. And so did Valentine.

'Let's sit down,' he said, helping her to a stone

127

bench. 'No one can see us here.'

He was right. They were on the opposite side of the house from where the kitchen was located, with the stables and courtyard between them. They could no longer hear the music. The garden was wrapped in silence. Valentine took Rosie's hand in his and they sat together, neither of them speaking.

Rosie relaxed and leaned against his shoulder, letting her earlier tension drain from her body. She felt neither happiness nor joy, just simple relief.

Valentine lit another cigarette and inhaled deeply. 'I'm sorry, Rosie,' he said at last.

'What for?'

'For not having sought you out sooner. For pretending to myself that you were better off without my company.' He paused. 'For convincing myself that I no longer loved you.'

He turned away from her and took a long pull on his cigarette. Rosie laid her face against his back. She could hear his heart pounding. Or was it her own? She waited. Had she heard him clearly? Was he saying he loved her? Eventually he turned back to her.

'Oh, but I *do* love you, Roisin Dove. And I hate myself for not having the courage to act on it. I yearn to bundle you up in my arms and race away with you to a place where no one knows us, and no one cares about our stations in life.'

Rosie's heart soared. Yes, he was telling her he loved her. How long had she waited to hear those words? Joy and anticipation flooded through her. He was asking her to run away with him. She was suddenly giddy. Of course, she would go with

128

him – how could he even doubt it?

She sat up and beamed at him. 'Oh, Valentine, I loved you from the first day I met you. I will follow you anywhere. Don't you know that?'

He seemed to hesitate. 'But I have no money, no inheritance, and no prospects...' he began.

She reached up and put her fingers on his lips. 'Ssh,' she whispered, 'I don't care about any of that. I just want to be with you.'

He sighed. She could not see his face in the darkness, but she sensed something was wrong.

'I know, Rosie,' he said at last. 'But the truth is while some men are able to ignore the constraints and duties of their stations, I have let them shackle me.' He took a deep breath. 'That's why I have decided to go to America after all. I've dreamed that if I could make my fortune there I could send for you and we would be free to live our own lives. But it would mean you would have to wait for me, and I will not ask you to do that. You are young and beautiful and have your whole life ahead of you. You must not let it pass you by while you wait for me.'

'Stop it, Valentine. Of course I will wait for you.'

Valentine bowed his head. 'You don't understand, Rosie. These dreams of mine may not be realistic, no matter how much I wish they could be. The reality is that I am not suited to business. I have no head for it and, as Papa is keen to remind me, I lack the backbone to stick with a challenge.'

Rosie sighed. How could he believe such things about himself? 'Valentine, all you need is to find your path – the thing that will make your heart sing. Don't listen to your papa. I have faith in you.'

Valentine ground out his cigarette under his foot. 'The problem is, Rosie, that I no longer have faith in myself.'

They sat in silence. The air was cold and still. No bird was yet awake, but a film of pale light crept over the black silhouette of Mount Nephin in the distance, signalling that dawn was approaching. A few minutes earlier Rosie had been afloat with happiness. Now Valentine was trying to snatch that happiness away from her. He'd told her he loved her and now he was pushing her away.

Suddenly they were embracing, kissing each other fiercely on the lips, their breaths coming in short spasms. Rosie locked her arms around his neck and pulled him closer as if by sheer force she could keep him with her forever. He did not fight her. Instead, his kisses grew more passionate and he clutched her so tightly that she could hardly breathe. She pressed her body hard into his as if trying to meld them into one. They stayed that way for a long time, and then with a groan he pushed her away from him. Although she could not see it, she groped for his face and felt his wet tears.

'Don't go,' she cried.

'Goodbye, Roisin Dove.'

He kissed her hands as she stroked his face then took her wrists and pushed her away more forcefully than before. Without another word he stood up and strode away without looking back.

Rosie whispered after him in the darkness, 'I would have waited for you, Valentine.'

But she knew he had not heard her.

She did not go to her room that night. Instead she went back to the Killeen Cottage. Her ma blessed herself when she opened the door and saw her daughter standing there in the cold and dark.

'Mother of God, what's wrong? Is it bad news?'

Rosie shook her head. 'No, Ma. Will you just let me in? I'm foundered with the cold.'

Rosie sat down. Her da snored in the settle bed beside the fire, and the boys were asleep in the back room. Ma set the teapot on the bank of turf to heat it up, then poured the tea into a mug, added milk and sugar and handed it to her daughter.

'Did you get sacked? Ah, Rosie, I often worried one of these days you'd let your temper get the better of you.'

'No, nothing like that, Ma.'

Rosie sipped the tea. How could she explain to Ma what had happened when she could hardly explain it to herself? How could she put into words what Valentine's betrayal had meant to her? Yes, it was a betrayal, even if *he* may not have seen it that way. He had betrayed her dreams. He had destroyed the hope that had kept her going all these months, down on her knees, humiliated.

'I'm racked with tiredness, Ma. Can we talk about it later? I just need to sleep.'

Rosie studied Ma's face. She had not realized how much she had aged in the past months. Deep lines carved her weather-beaten cheeks, and her eyes had lost their sheen. A wave of sorrow washed over her. She was about to break Ma's heart just as Bridie had done. But how could she help it? She had to go. She could never set foot near Ennismore again. And neither could she stay at the cottage. There were too many memories. Her spirit would die here.

PART THREE

DUBLIN

1912–1914

CHAPTER 10

It was dusk when Rosie climbed down off the train at Dublin's Westland Row Station on 2 January 1912. She was stiff from the long journey squeezed tight against the window by a country family who had boarded at Mullingar and spread themselves and their belongings out on the wooden seat as if she was invisible. She set her bag down on the platform, stretched her back and shook her shoulders.

'Wouldn't do that, miss,' shouted a porter, looking down at the bag, 'or it will be the last you'll see of it.'

Startled, Rosie picked up her bag and started walking. Crowds rushed past her – mothers with babies in shawls, rough men, some of them unsteady on their feet, and young girls her own age in cheap, gaudy clothes. She tried not to stare. That would give her away as the innocent country girl she was. She had heard enough from Sadie and the other staff about how the Dubliners would steal the eyes out of your head if they got a chance. She clutched her bag closer to her body and walked on, her head held high.

Out on the street, rivers of humanity assaulted her. Everyone was in a hurry, pushing by her as if she was standing still, bumping into her without apology. She was dressed conservatively in a long woollen skirt, and a high-necked blouse under a

135

tweed jacket with her hair drawn back into a bun under a small, brown hat. She could have passed for a teacher or a shop clerk, or maybe a lady's maid. The last thing she had wanted was to draw attention to herself but even now she was aware of occasional glances from men approaching from the opposite direction. She looked down at the scrap of paper in her hand on which she had written Bridie's address. She had copied it down before she left the Killeen cottage, creeping out into the darkness before anyone awoke. She had left a note for Ma on the table, explaining that she was taking a few days off to visit Bridie in Dublin. She knew such a brief explanation would hurt Ma and worry her, but what else could she have said? She could not bear even to tell herself the truth of why she must escape.

She paused from time to time to ask directions – deliberately selecting someone who looked kind, or at least harmless, and pressed on. Street-lights began to glow as the day drew in, casting ominous shadows in dark corners and alleyways. She left the main thoroughfare of Sackville Street, walked on to Montgomery Street and made her way through a warren of narrow lanes.

She became more apprehensive as the crowds grew scarcer and the light dimmer. At last she found Foley Court. She took in a deep breath. Whatever she had expected to see, this was not it. Four-storey tenement buildings lined either side of the short street, huddled together like weary soldiers at the end of a battle. Some were black-stained from fires, others grey and crumbling, all looked in danger of collapse.

Three small boys raced past her, chasing an emaciated dog. One of them pulled at her skirt as he went by and said something she didn't understand. She walked on, treading gingerly around the litter on the pavement, and stopped at number six, a soot-covered building just like the rest. A group of women, some old, some young, sat on the front steps passing around a bottle of gin.

'Excuse me,' she said, her voice shaking as they stared up at her with curious, hard eyes, 'I'm looking for Bridie Delaney.'

No one answered her.

'She's my sister,' Rosie tried again. 'She's married to Mr Michael Delaney.'

One of the women laughed, exposing ragged teeth. 'D'you hear that, girls? Mr Michael Delaney, if you please.' She peered up at Rosie. 'There's no such gentleman lives here. Now if it's Micko Delaney you're after, you can find him on the fourth floor – if he's not still in the public house.'

'And Bridie...?'

They shrugged and passed the bottle again, moving aside so that Rosie could climb the steps between them. Tentatively, she pushed open the front door and crept into the darkened hallway. The stench assaulted her first – urine and faeces, stale vomit and porter, bitter odours of boiling cabbage. Then the sounds teemed around her as she climbed the stairs – arguing, cursing, singing, crying, thudding and scraping. She tried not to breathe nor to look right or left as she ascended. At last she reached the fourth floor.

She raised her hand in the dimness and knocked

137

on the nearest door. It slid open at her touch. She stood looking into the interior, paralysed with horror and disgust. A figure that looked like an old woman knelt over a pile of rags in the middle of the floor, soothing an infant who lay there. The rest of the room was bare except for a rickety dresser, a single chair, some wooden boxes and a rumpled mattress beneath a grimy window.

'Excuse me,' she murmured as she backed away, intending to try the next door.

But as the woman raised her head at the noise, Rosie was horrified to see it was Bridie. She was stick-thin and sallow, her red-rimmed eyes bulging in her gaunt face. She rose to her feet, came closer and peered at Rosie, who stood rooted to the spot unable to utter a word.

'What are you after wanting?' she rasped. 'Well stare away and go back to Ennismore and tell them about the luxury I'm enjoying in Dublin, you nosy bitch you.'

Bridie turned away and went back to tend the infant. Rosie ventured farther into the room and set her bag down on the floor beside her. She gazed around, looking for a place to sit, but the only chair was covered in dirty clothes.

'I never thought I'd see Rosie Killeen at a loss for words. There's a first time for everything, so.'

Rosie fought back tears. 'Ah, Bridie,' she began, 'what happened? How...?' Again words failed her.

Bridie soothed the infant and pulled the rags up over it. She got to her feet and walked across the room away from Rosie, and leaned against the dresser. 'Best you go back where you came from. You have no business here.'

138

'Neither do you.'

Bridie shrugged. 'I belong here rightly. With me own kind.'

'Living in this filth? Among these people? How can you say that?'

'It's not Ennismore but at least I'm up off me knees.' Bridie uttered a bitter laugh.

Rosie's heart sank. 'What happened at all, Bridie? Where's your husband? In the name of God, sure I thought he had a good job at the bakery, and you too. Sadie said–'

'Aye, Sadie knows all, doesn't she?'

Rosie walked over to Bridie. She put a hand on her arm but Bridie pulled away. 'Get away out of this.'

Rosie saw she was fighting back tears. She tried hard to control her own. 'You're my sister, Bridie. I'll not leave you like this.'

A noise in the doorway made Rosie swing around. A short, heavy-set young man stumbled into the room. He might have been handsome once, Rosie thought, but the florid complexion, purple veins and slack mouth had changed all that. Rosie recognized the signs of devastation brought on by drink. She had seen plenty of it around the village where she grew up, and in some of the guests who came to Ennismore from time to time. 'The curse of the drink,' she heard her da's words echo in her head.

'Who the fuck are you?' said Micko. 'Another do-gooder?'

'She's not the Lady's League, Micko. She's my sister.'

He leered at Rosie and drew close enough to her

that she could smell his putrid breath. 'So this one got all the looks then? She'd do well down on Sackville Street. Earn a pretty penny off the soldiers, I'd say.' He turned to Bridie. 'Not like you, darlin'. Sure nobody would look twice at you.'

Rosie wanted to lash out but stopped when she saw the glint of fear in Bridie's eyes. Micko had the look of a thug.

'I've left home for good,' she said, addressing her words to Bridie. 'I was hoping I could stay with you until I got settled.' She paused and looked around. 'But I can see now that would be difficult.'

Micko burst out laughing. 'Difficult!' he said, imitating Rosie. 'D'you hear that, Bridie? She sees that it would be difficult to stay here. Did you ever hear such shite in your life?'

He shuffled over to the old dresser and rummaged in a drawer, withdrawing a fistful of coins.

'You can't take that,' said Bridie. 'I have it put by for the rent. We owe more than three months and–'

'I fucking earn the money, and I'll spend it how I like.' His face was red as he shoved the money in his pocket and moved towards the door. 'I'll leave you to it. A man couldn't have any comfort in his own house with you two biddies.'

Rosie and Bridie watched him go.

'You may as well sit down,' said Bridie at length, taking the pile of clothes off the only chair and throwing them in a corner. 'I'll make some tea.'

They sat up talking well into the night, Bridie perched on a wooden box beside Rosie cradling her infant – a girl whom Bridie had named Kate after their mother. In all their years living under

140

the same roof they had never talked so intensely or so honestly. All the jealousies and arguments of the past seemed to drop away like leaves from a tree. Bridie, laid bare now in front of her sister, left off all pretence of anger and resentment, and let emerge a truth purified by her shame. In response, Rosie dropped her mask of pride and admitted her fantasies about Valentine. So intent were they on each other that they ignored Micko's stumbling return as he collapsed onto the thin mattress.

Rosie slept fitfully. Bridie had laid a thin blanket on the floor for her and a rolled-up rag to use as a pillow. Though her body was exhausted from the long journey to Dublin, and the shock of what she had found there, still her mind would not rest. Her thoughts were a swirl of Valentine bidding her goodbye in the garden at Ennismore, Ma weeping in the small cottage and Bridie, red-eyed, kneeling over her sick infant. Micko's snores shuddered around the room, and ominous sounds of scurrying and scraping inside the walls made her cringe. When she could stand it no longer, she roused herself, dressed and slipped out into the cold, dark air.

The street was empty. She walked with her head down as fast as she could away from Foley Court. New thoughts tossed about in her mind. She must find a job and a place to stay as quickly as possible. The very thought of returning to Bridie's room made her stomach churn. And she must find a way to rescue Bridie and her child from that squalor. She realized with a start how this new urgency had replaced all her shattered dreams about Valentine. 'This is reality, Rosie,' she murmured to herself. 'You're no longer living on dreams.'

By the time the first rays of dawn appeared she had reached Sackville Street, the main thorough-fare of the city. Young boys in caps held out newspapers, shouting the headlines at passers-by. Iron gates rattled as shopkeepers pushed them aside to open their premises. An electric tram hissed past her and made her swing around. She had never seen such vehicles before, and was both mesmerized and alarmed by them. The riot of noises shook her nerves and she found herself longing for the familiar, mellow sounds of home.

She bought a newspaper and went into a dimly lit café where she ordered tea. She was starving, but ignored the array of tempting buns and other baked goods on display. She must conserve what little money she had. She scoured the newspaper for employment advertisements. The column for female 'situations vacant' was disappointingly short. She had expected rows of openings for shop clerks, postal clerks, seamstresses, teachers or governesses. She would even consider, if neces-sary, factory work, but even these vacancies were scarce. There were one or two openings for typewriter operators, but Rosie had no training. She didn't even know what a typewriter looked like. Most of the advertisements were for maids, and nannies, and one for a cook. She sighed. How could she ever return to domestic service again? She swallowed the last of her tea and left the café.

She started off each day the same way – an early departure from the dismal room before Bridie and

Micko were awake, a walk to Sackville Street and a tea in the café along with the day's newspaper. Then followed hours upon hours of entering premises to enquire for work, only to exit them again filled with disappointment. At first she was selective – dress shops, hat shops, flower shops, drapers and tobacconists. Then she became bolder – solicitors' offices, doctors' offices, banks. In desperation she tried butchers, pawn shops and even public houses. By turns she was sniffed over, ogled, ignored and laughed at. She was considered under qualified in some cases, over qualified in others, but in all cases unsuitable.

By day she walked the length and breadth of the city and each night returned exhausted to 6 Foley Court. She came to realize that Bridie's situation was the same as thousands like her in Dublin. The city was immersed in poverty. There was no work to be had. The only thriving occupation for a girl like her, as Micko constantly reminded her, was prostitution. Indeed, Rosie had seen the girls around the city – both in the area around Bridie's house, and also in the city centre. She came to understand that even the prostitutes had their hierarchy – the poorer ones working on Montgomery Street, and the better dressed ones on Sackville Street – and that the majority of their customers were British soldiers from the nearby barracks.

At last she came to a decision. She got up before dawn one morning two months after she had arrived at Bridie's. She dressed more carefully than usual, putting on her best hat and jacket, and polishing her boots. She put a perfumed handkerchief in her pocket, and made sure her hair was brushed. Washing her hair the night before had been no mean feat. A bucket of water had to be hauled up the four flights from a communal tap in the rear yard of the building. There was no chance of heating it, so she made do with the cold water.

Bridie was full of apologies for the state of things but Rosie waved her away. This was not her fault. Besides, Rosie was more concerned about Bridie's infant. The child had been sick with a fever ever since Rosie had arrived. There was no money for doctors, and all Bridie could do was wipe her down at intervals with a cold wet cloth. 'What if I lose her to the fever?' she blurted out one night. Rosie was unable to answer her.

It was living in this squalid, hopeless place that had helped Rosie make up her mind. She would go to visit Lady Marianne Bellefleur, aunt of Victoria and Valentine, and sister of Lord Ennis. Victoria had told her that Lady Marianne had extended an offer for either of the girls to visit her in Dublin, particularly if they wished to strike out on their own. Rosie had tossed and turned all night in a sweat, wrestling with her decision. How could she throw herself on the mercy of this woman she hardly knew? How could she go to a relative of the Bell family after she had run away so abruptly? What about her pride? But as she drifted in and out of sleep, listening to the rats scurrying inside the walls, she realized that all her pride had been used up during her days of walking Dublin's inhospitable streets. There was no choice any more. Her pride did not matter. What mattered was saving Bridie from this life.

It was a particularly cold morning, and Rosie pulled her jacket tight around her as she walked. She went into the café and bought a cup of tea. This morning she allowed herself a warm bun. She had time to kill. It would not be respectable to call at Lady Marianne's house before ten o'clock. Rosie had casually enquired of Bridie one evening as to where Lady Marianne lived.

'Fitzwilliam Square,' Bridie said, 'number six, just like here!'

She had laughed when she said it, but Rosie knew that Fitzwilliam Square would be nothing like Foley Court. Now she stared at the address she had written down. It should not be that hard to find. Bridie had said it was south of the city beyond the river. She ate and drank slowly, tucked away in a dim corner.

As the café grew more crowded the waitress began to glare at her, as did customers waiting for her table. She sighed and stood up and edged her way back out on to the street and began to walk south. The city had come alive while she was inside sipping her tea. Trams and horse-drawn cabs wrestled one another for space, while bicyclists and pedestrians dodged around them. As always, the noise was deafening – the blare of horns, shrill whistles, the whoosh of trams and the clip-clop of horses, the calls of errand boys. She had a fleeting image of the woods and pastures around Ennismore where the only noises were the calls of the birds, the lowing of cattle and the soft breezes from the lake and her heart felt heavy.

It grew colder as she reached the River Liffey which ran through the city. As she crossed the

O'Connell Bridge she looked down at the bustling dock workers hauling cargo on and off boats. It struck her that even amidst all these crowds she had never felt so alone. As she walked south she passed Trinity College. Valentine had spent a term there before being asked to leave. She looked now at the young men flooding in and out through the main gate – some hurrying as if late for a class, some dawdling, others stopping to greet their comrades. She slowed her step to look at them, blushing when several of them turned around after a tall young man had pointed at her.

As she walked on, her hands buried deep in her coat pockets against the cold, she noticed that the area had grown cleaner and quieter. The tenements and filth of Montgomery Street and Foley Court seemed a world away. Here, the four storey terraced houses were solid and well-kept, and no women beggars with babies in shawls occupied the pavements. There were no prostitutes either, she noticed, at least not obvious ones.

She came upon one square of houses with a small green in the middle. She glanced up at the brass plate on the corner building and saw it said 'Merrion Square'. Where had she heard this name before? Ah, yes, Lady Ennis had rented a house here for Victoria's first Season. She thought again of the rejection she had felt the morning Victoria had ridden off from Ennismore. How much she had wanted to go with her! She stood for a moment, wondering which house they had lived in, and imagined the parties that might have taken place there. Then, putting such thoughts out of her mind she pressed on.

At last she came to Fitzwilliam Square. Well-tended, terraced houses formed a square around an enchanting, tiny park. A pang of homesickness struck her as she thought of the Victorian garden where she and Victoria had played as children, where she and Valentine had kissed. There was hardly a sound as she walked around the square looking for number six. She admired the ivy-covered brick houses, each with a brightly painted door of blue, red, green or glossy black. Glass panels flanked each door, above which was an elegant arched window. Even though it was still winter, plants and flowers overflowed painted window boxes. Ornate wrought iron railings and window guards protected each house.

She stopped in front of the steps that led up to number six. She smiled when she saw the boot-scraper on the top of the steps – a memory of Ennismore. And she found herself taking pride in the observation that the steps had not been scrubbed up to Mrs Murphy's standards, or to her own, for that matter. Her brief sense of pride was immediately replaced by doubt. Was it the height of impertinence to arrive unannounced? What if Lady Marianne was away and she had come all this way for nothing? What if Lady Marianne was outraged at her boldness? Her hand froze as she reached for the brass knocker, a highly-polished brass circle with three stylized lilies. She recognized the design from a rug at Ennismore – fleur-de-lys, Victoria had told her, a French design.

Everything in her wanted to turn and run. But the spectre of Bridie and her baby in that squalid room at Foley Court kept her there. She lifted the knocker and let it fall with a thud.

The door opened and a girl about her own age in a grey maid's uniform with a frilly white apron and cap smiled down at her.

'May I help you, *mademoiselle?*' she said in a strong French accent.

Rosie swallowed. 'I am here to see Lady Bellefleur,' she said. 'I am a friend of her niece, Miss Victoria Bell.'

The girl eyed her with interest. 'And your name, please?'

'Miss Roisin Killeen.'

The maid stepped aside. 'Come into the drawing room please. I will let Lady Marianne know you are here. You have a card, no?'

Rosie reddened. She knew the proper form was to present a card when you came on an unexpected visit. 'I'm afraid I do not have it with me,' she lied.

'*D'accord.* You will wait here please.'

The maid disappeared, leaving Rosie standing in the drawing room. She looked around her, afraid to sit down. The colours in the room were a delicate concoction of blue and pink pastels set off by gilt-edged mirrors and rich, citrus-wood furnishings. The fleur-de-lys pattern on the front door knocker was repeated in the pale blue rug. There was a light, airy feel to the room, as compared with the heavy, substantial, faded grandeur of the rooms in Ennismore. Rosie was reminded of the ornate birdcages she had seen pictured in some of Victoria's books on France, and she smiled. A rustle behind her intruded on her

148

thoughts and she swung around.

Lady Marianne Bellefleur entered the drawing room wearing a pale green tea dress. Rosie was taken aback. She had never seen Lady Marianne up close. She was radiant for a woman her age. Her skin was white and flawless, and her hair, though blacker than may have been natural, formed a glossy frame for her delicate face. She offered her hand to Rosie.

'*Bonjour, Mademoiselle*. You are a friend of my niece Victoria? Is she well?'

Rosie took her hand and let it drop quickly. Lady Marianne seated herself on a carved, pink love seat beneath the window, and motioned for Rosie to sit on a delicate blue velvet side chair. Rosie sat down, and clutching her reticule leaned forward.

'Very well, ma'am, er, my lady,' she began. And then she spoke rapidly, afraid that if she didn't get all her words out at once she might flee from this place and never return. 'I am Rosie Killeen. I was Victoria's school companion for years at Ennismore until she came out for her first Season. I've been in Dublin for some time. I hoped to strike out on my own. I know that's something you encourage young woman to do. Victoria told me you said that. And, and she said that you told her either one of us could come to see you in Dublin. I wouldn't have come at all but for my sister Bridie's living in awful conditions and I have to find a way to help her and...'

Rosie ran out of breath and a sudden terror seized her as she looked at Lady Marianne.

'Does Lady Ennis know you are here?'

'What? No, my lady. Nobody knows where I am.'

'Was there a scandal?'

Rosie flinched. Could her running away in the middle of the night without notice or warning be considered a scandal?

'No, nothing like that,' she said, her voice louder than she intended, 'I just needed a change. I wanted to take charge of my future.'

Lady Marianne picked up a tiny bell from a side table and summoned the maid, asking her to return with tea. Rosie waited, her heart thumping.

'And just what is it you think I can do for you, Miss Killeen?'

A wave of misery washed over Rosie. What was the use of hiding the truth any longer? She began to sob.

'I don't know, my lady. You are my last hope. I can't go back to Ennismore. Valentine said he planned to go to America and for me not to wait for him and...'

Lady Marianne smiled. 'Ah, the truth at last. *Toujours l'amour.* Yes, dear Thomas came to visit me some weeks ago. As I had predicted he would, he told me he would be sailing to America on the *Titanic* with Miss Sofia Hoffman and her papa. I was delighted to hear his news. He mentioned that Valentine would be accompanying them. One would be pleased to see two fine young men going off on a great adventure.' She paused and sighed. 'Unless of course one happens to be in love with one of them.'

Rosie blushed. There was no turning back now. She was at the mercy of this woman whom she had never before met. She held her tiny china cup in a shaking hand while Lady Marianne

150

peered at her.

'You speak well and you are well groomed. You could possibly be mistaken for a lady.' Lady Marianne appeared to be speaking to herself as much as to Rosie.

'I just want help finding employment, my lady. Just to earn enough to pay my own way, and help my sister.' She took a deep breath. 'I thought maybe you could give me a reference. That's all I want.'

Lady Marianne leaned back on the sofa. 'Nonsense, my dear. A girl with your looks and bearing must set her sights much higher than that.'

She drained her tea and stood up, an impish smile on her face. 'I shall talk your situation over with dear Mr Kearney – he always has splendid ideas. Give me the address of your lodgings and I shall send a note letting you know when to return. At that time I shall tell you what we have planned for you.'

Rosie left the house on Fitzwilliam Square filled with a mixture of dread and excitement. She retraced her steps past Trinity College, along the bridge over the River Liffey and up Sackville Street. This time she was in too much of a trance to notice anything around her. By the time she mounted the stairs to Bridie's room her resolve had hardened.

'I don't care what the woman has in mind,' she said to herself, 'I'll agree to whatever it is. I can't spend one more night in this vile place.'

CHAPTER 11

On the same day Rosie visited Lady Marianne, Valentine, who had been in London since the beginning of the year, joined his brother on the journey home to Ennismore to say their goodbyes to the family. He and Thomas would board the *Titanic* when she docked at Queenstown in County Cork on 11 April – Sofia and her father having boarded the previous day in Southampton.

The young men chatted in the carriage all the way down from Dublin. It was only when Ennismore came into view that they grew silent and preoccupied.

'This is going to be difficult,' said Thomas, as if reading his brother's thoughts.

'An understatement, I think.'

'Mama will be the hardest to convince. I know she does not approve of Sofia.' Thomas straightened his back and jutted out his chin. 'Not that it matters. I mean to marry her. Still, I hate to see Mama distressed.'

Valentine studied his brother. 'You are braver than I am, Thomas. You will let nothing stand in the way of your love.'

'What could be more important?' said Thomas.

Their hired carriage drew to a halt in front of the house. Lady Ennis, Lord Ennis and Victoria came down the front steps to meet them, their sister rushing ahead of their parents.

'I'm so glad to see you!' said Victoria as she reached up and hugged each of them in turn. 'How exciting this all is. Do tell me your news. Oh, I so wish I was going with you, but Mama will not even consider it. She says I am too young, and–'

'Victoria!' Lady Ennis's tone was sharp.

Victoria stood aside as her brothers approached their parents. They each attempted to embrace their mother who, instead, turned a stiff, disapproving cheek towards them to be kissed. In contrast, Lord Ennis offered his hand and a pat on the shoulder in a friendly greeting. The family went inside as Brendan and Sean came out to fetch their bags while a groom led the coachman around to the stables so that he might water the horses.

Lady Ennis erupted into full hysteria as the family assembled in the drawing room. 'How could you boys do this to your mother?' she wailed, dabbing her eyes with a dainty handkerchief. 'I never thought to see the day when my sons would abandon me in such a manner.'

'I'm not abandoning you, Mama,' said Thomas and Valentine in unison.

'But you are. What else would you call sailing off to that uncivilized place from which you might never return? Who knows what calamities may befall you there? I hear the savages still run amok cutting off people's heads.'

'That was the French, Mama,' put in Valentine, forcing a smile. 'The American Indians take scalps.'

Lady Ennis descended into another paroxysm of sobs.

'Now, Thea, you are letting your imagination overwhelm you,' said Lord Ennis. 'Compose yourself, my dear. Louisa, please attend to her.'

Lady Louisa, who sat taking in the proceedings, gave a dry laugh. 'I can't think what *I* can do, Edward. She is beyond all reason.'

Victoria went to sit on the side of her mother's chair and put her arm around her. 'Please don't cry, Mama. This should be a celebration.'

Lady Ennis looked at her daughter as if she were mad. 'Celebration? What is there to celebrate about one son paying court to a totally unsuitable girl, while the other abandons us at the mere crook of that horrible little Jewish man's finger?'

'Mr Hoffman is not a horrible little man, Mama, and why would you care whether or not he's Jewish?' said Victoria. 'Besides, he is offering Valentine a chance to make something of himself.'

'Hear, hear, Victoria,' said her father. 'America may make a man out of your brother after all.'

Valentine bowed his head and said nothing.

Lady Ennis glared at her husband. 'And what of the fact that our sons are undertaking this journey together? What if that ship sinks? What if they both drown? Ennis Estates will be left without an heir. I don't see how you can permit it, Edward.'

'Nonsense, Thea. The *Titanic* is the soundest and most advanced ship ever built. I hear her engines are of the finest and most efficient design. There's never been a ship like her.'

'Besides,' said Louisa, signalling Burke for another glass of sherry, 'I daresay they have an adequate number of lifeboats!'

The *Titanic* sailed out of Queenstown on Thursday, 11 April, 1912 on her maiden voyage to New York. The Dublin newspapers were full of the story. Rosie sat in the café on Sackville Street reading every word of every article. She pictured Valentine standing on the deck looking out to sea. Would he think of her? she wondered. The pain she had felt last New Year's Eve in the garden when he had told her not to wait for him returned, more intense than before. In the midst of the rush of people around her she felt completely alone.

Back at Ennismore, the Bell family and the staff were lost in their own imaginings. Thomas and Valentine Bell and the younger footman, Sean Loftus, who had also sailed, were foremost on their minds. A vague restlessness had taken hold of Victoria since she had waved her brothers goodbye, jealous of their adventure. Her first two Seasons in Dublin had been a whirlwind of excitement, and her travels on the Continent unforgettable. She had thought at the time that life could not get better. She had acquired many suitors and enjoyed playing one off against the other. But by the time she had arrived home late the previous year, the excitement had begun to pale. Meeting Sofia had not helped matters. The young woman's free spirit and disregard of the stifling rules of the gentry had made Victoria realize how narrow and boring her own life was and would likely remain.

Below stairs, Thelma moped while a glum Sadie sat mending one of Lady Louisa's petticoats. Immelda fingered the flimsy pages of her prayer book, her head bowed. Mrs O'Leary set the lamb to roast in the oven and sank down on a chair, flapping her apron to cool her burning cheeks.

'Ye look like ye lost a shilling and found a farthing,' she said.

'I miss Sean,' said Thelma.

'Don't waste your time moping about that lad,' said Mrs O'Leary. 'Sure isn't he having the time of his life with all the pretty young girls?'

Thelma stuck out her bottom lip. 'I suppose he is.'

Sadie shoved her mending aside. 'I wish I'd gone with my cousins and the rest of the ones from below in Lahardane,' she said, referring to more than a dozen young people who had left from her own village. 'Just for the craic, that's all. And I'd have had me pick of the handsome lads on board.'

'Sure they're no more than grooms and stable hands and farmers' sons,' put in Mrs O'Leary, 'just like our Sean. I thought you had your sights set higher than that, Sadie.'

Sadie flushed. 'I don't mean the lads in steerage,' she said. 'I couldn't be bothered with the likes of them. I'd have been up on the first class deck as fast as my feet would carry me. Who knows, I might have met a count or a prince or maybe some rich Yankee boyo.'

Mrs O'Leary rolled her eyes. ''Tis dreaming y'are, Sadie Canavan. They'd have gates and guards to keep out the likes of you. You'd have been sent back down where you belonged.'

Sadie glared at the cook and resumed her mending, punching her needle ferociously into the gauzy material. Mrs O'Leary stood and blessed herself.

156

'Why are ye all sitting around with faces as long as a drink of water? 'Tis happy for them we should be. Seaneen, and Masters Thomas and Valentine too, and wishing them good fortune at the end of their journey.' She turned to Thelma. 'Get up, girl, and wipe that face off yourself. There's work to be done.'

By the following day, the torpor that had filled the house eased. The servants went back to their daily routines and the talk of America faded. Only Victoria continued to dwell on it. Not for the first time, she wished she had someone to talk to. She had tried to bring the subject up with her mother but Lady Ennis was distracted, indulging her overt outrage that her sons had had the temerity to go against her wishes by leaving. At times like this the pain of her lost friendship with Rosie was acute.

She wondered what Rosie was doing. Her friend had left so abruptly that no one had understood it. Valentine had roamed about the house as if in a daze. He was the last one to see her but insisted to Victoria that he had said nothing to upset her. In her frustration, she had gone to visit Rosie's mother at the Killeen cottage and had found the poor woman distraught. All she had was a brief note from Rosie saying she had gone to Dublin to check up on the welfare of her sister, Bridie. Victoria knew in her heart something more than concern for Bridie had driven Rosie away. She hoped her own neglect of her old friend had not been the cause. She pushed down the guilt that rose up at the thought.

On the following Monday unsettling news

began to trickle in about a ship that had sunk somewhere in the Atlantic. Speculation around Dublin was ripe. Details were scarce. There had been no confirmation yet that the ship involved was the *Titanic*.

Rosie was in a daze as she made her way to the offices of the White Star Line which owned and operated the *Titanic*. There, she was jostled by crowds of frenzied relatives and friends of the passengers, as well as reporters, all clamouring for news. She hoped against hope that it was some other ship that had met with disaster. But the longer she stood, the more the conversations swirled around her, the more her hopes were dashed.

She did not go back to Bridie's that night. Instead she sat on a bench outside the now darkened White Star offices. She had not eaten all day but food was the farthest thing from her mind. Valentine! Oh my God, let him be alive! She repeated the words to herself over and over like a prayer. She bargained with God. Let him live and I will give up all my jealousy. I will no longer desire him. I will put him out of my mind forever. I will never bother him again. If only you will let him live.

By the next day the *New York Times* had confirmed the news. The *Titanic* had hit an iceberg and sunk. The rescue ship, *Carpathia*, had picked up over seven hundred passengers. The White Star offices began to circulate lists of the survivors. Rosie scoured them, standing on tiptoe to see above the crowd, and straining her eyes to read the small print. At last she saw his name. Valentine Bell. 'Thank God,' she whispered. 'Thank God.'

While Valentine and the Hoffmans had all survived, Thomas was listed as missing, as was Sean Loftus. Like hundreds of others who had perished, their bodies had not been found. The house was plunged into mourning. Drapes were drawn to blot out the light. Visitors came to pay respects and servants crept about the house wearing black armbands. Lady Ennis's earlier hysterics gave way to stony silence. Reverend Watson arrived to make arrangements for the memorial service. Valentine had cabled to say he would not be coming home for the service. His duty, he said, was to stay and comfort Sofia who was inconsolable.

Below stairs, Mrs O'Leary dropped to her knees and wailed.

'Sweet mother of God. May holy St Brigid and holy St Christopher have mercy on all them poor souls.'

Thelma began to sob. 'Don't let Sean be dead.'

Sadie wept for her two young cousins who were also listed among the missing while Mrs Murphy muttered her prayers, and Mr Burke bowed his head.

'Well, I suppose we've all been spared then,' said Brendan, who sat at the table drinking tea. 'I mean if your man Valentine had drowned as well as Thomas there'd have been nobody to inherit the estate and that would mean we'd all have been out on our arses.'

Without warning, Mrs O'Leary jumped up and slapped Brendan across the face. 'How dare you?' she shouted. 'Have you no mercy in you at all?'

Brendan shrugged. 'What do I care what happens to the gentry?' he said. 'A few less of

159

them in Ireland would suit me. I'd rather they were all dead and buried. They have no rights in this country, and never did.'

Anthony stood up and leaned over Brendan, his face close. 'That's enough, me boyo. This is neither the time nor the place for your rebel talk. Save that for the public houses and show some respect for the dead.'

Sadie stood up. 'I have to go to Lahardane,' she said. 'I have to see my family. Surely they've heard the news by now. Ah, what am I going to say to them?'

'I'll come with you,' said Brendan, standing up. 'I have a spare bicycle. We'll ride down there together.' He turned to Mr Burke, as if in afterthought. 'I might have no sympathy for the gentry, but I feel for them poor souls below in Lahardane who never did any harm to anybody. And Sadie needs someone to go with her.'

Mr Burke nodded. 'As long as you are back by morning.'

He turned to the housekeeper. 'Some brandy, I think, Mrs Murphy,' he said. 'It would do us all good.'

CHAPTER 12

At the end of April Lady Marianne finally sent word for Rosie to return to the house on Fitzwilliam Square. Rosie had almost given up hope of ever hearing from her again. When the letter arrived she was weak with relief, but her relief turned to anxiety when she heard Lady Marianne's proposal.

'It will be such a wonderful experiment,' the good lady told Rosie when she went to see her. 'I will bring you out for the 1913 season. It is too late for the current one and besides, many are still mourning the *Titanic* disaster. I will introduce you to all the right people. I shall say that you are my poor orphaned cousin from the country whom I have adopted as my ward. I'm confident with my support we can find you a good match.' She paused and rubbed her hands together. 'It was dear Mr Kearney's suggestion. I told you he always has such marvellous ideas. And best of all, Miss Killeen, what a delicious deception to pull off under the very nose of my dear sister-in-law, Lady Ennis. Just the best ruse ever!'

Rosie was stunned. She slumped down on one of the velvet chairs, trying to take it all in. Her immediate reaction was to protest. How dare Lady Marianne use her just to amuse herself at the expense of her sister-in-law? She would refuse. She would hold on to her last shred of dignity. But as she opened her mouth to speak, she found herself mute. What good would it do her to refuse? What other alternative had she? Valentine was gone. Lady Marianne had told her that he had decided to stay in New York to comfort Sofia. She had no money and no prospects. She thought again of Bridie and her infant up at Foley Court. What right did she have to let her pride stand in the way of the only thing that might save them?

'Thank you, my lady,' she said, her head bowed.

'I am very grateful for your kindness.'

She did not tell Bridie the whole plan, only that Lady Marianne had invited her to stay until employment could be found for her. Tears welled in Bridie's eyes, and Rosie reached out and hugged her.

'Ah, don't be crying now, Bridie. Sure isn't this the best thing for all of us? As soon as I have money I can move you and Kate out of this place and we can all take a room together. I'll find a place that is clean and respectable. And we'll be able to pay for a doctor for the baby, and...'

Even as Rosie said these things she felt guilt rising in her. What if Lady Marianne's plan didn't work? How could she give Bridie such false hope? But she pressed on, 'It might take a bit of time, but I'll be back to visit as often as I can.'

She picked up little Kate and held her so tightly the child began to squirm in her arms. Rosie choked back tears as she looked into Kate's brown eyes, so like Ma's. 'I'll not forget you, Kate,' she whispered.

As she took her leave from Foley Court later that day, however, she pushed away all thoughts of false hope and allowed herself to enjoy a guarded optimism about what the future might hold.

Thus in early May of 1912, Rosie Killeen moved into the guest bedroom of 6 Fitzwilliam Square and threw herself and her future upon the mercy of Lady Marianne Bellefleur.

Her first months at Fitzwilliam Square were a whirlwind of visits to the best dress shops in Dublin, etiquette lessons from Mrs Townsend, a fierce matron whose business was to ready young ladies for the Season, and invitations to teas at the houses of Lady Bellefleur's acquaintances.

'We must bring you out slowly,' Lady Marianne had said. 'We'll start by introducing you to ladies whose influence is minor, just to see how you fare. Then we can work our way up to the more important houses.'

Lady Marianne had insisted that Rosie's name be given as Rosalind. 'Rosie or Roisin is entirely too native a name, my dear, lovely though it is,' she said. 'We must pay attention to such details.' Rosie had wanted to protest, but again she thought of Bridie and held her tongue.

And so she allowed herself to embrace her sudden good fortune. She remembered all the glittering fantasies of her childhood, imagining how it would be to live as a grand lady. And now that she was on the cusp of such a reality she could scarcely believe it. Lady Marianne's protégé, Mr Shane Kearney, sat with her every evening after dinner regaling her with the foibles of Dublin's high society. Rosie giggled as he recounted tales of illicit affairs, hushed-up scandals, 'unplanned' children, gambling, carousing and excesses of all kinds among the city's gentry.

'Is there no one who is respectable?' she asked.

Mr Kearney tossed back his hair with a smile. 'Oh, I'm sure there are, my dear, but where is the amusement in discussing them? I prefer the profligate and the scoundrels. So much more delicious, and usually so much better dressed!'

Rosie made quick progress. Her manners and diction were already refined from her years of being with Victoria and, she had to admit, from

Lady Louisa's tutelage. Not once did she betray her origins as a farmer's daughter. She spoke French adequately and played the piano quite well – both desirable attributes for a young lady entering society. Along with Mrs Townsend's guidance, she quickly mastered the appropriate behaviours when being introduced at teas and dinners. Lady Marianne was very pleased with her improvement.

But on the quiet evenings at Fitzwilliam Square, when Lady Marianne and Mr Kearney had gone out to the theatre or to dinner with friends, and Rosie sat alone in the small library, doubts began to creep into her mind. She had always known the strict schedule kept by the Bell family at Ennismore. Their days were punctuated by unwavering timetables – breakfast at eight, lunch at noon, dinner precisely at seven in the evening, sewing or reading until bedtime at eleven. Now, in living this routine herself, Rosie realized how confining it could be.

As time wore on it began to feel more and more as if she was acting out a bizarre pantomime. She had to change dress several times a day, always follow the cues of the gentlemen, and keep her opinions to herself. She could not even go out for a walk without a chaperone. Is this what life would be like as the lady of a grand house? Is this what life was like for Victoria? Is this what life would have been like if she'd married Valentine? She pushed away such thoughts as forcefully as she could.

Many of the people she met at the teas and dinners she attended she found boring. Had it not been for Mr Kearney's stories of their various scandals, she would have had difficulty making it through such evenings. She held her own well enough with discussions of horse riding and country houses and the latest fashions, careful not to slip into the point of view of a servant. Most of the girls her own age appeared to have less humour than even Lady Louisa at Ennismore, and their mothers, while polite, clearly viewed Rosie as competition for their daughters. She had never imagined how competitive this business of finding a husband could be.

One welcome exception to the succession of boring evenings was when Lady Marianne brought her to visit the Butler family at Temple Villas. There were three sisters, ranging in age from fifteen to twenty-one, daughters of a doctor and his artist wife. They were lively and entertaining, and interested in everything that was going on around them. And, despite their mother's urging, not one of them had a great desire to be 'brought out' into society. Instead of horse riding and fashion and country homes, they talked of the plight of the poor in Dublin, the growing labour unrest, and the swelling tide of nationalism.

Rosie listened intently. She could certainly attest to the state of poverty in Dublin, but could hardly mention her sister Bridie or Foley Court. Valentine had talked at times about the labour unrest and the rise of unions. Victoria had said that Jules Hoffman was so impressed with Valentine's knowledge on that subject that he had invited him to America. What surprised her was that these girls, daughters of a respectable Protestant family in

Dublin, were enthusiastic about Irish nationalism. Rosie had always thought that such sentiments were restricted to the likes of Brendan Lynch at Ennismore, and those lads like him down in the west of Ireland.

'Yes, our friends dear Lady Gregory and Mr Yeats of the Abbey Theatre are strong proponents of the nationalist movement, aren't they, Mr Kearney?' said Lady Marianne, beaming at her companion.

'Indeed. And they use the Abbey Theatre to that end to promote their views.'

'Oh, I love the Abbey,' said Kathleen, the youngest sister. 'I would so love to be an actress. But Papa says it would not be proper.'

'Last year you wanted to be an explorer,' said her oldest sister, Geraldine, 'and undoubtedly next year you will want to be a circus acrobat!'

'Don't tease her so, Geraldine,' said Mrs Butler. 'The child is blessed with a vivid imagination.'

'Well, I for one want to be a journalist,' put in Nora Butler, the middle daughter and the plainest of the sisters, 'and I won't change my mind. I plan to write articles about the coming revolution. I've already shown some of my work to Mr Griffith who publishes the Sinn Fein newspaper. He was very complimentary.'

'Sinn Fein?' asked Lady Marianne.

Dr Butler sighed and looked at Nora. 'It means "Ourselves Alone", a term that has become popular with nationalists who want an Ireland free from British rule. From what I hear Griffith is a very passionate revolutionary. I think he will emerge as one of their leaders someday.'

166

On the way back to Fitzwilliam Square Rosie spoke up. 'What a delightful family they are. So different from everyone else I have met.'

'Yes,' said Lady Marianne, 'I admire those young ladies for their independence, and their parents for letting them live their own lives. I wish our Victoria could be more like them. But, of course, with Lady Ennis for a mother...'

They rode in silence for some time. Then Lady Marianne spoke again.

'I do hope you are not planning to follow their lead, Rosalind, at least not for the present. We must see you launched into society first. After you have made a suitable marriage you can use your influence, and your husband's money, to further whatever cause you please. But as it is, in your present circumstances, such a path would be a grave mistake. And after all I have done for you it would be most ungrateful of you to pursue such a course, would it not?'

Rosie flinched. 'Oh, please, Lady Marianne, I had no notion of it. I am more grateful than you know for all you have done. I will not let you down.'

'I hope not.'

While Rosie was being groomed for the forth-coming Dublin Season, the spectre of Thomas Bell still hovered over Ennismore. Most of the servants were convinced that his ghost had joined that of a suicidal ancestor of the DeBurcas – the original owners of the house – who haunted the attic. Thelma refused to venture up there, even if accompanied by another one of the staff. She

167

insisted on sleeping in the scullery instead. Even Sadie blessed herself as she rushed, head down, along the corridor to the bedroom she had once shared with Rosie.

Lord Ennis spent as much time as he could in London and Lady Ennis lost all interest in entertaining. The Reverend Watson took the opportunity to visit the house often to bring, as he said, 'solace to the suffering members of his flock.' Lady Louisa, her blatant overtures towards the recently widowed clergyman having proved fruitless, now regarded him with unconcealed hostility. Lady Ennis refused to emerge from her seclusion. It fell, therefore, to Victoria to receive him as politely as she could.

As the prospect of living in a house in mourning stretched out before her, Victoria grew increasingly restless. At first she did all she could to ease the overt tension between her parents – forcing herself to make amusing remarks at dinner, recalling memories of happier times, expressing hopeful predictions for the future – but nothing could melt the chill that had formed between them. In the end she gave up, but the silent formality that pervaded their encounters weighed heavily upon her. She yearned for someone to confide in. Oh, where was Rosie? Why had she left her alone? Victoria wished she could tell her friend how stifling living in this house of sorrow had become, how odd and out of place she felt. It was as if she no longer fitted in anywhere. Even her clothes felt strange, as if they were meant for someone else.

Perhaps it was loneliness or boredom that brought it on, Victoria couldn't be sure, but her mind became more and more occupied with thoughts of Brendan Lynch. Rosie had often joked that Brendan had a notion for her but Victoria had dismissed it.

'Think what you like, but the only time I've ever seen him smile is when he looks at you,' Rosie had insisted.

Now Victoria began to piece together snippets of memory – the time he smiled and wished her 'Happy Birthday' when she turned thirteen, the time he held on to her elbow for longer than was necessary when he helped her into the carriage as she departed for the Season, the times she caught him looking at her under lidded eyes as he served dinner. Were these all signals that he did indeed have a 'notion' for her as Rosie had suggested? Or maybe she was imagining things. One thing she was sure of was that he was a great deal more interesting, not to mention more handsome, than the young men she had met during her Dublin season or on her trip abroad.

She tried to put such thoughts out of her head. It was not proper, she told herself. Only trouble could come of it. But much as she tried to avoid his eyes each evening in the dining room, the more compelled she felt to look at him. Unfortunately, there was nothing else to distract her from this preoccupation and she began to think she might go mad. Thus, when Christmas Eve arrived, she willed herself to confront him. She must put an end to this fantasy once and for all. Gathering her courage, she marched down to the servants' hall.

The staff were gathered around the big table about to make a half-hearted toast to the Season.

They fell silent when Victoria appeared in the doorway. Mr Burke stood up and approached her.

'May I help you, Lady Victoria?'

Victoria shook her head, slightly flustered. Now that she was here she was at a loss for words. It seemed that the torpor that pervaded the upstairs rooms had found its way down here also. 'I was hoping you might be playing some music,' she began. 'The rest of the house is so very quiet, and...'

Mr Burke smiled. 'Come on in, then,' he said. 'We're just having some wine, and I think Anthony would be glad to play something if you asked him.'

He took Victoria's arm and led her into the room. The staff all rose to their feet. 'Lady Victoria wishes to join us for a few minutes,' he began, looking at the blank faces. 'She wants to wish us all the blessings of the season.'

Victoria nodded. 'Yes,' she whispered, 'my family wishes to thank you for all your devoted service during the year. And ... and they hope you will not let their sadness interfere with your own celebrations. Please play some music. And please sit down, everyone.'

Mr Burke pulled out a chair for her while Anthony clapped his hands. 'Fair play to you, Lady Victoria. Sure we'll get a wee tune going for you, won't we, lads? God knows a bit of music might cheer this crowd up, they've been so sour even the divil himself would hardly come near them.'

In spite of her nervousness, Victoria suppressed a smile.

'Yes, of course,' said Mr Burke, standing to take

170

charge. 'Welcome, my lady. Brendan? Fetch your instrument. You too, Mrs Murphy.'

Soon, the music swirled around the room. Victoria sat entranced as she watched Brendan play. Rosie had told her he played the fiddle but she had never seen him do so. Brendan fixed her with a stare as he played. She thought she detected a hint of fire in his eyes. Could it be aimed at her? But she quickly dismissed the thought. Surely it was his passion for the music and not her that made his eyes glow. She sat, unable to tear her gaze away from him. Suddenly, as if coming out of a trance, she was aware of the others watching her intently. Could they read her mind? Flustered, she gathered up her skirts and fled from the room, mumbling apologies.

'Well, doesn't that beat the band altogether?' said Mrs O'Leary. 'To think Miss Victoria would prefer our company to that of her own family on Christmas Night.'

'Can you blame her?' said Sadie. 'Every one of them's walking around with a stick up their arse.'

'Sadie!' said Mrs Murphy. 'Show some respect.'

'It's true,' put in Thelma, emboldened by the wine. 'I've seen it meself. His lordship and her ladyship don't even sleep in the same bed any more. His lordship is always lying in the chaise longue in his study when I go in to make up the fire of a morning.'

'Maybe he slips in and out in the middle of the night, so,' said Brendan.

Mr Burke banged his fist on the table. 'That's enough! We will not speak of our superiors in that manner.'

'They're not *my* superiors,' said Brendan.

'Nor mine,' echoed Sadie.

'Nor mine either,' giggled Thelma. 'Me da says the Irish are inferior to nobody, particularly the English.'

Mrs O'Leary gaped at Thelma. 'That's enough talk, girl. And enough wine, too. Get yourself up to bed.'

Mr Burke glowered. 'I will put this kind of talk down to the fact that everyone has had too much wine. But if I ever hear it from any of you again ... there will be consequences. Mark my words. Now get to bed, all of you.'

As the grumbling servants rose to make their way to bed, Victoria had already reached her own bed and pulled the covers up around her head. She lay trembling with a mix of fear and excitement. I can't go down there again, she told herself, but as she drifted off to sleep she knew that she would.

CHAPTER 13

In February of the New Year a cable arrived and its news ricocheted through Ennismore like an echoing rifle shot. In the library, Lady Ennis cried out and dropped the cable as if it were on fire.

'What on earth is it, Thea?' said Lord Ennis, rushing into the room. 'What has come over you? Should I have Louisa fetch the doctor?'

He tried to ease his wife on to a sofa but she

had grown stiff as a corpse, and as white. Lady Louisa bent to pick up the cable. She scanned it rapidly and held it out to her brother-in-law. 'Perhaps this will explain it,' she said.

Lord Ennis took the cable, which was dated 14 February 1913, and read it, his eyes widening as he did so. When he looked up at the women, his face flushed with pleasure.

'What capital news!' he exclaimed. 'What a wonderful outcome. God has blessed the Bell family at last.'

His wife let out another cry. 'Surely you can't mean that, Edward? It's the most awful news imaginable.'

'What? That we have a new grandson? That Valentine and Sofia are married? That they will be returning soon to Ennismore? I don't understand, Thea.'

Lady Ennis slumped on the sofa, fanning herself furiously against a sudden burst of flames that had erupted from the fire in the grate. 'Edward, how can you be so blind? A marriage between our son and that vulgar American woman and we knew nothing of it until now? We are disgraced, Edward. How shall we ever explain it?'

Lord Ennis grew irritated. 'Our son has made a profitable marriage. A child has been born – a boy to secure our lineage well into the future. Ennis Estates may well have been saved from the auctioneer's gavel. The future of the Bells is secure. For God's sake, what more could we wish for, Thea? I don't give a damn about the wagging tongues. Our legacy is safe, and that is what matters. Jules told me Sofia will have five thousand pounds a year, not to mention the settlement he will have made on her upon her marriage – a generous amount, no doubt, since she is his only child.'

'All you think about is money,' said Lady Ennis, dabbing her eyes.

Lord Ennis glared at her. 'You would do well to give it more thought, my dear. Your extravagances over the years have almost bankrupted us. You should welcome Sofia with open arms. She is your saviour as well as mine.' He walked across the room and rang the bell for Mr Burke. 'Now let's stop this nonsense and raise a toast to Valentine and Sofia, and our new grandson!'

For the first and only time, Rosie Killeen and Lady Althea Ennis were in agreement. Though their reactions to the news stemmed from very different reasons, both were equally devastated. Lady Marianne was triumphant when she announced the news to Rosie.

'It is wonderful, is it not, Rosalind? Although I'm sure Althea is beside herself because those young people had the temerity to go their own way without asking her permission. I was impressed the moment I met Sofia – such an independent young woman and so full of life. She will be more than a match for Althea. My brother is over the moon, particularly about the money she brings with her. And I can't wait to meet my new grand-nephew. Julian is his name and...'

Rosie did not hear the rest of Lady Marianne's words. She watched her mouth moving, but a high-pitched humming in her ears had suddenly deafened her. A current of pain burned from her

174

groin to her throat and she felt her heart compress. She sank down in a chair, clutching its arms to prevent herself from fainting. Lady Marianne regarded her with alarm.

'Oh, my dear girl,' she began. 'Oh, how thoughtless of me. I did not realize you still cared for Valentine so much.' Lady Marianne came closer. 'Mourn him, my dear,' she said, 'but not for too long. Then you must move on. Go upstairs now and rest. I will send Celine up with some tea.'

Rosie lowered her head. Her face burned and her eyes itched as if filled with gravel. She was not sure she could move but she knew she had to get away from Lady Marianne. She rose slowly and made her way out of the room. Gripping the banister to steady herself, she climbed the stairs and stumbled into her room. She lay down on the bed fully clothed, her fists clenched at her sides. As she stared at the ceiling, hardly breathing, she imagined she lay in a coffin. If she could be still enough, she thought, she could keep the pain at bay.

Evening fell and the light outside the window dimmed. In that unreal pocket of time between day and night she allowed her thoughts to form one at a time – anger with Valentine for his betrayal, anger with herself for her naivety, anger with the Bell family, and finally anger with God. When those thoughts subsided she admitted to herself that, despite all the facts pointing otherwise, she had nursed the hope that one day he would come back for her. How could she go on now, she wondered, without the hope of him?

When she arose the next morning and washed

herself and dressed in fresh clothes, she felt cleansed. But she perceived a change within her that she could not name. The tenderness, fuelled by her love for Valentine which she had once carried in her heart, had transformed, tempered by disappointment into some rougher thing. Love had simply fled, leaving her with a firm resolve to accept what fate held for her. All she could do now was pray that the upcoming Season would be a success and that she would make a good match with some well-off suitor. She didn't care if he was young or old, homely or handsome, as long as he could offer security. A small voice inside her told her that she deserved better.

July arrived and with it the major social event of the 1913 Season – a ball at the gracious Hotel Metropole in Dublin. Lady Marianne surprised Rosie with a beautiful gown from House of Worth in Paris.

'Monsieur Worth was French, my dear,' Lady Marianne said, ignoring the fact that Charles Worth had actually been born an Englishman. 'Nothing less will do for your formal entry into society.'

The gown so took Rosie's breath away that she was almost afraid to touch it. She hung it up in her room and stared at it. It was a soft, pale green charmeuse covered with beige silk tulle and embroidered with crystal brilliants like so many tiny stars. It was low cut with a high waist and its long narrow silhouette fell in drapes to the floor. Rosie had a sudden memory of the day in Victoria's room at Ennismore when she had admired the gowns Victoria held up to her – each more beautiful than the last. She had never imagined owning anything as grand. And now here she was, staring up at her very own gown, more lovely than any of the ones Victoria had owned. She allowed herself a small shiver of pleasure.

On the evening of the ball, Lady Marianne's maid, Celine, dressed Rosie and arranged her black curls into a glossy swirl on top of her head into which she placed some pale green feathers the exact colour of the gown. Rosie could not believe what she saw in the mirror. The gown had been tailored to exaggerate her tall, slim figure and brought out the green hues in her hazel eyes. Her skin was pale – her freckles imperceptible from not having been allowed in the sun without a parasol – and her lips full and red. She regarded the exceptionally pretty girl reflected back at her. Was that she? An unexpected fear gripped her and for a moment she could not breathe. The image in the mirror could not be her but some stranger, some imposter. Rosie, the servant, belonged down on her knees scrubbing floors, not standing erect in a ball gown.

'*Magnifique*,' said Celine, interrupting Rosie's thoughts. 'You look beautiful, *mademoiselle*. Your dance card will be full in no time.'

Lady Marianne clapped her hands as Rosie descended the stairs.

'My dear, you are a vision. Is she not, Mr Kearney?'

Mr Kearney, debonair in a dark blue evening jacket with blue silk lapels, grey silk waistcoat and a crisp white bow-tie, bowed.

'A vision indeed, my dear,' he said, turning to Lady Marianne, 'and a credit to your foresight and good taste. I'd wager we could pass her off as distant royalty, if necessary.'

Rosie trembled as a cold shiver ran through her.

'Let us go out to the carriage,' said Lady Marianne, sweeping past Rosie in a stunning dress of white satin covered with rhinestones. 'We do not want to be late.'

Outside the Hotel Metropole, Sackville Street was choked with horse-drawn carriages and cabs. As Rosie stepped down, she looked up at the grand Georgian building with its façade of decorative ironwork balconies and trembled with excitement and dread. Young women, some in demure white gowns, others arrayed in colourful silks, satins and plumes like so many tropical birds, surrounded her on the pavement. They trilled and giggled as they greeted one another. Rosie saw that most were younger than she by several years. Even though she was only just twenty-one, she felt like a matron compared to them. There were a few older girls, however – quiet and serious, some with looks of mild desperation, others fierce as if preparing for battle. For many of them this would be their last Season, and if they did not secure a match they would be given up to a life of spinsterhood, like Lady Louisa. Rosie felt a sudden rush of pity for them, and for her old teacher.

Lady Marianne and Mr Kearney each took her elbow and guided her between them up the red-carpeted staircase that led to the ballroom. Outwardly, Rosie appeared composed and serene,

178

but inwardly she struggled not to gape open-mouthed at the scene around her. She took in the evergreens woven into the balustrades of the staircase, the red and pink hydrangeas in brass urns and the elegant white lilies in tall vases. The high-ceilinged ballroom was ringed with globe lamps which cast a golden light on the pale yellow walls and rich maple floor. Archways gave way to side rooms where white-clothed tables were set with platters of food and shining crystal punchbowls. In the far corner of the room, atop a flower-bedecked platform, musicians played a soft, slow melody.

A sharp tug on her elbow brought her back to reality.

'Prepare for your introduction, Rosalind,' directed Lady Marianne.

The ball was being given by Lord and Lady Mountnorris in honour of their eldest daughter, Caroline. Lady Mountnorris was considered the premiere hostess in Dublin society, and Lady Marianne had been delighted to receive the invitation. She had immediately stepped up Rosie's instructions, securing extra etiquette tutelage from the estimable Mrs Townsend.

'May I present my ward, Miss Rosalind Killeen,' said Lady Marianne as she extended her hand to her hosts.

On cue Rosie smiled, eyes cast downward, and gave a small but perfectly executed curtsey.

'Charming,' said Lady Mountnorris in a throaty voice as she eyed Rosie and then Mr Kearney who had bowed, one foot forward in the manner of a courtier.

Rosie suppressed an urge to giggle. She had grown quite fond of Mr Kearney whose outrageous behaviour never failed to amuse her. She smiled instead at Lady Caroline, who regarded her for a moment, taking in Rosie's gown, and then dismissed her with a sniff of her long, beaky nose. Lady Marianne and Mr Kearney led Rosie away from their hosts and settled her on one of the upholstered love seats that lined one side of the ballroom. Lady Marianne stood behind her, while Mr Kearney was dispatched to fetch champagne. Rosie, unsettled by Lady Caroline's reaction to her, sat erect, clutching her dance card in sweating fingers. She had two entries on her card, arranged in advance by Lady Marianne so that she would not be sitting for long 'unclaimed' as the good lady put it.

Mr Kearney returned with champagne in two tiny crystal glasses. Rosie sipped hers carefully, not daring to imbibe too quickly. She must keep her wits about her. She relaxed when two young women she recognized as two of the Butler sisters approached. Geraldine, the oldest, wore a pair of pale blue silk trousers embroidered with crystals. Her sister Nora had not even tried to dress up for the ball. She wore a long black skirt and a high-necked white blouse with a black ribbon tied at her throat. The girls greeted Rosie with delight.

'You look beautiful, Rosalind,' said Geraldine. 'I'm afraid I am causing a bit of a scandal with my trousers, but I'm having such great fun.'

'We're only here because Mother insisted,' said Nora, 'but I refused to dress up like a ridiculous bird of paradise – no offence, Rosalind.'

'None taken,' Rosie smiled.

At that moment a short, pudgy young man approached Rosie.

'I'm here to claim my dance,' he said.

Young Lord Gillespie had been coerced into the dance by his mother and Lady Marianne and Rosie could see by his expression that he was not pleased at the prospect. She rose and allowed him to lead her out onto the floor and the musicians struck up a slow waltz. Lord Gillespie was a sullen and awkward partner. He had a poor sense of timing and he stepped on her toes several times. Rosie smiled as graciously as she could and tried to make light conversation, to which he grunted in reply. She could not wait for the dance to be over.

Her second 'arranged' partner was even more distasteful, an older man with wispy, grey hair, who held her too tightly as he grinned at her through yellowed teeth. He was a good dancer though, and Rosie glided around the floor with him. She closed her eyes so she would not have to look at him, instead allowing herself to get lost in the music. She smiled broadly when the dance ended which he mistakenly took to be encouragement.

'I *do* hope you will keep your card open for a dance later,' he said. 'I do so adore the mazurka.'

Rosie nodded and sat down. If all her partners were to be like those two, she thought, she would just as soon sit here all evening. But she did not realize that she had attracted a lot of interest. One by one, an array of handsome young men approached her and introduced themselves. Many were from Trinity College, some from Cambridge and Oxford, all of them from prominent Anglo-Irish families. Lady Marianne insisted on helping her fill out her dance card, advising as to who was suitable and who was not. And before long, Rosie's dance card was full.

'I knew it,' said Lady Marianne, beaming at Mr Kearney. 'I just knew we were going to make this evening a success.'

For the next hour Rosie danced every dance – waltzes, polkas, and mazurkas. Breathless, she excused herself, pleading the need for rest. Lady Marianne had made sure that she left open intervals between dances, lest she appear too anxious. Rosie sat down on the love seat, fanning herself. She was exhilarated. Her partners were very complimentary, many hinting they would like to call on her in the future. She had smiled and made no commitment, as she had been taught. Protocol required the young man to follow up after a ball by sending his card to the young lady's residence and asking if he may call. Rosie was sure some of them would indeed do so. She was already weighing which ones interested her the most. She was lost in thought, her head down as she read the names on her dance card, when a voice interrupted her.

'May I have this dance?'

She would have known his voice anywhere. Her heart squeezed tight in her chest. Perspiration ran down the back of her neck and her hands began to tremble. With effort she took control of herself and looked up. He was even more handsome than she remembered, his boyish slenderness forged now into a robust, muscular frame beneath his dinner jacket. His bright, blond hair had darkened a little but his blue eyes were as clear as ever. Rosie fought back her urge to throw herself into his arms. Instead, she gathered herself and arranged her features into a bland expression.

'I'm sorry, I've already promised this dance,' she said as if addressing a stranger, 'and the rest of my card is full.'

'But my dear that is not true,' said Lady Marianne, snatching Rosie's dance card from her and pointing to it. 'See, we left this one dance open so that you could rest. But this is dear Valentine who is asking you. You can hardly refuse him.'

Rosie wanted to shout that she could and she would. But she did not want to create a scene. She glared at Lady Marianne and then at Valentine.

'Of course not,' she said.

Valentine led her to the middle of the dance floor. Rosie hoped it would be a fast dance, a polka or a mazurka, or even the new dance craze, the tango, so that she would not be obliged to talk to him. But the musicians began to play a slow waltz and Valentine took her in his arms.

'You look exquisite, Rosie,' he said, looking straight into her eyes. 'I've never seen you look more beautiful.'

Rosie said nothing, but stared over his shoulder, determined not to betray her feelings. They danced around the floor in silence. Rosie felt as if she were floating. She had never danced with him before, although she had often imagined what it would be like. And now here he was... She began to tremble as a panic gripped her. Why was he here? Who was with him? Was he here with Sofia?

Worse yet, was he here with Lady Ennis or Lady Louisa or Victoria? Rosie felt faint and stumbled. Valentine steadied her and held her tighter.

'I've missed you so much, Rosie,' he whispered into her ear.

'That's no way for a married man to talk.'

Valentine sighed. 'Oh, Rosie, I want to explain...'

'There's nothing to explain. You went to America and you got married and now you have a son. It sounds straightforward enough to me.'

'But it's not. There's so much you don't know.'

Rosie looked at him. 'I know all I need to know.'

She stopped in the middle of the floor, heedless of the stares around her. 'Go and dance with your wife, Valentine, and leave me alone.'

'Sofia is not here,' he said, his head bowed.

The mention of Sofia's name chased away every last wisp of fantasy Rosie might have harboured surrounding Valentine. As long as she had not heard him actually say that Sofia was indeed his wife, she had hung on to a fragile shred of possibility that it had all been a mistake. Now the sound of Sofia's name on his lips slammed against her like a fist knocking the breath out of her. She stumbled backwards again and would have fallen had he not steadied her once more. She gave him one last frantic push and ran back to where Lady Marianne stood.

'I have to go,' she said. 'I am not feeling well.'

Lady Marianne's face darkened. 'You cannot go, Rosalind, it is bad form. You must stay and fulfil your dance promises.'

'I don't give a feck if it's bad form,' said Rosie, directing all her frustration at Lady Marianne,

184

'and my name is not Rosalind.'

'No, it most definitely is not!'

A voice behind her made her freeze. It was Lady Ennis. 'Turn around, young lady, and explain yourself.'

Slowly, Rosie turned to face her accuser. There stood Lady Ennis glowering at her as if she were beholding an unwelcome vermin. Beside her stood Victoria, open-mouthed, and behind her, Valentine, his head bowed.

'How dare you attempt to pass yourself off as a lady, you young trollop! The impertinence! Who on earth do you think you are?'

Victoria, recovering from the shock of seeing Rosie, placed herself between her mother and her friend. 'Stop it, Mama,' she said. 'Just leave her alone. There's no need to make a scene.'

Lady Ennis glared at her daughter. 'Step away from her, Victoria. Everyone is watching us. Do you want to jeopardize your reputation by taking a servant's side against her own mother?'

Victoria flushed in anger. She put her arm around Rosie. 'You've never understood, have you, Mama? She is not a servant, she is my friend.'

Before an outraged Lady Marianne could intervene, Lady Ennis turned her wrath upon her and Mr Kearney.

'And you,' she said, 'how dare you and this ... this *gentleman* disgrace us in this way? We shall be the laughing stock of Dublin society! Attempting to pass off a servant girl as a lady of quality? It is beyond comprehension. I would wager you have done it to disgrace me. You have always gone out of your way to embarrass me, and now this...'

By now, even though the orchestra continued to play, a large crowd had left the dance floor and gathered around them, the ladies gasping, whispering and giggling behind their fans. The room began to swim in front of Rosie's eyes. She gripped the back of the love seat to stop herself from fainting. Everything began to close in around her and she could hardly breathe. She had to get away. With effort she shook off Victoria's arm and pushed her way through the crowd, ignoring the cries behind her. She stumbled down the staircase and out through the front door of the hotel. Outside on the pavement she stood, confused. Where was she to go?

A hand on her elbow startled her and she swung around like a cornered animal ready to pounce. There stood Valentine. 'Come on, Rosie, I'll escort you home.'

'Home?' she said, pushing him away. 'Thanks to you and your family, I have no home. I can't go back to Lady Marianne's after this.'

'But you must,' he said. 'Where else have you to go?'

Rosie looked down at her beautiful gown. How could she go up to Bridie's rooming house looking like this? 'God help me,' she whispered.

Valentine signalled for a carriage just as Victoria appeared beside them.

'I'll take her, Valentine,' she said.

Valentine hesitated. He looked from his sister to Rosie.

'It's best,' persisted Victoria. 'You need to get Mama away from here as quickly as possible. It is your duty as her escort.'

He nodded and with one last glance at Rosie turned away.

'Very well.'

A carriage pulled up to the kerb. Rosie allowed Victoria to help her into it, but pushed her away as she attempted to climb in after her.

'No, Victoria,' she said. 'Leave me alone. Please.'

She flinched at the sight of Victoria's crestfallen expression. How could she explain to her that the very sight of her sharpened the pain in her heart? She was a Bell, and innocent as she might be, she still represented all the hurt Rosie had suffered at the hands of that family. She closed the carriage door and set her gaze straight ahead so that she could no longer see her old friend.

CHAPTER 14

Rosie awoke the next morning with a start. She looked down at herself and realized she had not properly undressed. Her gown, so beautiful the night before, lay in a heap on the floor and she still wore her petticoats. Memories of the previous night's events began to filter into her consciousness, but most of it was still foggy. Her conversation with Valentine was a jumble. She recalled Lady Ennis's anger as she confronted her, but she did not remember exactly what was said. How had she made her way back to Fitzwilliam Square? Oh, yes, Valentine had called a carriage for her.

She lay back down on the pillow. There was not

a sound in the house or on the street outside. She must think. The first thing she had to do was dress in her old clothes and pack the belongings she had brought with her. Everything else – all the dresses and jewellery which Lady Marianne had bought her – must be left behind. They did not belong to her. None of it had ever been hers. Once more she had been given the promise of happiness, only to have it snatched away at the last minute.

She allowed herself a few minutes of self-pity. How could Lady Marianne have been so cruel as to involve her in this charade? Had she known all along that Lady Ennis and Victoria and Valentine would be at the ball? No, that didn't make sense – Lady Marianne's triumph would have been so much greater had she actually succeeded in procuring a husband for her. Still, she wanted to direct her anger at someone. But as she lay there, Rosie knew that the true object of her anger was herself.

She drifted off to sleep until a knock on the door startled her.

'*Mademoiselle?*' It was Celine.

'Go away.'

'But, *mademoiselle*, you are wanted downstairs.'

'No. Tell them I am not well.'

'*D'accord.*'

Rosie jumped out of bed. She couldn't bear to face anyone. She would sneak down the back stairs and out through the rear garden. Hurriedly, she dressed in her old clothes and threw her few belongings into a bag. She tried not to think about going back to Bridie's hovel on Foley Court, but it was her only alternative. When she was ready she crept towards the door and unlocked it. Taking a deep breath she opened it to step out and bumped into Victoria.

'Rosie?'

Rosie tried to shove her aside. 'I have to go before anyone sees me.'

But Victoria grasped her arm. 'Please, Rosie. Please stay and talk to me. And then if you want to escape I'll help you. But please talk to me first.'

Rosie looked at Victoria's earnest face. What harm could it do now to talk to her? Nothing was going to change. She shrugged and turned back into the room, dropping her bag on the floor and sinking down on the bed. Victoria closed the door quietly behind her and locked it. She walked over to a side chair and sat down facing Rosie.

'I'm so sorry, Rosie—' she began.

'You've nothing to be sorry for,' Rosie interrupted. 'It wasn't you made a fool out of me. It was myself did that.'

'No, it was Aunt Marianne and Mama and...'

'Aye, and Valentine.'

Victoria sighed. 'Yes, it was all of us, I suppose.' She leaned forward in her chair. 'It wasn't planned, Rosie, honestly it wasn't. Mama and I had no idea you were at the ball, and even when Valentine spotted you we didn't recognize you. We just thought you must be a friend of his from his days in Dublin. A beautiful friend, I might add.'

Victoria glimpsed Rosie's gown crumpled on the floor. She reached for it and held it up in front of her. 'Oh, Rosie, this is so beautiful. It looked stunning on you. What was it doing on the floor?'

189

Rosie shrugged and said nothing. Victoria laid the dress across her knees and began smoothing it.

'As I said, none of us knew you were going to be there. It was Mama's idea that we should come to Dublin and take the house on Merrion Square. It was the first sign of life she's shown since Thomas's death and I didn't want to disappoint her. Valentine volunteered to accompany us.'

A frown passed over Victoria's face as she mentioned her brother's name. 'He seemed very eager to get away from Ennismore. I don't understand why he would leave Sofia and the baby behind in order to be our escort. In the past it was like pulling teeth to get him to come with us.'

'Are Sofia and the baby well?' Rosie forced the words from her lips, unable to hold back her curiosity.

'What? Oh yes, they seem so. Well I must say that Sofia is very subdued compared to the carefree girl she was when we first met her, but she appears content. And baby Julian is delightful. He has won over everyone in the house with his happy laughter.'

They sat in silence for a moment.

'Rosie, why did you run away from us?' said Victoria suddenly.

Rosie stiffened. 'I didn't run away. I came to see to my sister. I was worried about her. We all were.'

'But you could have warned us, Rosie. You could have told us where you were going. We were all so worried about you.'

'I doubt that.'

'But we were. At least I was, and so was Valentine. And the staff was always asking if we had news of you.'

'Aye, probably Sadie Canavan looking for gossip.'

'I finally went to your cottage. Your poor mama was distraught. Apparently you had given her no warning either. She said you just left a brief note saying you were going to see Bridie in Dublin. But she'd had no letter from you since.'

Rosie shifted on the bed, fighting the guilt that crept over her. Poor Ma.

'Rosie, what did we do to you? If you'd explained what was wrong we could have fixed it. You didn't have to run away.'

'Nobody could fix it,' Rosie blurted out. She immediately wished she could take the words back, but pressed on, hoping Victoria hadn't heard her. 'And I told you, I didn't run away. I sensed Bridie was in trouble and I was right, she is. She's living in poverty here in Dublin with a drunken husband and a sick child. I'd been trying to find work so I could help her, but there was no work to be had. And when your aunt offered me the chance to find a husband I grasped at it. There seemed no other choice.'

Victoria reached over and patted Rosie's arm. 'That's terrible, Rosie. Poor Bridie. Could you not have arranged to bring her and the child back home with you?'

'No, the shame would be too much for her, God help her. Besides, that drunken lout she's married to would find her and drag her back. And even if he didn't, I don't think she would leave him. He's her child's father, after all, and

191

she believes she's made her bed and must lie in it. Poor Bridie.'

Victoria leaned back on her chair. 'Valentine and I were both hoping we would run into you in Dublin. He told me he had found out from your mother where Bridie lived.'

Rosie was appalled. 'For God's sake, he didn't go there, did he?'

'Not yet, we only arrived a few days ago. But I know he intended to. And then there you were, at the ball at the Metropole Hotel. I'm sure he was delighted to see you. You two used to be such great friends.' Victoria paused. 'He's downstairs,' she went on. 'Won't you see him?'

Rosie shook her head vigorously. 'No.'

They lapsed into silence again. Voices drifted up from downstairs. Rosie stood up.

'I have to be going.'

Victoria rose and grasped Rosie by both arms. 'Please, please, Rosie, come back with me to Ennismore. There's nothing for you here, you said yourself you can't help your sister and there is no work. Where else is there for you to go? Come back home where we care about you.'

Rosie fought back tears as she looked into her friend's solemn face. The word 'home' had moved her more than she could bear. She knew Victoria meant every word she said. Dear Victoria.

'No, I can't, Victoria. I can't face them.'

Victoria grasped her harder. 'Come for my sake then. You have no idea how lonely it is for me. I have no one to talk to, no one to confide in. Sofia is preoccupied with the baby, and you yourself know there's no talking to either Mama or Aunt

Louisa. And Valentine has changed. We used to be able to laugh together, but I haven't even seen him smile in an age.'

A flash of anger hit Rosie and she pulled away from Victoria.

'Come back just to keep you company?' She let out a bitter laugh. 'Nothing changes, does it, Victoria? That's all you ever wanted me for, isn't it? And when you went off to Dublin and made your new friends you cast me aside. Now you're stuck back at Ennismore, bored and lonely, and you think you can snap your fingers and I'll come running. Well I won't do it. I'll not let you use me any more!'

Victoria bowed her head. 'You're right, Rosie. I did use you. I suppose all of us did.'

Rosie shrugged. 'None of it matters now anyway. I have to go.'

Victoria nodded. Tears clouded her blue eyes.

'I'll go down and distract them so that you can get out without being seen. Goodbye, Rosie. I wish you all the best.'

With that, Victoria left. Rosie waited until she heard her enter the drawing room and then, quietly as she could, crept down the back stairs and out through the gate in the wall of the tiny, rear garden. She did not look back at the house on Fitzwilliam Square.

While Rosie and Victoria were talking upstairs, Lady Ennis paced back and forth across Lady Marianne's drawing room. Neither Valentine nor Victoria had been able to dissuade her from coming to Fitzwilliam Square to confront her sister-in-law once more.

'You said all there was to say last night, Mama,' said Valentine. 'Please leave things as they are.'

'He's right, Mama,' Victoria echoed. 'You have done enough harm.'

Lady Ennis glowered at her children. How dare they both turn against her in this manner?

'That peasant girl has a hold on you both that I cannot understand. If I were foolish enough to believe in all the tomfoolery the native Irish spout I would wager that she had put a curse on you. How else could she persuade you to turn against your family and your class?'

'That is an exaggeration, Mother,' said Victoria, 'but if we have it's because of the scandalous way you have treated her.'

Lady Ennis set her face in a hard line. She refused to argue with her children any more. 'Fetch the carriage, Valentine.'

As she rode to Fitzwilliam Square, Lady Ennis savoured thoughts of the encounter ahead. So often she had wanted to express her outrage at Edward's sister for all the embarrassments, the slights and the petty, veiled criticisms the woman had tossed her way, but for the sake of harmony, and concern for Edward's temper, she had restrained herself. If she were honest, she would admit that she was less concerned with the fact that the servant girl had dared to behave above her station than the fact that Lady Marianne had orchestrated it. But in doing so, Lady Marianne had finally handed her the perfect opportunity to confront her sister-in-law with all the venom she had accumulated towards that lady over the years of her marriage.

When they arrived, Victoria excused herself to go upstairs, while Valentine slumped sulkily on a corner chair. Lady Ennis had refused to sit down and have tea when Lady Marianne offered it. She was primed for battle and did not want to lose her momentum. She did not notice that Lady Marianne's expression was as fierce as her own.

'As I said last night, Marianne, I am outraged that you should have undertaken such a ruse. You have no doubt tarnished your reputation irrevocably, and by doing so have compromised that of the Bell family also.'

'You mean tarnished *your* reputation, you insufferable snob!'

Lady Marianne's outburst took Lady Ennis aback. How dare this woman address her this way? She looked around for an ally but her son sat mute while that insufferable Mr Kearney laughed out loud. Well, she was not having it.

'I shall ignore that remark, Marianne. Nothing excuses what you have done to this family. What on earth would possess you to do such a thing other than to embarrass me? I am certain it was not out of concern for that girl's welfare. You didn't even know her.'

'No, I did not know her, but there was something appealing about her. Perhaps it was her honesty and total lack of guile that drew me to her. I saw immediately what huge potential she had, and she was so humble she did not even recognize it in herself.' Lady Marianne paused and sighed. 'But how could someone like you understand the idea of wanting to help a person less fortunate

195

than yourself? You live in a world, Thea, of which you are the very centre, and no one, not even your own children, can breach that position.'

'Do not change the subject! If it wasn't your idea to embarrass me then it must have come from this odious little man who follows you around like a pet poodle.'

Lady Ennis glared at Mr Kearney who, rather than cowering or showing anger, stood up and bowed, flourishing the brightly coloured silk hand-kerchief from his suit pocket in her direction.

She took in a deep breath. She felt her face grow hot, and sweat began to trickle down the nape of her neck. This was not going as well as she had expected. If only Edward or Louisa were here to support her. But as she thought about it she realized that neither of them would have backed her up. Weaklings, all of them. Her anger threatened to explode. It was all that peasant girl's fault. She had been a curse on the family since she had come to Ennismore.

'Where is that young trollop now?'

Valentine jumped up and stormed to the door. 'I can't listen to any more of this. I am going for a walk.'

'She is upstairs,' said Lady Marianne, sitting down next to Mr Kearney. 'I intend to go up and apologize to her as soon as you leave.'

Lady Ennis's legs grew weak and she felt all the air ebb out of her lungs. Holding on to a side table, she eased herself onto a chair. What on earth was wrong with these people? Apologize? To a servant? Had the world turned suddenly upside down?

Lady Marianne kept speaking, as if to herself. 'I

must admit, in the beginning I thought of the whole idea as a lark. What fun to be able to put one over on the stuffy society matrons of Dublin? And Rosalind – er, Rosie – was perfect. She was beautiful, well-spoken, and her manners were impeccable. Anyone meeting her would have readily assumed she was a lady.'

Lady Ennis sniffed. 'All thanks to the education and grooming she was given at Ennismore, and still she was ungrateful. She refused to become Victoria's maid when she was asked, and then ran off because the life of a servant did not appear to suit her.'

Lady Marianne ignored her. 'As I said, it would have been so easy with a girl like her, and we were well on our way before you interfered, Thea. So many young men were showing an interest.' She reached for Mr Kearney's hand. 'But what we did not stop to think about, dear Mr Kearney, was the disservice that we were doing to Rosie.'

Mr Kearney nodded. 'She would have been found out sooner or later, I suppose.'

'Yes,' said Lady Marianne, 'but I had hoped by then her suitor would have been so much in love with her that her station would not have mattered to him.' She turned to Lady Ennis. 'What I did was rash, Thea, but not because it tarnished your reputation. Or mine! I don't give a fig what the Dublin matrons think of me. No, what I have done has devastated an innocent young woman who put her trust in me. I am determined now to make it up to her in any way I can.' She stood up. 'If you will excuse me, I will go up and talk to her now.'

Just then Victoria entered the room.

'It's too late, Aunt Marianne,' she said, 'Rosie's gone.'

Lady Marianne sighed. *'Quel dommage!'*

Lady Ennis took the opportunity to make her exit. She stood and smoothed out her skirts. 'Victoria,' she said, 'your brother has rudely deserted us. Go and fetch the carriage. We are going back to Merrion Square and have Fox pack our things. From there we shall leave immediately for Ennismore. I have had enough of Dublin. Goodday, Marianne.'

CHAPTER 15

She saw him as soon as she turned the corner into Foley Court. He sat on the front steps of number six, leaning to one side away from the dishevelled women who had settled beside him. She could only imagine what vulgar remarks they were making at his expense. A few hours before she would have enjoyed seeing his discomfort, believing he deserved this and more. But now, her anger blunted, a faint wave of pity filled her. He was clearly enduring this humiliation in order to see her, the least she could do was rescue him. Taking a deep breath, she marched up to the steps and, ignoring the taunts of Bridie's neighbours, took him by the arm and pulled him up.

'You've no business here.'

Valentine looked up at her 'I came to see you, Rosie. I was prepared to wait all day.'

'Be glad your wait's over then. Come on out of this before these ones eat you alive,' she said, ignoring the women's lewd gestures. 'We'll go and have a cup of tea.'

Valentine reached for her bag and allowed her to lead him away from number six towards Sackville Street. They must have looked an odd pair, Rosie thought, as they walked arm in arm – he an obvious gentleman, she, at best, a lowly clerk or shop girl. It wasn't just their clothes that gave them away – his well-cut grey suit with crisp white shirt and silk cravat, her well-worn, un-fashionable wool skirt and tweed jacket – but rather their bearing. Valentine carried himself in the confident, upright manner of the gentry, while Rosie's head was bowed in the way of poor country-folk self-conscious in the company of their betters. Some of her old anger shot through her at the thought. She raised her head and stuck out her chin in stubborn, silent confrontation directed at everyone who looked at her.

They reached the café where Rosie had spent so many mornings in the past perusing the news-papers in desperate hope of work. She was glad to get away from the clamour of traffic and the humidity of the July afternoon, but inside there was no refuge to be had. The heat from steaming kettles and hot ovens was worse than outside. Her skin turned clammy with sweat and she longed to remove her jacket, but to do so would be bad form. Enviously, she eyed other young women fanning themselves, sleeves of blouses rolled up and buttons undone at their throats. Valentine ordered tea from a thin-lipped waitress

199

who eyed Rosie with suspicion.

They sat staring at each other, their silence punctuated only by the clang of the bell as the café door opened and closed. Rosie found herself flushing beneath his scrutiny. She tried to summon her anger towards him – anger that was so easy to conjure when he had not been sitting in front of her, his blue eyes fixed on her face. She must not let her guard down, she thought. God help her she must not let herself be hurt again. She could not bear it. She gathered her strength.

'What do you want, Valentine? Surely there's no more to be said between us.'

He reached for her hand but she pulled it away. 'I want your forgiveness.'

'You have nothing to be forgiven for,' she said. 'You told me not to wait for you. You were very clear about that.' The waitress set a cup of tea gently in front of Valentine, then slammed a second cup in front of Rosie so that the liquid splashed out into the saucer. Rosie ignored the slight and went on speaking. 'I was the one who didn't believe you. I was the one who held out hope you might come back to me.'

She realized she revealed more than she meant to. But what did it matter now? Her hand shook as she picked up her tea cup, sending more liquid spilling into the saucer, but Valentine did not move.

'I really did love you, Rosie. I still do.'

She wanted to tell him that she loved him too, that she would never love anyone else, but she could not force those words out of her mouth. She had been humiliated enough. Her old friend, anger, came to her rescue. She pushed the teacup away and stood up.

'Stop it!' she said, ignoring the customers who had turned to stare. 'What is it you want, Valentine? To have a mistress as well as your wife just like the rest of your kind? Well I won't do it. If you love me as you say, you would never ask me to stoop to that.'

Valentine leaned forward his hands out as if pleading. 'No, you have it wrong, Roisin Dove. I am only telling you what my heart feels, and God help me I can't change that.'

'What about your wife? What about Sofia? Do you love her?'

Valentine bowed his head. 'She is my wife.' He looked up again at Rosie. 'But it's not the same.' He took a deep breath. 'I married Sofia because it was my duty, not because I was in love with her – or she with me. You have rebuked me in the past about my sense of duty, and it may not mean much to you, but it means everything in my world.'

Rosie sat down abruptly. Anger and confusion warred within her. She opened her mouth to protest, but he kept on speaking.

'No, hear me out, Rosie. Sofia had conceived Thomas's child. When he drowned she was utterly distraught. Don't you see, I couldn't have left her alone in that circumstance? I owed it to Thomas to take care of her – and his child.'

'And save your family's reputation!' Rosie spat the words at him.

Valentine nodded. 'Yes, that too, I suppose.'

Rosie pushed her chair back and stood up, exasperated. Duty, she thought, always fecking duty! 'Well you made your choice and that's an end to it.' She tried to speak firmly although her voice quavered. 'Whatever your reasons, I don't want to know.' She went on as if speaking to herself. 'If it wasn't her, it would have been another one of the gentry. You made up your mind to fulfil your duty to marry a wealthy woman once Thomas died. I've learned a lot since I've been in Dublin, and I understand things better than I did back at Ennismore. You would never have married me, just as none of the men from the Metropole Ball would have married me once they found out who I really was.'

The effort of facing the truth exhausted her and she sat back down. She put her hand on his arm. 'I accept that you believe you love me, Valentine,' she said gently, 'but whatever those feelings are, they are no good to me.'

He looked at her, his eyes glazed with tears. 'I'm sorry.'

She swallowed the pity for him that rose in her heart. What she needed now was pity for herself. 'I don't hate you. I could never do that. But if you truly love me, you have to let me go.'

She stood up and he began to rise from his chair. She put her hand on his shoulder and eased him back down, then bent and picked up her bag.

'Don't follow me.'

He nodded. 'One day I will put it right–'

Before he could finish she put her finger on his lips. 'Goodbye, Valentine. Keep well.'

She turned and walked towards the door. While everyone's eyes in the café watched her go, the only eyes she could feel on her belonged to him. She squared her shoulders, pulled open the door and resolutely stepped out onto the street.

As Rosie walked, she tried to brush aside the thought that Bridie might not even want her back. After all, a year had slipped by since she had set foot in Foley Court. Because of the restrictions on her movements, she had not been able to keep her promise to Bridie to visit. Desperate, she arranged with Celine to get several notes delivered, but had received no reply. She feared her sister had lost faith in her. She imagined Bridie sitting with baby Kate in that wretched little room on Foley Court, cursing herself for ever having believed in Rosie's promises.

Bridie opened the door and eyed her up and down. 'So ye got fed up living with the gentry, did ye? Did they throw you out or were you just lonely for the luxuries we have here at Foley Court?'

Rosie ignored her sister's sarcasm. How could she blame her? After all the promises she had made, she had let her down. She had no money to give her. Instead she was throwing herself on her sister's charity.

'I heard you had a fancy man sitting here waiting for you,' said Bridie, her face red with indignation. 'Doesn't look like he rescued you though. I suppose once he saw the class of people you *really* come from he ran back to his own people.'

Rosie's heart wrenched at Bridie's words, but she did not argue with her. After all, when she thought about it, her sister spoke the truth.

Micko's reception was bitter. 'Will ye look at

what the cat's dragged in? Miss high and mighty. Oh, I've friends in high places, Bridie, says she. Sure they'll be setting me up in no time and I'll have bags of gold to bring ye, says she.' He spat at Rosie's feet. 'Get to fuck away out of this and don't be coming back annoying us.'

Rosie picked up her bag. Micko was right. She must leave. She had no idea where she would go, but knew she was no longer wanted here. As she turned away from the door, Bridie called out after her.

'You can stay for now, until you get a place. I wouldn't want to see you on the streets.'

Micko spat again. "'Tis where she belongs.'

Ignoring his remarks, Rosie stepped into the squalid little room and set her bag down on the floor. She stifled the nausea that rose in her throat as she looked around her. The fetid smell of poverty filled her nostrils and the sight of little Kate lying listlessly on a soiled pallet on the floor made her want to cry out in protest. Had it been this wretched before, she wondered, or had her year of living in the clean comfort of Lady Marianne's home erased her memory of this raw reality? She struggled with the horror she felt, trying not to let it show. How on earth was she going to endure it?

She walked over to where little Kate lay on the floor and bent and picked her up. She sighed. The child was skin and bone. She seemed to have shrivelled since she last held her. Absently, she cradled her to her chest, crooning a lullaby that Ma used to sing. Tears rolled down her cheeks.

In the days that followed, Rosie took up her old

routine of leaving Foley Court early, spending the day looking for work, only to come trudging back empty-handed and weary each night. She was prepared to take any kind of work now, even domestic service, but there were no vacancies listed even for those positions. People seeking work were becoming anxious, even desperate.

A curious tension permeated Dublin. There was talk of labour unrest, and the likelihood of strikes. The newspapers were full of it. James Larkin, the leader of the Irish Transport and General Workers' Union, was in Dublin organizing unskilled workers. Many employers believed Larkin was trying to bring about a social revolution through unionizing workers and calling general strikes for better wages and conditions. As a result, many of them ordered their workers not to join the union and dismissed those who already had.

The powder keg finally erupted in late August, 1913. In protest of the ban on unions, tram drivers and conductors stopped their vehicles in the middle of Sackville Street and walked off the job. They were followed by thousands of workers, both men and women, across Dublin who went on strike, Micko among them.

'But we have little enough to eat as it is,' sobbed Bridie. 'How will we survive without your wages?'

'I'll not break the picket line. I'll stand up with my comrades, the men of Ireland,' Micko said. 'I'll starve before I'll be a scab.'

'And let your wife and child starve along with you?'

Micko did not answer her.

Bridie peered up at Rosie. 'Ah, Rosie, what will

we do?'

Rosie had no answer for her, either. She thought of the similar conversations that must be taking place in every slum in the city. The workers had little enough to live on and now they were being forced into a choice between feeding their families and a chance that by striking they could in some way improve their lot. They also risked losing what little they had, and for once she felt sympathy for Micko.

She also had her own conscience to wrestle with. She could probably secure a job if she were willing to cross the picket lines. Strikebreakers were being attacked by striking workers but that was not what made her hesitate. What stopped her was an unfamiliar feeling of anger that rose in her and took hold. For the first time she saw clearly how the poor, like herself, were being treated in Ireland, and she did not like it.

At the height of what came to be called 'The Lockout', over twenty thousand men and women were on strike. Riots broke out. People were killed and injured. The already dire poverty turned deadly. The small stipend that the strikers received from their unions was woefully inadequate. People, desperate for food, clogged the Dublin docks fighting for food parcels being sent by union organizers in the United Kingdom.

In the end, Rosie realized that food was more important than principle. One morning she made her way down to Boland's bakery where Micko had worked, and walked through the gauntlet of protesters, ignoring their taunts and curses, and presented herself for employment.

She was careful to arrive early in the morning before Micko made his way to the picket line so that he would not see her. She found a job on the night shift.

While tensions had erupted into open turmoil in Dublin, back at Ennismore they remained subdued beneath a veneer of polite gentility. A casual visitor to the house would have detected nothing amiss – amiable hosts, efficient servants, enviable adherence to order and convention. But for those living under its roof the sour odour of lurking misfortune was palpable.

The odour wrapped itself around Victoria like a heavy, damp blanket. Ever since she returned from Dublin she had been uneasy. The earlier feeling of not belonging in her own skin that had begun before Rosie left returned with a vengeance. The memory of Rosie's anguished face when Lady Ennis had confronted her at the ball came back to haunt her again and again. How could Mama have been so cruel? How could Aunt Marianne have not seen that her well-intentioned thoughtlessness would destroy Rosie? For the first time in her life, Victoria felt ashamed of her family, and her class. She knew now that for her the ritual of the Season was over. She could never go back to the grand balls, teas and excursions on the continent without thinking of the underlying cruelty that accompanied them.

Lady Ennis, still seething with outrage over the actions of Rosie and Lady Marianne, launched forth once again into a tirade.

'I wouldn't have believed it if I hadn't seen it

with my own eyes!' she declared again, never tiring of making the same point.

The Bell family sat around the dinner table on a late August evening but despite the warmth outside, a distinct chill hung over the diners that had nothing to do with the civil unrest in Dublin. While Victoria picked at her food her Aunt Louisa bristled with indignation at the veiled slights tossed in her direction by her sister. Valentine glared at his mother but said nothing.

'It all goes back to your decision to let that girl study with Victoria,' Lady Ennis continued, glaring at her husband, 'and Louisa failed to remind her of her place. I'm sure Louisa thought she was doing the right thing, but...'

Lady Ennis let the question hang in the air.

Lord Ennis did not answer. Instead he focused all of his attention on the fish course that was set before him, pausing only between mouthfuls to drain his wine glass and signal for more. His new daughter-in-law, Sofia, toyed with her consommé, having waved away the main course.

'Is that all you're eating, Sofia?' asked Valentine. 'You need more than that to recover your strength after the baby.'

Sofia gave her husband a baleful look. 'I have little appetite, Valentine. Please don't fuss.'

Valentine sighed and turned to stare glumly out the window.

'This fish is spoiled, Burke,' said Lady Ennis. 'The smell is overpowering!'

The butler rushed to her side and stared down at the fish, sniffing conspicuously. 'My apologies, my lady, but I am assured it was caught fresh this morning. Perhaps there are spices in the white sauce that are not to your liking. However, I will bring you some more straight away.'

Lady Ennis waved her hand impatiently. 'No, no. Just bring the dessert.'

'There's nothing wrong with the fish, Thea,' said Lord Ennis. 'You are just looking for something to complain about, now that you have finished berating me.'

Lady Ennis stiffened. 'Why should I not berate you, Edward? After all, it was *your* sister who caused this scandal.'

Victoria could not contain herself. 'I do think you're making too much out of this, Mama. I for one feel sorry for Rosie. She didn't deserve what Aunt Marianne did to her, and you made things worse by causing a scene.'

'I agree with Victoria, Mama,' said Valentine. 'You brought more attention to the situation than was necessary. Why could you not have let the evening finish and then confront Aunt Marianne? Instead you shamed poor Rosie in front of everyone at the ball. No wonder she ran away.'

'Good riddance,' muttered Lady Louisa.

'And your sister has not finished humiliating us yet, Edward,' went on Lady Ennis. 'She says she feels guilt over what happened and has vowed to help the girl. Can you imagine feeling guilty towards a servant? It is beyond understanding.'

'Rosie looked every inch a lady, you must admit, Mama. Aunt Marianne's plan may well have worked if you hadn't interfered,' said Victoria.

Lady Ennis sniffed. 'It would have worked only until her suitor discovered she was a peasant. No decent man would have married her.'

Valentine flushed and bowed his head.

As silence fell on the company, small sounds were magnified – the scraping of silverware against china, the whoosh of Lady Louisa's fan, the rattle of the dumb waiter as it descended into the kitchen, and from beyond the open windows the echo of horses' hooves as grooms rode back to the stables. A sudden breeze snuffed all the candles out, leaving a lingering smell of smouldering wax.

Sofia rose abruptly. 'If you will excuse me, I believe I hear Julian crying.'

'I didn't hear anything,' said Valentine.

Sofia gave him a long, studied look. 'I'm sure you didn't, Valentine. Your thoughts appear to be elsewhere.'

Valentine opened his mouth to reply but thought better of it.

Lord Ennis rose. 'Care to join me in the library, Valentine?'

As the men left the dining room, Lady Louisa declared that she had a headache and needed to lie down. Victoria seized her chance. The last thing she wanted was to be left alone with her mother to listen to her complaints.

'I need some fresh air, Mama,' she said. 'I think I will walk in the garden. It's such a fine evening.'

Lady Ennis shrugged and rose regally. 'I shall be in the drawing room if anyone cares to join me. Burke, bring me some tea.'

In the library, Lord Ennis poured a brandy for himself and handed one to Valentine. 'This damned business in Dublin is getting out of control. Twenty thousand workers walked off the job and now they're begging for food down on the docks. That socialist Larkin should be hanged!'

'You should see the conditions the poor live in, Papa. It's unconscionable. I went up to the area where Rosie lives with her sister. I could hardly believe the filth and squalor. The building looked as if it was ready to collapse.'

'And did you find her?'

Valentine swung around at the sound of Sofia's voice. She was staring at him with a mixture of sadness and curiosity.

'I just came in for a book,' she said dully. 'Go back to your conversation.'

Valentine spoke, as if to himself. 'Yes, I found her. We talked. I doubt that I shall see her again. And I am certain she does not wish to see me!'

When Sofia had gone, Lord Ennis looked at his son. 'Is anything amiss, Valentine? I don't wish to pry but I sense that Sofia is rather unhappy these days. I put it down at first to homesickness for New York, but I wonder if there is not more to it.'

Valentine shrugged. 'I think she is just a little tired. I expect it will pass.'

His father chuckled. 'Quite so, dear boy. I wish I could hope the same for your mama, but she seems to be rather enjoying her bad temper.'

'Will you look at all this food coming back and me after sweating the arse off meself to make them a decent supper? Bloody ingrates!' Mrs O'Leary wiped the sweat off her face with a dishcloth.

'That will be enough, Mrs O'Leary,' said Mr Burke. 'I understand your disappointment, but that is no way to speak of your superiors.'

211

'Superiors my arse,' muttered Brendan under his breath.

'Imagine now how many poor starving craturs in Dublin would welcome such a fine supper,' said Anthony Walshe, lighting his pipe. ''Twould remind you of the famine times when the landlords had tables so filled with food they almost collapsed under the weight of it and people beyond in the bogs dying for want of a crust of bread!'

'That's enough of that sort of talk,' snapped Mr Burke. 'I'm surprised at you, Mr Walshe.'

'Aye, so am I,' said Brendan. 'Aren't you the man always telling me that kind of talk belongs in the public house?'

Anthony took a long draw on his pipe. 'I did surely, Brendan. But that was before all the stories of the hardships them poor strikers in Dublin are suffering. 'Twould cause any decent Irish man to rise up against the overlords. The hell of the famine times is never far from our memories.'

Mrs O'Leary sank down on a chair. 'I wonder about our Bridie up there. I hope she has enough to eat. Her ma's astray in the head with worry over her. And now Rosie too. I say prayers for the two of them every night.'

'Well you may save your prayers for the Rosie one,' put in Sadie, who had just come in to the kitchen. 'Lady Louisa's after telling me the whole story. You'll never believe it.'

Immelda Fox shot Sadie a sour look. 'You've no business talking about it.'

Sadie smirked. 'I suppose her ladyship told you all of it as well, Immelda, since you were up there with her in Dublin. On my oath, I'd swear you're not keeping the story to yourself just to protect her ladyship. I'd say you have another reason altogether.'

Immelda reddened. 'I don't know what you're on about, Sadie Canavan.'

'Will you get on with it, Sadie?' said Mrs O'Leary. 'Don't leave us hanging.'

Sighs and gasps followed as Sadie related the story of how Lady Marianne had tried to pass Rosie off as a lady and how Lady Ennis caught them out at the grand ball at the Hotel Metropole. Thelma dropped the pot she held into a sink full of suds and stood open-mouthed.

'Ah, there was ructions altogether,' said Sadie, embellishing the story for her audience. 'Supposedly she wore a dress that cost a thousand pounds and danced with all the young toffs without a care in the world, and then boom – down comes the whole kit and caboodle – when her ladyship recognized her.' Sadie paused for breath. 'Actually, it was Master Valentine saw her first and asked her to dance, and she was bold enough to get out on the floor with him. The nerve of herself!'

Mrs O'Leary blessed herself. 'Jesus, mother and Mary.'

Mrs Murphy, who had entered just as Sadie had begun her story, gasped.

'What in God's name was she thinking? Did she not know she'd be caught out?'

Immelda scowled. 'She would have got away with it if her ladyship didn't make such a fuss. Just goes to show you *can* make a silk purse out of a sow's ear. Just because a girl's born poor doesn't

213

mean she's not as good as the rest of them.'

Mrs O'Leary smiled dreamily. 'I'd say our Rosie looked beautiful all the same. Such a lovely girl. Always was.'

Sadie glowered.

'Ah, sure you're only jealous, Sadie,' put in Brendan. 'You wish it had been yourself there at a grand ball wearing a fine dress.'

'Ah shut up, Brendan, and mind your own fecking business!'

'Was there any word of Bridie?' asked Mrs Murphy.

Sadie shrugged her shoulders. 'No. Unless Immelda here heard something.'

Immelda shook her head. 'Not a word,' she said.

CHAPTER 16

As time went on, Victoria's resentment of her family grew like a slowly rising fever. Her rebellions were small at first – arriving late for dinner, ignoring young male suitors to the point of rudeness, contradicting her mother in front of guests. In time she cut her hair into a short bob, scandalizing her mother as she knew it would, and refused to wear a corset. Valentine watched her with amusement, while Sofia smiled for the first time in months. Lord Ennis found more and more excuses to absent himself from Ennismore. Lady Louisa greeted Victoria's behaviour with a mix of glee and contempt.

'Since there will be no more Seasons for you, my dear, if this dreadful war they are predicting begins, you may well reconcile yourself to life as a spinster dependent upon your relatives for support.'

Victoria had sensed the vindictive pleasure with which her aunt uttered these words.

'I can bear witness to the fact that it is not an easy life. It will require patience and fortitude. Society is particularly harsh towards single women like us. The worst of it is the pity in their eyes.'

At first, Victoria was appalled to think that Lady Louisa was condemning her to the same category as herself, but as she thought about it she realized her aunt was right. At almost twenty-one she was perilously close to the age at which girls who had failed to make a match were written off by society. She had seen the panic often enough in the faces of the older girls at the balls, desperate for a last chance to find a husband. Now she realized that she would be at the mercy of men like the Reverend Watson who, having deemed his mourning period as a widower to have been of a suitable length, was now actively pursuing a new wife. She had done her best to avoid his overtures. She still found the man as distasteful as when she had first met him at thirteen. Moreover, his attentions towards *her*, while apparently ignoring Lady Louisa's existence, had increased her aunt's bitterness towards *her*. At those times her annoyance with her aunt had melted into pity – which on reflection, Victoria realized, proved the truth of Lady Louisa's words.

As she mused upon Lady Louisa's dire predictions, Victoria's thoughts turned back to Brendan Lynch. For the last year she had made a deliberate effort to keep him out of her daily thoughts, refusing to meet his eyes during dinner, and staying away from the servants' quarters. But at night he still invaded her dreams – a dark, sullen lover with hypnotic eyes who made love to her so passionately that she often awoke soaked in sweat. Now she found herself wondering what he would be like as a real-life lover. Each time it happened she chased the fantasies away, flooded with hot embarrassment.

While she still ignored him at dinner, she began to time her evening walks to coincide with when she thought the servants, including Brendan, would have finished their work and have a bit of leisure time before bed. She knew she was taking a risk, but the excitement of the forbidden had taken hold of her and she felt helpless against it. She hadn't thought clearly about what she would do when she actually ran into Brendan, as was inevitable.

On New Year's Eve 1913, Mr Burke invited her to join the staff for their annual celebration. 'You seemed to so enjoy it last year, my lady,' he said.

'Oh, I wouldn't dream of it, Mr Burke,' she protested. 'I do not wish to intrude on your private time.'

Even as she said the words, she yearned to see Brendan playing his violin. What could it hurt? She told herself she would leave after he performed.

'Perhaps just for a little while then. I could

accompany the musicians on the piano. I haven't played in so long and I'd love to learn some of your Irish tunes.'

The rest of the staff had no choice in the matter but to let her stay. Mr Burke nodded to all of them to carry on as usual. But there was a strain in their conversation and laughter, and while their resentment did not show on the surface, it was palpable.

Brendan nodded at her as she sat down at the piano, a faint smile playing around his lips as he took up his violin and began to play. Victoria sat transfixed, her fingers resting on the keys without playing. She watched his every move – the set of his shoulders, the arc of his elbow, the long, thin fingers, caressing the bow. She watched his face as its hard lines melted into soft contours and his dark eyes became lit from within as if by a distant flame. Even after he had finished and set down his instrument she was unable to move. He stared straight at her and she returned his gaze without blinking. Had it not been for Anthony Walshe shouting, 'Good man yourself, Brendan,' she wasn't sure how long she would have sat there. Recovering herself, cheeks aflame, she muttered an excuse and got up from the piano and left.

'Your playing must have turned the young colleen's stomach, Brendan,' joked Anthony in an effort to break the tension.

Brendan smiled back. 'Ah sure, music will do queer things to the soul, Anthony.'

Outside, Victoria stood trembling, her heart thumping in her chest and her breath unsteady. What had she been thinking? Her family would be horrified if they knew where she was. But deeper in her soul, in the rebellious region that had awoken following her visit to Dublin, she realized that a strange insanity had taken possession of her, against which she was powerless.

'Are you all right there, Lady Victoria?'

Brendan's voice cut through the darkness. Victoria swung around.

'I am,' she said.

'Will I walk you back to the house so? 'Tis powerful dark to be out on your own.'

Without waiting for an answer, Brendan took her elbow and steered her towards the house.

'I hope my music didn't offend you, miss.'

'Of course not. You play beautifully, Brendan.'

She realized with a start she had just used his name for the first time. She stole a look at him and saw under the moonlight that he was smiling.

'I wasn't sure the likes of yourself would enjoy music like mine – Irish music, that is.'

'And why wouldn't I? I'm Irish too.'

He grinned then, and pulled her closer to him. 'I always knew you were different,' he said.

Her heart jumped at his words, even as alarm bells sounded in her head. This wasn't right. She should not encourage him. And yet all she wanted was to walk with him, feel the pressure of his hand on her elbow, and the nearness of his body next to hers. She noticed that he slowed his step as they approached the house. Then he turned to face her.

'Why have you been avoiding me, Victoria?'

She immediately wanted to deny it, but the truth tumbled out instead. 'I was afraid,' she said simply. 'We're not supposed to like each other. There are rules.'

He put up his hand and caressed her cheek. 'Those rules are for the others,' he said, 'not for you and me.' He pressed closer. 'These last few months have been torture for me. I thought you no longer cared about me. Or that maybe you'd fallen in love with some fancy suitor. But tonight, tonight I saw in your eyes how you feel about me.'

Victoria let out a small whimper. What was she to say? Again, the truth won out. 'You're right. I do have feelings for you, Brendan. And I can see that you have them for me.' She drew a deep breath. 'But we can't act on them. Don't you see it would be wrong?'

Brendan drew back from her and was silent for a while. 'We can be friends, so,' he said at last. 'Sure there'd be no harm in that.'

She smiled. 'No. No harm at all.'

Later that evening, Immelda Fox slipped out of the kitchen and walked towards the stables behind the house. In her wake the sound of voices streamed from the kitchen – Mrs O'Leary giving out about one of Thelma's frequent blunders, Sadie gossiping about Lady Louisa, Mr Burke attempting to impose civil order. The moon's face now hid behind a fan of clouds as she strolled through the courtyard. The soft neighing of horses greeted her as she drew closer to the stables. She wrinkled her nose.

'How do ye bear the smell of dung?' she said to Brendan Lynch who sat smoking on an upturned barrel.

'Smells better than the gentry,' he said.

'Give us a fag.'

'Jesus, would you ever buy your own, Immelda? You get wages the same as meself.'

'Just give it to me.' Immelda's tone was rough and filled with irritation.

Brendan shrugged and passed her a cigarette and a box of matches.

Immelda lit the cigarette and took a long drag. 'I've a powerful headache after listening to herself,' she said. 'All *that* woman does is complain. If it's not about the Victoria one, then it's about the rest of them ignoring her outrage at Lady Marianne.'

Brendan grunted as Immelda took another long puff.

'Ye could almost feel sorry for himself married to the likes of her,' she said. 'No wonder he stays away as much as he does.'

'I wouldn't feel too sorry for him. Probably has a fancy woman over in London.'

Immelda gave Brendan a sharp look. 'What would you be after knowing about that?'

Brendan shrugged. 'Nothing. But it's what they all do, isn't it? People like him think they own the world and they're entitled to take anything or anybody that suits them. Why should himself be any different?'

Immelda's voice grew hard. 'God forgive me. I hate them all, so I do.'

'Fine way for a nun to be talking.'

'I was never a nun.'

'Ye might as well be, for all your bloody piety.'

'And you're no saint, Brendan Lynch. I see how you've been looking at the Victoria one.'

'Arrah, for fuck's sake, you're full of shite.'

'I'm not. I've seen the way you follow the trollop with your eyes.'

'She's not a trollop. And 'tis none of your bloody business.'

Immelda leaned against the stable wall and took a long puff on her cigarette. Her tone softened. 'I'm just trying to warn you, Brendan. You could lose your job over the likes of her and then where would you be?'

Brendan chuckled. 'Ah, so you're only concerned about me welfare, is that the way of it? Are you sure 'tis not a wee bit of jealousy on your part? After all, you have to admit I'm a fine-looking feller.'

Immelda's cheeks reddened as she bent to grind out her cigarette butt on the ground. When she looked up anger had replaced her embarrassment. 'I'd never go lowering myself for a vain eejit the likes of you.' As she turned to walk away she called back over her shoulder, 'Just remember, pride goes before a fall. Don't be saying I didn't warn you!'

After their encounter on New Year's Eve, Victoria and Brendan grew more emboldened. In the early months of 1914 they arranged meetings, sometimes at the stables, sometimes in the garden, sometimes at the estate gates, always late at night and in darkness. At times he was gentle but other times a fierce anger seemed to overcome him and he was sarcastic and impudent.

'What is it you're wanting from me, miss? Is it a new plaything you're after – a feller with rough hands and a rough brogue to excite you?'

Oddly enough, his occasional rudeness only made him more fascinating to her. She had expected at any moment he might lunge at her and press hungry lips over hers. She found herself vaguely disappointed when he did not. Instead, he seemed content to talk.

'Why are you always so angry, Brendan? Why do you resent my family so much? Rosie explained to me all about how the aristocracy drove the Irish off their lands, but that was a long time ago. And the rest of the servants don't seem to hate us as much as you do.'

Brendan had shrugged. 'They're just better at hiding their feelings.'

'I don't think that's it. I think there's something more.'

Little by little, Victoria drew the story from Brendan like an unravelling thread. At first he spoke in general terms. England's Oliver Cromwell and his men had driven the Irish off their lands. The penal codes had denied the Irish their rights to hold property, or vote, or have an education. On top of that, the landlords starved the people. County Mayo was hit the worst, he said. Nearly a million people had died there. Many of those who did not die by the roadside had died on coffin ships bound for America. After the famine years, the population of Ireland was only half of what it was before.

Brendan's voice took on a faraway tone as he talked of such tragedies. Although she could not see him in the darkness, Victoria imagined his face softening and the light in his eyes glowing as he spoke in the way that they did when he played his fiddle.

'I've heard those stories,' she said softly. 'And I believe them. Some of our society says it's all exaggerated, but I have seen their cruelty up close. I saw how they treated Rosie in Dublin.' She paused, remembering the night of the ball and Rosie's despair the next morning. 'But I still think there's something else.'

It was early April 1914, the second anniversary of the *Titanic* sinking, and the deaths of Thomas and Sean and so many others, when Brendan finally revealed the 'something else' that Victoria instinctively knew he was holding back. She had slipped out earlier than usual after dinner to meet him. They sat in the Victorian garden on the bench that had been Victoria and Rosie's favourite place to talk. At this time of year the evening light lingered. She knew she was taking a risk that someone would see them, but ignored it. She had longed to see Brendan's face clearly as they talked, and tonight she could.

'Me ma drowned herself,' he said out of the blue.

His voice was harsh as if his throat hurt and he looked past her to some invisible space beyond.

'She was only thirty years of age,' he continued, as if speaking to himself. 'She left me da, and me and four more children behind her. Me da turned to the drink and left me to rear the rest of them. I was the oldest.'

He paused, and Victoria held her breath. She had no words for him. She knew he expected none. Without thought she reached out and took his hand in hers. It was rough to the touch, and

223

the feel of its roughness moved her to tears more than his words had done. She waited.

'Her ma before her did the same thing. So maybe the madness runs in the family.'

He swallowed hard. His hand gripped hers.

'Me granny and granda were alive during the famine. They were starving like everybody else. When he found out she was pregnant he climbed over the walls of the local estate and stole a few vegetables.' He turned his face towards Victoria. Tears filled his eyes. ''Twas only a cabbage and a bunch of onions. Nothing anybody would miss. But the master himself, may he burn in hell, caught him and shot him stone dead.'

Victoria gasped.

Brendan didn't appear to hear her. He had turned away again. 'After that, Granny was never the same. She survived and so did me ma, but she was never right. She walked into the lake when Ma was only ten.' He laughed gruffly. 'Come to think of it, the same age as I was when me own ma died. They say history repeats itself.'

Victoria spoke up. 'Whereabouts was your grandfather shot?'

She prayed that it had not been on the Ennis Estates.

Brendan looked at her suddenly as if surprised to find her there. 'What? Ah, 'twas over in Killalla.'

They sat in silence. At last Victoria leaned forward and took his face in both of her hands. She kissed him softly on the lips. 'I'm so sorry, Brendan,' she whispered, 'I'm so sorry.'

Immelda Fox accosted Brendan as he came

through the kitchen door.

'You were missed at dinner,' she said. 'Mr Burke was asking where you were.'

Brendan shrugged. 'I wasn't hungry.'

He tried to push past her, but she blocked his way.

'Aye, just hungry for that Victoria one. I saw ye from her ladyship's window,' she said, 'kissing on the garden bench like two lovers.'

''Tis none of your bloody business.'

This time he pushed roughly past her and went into the kitchen. But she followed him through the kitchen and into the back hallway to the room where the footmen slept.

'What is it ye want, Immelda?'

'I want to hear you've ruined her for anyone else.'

Brendan stared at her. 'You're not right in the head, Immelda. Get away from me before I slap the face off you.'

Immelda backed away and spat on the floor where Brendan stood. 'Don't tell me the fierce Irish rebel let himself be sweet talked by a gentry girl who was just playing with him. Are you that much of an eejit? She doesn't give a shite about you. She's just amusing herself. Mark my words. The minute an eligible feller of her own class comes along she'll pretend she never even knew you.'

'That's not true,' Brendan began, 'she's different...'

But Immelda turned and strode away. Brendan let loose a string of curses in her wake.

CHAPTER 17

The following evening the Bell family, except for Valentine who was away on estate business, gathered after dinner in the library. Although the room was stifling hot, Lady Ennis had forbidden Mr Burke to open the windows.

'I will not have idle ears outside eavesdropping on our conversation,' she said.

Victoria sat upright in a leather chair beside the game table. Her hands were clammy, and a trickle of sweat ran down the back of her neck. She dared not think of what might be coming. Her first inkling of trouble was when Brendan had not been present at dinner. Sadie Canavan had helped Mr Burke serve. Victoria had caught her sly smirk as she ladled the soup into her bowl. Dinner was a glum affair. Her mother and aunt had avoided looking at her, and her father had gulped down more wine than usual. No one had spoken. Sofia had looked bemused but shrugged and concentrated on her food. When the last dish was cleared, Lord Ennis had risen, grim-faced, and asked everyone to join him in the library. Mr Burke had followed with brandy and sherry, which he served and then disappeared, unbidden.

Lord Ennis stood in front of the fireplace and looked about him. Victoria held her breath.

'I scarcely know where to begin,' he said, 'so disturbing is the news that has reached my ears.'

His wife uttered a low sigh which he ignored. Instead he set his gaze squarely on Victoria.

'A man expects his sons to disappoint him now and then. It's part of their process of growing up and asserting themselves as men. They often test the rules. God knows, your brother Valentine has done it often enough. But a man does not expect his only daughter to behave in a way so disgraceful that it dwarfs any misdeeds of his sons. You have not just disappointed me, Victoria, you have pained me deeply.'

Victoria shrank inside. Deep down she knew what he meant, yet out of a bleak hope she was wrong she asked the question anyway.

'What have I done, Papa?'

Lady Ennis, unable to control herself any further, erupted.

'You know very well what you have done, Victoria. I have tried to overlook your rebelliousness these last twelve months – your scandalous dress, your rudeness to me and our guests, your sullenness. I put it down to your unhappiness about not yet securing a husband and your loneliness for company your own age.' She paused and sighed dramatically. 'I tried to put myself in your position and to be patient with you. But this ... this ... I can hardly bring myself to say the words.'

Victoria's frustration rose. She wanted to embarrass her mother into describing the accusation aloud. 'Tell me, Mama. Tell me what I have done.'

But Lady Louisa jumped in.

'For God's sake, Victoria, do stop playing the innocent child. You have been consorting with a footman in front of everyone. You didn't even have the decency to be discreet. You have been seen loitering around the servants' quarters and the stables stalking him like a bitch in heat, and last evening you were seen in broad daylight kissing him in the garden. Where else you have been with him and what else you have done we can hardly bear to consider.'

Anger surged through Victoria. A strong compulsion to defend herself and Brendan fuelled her and she stood up.

'How dare you accuse me of such behaviour? Brendan Lynch and I are friends, nothing more.'

Lady Ennis put her hand to her throat. 'Friends? With a footman?'

Victoria ignored her.

'Who told you these lies?'

'Your mother's maid Fox has seen you together on numerous occasions,' said Lord Ennis.

'Immelda Fox? You can't believe her. She hates me!'

'Mr Burke has confirmed it. In fact, he confronted the man in question this afternoon and he admitted it. He has been sent away.'

'You can't sack him, Papa,' cried Victoria. 'He did nothing wrong. Neither of us did anything wrong.' Tears began to roll down her cheeks. 'Can't you see how it has been here for me? I feel like a prisoner. I have no one to talk to. You are all so wrapped up in your own lives you have no time for me. I have no money of my own or I would have run away long ago.'

Lord Ennis moved closer to his daughter and his voice grew softer.

'If you were that unhappy, Victoria, you should

have come to me.'

'You're never here, Papa. You can't wait to get away from this gloomy place, and I don't blame you. I would think you'd understand.'

In contrast to her husband, Lady Ennis's tone was cold.

'Mere unhappiness and boredom do not give you licence to disgrace yourself and your family. What would society think if they heard of this behaviour?'

'That's all you care about, Mama. What will society think? Well I don't care what society thinks. Brendan is a good man. But you do not see him as a person. None of the servants are people to you. They do not count as equal – they do not count as living, breathing souls with feelings and hopes and disappointments and joy, just like the rest of humanity. You hardly acknowledge their existence at all. The only time you notice them is if they fail to serve you in some way. You are the ones whose behaviour is disgraceful, not me.'

Lady Ennis turned to her husband.

'This all started with that peasant girl, Edward. You see now what evil she sowed in this girl's head, and in our lives?'

'This isn't Rosie's fault,' said Victoria. 'Don't blame it on her. I was as caught up in this life as all the other girls my age, going to balls, travelling on the continent, having servants. It took my witnessing how you treated her in Dublin to see how cruel you are – we all are – to people like her. And I don't want to be part of that any more.'

Lady Ennis's expression hardened. She waved her hands in agitation.

'What matters now, Victoria, is saving your reputation, or what is left of it. You may not realize, but if this "dalliance" were known you would be an outcast in society.'

'Spoiled goods,' said Lady Louisa.

'When you come to your senses, and you will,' her mother continued, 'you will see that I am right. Your father and I have discussed it, and we feel the best course of action is to send you away from here for a while.'

'Good. I'll leave tonight.'

'Don't be impetuous, Victoria,' said Lord Ennis. 'We have thought about this and what is best for you. Many young ladies of quality are now entering the profession of nursing, so I'm told. They are doing this as part of preparation for the war which appears inevitable. They are training to nurse soldiers when they come home from the front. Therefore, such pursuits are looked upon as appropriate while the war persists.'

Victoria waited. A faint hope rose in her heart.

'I have a good friend in Dublin, Dr Cullen, who is a fine physician. He runs a small but elite clinic. I spoke with him by telephone today and he has agreed to take you on and give you training. My sister, Lady Marianne, has agreed to let you stay with her.'

Lady Ennis began to protest but her husband put up his hand.

'It has been settled, Thea. It will attract less attention if Victoria is staying with her aunt. You know how these society matrons can be if they sniff a scandal. This matter must be kept within the family.' He turned to Victoria. 'You will travel to Dublin with me next Sunday. I shall see you safely settled with Lady Marianne and Dr Cullen before I leave for London and Parliament.'

Victoria nodded. 'Very well. May I be excused now?'

'Well, that's the young miss gone as well. Ennismore will be a lonely place with just themselves left. If it wasn't for the gossoon, Julian, there'd be no life here at all!'

Mrs O'Leary sat down on a kitchen chair. An unexpectedly violent late spring storm had made her legs swell and thrown her into a foul mood. She chastised young Thelma so often that the maid had threatened to leave and join the convent. The rest of the servants were glum as well. Sadie was particularly upset.

'Now that Brendan's gone, I don't suppose they'll be taking on a new footman. After all, his lordship was too tightfisted to replace poor Sean after he drowned, God rest his soul. Now, it looks like I'll have to do two footmen's jobs as well as my own, and not a penny extra will I get for it.'

Mr Burke appeared behind her.

'You should be honoured to do your bit for King and country, Miss Canavan. As you are well aware, there will be no suitable young men to be found when the war comes. All of the great houses will have to make do with fewer staff.'

Sadie glowered at Mr Burke, while Mrs O'Leary laughed aloud. 'Do ye hear that now? We've been slaving in a great house all these years and none of us knew it.'

Mr Burke pulled himself up straight and

frowned. 'Ennismore may not be as grand as West-port House and the like, Mrs O'Leary, but the Bell Family are as fine as any aristocrats in Great Britain.'

'You're forgetting we're in Ireland, not Great Britain,' put in Anthony Walshe, who had just come in to the kitchen.

Suddenly, Mr Burke pounded his fist on the table. His face turned crimson and his eyes blazed like a man finally pushed beyond his limits.

'I will not have this constant defiance from all of you,' he shouted. 'God knows you were always inclined to unruliness. I have managed to maintain order only by wielding a strong hand. But lately ... lately your attitudes border on insubordination. I will have no rebellion in this house!'

The staff stared at him in shocked silence. Not even Anthony could manage his usual witty response. They watched as the air seemed to seep out of the butler, as if the effort at control had been too much for him. Mrs Murphy, who was watching from the doorway, went over and took his arm.

'Come on now, Mr Burke,' she said. 'I have household matters that need your attention.'

With that, she led him away towards his study.

Sadie let out a sigh. 'Would ye believe the likes of that if ye hadn't seen it with your own eyes?'

Anthony sat down near the stove and lit his pipe. 'Ah, sure isn't everybody out of sorts over this bloody war. We're all anxious over what's going to happen to us – even the gentry. His lordship and her ladyship have lost one son to drowning and may stand to lose another one to the war. And the rumours of an uprising here at home are all around us.'

Immelda, who had remained silent and expressionless up until now, suddenly spoke up.

'Well, I for one have no pity for the gentry. Look at what they're after doing to poor Brendan, turning him out without a penny on account of the lies that young one told about him. I tried to warn him, but he wouldn't listen.'

'Ah, you're wrong there Immelda,' said Sadie. 'I'd say there was fault on both sides. Brendan had no business taking up with her, and she had no business allowing it.'

'Aye,' said Immelda, 'but who's the one who got the punishment? Brendan, not herself. She'll be away now to live a fancy life in Dublin, and he'll be out on the road like a beggar. He'll never get another job in service.'

Anthony tamped down the tobacco in his pipe. 'Sure he was never a great man for service anyway. He hated the gentry.'

'Except for Miss Victoria,' put in Sadie.

'Aye, well, be that as it may,' continued Anthony, 'I'd say Brendan is well on his way to joining up with the Irish Volunteers. Revolution was all he ever talked about. And now he has even more reason to want it.'

Mrs O'Leary shook her head. 'I admit I had no love lost for Brendan, but I have to agree with Immelda. "Twas him got the short end of the stick this time. The same thing could happen to any of us. Themselves will always stick together when trouble comes – we're the ones they'll take it out on. We should never forget our place.'

Silence fell upon the kitchen as the servants became lost in their own thoughts. The rest of the house was often silent but the kitchen and servants' hall always pulsed with life. Now, on this late spring evening of 1914, it seemed that the very heart of Ennismore had stopped beating.

CHAPTER 18

The Dublin strikes ended and Micko returned to his job at Boland's Bakery. Rosie was sacked. She had never disclosed to Micko where she was working for fear of his wrath. Because she worked nights he assumed she had taken his advice and become a prostitute on Sackville Street. She let him think it, enduring his lewd remarks for the sake of peace. While she had grown thin because she ate little so there would be more food for Birdie and Kate, her bearing of gentrification had become so much a part of her she could not shed it. The other workers took her for an outsider and looked on her with suspicion. She did her best to ignore their taunts. It was worth putting up with them for Bridie's sake. For all this, the months of work had been good for her, giving her a sense of purpose.

Dublin was filled with talk of war. Many young men looked forward to signing up with the British Army, and not all for patriotic reasons. A stint in the army offered steady pay and the possibility of adventure in foreign lands. Micko dismissed the idea.

'I'll not sign up to take the King's shilling,' he declared, 'and I curse them that does.'

Rosie wondered if Valentine would sign up when the time came. He had always talked about the obligation of duty. But he had a wife and son now, and he was the only surviving son of the Bells. She dismissed the thought. Anyway, she had herself to worry about since she was out of work again. She tried to imagine her options, but realized she had none. She had ignored invitations from Lady Marianne to come and see her. The lady had said she wanted to help her, but after the last humiliation, how could Rosie ever trust her?

One late April evening, after a long day of searching for work, Rosie dragged herself back to Foley Court and wearily climbed the stairs. She opened the door and froze where she stood. There, in the middle of the room, stood Victoria and Lady Marianne's maid, Celine. She saw that the shock on Victoria's face equalled her own. Whether it was from exhaustion, embarrassment or Victoria's striking likeness to Valentine, Rosie didn't know, but a hot anger blazed through her at the sight of her old friend.

'What is it you want?' she said

Rosie was aware of her shabby dress, thin, drawn face and aura of desperation, but in spite of all of it she thrust her chin out stubbornly and stared at Victoria.

'I asked what you want,' she said again.

Victoria fidgeted with her reticule. 'I came to see you, Rosie,' she said, and then, looking around the room, 'Is there somewhere we can go?'

Rosie's stubbornness grew. 'Whatever you want to say you can say it here in front of Bridie.'

Bridie had picked up Kate and moved to a corner of the room. Micko was not at home, for which Rosie was grateful. She took a shiver of pleasure at Victoria's obvious discomfort. Celine was expressionless, but then Celine had been to Foley Court before. Victoria looked around for somewhere to sit and Bridie hurriedly wiped off the only chair. Victoria sat down gingerly. Rosie closed the door behind her and leaned against it.

'If you've come with more word from your aunt that she wants to help me, you've wasted your time. I already told her no.'

Victoria's face paled. 'I-I came to tell you good news, Rosie. I have come to Dublin for good. I shall be taking up nursing.' She paused and looked down at her knees. 'I was hoping you'd be pleased to see me.'

Some of Rosie's anger diminished as she looked at Victoria's earnest face.

'Why have you come to Dublin?' she asked. 'Was it of your own accord?'

A faint flush spread across Victoria's face and throat. 'Not exactly,' she said. 'But I was glad of the excuse.' She hesitated for a moment then drew a deep breath. 'Do you remember Brendan Lynch?'

'The footman? Yes.'

'Well, he and I became friends. And Papa and Mama found out about it and they insisted on my being sent away. They arranged that I should come to Dublin.'

Rosie sensed there was more. 'What do you

mean by "friends"?'

Victoria flushed again. 'It was more than that. I grew very fond of him. And he of me. And then that troublemaker Immelda Fox saw us kissing in the garden and...'

'What happened to Brendan?'

'They sacked him,' Victoria said in a whisper.

There was silence for a moment and then Rosie's wrath burst like a thunderclap over the room. 'For the love of God what is wrong with you and your kind? Do you not see that the likes of Brendan and myself are real people – not your playthings to toss aside when you have done with us? Get out now! I want nothing more to do with the Bell family. I will never trust any of you again.'

Rosie trembled as she opened the door wide.

'Please, Rosie,' Victoria said, 'please don't reject me. I have done nothing wrong. I loved him.'

'Just as Valentine loved me?'

Victoria looked around in desperation. 'Please, Rosie,' she said again, 'I need your friendship. I even risked coming to *this* place to find you.'

It was the worst thing Victoria could have said. Even Bridie sensed the danger as she reached out to restrain her sister.

'She doesn't mean anything by it, Rosie. Let her go.'

Rosie looked from her sister to Victoria and around the room, observing the scene through her old friend's eyes. Of course Victoria was disgusted by what she saw. Hadn't she herself been when she first entered Foley Court? But all Victoria's words had done was reinforce how different their two worlds were, and how the two could never be reconciled. She bit back the angry words she was about to hurl Victoria's way. What good would it do to scold her for her honesty?

She opened the door wider and put out her arm, pointing to the hallway. 'You'd better go now,' she said, 'both of you.'

Rosie had expected Victoria to slink away full of apologies, as she always did after an exchange like this. But this time she was wrong. Victoria stood up but did not move. Her face bore an expression of defiance Rosie had never seen before.

'For heaven's sake,' Victoria began, 'can you not let bygones be bygones? Stop blaming me for what my family and society has done to you. I am not my mother, or my brother, or my aunt, all of whom you rightly claim have treated you badly. I am Victoria and I am your one friend. And I am tired of apologizing to you.'

Rosie opened her mouth to protest but Victoria held up her hand. 'We are not children any more and we need to accept our lives as they are. Yes, you have suffered, but so have I in ways you can never understand. We have both been prisoners of our class. But what good is dwelling on the past? We have it within our power to change our futures. If you insist in wallowing in the wrongs that have been done to you, you will only succeed in destroying any chance our friendship may have to survive. It's your decision, Rosie.'

With that, Victoria marched out of the room, Celine behind her, leaving Rosie and Bridie to stare after her.

After Victoria and Celine left, Rosie slumped

down on the chair. Bridie watched her in silence. An hour passed and Rosie felt the room closing in on her. She began to sweat and fought back nausea that rose in her throat. She had to get out. Abruptly, without saying a word, she jumped up and ran for the door. She took the filthy stairs two at a time and, ignoring the shouts of the women on the front steps, ran up Foley Court and around the corner. She ran until she reached Sackville Street and, without any thought of where she was going, kept on until she came to the River Liffey.

It was only when she reached the O'Connell Bridge that she let herself relax. She bent over, struggling to regain her breath which came in jagged waves. She reached for a nearby bench and sank down on it. She felt her essence – the Rosie she had been – ebb out of her, her emotions flattened like bread dough pounded under her mother's hand – all the air gone out of them.

Passers-by glared at her as if she were one of the shawlie women who lined the bridge, begging. She sat motionless, head down, unaware of time passing, lost in images of her past – the classroom at Ennismore, waving farewell to Victoria as she rode off to Dublin for the first time, Valentine's last kiss on New Year's Eve. Then more recent memories surfaced – her disgrace at the Metropole Ball, her last meeting with Valentine and today's confrontation with Victoria. She sighed. Her final connection with the Bells was broken. She no longer hung suspended between two worlds. It was as if all those memories were now erased and she had landed squarely back in the world she had left when she was eight years old.

The smell of cheap perfume began to choke her and she lifted her head. Two women leaned over her, their painted faces so close she could smell their putrid breaths. One grabbed her arm, fingernails piercing her sleeve and digging into her flesh.

'G'wan outta that,' she hissed, 'ye fuckin' hooer. Who said you could sit there?'

Rosie looked at the woman and then at her companion who stood, hands on her hips, glowering down at her. She realized at once that they were Dublin prostitutes and that she sat on the bench they had claimed for themselves. She knew from her many walks through the city that prostitutes marked out their territories and fiercely defended them from newcomers. In the past she might have refused to move, but tonight she was weary. She began to stand up but not before the two women set upon her and began pummelling her, their curses heating up the cold air.

'Ah, now, now, ladies. Is that any way to behave?'

A deep, resonant male voice penetrated the air and the women stopped their beating and turned around. Rosie blinked to make out the man who had spoken. He was tall and broad-shouldered with an angular face and longish brown hair. He wore a long, dark overcoat, which swung open as he strode towards them. She judged him to be in his early forties.

'Sure there's plenty of room for all of ye in Dublin. No need to be beating the bejasus out of one another. Off ye go now.'

The two women glared at him and then at Rosie

before walking away arm in arm. Rosie made to move as well, but the man caught her arm.

'What's your hurry, darlin'? Sure the night's still young so.'

Rosie recognized his County Mayo accent immediately.

He pulled her down beside him on the bench. 'Sit down, love. Sure I'd enjoy your company. 'Tis lonely here sometimes even though the streets are choked with people.'

Rosie stood up. 'I am no harlot, if that's what you're after thinking,' she began, gathering energy from her outrage at his insinuation. 'You'll find plenty of the kind you're looking for beyond on Sackville Street. Just follow the two of them you're after chasing away.'

The man let out a loud guffaw, throwing his big head back. 'Ah, 'tis a Mayo woman that's in it if I'm not mistaken. And a fine one at that.'

Rosie was a little taken aback that he had recognized her accent so readily. She shrugged. So much for all of Lady Marianne's and Lady Louisa's efforts to stamp out her country brogue.

He stood up and bowed. 'Cathal O'Malley at your service, miss. Lately come from the fine Mayo town of Westport on the shores of the Atlantic Ocean. Would ye not sit and talk a while with a pilgrim like yourself?'

Rosie studied him. He was handsome for a man of his age, and something about his deep, soft brogue and his demeanour charmed her. Suddenly self-conscious, she smoothed out her dress and pushed her stray curls up under her hat. She might not be a beauty, she thought, but at least

241

she looked respectable. If Rosie could have seen herself through others' eyes, however, she would never have questioned her beauty.

She sat down on the bench again and extended her hand to him. 'Roisin Killeen from the village of Ennis in County Mayo,' she said.

He shook her hand and sat down beside her. 'Pleased to make your acquaintance, Roisin Dubh.'

Rosie started. 'My da used to call me that,' she said, without thinking.

He leaned back on the bench, strong legs stretched out and crossed at the ankles, his feet shod in leather boots. His hands lay in his lap. Rosie noticed that they were elegant and well-manicured, at odds with his sturdy appearance.

'Ennis?' he said. 'I know the place well. Fine big house there named Ennismore. I'd say you know it.'

'I do,' said Rosie, flinching slightly at the name.

'And what brings you to Dublin?'

Rosie hesitated. 'My sister's been ill. I came to help her.'

'Has she seen a doctor?'

'The public hospital only.'

'Ah, the Union. I know it well.'

He lapsed into silence for a moment. Rosie could not contain her curiosity.

'And yourself?'

He seemed to return from a faraway thought. 'Me? Ah, 'tis a long story. Too long to be told while sitting here on a cold bench.'

He turned to stare at her, a smile playing about his lips. For a moment she felt herself unable to turn away from him. Then alarms sounded in her head and her curt manner returned.

'I have already told you, Mr O'Malley, I am not the type of woman who keeps company with men at night.'

He threw his head back and laughed again. 'Aye, you made that very clear, Roisin Dubh. And I had no intention of inviting you to spend a sinful evening with me. I'd never think of corrupting a lovely, pure Mayo girl like yourself.'

Rosie stood. 'I'm glad to hear it. Goodnight, Mr O'Malley.'

He stood up and bowed, still grinning. He took her hand. Again, Rosie was struck by the smoothness of his hands.

'Goodnight, Rosie Killeen,' he said. 'Perhaps our paths will cross again.'

'I doubt it,' she said.

On the way back to Foley Court, Rosie thought about the encounter. Something about Cathal O'Malley had piqued her interest. She was sure he had mistaken her for a prostitute, but when she had protested he had been gracious, even though he poked a little fun at her. Perhaps it was his connection with Mayo that had drawn her to him. She had not realized how lonely she was for some connection with home.

A sense of purpose began to infuse her as she walked. She was glad she had set him straight. No matter how low she fell, she knew she would never stoop to that. She would never allow herself to be used again. A new resolve flooded through her. Victoria was right – she had a chance now to forge her own future. From now on she would no longer be a victim. She would no longer allow the gentry to hand her gifts only to snatch them away again. She would take charge of her own life. No matter what it took she would never again subject herself to the humiliations she had experienced at the hands of the gentry. The young starry-eyed country girl with unrealistic dreams was gone.

PART FOUR

REBELLION

1914–1916

CHAPTER 19

Victoria bid goodbye to her father outside 6 Fitzwilliam Square.

'Thank you, Papa, for all you have done.'

Lord Ennis smiled at his only daughter. 'You will thank me by doing your best, Victoria, and applying yourself to your training with Dr Cullen. It is most generous of him to take you on.'

Victoria bowed her head. 'Yes, I know, Papa, and I promise I will work hard.'

Lord Ennis bent and kissed her on the cheek. She noticed that his eyes were moist and she reached over and hugged him tightly. He pulled away, looking somewhat embarrassed. 'There, there, Victoria. I must be off now. Don't forget to write to your mama.'

With that he called to his driver and climbed into the carriage. Victoria watched as it took off up Sackville Street, looking old-fashioned and somewhat out of place among the electric trams. Just like Papa, she thought to herself, still clinging to the old-fashioned habits of the past.

She lingered on the pavement until the carriage disappeared. Then a sudden and unexpected fear overwhelmed her. She did her best to quell it, but without the promise of Rosie's companionship she felt utterly and miserably alone. Renewing their friendship was the thing she had most looked forward to in coming to Dublin, and that hope had been dashed. She couldn't see how things could be mended now.

She allowed her thoughts to turn to her visit to Rosie in Foley Court, even though the memories of the sights and smells of the place still sickened her. Celine had warned her that Bridie lived in a Dublin slum, but she had not been prepared for the squalor and despair she found there. It was all she could do to keep her rising nausea at bay. Her earlier euphoria at her new-found courage in standing up to Rosie had begun to ebb. She understood that Rosie's antagonism towards her stemmed from embarrassment, but still her old friend's words had stung.

For a moment she wished she was back in the safety of Ennismore where she was sheltered from the vagaries of the world. She found herself craving the very protections under which she had so recently felt stifled. She began to question her ability to survive in the real world outside that sweet prison in which she was brought up. Sighing, she entered the front door of her aunt's house and closed it tightly behind her.

That night, she dreamed of Ennismore, where she was playing in the garden with Rosie while the sun shone down on them. Valentine was nearby, laughing. Suddenly she was twirling in her bedroom, showing off her new dresses to Rosie, excited at the prospect of her first Season. But now Rosie was crying. She put her arm around her to comfort her but Rosie pushed her away and ran out. She ran after her, calling her name, but Rosie would not look back. Then she was back sitting in the garden, this time with Brendan, kissing him passionately, but in the middle of the kiss he got up and walked away from her.

She awoke before dawn, exhausted from her dreams and bleary-eyed, and for a moment she was not sure where she was. Then she remembered. She sat up in bed. She must turn her mind to the future. Today she was to begin work as a trainee nurse volunteer in Dr Cullen's clinic. She had no idea what kind of nurse she would be but was determined to try her hardest. She hoped the sight of blood and suffering would not weaken her resolve to succeed.

True to her promise to her father, she applied herself with zeal to her new duties. The nurse who trained her was firm but kind and Victoria's natural gentleness won her favour with patients. She was anxious to learn as much as she could but soon grew bored with the society matrons and their daughters whose genteel complaints of nervous conditions, digestive disorders, fatigue and the like made up most of Dr Cullen's practice.

She grew a little disappointed as she realized that while she was no longer at Ennismore she was still trapped in the same circles of society as before. The only welcome change was the freedom to come and go from Lady Marianne's without a chaperone – a matter on which she was most insistent. She must fight to regain her courage.

'I am no longer a child, Aunt Marianne. I have come to Dublin to find independence and to learn a skill that in time may help me earn my own living. I thought that was something you encouraged.'

'But I do, my dear. I am all for modern young

women becoming independent. It's just that I am responsible for you here. And you are not aware of the hidden perils of a city like Dublin. If something should happen–'

'I will take full responsibility for my own safety,' Victoria interrupted.

Aunt Marianne uttered a defeated sigh. '*D'accord,* Victoria. I see you intend to have it your own way. I will not interfere.'

CHAPTER 20

The summer passed uneventfully at Ennismore, but the underlying tension arising from distant events continued to grip it. The trouble brewing on the continent of Europe grew and, as Lord Ennis had predicted, when Germany declared war on small, neutral Belgium, Prime Minister Asquith delivered an ultimatum to Germany – stay out of Belgium or we will declare war against you. The ultimatum went unanswered and on 4 August 1914 Britain entered the war.

Valentine Bell decided to sign up.

'Out of the question,' thundered Lord Ennis. 'We have lost one heir to the Ennis Estate. We shall not lose a second!'

'Its future is safe with Julian,' said Valentine, his voice even.

Lord Ennis moved closer to his son, his face florid. 'Julian is a mere infant. Who will look after things if you don't return? I shall certainly not be up to it for the next twenty years.' He shook his head. 'I don't understand you, Valentine. I thought you had changed but I see now you are just as immature as ever.'

'I'm sorry, Papa, but I believe it is my duty.'

'Your duty is here,' shouted his father. 'Your duty is to this family and this estate. What of Sofia and Julian? Would you put them in such peril? And what of your mama? Didn't she suffer enough with Thomas?'

They were standing in the library where they had repaired as usual after dinner to discuss the affairs of the estate and other news of interest. Valentine left his father and went over to look out the window and down to Lough Conn in the distance.

'I shall not be gone for long, Papa. Everyone says the war will be over by Christmas.' He gave a wan smile. 'I fully intend to return safe and sound.'

Lord Ennis gave his son a long, penetrating look.

'Unless, of course, you think I'll fail as a soldier, just as I failed at everything else.'

'No, Valentine, of course I don't!'

'Oh, I think you do, Papa,' Valentine said aloud, then whispered 'and well you know it,' under his breath as he turned away.

Below stairs the news of war was met by argument, excitement, concern and prayers.

'There's not many will be going,' declared Anthony Walshe. 'There's few boys will be risking life and limb for an English king. *I* won't go if they ask me.'

''Tis a good job you're the age you are and they'll not be calling you,' snapped Mrs O'Leary,

251

'because I'd have no cowards around *my* kitchen.'

Anthony looked offended. 'I'm not so old I can't stand and fight against any man. But this is a different kettle of fish altogether. Why should our Irish lads fight for England? What has England ever done for them?'

'Arrah, you sound more like Brendan Lynch every day of the week. I thought we'd heard the end of that talk when he left.'

Mr Burke, who had been watching the proceedings from behind his office window, stepped out into the servants' hall.

'There has been no word of conscription for Ireland, but if it comes I would expect all able-bodied young men to do their duty.'

'Hear, hear, Mr Burke,' said Mrs Murphy.

''Twould be exciting all the same,' said a young stable hand. 'Anything to get away from the monotony of this place.'

Anthony glared at him. 'Take the King's shilling, would you? Just like Judas Iscariot!'

'Don't be blaspheming, Anthony,' said Immelda.

'I can't believe Master Valentine's going,' put in Sadie, 'and him just married and a new father. I've said it before and I'll say it again, something's not right with them two.'

'That's enough of that, Miss Canavan,' said Mr Burke.

In the end Valentine could not be dissuaded and he entered the newly formed Second Battalion of the Irish Guards as a second lieutenant. The family and servants stood on the steps of Ennismore to bid him farewell. He was resplendent in his dress uniform of scarlet jacket with two shamrock insignias on the collar. Lady Ennis presented her son with a cold cheek to kiss, while Lord Ennis gave him a formal handshake. Sofia stood expressionless, baby Julian in her arms, while Lady Louisa regarded the proceedings with a faint hint of satisfaction on her face. The assembled servants waved goodbye as the coach clattered away down the gravel path towards the estate gates.

'Well, there's another one gone then,' sighed Mrs O'Leary, holding her hand over her brow to block out the sun as she watched the coach disappear.

'He looked so handsome,' said Sadie. 'I'd be dying if he was *my* husband going off to war, but herself just stood there like a statue.'

'Ah now,' said Mrs O'Leary, 'not everybody shows their feelings in public. You've no notion what Miss Sofia is thinking, Sadie Canavan.'

'Maybe that's the way Americans are,' said Thelma.

''Twill be a terrible cold place here without himself or his sister, all the same,' said Anthony. 'If it wasn't for the gosoon, Julian,' he added, not for the first time, 'there'd be no life left in the house at all.'

CHAPTER 21

In Dublin, following the declaration of war, Rosie overheard arguments for and against it as she went about her business from day to day, but took little interest. Had she been a man she might have agreed with those who hoped to join the army – after all, a secure job at this point in her life would mean a lot more to her than loyalty to Ireland. But she kept such thoughts to herself. She was beginning to despair of ever finding permanent work. She'd had a series of low-paying, temporary jobs, but the likelihood of a well-paying, permanent position seemed as far away as ever. The prospect of having to remain living with Bridie and Micko sapped whatever energy and resolve she had left.

And so when yet another note came from Lady Marianne Bellefleur inviting her to tea, Rosie did not automatically tear it up. Instead she held it in her hand and read it over and over again, warring with herself as to what to do. She had made a vow that she would never again let herself be used by the gentry. The humiliation of her exposure at the Metropole Ball had never really left her, much as she had tried to suppress the memory. Re-entering their world would once again expose her to all the hurts and betrayals that had almost destroyed her. She remembered the night she had walked back from O'Connell Bridge to Foley Court and had resolved to take charge of her life. Well, she had done so and what good had it done her save to reinforce that most dreams were pointless when subjected to the harsh beam of reality.

But as she lay in the darkness of Foley Court that night a new resolve filled her. Why not use the gentry rather than allowing them to use her? After all, would not turnaround be fair play? As long as she kept her wits about her, why not let Lady Marianne assuage her guilt about the Metropole

Ball fiasco by helping her? And besides, she needed to find a way to help Bridie, particularly after all the promises to her sister which she had not kept. Comforted by these thoughts, she turned over and drifted into a sound sleep.

The following week, Rosie sat once again in the drawing room of Lady Marianne's house on Fitz-william Square. The first time she sat here she had thrown herself on the mercy of this lady whom she had never met. She had been desperate and vulnerable and ready to accept any help that might be offered. Now, while still somewhat desperate, she no longer felt vulnerable. The lessons of the last year were hard-learned and the Rosie who sat here now was sceptical, practical and wiser.

Her only trepidation upon entering was that Victoria might be present and she was reluctant to face her old friend after their quarrel at Foley Court. However, Lady Marianne eased her concerns immediately.

'I'm sorry that Victoria cannot be here to greet you, my dear. She has been gone since early morning tending the sick. It truly amazes me how diligent my niece has turned out to be. I don't believe she has missed a single day.'

Rosie nodded, but made no comment. She stole a glance at Celine when the maid came in to serve tea, but Celine made no eye contact with her.

'I don't know if you have heard, but Valentine has joined the army, much against his parents' wishes I am told.' She paused and looked at Rosie who kept her expression as bland as she could manage. 'He has entered the Irish Guards,' continued Lady Marianne. 'I can just imagine how handsome he looks in that splendid scarlet uniform.'

Rosie sipped her tea. She sensed Lady Marianne was waiting for a comment. 'Has he shipped out yet?' she asked.

'Not from what Victoria tells me. He is at training somewhere in England. I'm sure he will visit us before he leaves for France. I can send you a note if you like. I'm sure you would like to wish him well.'

'Of course.'

Rosie tried her best to stem the blush that was spreading over her cheeks. She knew that Lady Marianne was testing her to see if she still had feelings for Valentine, and was determined to betray nothing. She had tried not to think of him at all over the last few months and hoped she was indeed over him. But the blush just reaffirmed that he would never be truly out of her thoughts or her heart.

The buzz of the doorbell brought her relief. Lady Marianne smiled at her and stood up. 'That will be the dear Butler sisters,' she said. 'I invited them to come and visit you. They have pestered me with questions about you ever since the ... ever since last year. And I know you admired them so.'

After some bustling in the hallway, Celine ushered in Geraldine and Nora Butler. They both rushed towards Rosie at once.

'Rosie!' declared Geraldine, the elder of the two. 'How wonderful to see you at last. We have been so worried about you.'

Rosie looked from one to the other and smiled. She was pleased to see them. They had been so kind to her the night of the ball, and she had never forgotten it. She took their hands by turn. 'What a lovely surprise,' she said, 'I never expected to see you again.'

Nora removed her hat and sat down. 'Neither did we. We thought Victoria might lead us to you, but she said she has only seen you once. I was surprised at that, but I understand she is spending all of her time at the clinic.'

Geraldine chuckled. 'Yes, seeing to the digestive plumbing of our fine Dublin ladies. I visited Dr Cullen with Mama recently and saw her there.' She paused. 'She is as lovely as ever, but something about her has changed. I can't put my finger on it.'

'She has found a new passion, I think,' said Lady Marianne after tea was served to her guests. She waved her hand. 'But enough of Victoria,' she continued. 'I have invited you here to discuss an idea I have for helping Rose. Dear Mr Kearney came up with the general idea, actually, and together we have refined it into what I believe is a most appealing plan.'

Rosie felt herself grow pale. She must keep her wits about her. She must not let herself get dragged into another of Lady Marianne's 'ideas'. She took a mild satisfaction that her hostess was no longer addressing her as 'Rosalind'. Now she breathed deeply, braced her back and shoulders and, remembering her latest resolve, put on her most charming smile.

'How exciting, Lady Marianne! Please tell me what you have in mind.'

CHAPTER 22

Meanwhile, diligent as Victoria was about her job at Dr Cullen's clinic, fault lines of dissatisfaction were beginning to appear. At first they were insignificant and could be dismissed as the result of fatigue and the stress of mastering new skills. But as time went on she came to realize that they were growing, threatening to erupt into an open rebellion. She yearned for more challenging work beyond the repetitive and routine complaints of the Dublin matrons who frequented the clinic. Each morning's walk to the clinic became increasingly exhausting.

When war was declared she hoped it might offer a reprieve. Nursing injured soldiers would surely renew her sense of purpose. Returning wounded soon began to appear, not at the clinic, but at the small, private hospital where Dr Cullen's seriously ill patients were sent for treatment. Victoria pressed for a transfer from the clinic to the hospital and it was granted. She was delighted, hoping she might now be able to make a difference.

Like Dr Cullen's other patients, the returning soldiers were all from well-to-do families. Although they were officers, their privilege had not protected them from the same ravages of battle – amputated limbs, head wounds, infection, gangrene, and shell-shock – as enlisted soldiers. She did her best to make them comfortable. Often she sat with them, holding their hands and listening to their stories, or writing letters for those who were unable to do so for themselves. She thought of Valentine, and hoped some nurse would be kind to him if he were ever in need. But even as she nursed these men she thought of the thousands of other less fortunate young men who would be returning to Ireland and left to the mercy of the state to languish in miserable, overcrowded hospitals. Maybe those boys needed her more. She tried to push away the nagging thoughts.

She wished she could share her feelings with someone and, as always, Rosie came to her mind. Her earlier anger with her friend was long forgotten. She had even thought of going back to find her at Foley Court, but the memory of the place made her shiver.

'It's just that I'd like to see her,' she said one evening to Lady Marianne. 'I went to see her once at her sister's lodgings. The conditions there were shocking, and Rosie looked so defeated. I am really afraid her despair may throw her into a life of...' She could not finish her thought.

Lady Marianne smiled. 'Rose has too much backbone and spirit to ever stoop to that, Victoria. I have been amazed at her resilience.' She put her hand on Victoria's arm. 'Don't worry about her. She will make her way. I doubt that pursuing this friendship with her is in either of your best interests. She needs to find her own path. I have put a plan in place for her and she has agreed to go along with it.'

Victoria was filled with sudden alarm. 'But, Aunt, you cannot possibly interfere in Rosie's life again after what happened last year. How could you?'

Lady Marianne laughed. 'Don't worry, dear, I was merely the broker in this matter. I have left Rose and her future to the good offices of the Butler sisters.'

'To what end?'

'Ah, I will give you the details in good time. But I am optimistic Rose will find her place at last.' She turned away, indicating the subject closed, and sat down. 'Now, about you, my dear. You too must look to your future. Perhaps you will find a suitor amongst those nice military officers you are nursing.'

Victoria shrugged. 'I doubt it, Aunt.'

She could have told her aunt about the brutish behaviour some of the men had exhibited towards her, assuming she was just a working-class nurse. They were polite enough when they were sick, but once they were on the mend their true natures had come through – the major who had outright propositioned her, the captain from Wicklow who pinched her bottom every time she passed him, the two lieutenants who discussed her physical attributes even though she was within earshot. But even had they behaved like perfect gentlemen, she knew she would have had no interest in them. Brendan Lynch, even though she tried to put him out of her mind during the long days, was the one who came back to haunt her dreams every night. She did not know if she would ever see him again but while his image and memory was still so vivid she knew no other man could take his place.

CHAPTER 23

One freezing night in November 1914, Rosie climbed the dark stairs in the large home of a Dublin district justice to attend a meeting of the Gaelic League. Geraldine Butler had pestered her several times since their meeting at Lady Marianne's home to attend one, sending her notes and threatening to come to Foley Court and escort her to a meeting herself.

'Do come,' Geraldine had said. 'I know the position of secretary we have offered you does not pay much, but you will meet some fine people, and learn all about what is going on in Dublin and across Ireland. It is very exciting, Rosie. And my hope is that such introductions will lead to an even better opportunity for you, one where you can employ all your talents.'

'She's right, Rosie,' Nora had said, and proceeded to give her the background on the Gaelic League, an organization of people with nationalist leanings, while Lady Marianne had nodded her approval.

When Lady Marianne had first broached the details of her 'plan' to Rosie she had been disappointed. Despite her scepticism, deep down she had harboured hope that the lady had conjured a miracle which would lift her out of her present situation and launch her on the road to success. A low-paying position with the Gaelic

League, an organization she had never even heard of, fell far short of a miracle.

'But I don't even know how to use a typewriter,' she told Lady Marianne, flustered. Then recovering herself she went on, 'I truly appreciate all of your efforts on my behalf, but I hardly think...'

At the time, she had not even been able to finish her sentence. Doubts were already creeping in. Was she a fool to reject the offer? But as she listened to Nora's impassioned description of the merits of the Gaelic League her scepticism returned. These were rich people playing pretend revolutionaries, she thought. They know nothing of the real world of the Irish poor. They are the same people who mocked me at the Metropole Ball. I want nothing to do with them. She had thanked Lady Marianne and left.

When she returned to Foley Court that afternoon, despair, as always, overcame her. Had she let her pride prevail over common sense? And as the days went by with no more likelihood of a secure job than before, Rosie realized she had made a mistake by refusing Lady Marianne's offer and with it a new chance to help Bridie and Kate. She could hardly go back begging to her now. She was saved the embarrassment of having to do so thanks to Geraldine's persistence. She decided to attend one meeting.

Now, climbing the stairs, she was unsure of what she would find. Noises drifted down from the rooms above – melodic strains of Irish music, the hubbub of voices raised in conversation and argument, the tap of feet dancing on wooden floors. She had dressed as carefully as she could, choosing the least worn of her dresses and a wool cape, darned on the inside so no one could see the stitches. Setting her chin firmly, she entered the main room at the top of the stairs. A young, pale bespectacled man sat at a table taking attendance.

'Roisin Killeen,' she said. 'Miss Geraldine Butler invited me. Is she here?'

The young man's face lit up. 'You are very welcome,' he said.

Rosie recognized his upper class, Anglo-Irish accent, so reminiscent of the young men she had danced with at the Metropole. She clenched her fists to her sides.

'Geraldine is busy at the moment,' he went on, 'rehearsing a vignette which will be presented later. Please go on in. There is tea and refreshments, or sherry if you prefer.' He smiled up at her. 'I would suggest the sherry to warm you up. You look positively frozen.'

Rosie murmured her thanks and turned away from the table. She forced herself to move through the crowd towards the refreshments. She was not used to crowds, particularly where she knew no one. All around her people were engaged in animated conversation. Young women, about her age, appeared confident and engaged, holding their own in arguments with equally intense young men. The young men appeared to be students and reminded her of the boys she had seen milling about Trinity College. The older men, all of them well-dressed and well-spoken, were gentry, although she allowed that some of them could well be teachers, solicitors or journalists. She had met many men like these over the years at Ennismore or at Dublin soirées she had attended with Lady Marianne. But the women were nothing like the girls she had encountered in the past – girls who loved to talk only about fashion, and travel, and their chances of making a good match. Although these women appeared to be from the gentry, they were like a different species.

She picked up a small glass of sherry and sipped it. She stood back in the shadows and listened to the snatches of conversation that drifted her way. There was talk of a recent 'Buy Irish' campaign which had taken place over Christmas at the Rotunda in Dublin where only Irish manufactured goods were sold. There was talk of language classes, debating societies and upcoming concerts. One young woman handed out pamphlets promoting a Ceili – a festival of Irish dance – to take place at a nearby church hall. Rosie took one and read it with interest. Sponsored by the Gaelic League, it was to be open to everyone and admission was free.

Nora had explained that the Gaelic League was the largest of the many 'Celtic' societies formed to support a Gaelic reawakening. Such societies were dedicated to the revival of the Irish language and culture, including poetry, plays, dancing and sports. By doing so, she had said, they hoped to re-instil in the native Irish a new pride in their culture and heritage.

'It's been beaten out of them over the centuries of English rule,' Nora had said, 'and we believe it's time to restore it.'

Rosie had never heard of such a movement. At Ennismore it would have been unthinkable that the Bell family or their neighbours would have encouraged the revival of Irish culture. From her own experience, Rosie knew the rural gentry viewed the native Irish as peasants – servants to cook for them and clean their houses, labourers to look after their estates and their livestock, tenants to till their fields and grow their crops. Once more her scepticism rose – did these Gaelic Leaguers really want to champion the native Irish culture or were they just engaged in some cruel pantomime for their own amusement?

Geraldine and Lady Marianne had also mentioned that the mission of such societies as the Gaelic League was expanding to include a political element. The plethora of Irish Nation-alist newspapers, such as *The Irish Volunteer* and *Irish Freedom* which were filled with anti-English propaganda, were stirring up the populace.

'The Irish are growing impatient waiting for Home Rule to be implemented,' Geraldine had explained. 'They are beginning to organize and arm themselves. The talk of a rebellion is growing louder.'

An older woman clapped her hands and invited everyone into a large adjoining room, where a small stage had been erected, and wooden chairs set out for the audience. A curtain concealed the stage. A tall young man with broad shoulders and a rich, mellow voice faced the audience and began to recite a poem in Irish that Rosie recognized straight away. It was called 'Dark Rosaleen', or 'Roisin Dubh' in Irish, and while it appeared to be a love poem to a young girl, it was in fact a poem about Ireland and her troubles. Rosie's da had recited the same poem to her many times in childhood. She wiped away a sudden tear as she listened.

The curtain was then drawn back and four young women, Geraldine included, appeared. They were dressed in black and red cloaks, each emblazoned with a rose, and performed a simple choreography behind the poet as he read.

'They're portraying the Four Provinces of Ireland,' whispered a young man next to Rosie. 'How clever of them.'

She applauded as loudly as the rest of the audience when the players and poet took their bows. She rose to go and find Geraldine. But instead of returning to the first room she found herself being carried with the crowd towards another, smaller side room. A knot of young men of a rougher hew than those she had encountered earlier sat drinking ale and laughing. Some were wearing ordinary street clothes, while others appeared to be in a uniform of some sort. A tall man in a long overcoat stood up and called for order. He had his back to her but she thought she knew him. She manoeuvred around the crowd to get a better look. When she saw his face, she knew him immediately. Cathal O'Malley, the man she had met on O'Connell Bridge the evening she had quarrelled with Victoria, began to speak in his clear, Mayo accent. The men quieted down and gave him their full attention. She grew flustered as she recalled their encounter. What would she say to him? She looked around for an exit and was about to make for the back staircase when Geraldine appeared.

'Rosie! How wonderful, you have come.'

Geraldine's voice broke the spell.

Rosie took a deep breath and smiled. 'Oh, yes. I've been looking for you. You were wonderful on stage.'

Geraldine shrugged. 'It was just a little tableau. But it was such fun.'

She reached for Rosie's hand. 'Come on downstairs with me, I want to introduce you to some friends. And besides, we're interrupting Mr O'Malley's speech.'

He must have heard his name because he turned around abruptly. His eyes caught Rosie's and held them. She stared back, unable to look away, just as had happened the first time they had met. A wide grin creased his face as he bowed towards her. Had Geraldine not pulled her away, Rosie could not say how long she would have remained standing there.

Geraldine Butler arranged Rosie's employment as secretary for the Gaelic League in short order. She was settled at a table in a corner cubbyhole within the larger offices of the *Sword of Light,* the official newspaper of the Gaelic League. Known to all as the *Sword,* its offices occupied the ground floor of a terraced three-storey house on Moore Street, off Henry Street in the north section of the city. Outside, Moore Street bustled with wagons, bicycles and pedestrians. Tradespeople, their carts laden with fruits, vegetables and flowers, hawked their wares with ribald cheer. The noise filtered into the League offices through the constantly swinging front door and merged in a merry cacophony with

267

the clack of typewriter keys, screech of ringing telephones and din of strident voices.

Through the glass partition that separated her cubbyhole from the main office, Rosie watched with fascination as a stream of people came through the door each day, bringing a cold blast of air with them. Journalists, writers, poets and illustrators mixed with well-dressed female members of the Gaelic League. Tradespeople and prostitutes alike warmed themselves with a cup of tea, while young lads in cloth caps hovered in the hope of some paid errand. It seemed to her that the whole of Dublin came and went through the door.

It occurred to her at times as she peered out through the glass pane that she was like Mr Burke, butler at Ennismore, who used to sit at his office window watching the servants in the servants' hall. She smiled at the memory. Her cubbyhole only had space for a small table, the chair on which she sat, and another for visitors. Any papers and records she needed resided in a cardboard box at her feet. From here she greeted League members bringing notices of events to be advertised, pamphlets to be typeset, and donations, dues and expenses to be recorded. Rosie had no typewriter, instead making do with paper and ink to make notes and a ledger in which to record the financial matters of the League. In time, she grew bolder in making grammatical corrections to the notices presented to her and suggestions for improvement in the layout of pamphlets. On evenings, when things were quieter, she stayed late to practise on a typewriting machine that sat on the editor's desk, and over time she was pleased with her progress.

One such Friday evening she sat practising at the machine. The newspaper staff had all left to celebrate the 'putting to bed' of yet another issue. The old printing press in the basement had groaned and grunted all day as the pages were prepared and now the new edition lay, bundled and banded, waiting for the boys who would come in the morning to distribute it across the city. For once, the offices were quiet.

The two upper floors of the Moore Street house were residential apartments. Rosie had no idea who lived up there, but the floor directly above was a frequent venue for meetings. She had seen men with serious faces, young and old, tramping up and down the staircase so often she paid little attention to them. Someone had mentioned they were Irish Volunteers who met to discuss politics and strategy. She had seen them at her first meeting of the Gaelic League, gathered in the small, side room, where she had also seen Cathal O'Malley. At times she wondered if he might be with them, but she had not seen him, and was by now so engrossed in her work that she gave little thought to them.

She was getting ready to leave when she heard the shuffle of feet on the floorboards above, and the door to the upstairs apartment open. The sound of voices drifted out onto the landing followed by feet on the stairs. She reached quickly for her coat, hoping to get out the door ahead of them, but they were already streaming past her. She sighed, deciding to wait until they were all gone, and make sure that the door was securely locked behind them. They had a habit of leaving the door wide open swinging on its hinges. She nodded to the last of them and moved again to pick up her coat but a heavy tread on the stairs made her pause. There was always one more dawdling behind the rest.

'Upon my word, if it isn't Miss Roisin Dubh from County Mayo herself!'

Rosie froze in the midst of putting on her coat and swung around.

'Mr O'Malley!'

He gave her a small bow and moved towards her. 'The very same.'

She looked up at him. He was as handsome as she remembered – strong, angular face, longish brown hair – but she saw now that his eyes were a startling emerald green, unlike her own hazel ones. She stared into them for longer than was polite.

'Is it editing the paper you are? Sure I took you for a clever one the first time I met you.'

He drew closer and she could smell the good, clean soap he used, the starch of his linens and the woolly damp of his long overcoat. There was a faint smell of pipe tobacco and whiskey on his breath.

'No, I'm just practising,' she said, trying to stem the blush that rose on her cheeks. 'I'm working for the Gaelic League as their secretary. That's my office over there.' She smiled. 'It's not much, is it?'

'With a queen such as yourself in it, it's a palace indeed!'

She blushed again and began to fidget with the buttons of her coat, growing nervous under his scrutiny. He came closer to the desk, pulled out a chair and sat down, so that she felt obliged to sit down as well.

'I saw you at the recent League meeting,' he said, 'but you scurried away like a rabbit before I could speak to you.'

'I didn't scurry! Geraldine Butler pulled me away. Anyway you were in the middle of a speech.'

'Ah, I was that. Well, we can have a chat now.'

He leaned back in the chair and stretched out his long legs, crossing them at the ankles. He gazed at her expectantly.

Rosie's nervousness grew. She tried to think of something to say but no words came. He waited in silence, openly appraising her.

'Are you a member of the League, then?' she managed.

He laughed, showing strong teeth. 'Ah, nothing that grand. I'm in charge of a squadron of volunteers – trying to take some eager young lads and tell them what soldiering is all about.'

'You're a soldier then?'

'Not officially, no. But I've seen a lot more of army life than those lads. Some of them are no more than farm lads come to the big city in search of adventure. They want to fight for Ireland. I tell them if you want to fight, join the British Army and get paid for it.' He paused and grinned. 'But, no, 'tis Ireland they want to liberate. I admire their passion, but I wouldn't want to be responsible for sending them to their deaths, and them not much more than babies.'

'Do you think it will come to that? Sure Home Rule's been passed already.'

'So it has, but people are growing impatient. Nothing will come of it while the war's on.'

'Everyone says the war will be over by Christmas.'

He shrugged. 'They're talking through their hats. 'Twill drag on for years.'

A fleeting image of Valentine passed through Rosie's mind, but she chased it away. She stood up again and began buttoning her coat, deliberately closing them one by one and turning up the collar. He rose to help her with it, but she shrugged him off. 'I have to be going home,' she said, 'it's late.'

'Aye, far too late for a young lady to be walking the streets on her own. I'll escort you, so.'

'That's not necessary,' said Rosie, 'I will be perfectly all right.'

He laughed aloud. 'Ah now, I remember how perfectly all right you were the night I met you on the O'Connell Bridge with them two ruffians beating the living daylights out of you.'

Rosie blushed. At first she wanted to berate him for having the bad manners to bring the matter up. But for some reason she suddenly saw the funny side and laughed with him. 'Aye, you have me there,' she said.

She walked towards the door. He stood and followed her. She allowed him to put his hand on her elbow as she stepped out into the street.

'Make sure the door's locked,' she said.

The wind seared through her as she walked with him in the darkness. She could barely see him but felt his rhythmic stride beside her and the pleasant sensation of his hand on her elbow.

She pulled her coat more tightly around her, looking enviously at his greatcoat. It would be a lot warmer than her own, she thought. But he had not even buttoned it up. It swung open as if he were impervious to the elements. They said little as they walked, and Rosie found his presence comforting. For once no drunks lunged towards her and no prostitutes spat at her. She allowed herself for a moment to sink into the sense of safety he provided. It was only when they neared Foley Court that she began to fret. She would need to stop him at the corner. She could not allow him to see where she lived. It was bad enough that Valentine and Victoria had both been exposed to Foley Court's horrors, she didn't want yet another person whose opinion she cared about to see it and pity her too.

'I'm just around the corner here,' she said, stepping away from him. 'This will be grand.'

But he ignored her and took her elbow once more, gently urging her forward. She had no choice but to keep walking. She bit her lip as she walked and sped up. They were nearly at number six. It would be over soon.

Cathal O'Malley looked up at the building. Even in the darkness it provided a ghostly spectre, as if proclaiming all the horrors within. His touch became gentle on her arm as he turned her towards him. 'Nothing shocks me, Roisin Dubh. I'm sorry you thought it would.'

Rosie blushed scarlet in the dark. He had detected her shame. Part of her wanted to burst into tears, but she was saved by a sudden anger.

'It's too bad the League doesn't see this,' she

said. 'They're too busy writing about the grand Irish culture – the lovely music and poetry and theatre and dance. Well this is Irish culture too. Why don't they write about *this?*'

She trembled now, still fighting back tears. He had not let go of her so she wrenched herself away and turned toward the house.

'Why don't *you* write about it?' he said from behind her.

She hurried up the steps. 'Good night, Mr O'Malley,' she said without turning around.

'It's Cathal,' he called after her.

CHAPTER 24

1915 dawned and with it Rosie's optimism about the future. She had settled well into her role as League secretary, and now had seen her work in print in the *Sword*. She had taken Cathal O'Malley's suggestion seriously that she write about the poor in Dublin. Tentatively, she presented her first article, a piece about the hardships endured by the poor during the Lockout, to the editor, and signed the piece 'Roisin Dubh'. She stood nervously beside him as he read it, frowned and read it again. Eventually he had looked up at her in astonishment.

'You're after writing this yourself?' he asked.

Rosie nodded.

'Have you more?'

'No. But I can write more.'

In the end the editor agreed that she should write one piece a month. Rosie was filled with pride when she saw her first article in print with her pen name 'Roisin Dubh' on the byline. She rushed home to show Bridie who read it with tears in her eyes. She wished she could also have shown it to Valentine, but quickly put the thought out of her mind.

Cathal O'Malley was filled with praise.

'Fair play to you, Roisin Dubh,' he boomed at her on the day her article appeared. 'I knew you had it in you.'

He was much too big to squeeze himself into her small space so he stood outside her cubbyhole peering in like a giant in a fairytale. Rosie blushed as she looked up at him. His loud voice attracted the notice of others in the outer offices. The editor of the *Sword* winked at her from his desk.

'Thank you, Mr O'Malley ... er, Cathal. It's nice of you to say so.'

She tried to busy herself with the papers on the table, but he was not to be put off so easily.

'I'd say this calls for a celebration. Come with me now to Toner's and I'll buy you a drink.'

'But, it's the middle of the afternoon,' said Rosie, flustered.

He laughed aloud. 'You can have a cup of tea if you're not up for the drink this early.'

'No. I mean I can't just leave. I'm on duty till five.'

But Cathal was still not dissuaded. 'Get your coat,' he said, leaning in to take her by the arm. 'You've earned a few hours off.'

A short time later they entered Toner's on

275

Baggot Street. The pub was a well-known gathering place, frequented by writers and journalists. Rosie would never have stepped into such a place alone. Not so for Cathal O'Malley. He was apparently a regular there, judging by the hearty greeting from the barman when they entered. It was a small, dark and aromatic place with a stone floor, a long bar with brass taps, and an area stocked with groceries at one end. The barman led them to a snug – a small private space enclosed by a door – the sort of place a man might bring his mistress, or politicians might engage in whispered conversation. Rosie wondered if the barman thought she and Cathal might be lovers and the fact that she had such a thought shocked her. She took a deep breath and steadied herself.

Cathal ordered a stout for himself and a glass of sherry for Rosie. As they waited for their drinks they sat regarding one another across the rough wooden table. Rosie again felt her colour rising under his scrutiny. She was glad when the barman interrupted the silence to set their drinks in front of them.

'Slainte,' said Cathal.

'To your health,' she replied.

Rosie thought back to the days when she had been very tongue-tied around Valentine. But she was only fourteen then. Now she was a grown up woman. There was no need for her to be acting like a love-struck girl. She took a deep breath.

'Tell me about yourself, Cathal,' she began. 'All I know is that you are from Westport, and you are training Irish Volunteers.'

Cathal smiled. 'That's about the size of it,

Roisin Dubh. Nothing much more to tell.'

Rosie smiled back. 'I'd wager there's a lot more to tell.'

'I could say the same about yourself, Miss Killeen.'

'Ah, but I asked you first.'

Cathal drained his glass and ordered another. Rosie sipped her own drink slowly. She could see that he was arranging his thoughts. He's a dark horse, so he is, she thought. He's deciding which of his secrets to tell me and which to keep to himself.

'I was born in Westport where my da was a doctor,' he began. 'I had a fine Catholic upbringing. As a young man I got into more than a few scrapes, owing to me bad temper. I was tossed out of a few schools, then sent to the military. In the end me da disowned me and I came on up to Dublin. I made a bit of money here and there – enough to buy a house on Moore Street next door to where you work.' He leaned back and gazed at her, his green eyes clear. 'And that's the story. I said there wasn't much to it.'

Rosie didn't know whether to laugh or rage at him. In the end she laughed.

'I've met donkeys have more to say for themselves than that,' she said.

He laughed along with her, appearing relieved. ''Tis not much, but 'tis all true,' he said, grinning like a schoolboy.

Rosie shook her head, finished her drink and accepted another glass. She realized he was going to tell her nothing more.

'Now what about yourself?' he began.

Rosie put up her hand. 'Ah, fair's fair, Mr O'Malley. The more you tell me, the more I'll tell you. And since you've told me nothing so far, I'll be telling you nothing either.'

He burst out laughing. 'You have a bargain, Roisin Dubh.'

As they were finishing their drinks, Cathal's expression grew serious.

'There is one thing I would like to talk to you about, Roisin.'

Rosie waited. Again, Cathal appeared to be arranging his thoughts.

'Now don't take this the wrong way, but I've been thinking a lot about it ever since I saw where you're living.'

Rosie's spine tightened.

'I know I said you've nothing to be ashamed of, and I believe that. But ... but 'tis a terrible slum altogether, and 'tis not safe for a girl like you on her own to be walking up to that place night after night.'

Rosie rose to her own defence. 'I can take care of myself. I've been doing it for a long time now. I'm no stupid girl up from the country with stars in her eyes.' Cathal put his hand on her arm. She let it rest there. 'And I never said I was ashamed of it! It's where my family lives and it's where I belong.'

''Tis *not* where you belong,' he said. 'But before you say anything else I want you to consider my suggestion. As I told you, I own a house on Moore Street. I only need the first and second floors. There's an acre of empty space up on the third floor. You could live there for no charge.' He paused and grinned. 'And I promise I'd behave like an altar boy, so you'd have nothing to fear from me. I don't expect anything from you in return.'

A range of emotions tore through Rosie as she listened – embarrassment, followed by anger, followed by outrage. How dare this man make such a proposal? What kind of woman did he take her for? Colour suffused her cheeks – this time not from shyness but from outrage. She opened her mouth but no words came forth.

He tightened his hold on her arm. 'I know what you're thinking, Roisin, that if I respected you I would never suggest such a thing. But 'tis out of respect for you that I'm doing it. I realize you have no reason to believe that I'm nothing but a blackguard out to take advantage. But I beg you to believe that my intentions are honourable. You have my word on it.'

Rosie pushed his hand away and stood up. '*Your* word?' she cried. 'I hardly know you. What good is *your* word to me?' She talked hurriedly as she pulled on her coat. 'I've never been so insulted in my life, Mr O'Malley. I want to hear no more from you on the subject. In fact, as of now, I would thank you to never speak to me again!'

With that she tugged open the door of the snug and strode out, leaving Cathal staring after her.

Rosie might well have never spoken to Cathal O'Malley again had it not been for an incident that took place early in the spring of 1915 – something she had long feared might occur and long prayed that it would not.

It was an unusually warm night for May. Not a

breeze fanned the humid air that pressed down on Dublin like a leaden hand, poking its long, damp fingers through the crevices that riddled the rotting window frames of the city's tenements. Rosie sweated with the rest of the citizenry as she made her way home from the League offices. The women of number six Foley Court sat as usual on the front steps, fanning themselves, and passing around a bottle of gin. They glared at her as they did every night but said nothing. She nodded back at them and climbed the steps to the front door.

The damp heat assaulted her as soon as she entered the dank, airless building and she gasped for breath. It would be a long, uncomfortable night, she thought, and once more cursed the fate that had landed her here. She thought, as she did every time she came back to Foley Court, about Cathal O'Malley's offer of accommodation, and once more she dismissed it. Such a thing was out of the question. She hoped that with the extra money she earned from her articles she would in time have enough money to persuade Bridie to leave Micko and move out of this squalor with Kate and herself. Until then she must bide her time.

The room was empty and dark. At first she wondered what had happened to Bridie, but then remembered that her sister had taken Kate to the hospital with yet another one of the child's frequent fevers. Wearily, she lit a candle, took off her jacket and then took a bucket down to the tap in the yard to fetch water. The water was luke-warm and rusty, but she was used to it by now. She had planned to wash her hair, but by the time she returned to the top floor she was too exhausted. She set the bucket down and went behind a bamboo screen to undress. She had bought the screen back when she worked at the bakery. She needed some privacy in such cramped quarters. She had bought a thin mattress and pillow, as well, which she had placed on the floor in a corner behind the screen. It occurred to her sometimes that she lived her life these days constrained in very small spaces – the cubbyhole at the League offices and this cramped floor space behind the screen.

She undressed, and lay down on the mattress in her thin shift. Soon the mattress was damp with the sweat of her body and her shift was soaked through. She sighed. She was beginning to drift off to sleep when the door opened. Bridie must be back with the child, she thought, but she was too weary to get up and see. Loud coughing and cursing signalled that it was not Bridie but Micko who had come home. Rosie stiffened and held herself very still. The cursing grew louder when Micko realized Bridie was not there. Rosie listened as he sat down heavily on the chair and gurgled as he greedily swallowed a beer. She waited for the thump of his body as he hit the mattress where he and Bridie slept. But he did not move. She prayed he would not realize she was there.

'Rosie, Rosie, ring around the Rosie.'

She started at his simpering voice. She must have fallen asleep. Now it took her some seconds to take in what was happening. Micko knelt on the floor leaning over her. His putrid breath made nausea rise in her throat. She lay still in the darkness, hoping he would think she was asleep.

'That hooer, Bridie, is not in her bed,' he went on, 'and no man should have to sleep in a cold bed.' He leaned over closer to her. 'But she left her lovely sister here for me, didn't she?'

Panic gripped Rosie. Night after night she had lain listening to Micko grunting and rutting as he assaulted her sister after a night of drinking. He had made many lewd remarks to Rosie but thank God he had never touched her. Bridie had always been there and he had taken his needs out on her. But Bridie was not here tonight.

'Please God,' she whispered, 'please God don't let him touch me.'

But even as she prayed she knew exactly what Micko intended to do, and no amount of prayer was going to stop him. Within seconds he lay on top of her, tearing at her shift with his rough hands, his breath coming in thick gasps. He thrust his wet tongue into her mouth so deep she thought she would vomit. With one hand he shoved her shift up above her hips and with the other began unbuttoning his trousers. A bright red flame filled Rosie's eyes and an anger she had never known before infused her. All senses left her and pure instinct took over. She began to kick her legs, her right knee aiming at his crotch. With balled fists she pummelled his head and back while he grasped her, his ragged nails tearing into her shoulders and down her back. She seized his jaw and pushed it back as far as she could so that he was forced to remove his tongue from her mouth. Then she screamed as loud as she could, all the while still kicking him. Her knee eventually found its target and he leaned sideways, cursing her.

With all the strength she could muster, she shifted herself from under him and pushed him to one side. Already off balance and inebriated, he rolled onto the floor. Before he could move, Rosie scrambled up and grabbed her dress and jacket that were hanging on the bamboo screen. Then she pushed the screen down on top of him. Half-crying, half-whimpering, she found her shoes and holding them and her clothes in her hands ran for the door and down the stairs. From the room above she heard the clatter of the water bucket as Micko Delaney crashed into it and the thud on the floor as he fell.

She was outside before she stopped long enough to struggle into her clothes and shoes. Then she took off up Foley Court and on to Montgomery Street. There were few people about that time of night, but Rosie didn't care who saw her. She ran on without thought of where she was going. When she finally stopped, bent over and exhausted, she was at the door of the house on Moore Street where Cathal O'Malley lived.

It took him some minutes to respond to her persistent pounding. By the time he opened the door he found her collapsed on his doorstep.

'Mother of God, what happened to you?'

Rosie looked up at him. She could not speak. She hoped he would not make her explain. She allowed him to lift her to her feet and lead her down a hallway and into a dimly lit room. He sat her down in a tall armchair beside a flickering fire.

'Stay there,' he said, his voice gentle, as he disappeared into another room.

Rosie shrank into herself, hardly aware of where she was. She noticed a half-drunk glass of whiskey on a table beside the armchair, and an open book, but very little of it registered. He returned with a glass of cool water, and a glass of brandy, which he set down on the table. He went out again and came back with a small box which contained bandages and ointments and other items. She stared at him, her eyes wide.

'Drink the brandy,' he said, ''twill do you good. Now let's have a look.'

Rosie whimpered and shrank away from him. ''Tis all right, Roisin Dubh,' he whispered. 'I'll not hurt you. Let me see you.'

She let him remove her jacket but as he began to unbutton the front of her dress a vague panic engulfed her. Was it going to happen again? She cried out.

'Ah, hush now, love. You'll be all right. But you're bleeding through your dress. I'm only trying to see your wounds.'

She beat the panic down. Bleeding? She hadn't felt anything. But there again, she was numb. She watched as he slipped her dress down over her shoulders. The material had stuck to her back with sweat and blood, and he eased it gently away from her skin.

'Jesus, Mary and Joseph,' he breathed. 'Who's after doing this to you?'

She shook her head and remained silent.

'Ah 'tis all right. You don't have to speak of it now.'

He reached into the box and took out cotton wool and a bottle of antiseptic and gently applied it to her cuts. There were several on her back and shoulders and upper arms. Her hands were scraped as well, as were her lower legs. She kept still while he cleaned and applied salve to her wounds. His touch was gentle. She was vaguely aware of the firelight that turned his brown hair to copper as he bent over her. He was in his shirtsleeves. She realized she had never seen him without his long, heavy overcoat.

The brandy began to do its work. Drowsily, she nodded and closed her eyes. She thought of how her da used to tend to her scraped knees when she was a child, joking with her so she wouldn't cry when he applied the antiseptic or iodine. Then he would kiss her on the forehead and tell her everything was better. She felt her da's kiss. It was so real she opened her eyes. But the only one kneeling in front of her was Cathal O'Malley.

CHAPTER 25

While the New Year of 1915 had promised optimism for Rosie, for Victoria it promised only spiritless dejection. Her earlier hope that nursing wounded soldiers at Dr Cullen's private hospital would bring her satisfaction was fading. There was no shortage of military officers needing her attention, but Victoria could not stamp out the thought that she could be doing more. Lady Marianne had shown Rosie's articles to her, filled with pride that her protégée was making such progress. And while Victoria felt a pinch of envy she also was horrified at the desperation that Rosie's articles were describing.

Perhaps Rosie's pieces were the catalyst that finally crystallized Victoria's resolve. A week earlier she had been reassigned back to the clinic after the head nurse at Dr Cullen's private hospital had complained that Victoria's youth and beauty were an unwanted distraction for the recovering officers. Now she was back to caring for genteel ladies with delicate health problems. Her vague yearnings to do something more soon became howling cries she could no longer ignore. So, one summer morning, instead of going to the clinic as usual, she made her way to the South Dublin Union Hospital and offered her services as a nursing volunteer.

The hospital was part of a group of buildings on James Street, which included a workhouse and infirmary. The South Dublin Union was officially established in 1839, but the workhouse and foundling hospital dated back over one hundred years before that. By the time Victoria went to work there, the hospital had become a vital resource for Dublin's poor, like Bridie and her child, who could obtain care free of charge. Besides nurses and women of various religious orders, the hospital was staffed by many volunteer doctors, some of them well-renowned.

The contrast between Dr Cullen's private clinic and the Union was stark. The grim, granite-faced building Victoria entered each day through a wide archway was a far cry from the discreet Georgian townhouse that housed the clinic. The

286

hospital was grimy, noisy, odorous, and overrun with patients. For the first time since coming to Dublin Victoria began to feel an inexplicable pleasure each morning. Her nursing skills were put to rigorous test straight away. No more the genteel complaints of gentlewomen and their daughters, her patients now presented with real sickness – much of it arising from poor nutrition, filthy living conditions and hopelessness – and she was making a difference in their lives. Within her first week she had treated cases of boils, scurvy and rodent bites, as well as whooping coughs, fevers and respiratory ailments. She was shocked at the number of women, young and old, who arrived with bruises and broken ribs and limbs – all of them claiming to have 'fallen'.

The days at the Union were long and demanding. She was grateful for the exhaustion that caused her to fall into a deep sleep each night. The bliss of sleep allowed her to blot out all thoughts of Brendan and the sadness that he was lost to her. During the day at the hospital she thought about Rosie often – she half expected to see her appear in the crowded waiting room with Bridie or the baby. The more she became aware of the price of poverty in the city, the more she began to understand why Rosie wrote the kinds of articles that she did.

One spring morning in May, the Union was as bustling as ever. By ten o'clock the vast waiting room overflowed with Dublin's poor. There seemed to be no end to the stream of humanity that struggled through the doors each day in search of care and compassion. She was securing a bandage on the arm of a young boy when she felt someone watching her. She swung around. A dark-haired man peered through the window. Something about the set of his head was familiar. She dropped the boy's arm abruptly.

'Hey, missus,' he protested, 'will you watch what you're after doing.'

But Victoria did not hear him. A buzzing filled her ears, hot sweat collected at the back of her neck, and her palms were wet and clammy. Shock seized her as she stared at the man. No, it could not be him. She must be imagining it. She stood rooted to the spot as he opened the door and came into the room.

'Well, well, Miss Bell. You've come down a peg or two, I see.'

Brendan Lynch's tone was surly.

A rush of emotions flooded through her – embarrassment at the images that pervaded her dreams, even though she knew he could not possibly know of them; delight that he was here, standing in front of her; fear that he would reject her because of how her family had treated him. Her heart thumped in her chest and she struggled to speak.

'Brendan?' she managed, though her mouth and lips were parched. 'What are *you* doing here?'

He shrugged and looked down at a blood-soaked handkerchief wrapped around his fingers. 'Looking for a nurse like everybody else. I was a bit careless with a knife.'

Victoria instinctively reached for his wounded hand but he drew it back. 'I'll wait me turn.'

Although his tone was sullen, Victoria thought

she saw his old passion burning in his eyes, but she dismissed it as wishful thinking.

'I'm sorry about what happened, Brendan.' The words burst out of her. 'I never meant for you to lose your job.'

She studied his face for any hint of hostility. Surely he must resent her, hate her even, for how he had been treated at Ennismore. He had been sent away without any chance to explain. How that humiliation must have fed into his hatred of the gentry. Did that resentment now include her? She waited for his judgement but it did not come. Instead he shrugged.

''Tis myself acted the fool,' he said. 'I should have known better than ever to trust the gentry.'

Victoria winced. Had the bond of trust between them been broken? She fought back tears.

'Ah, sure 'twas the boot in the arse I needed to get away from there,' he went on. 'Anyway, the company is better in Dublin. There's plenty of lads here like meself. They're a far cry from the likes of the brown-nosing oul' weasels beyond at Ennismore. And I've joined the Volunteers.'

'I'm glad you've found your place, Brendan.' She smiled, trying to lighten the mood. 'No one ever thought you were cut out to be a footman.'

'Aye, you're right there. But 'twould have made no difference soon enough. When this war's over there'll be no footmen left in this country or in England. Young fellers will have been out seeing the world, fighting alongside their supposed superiors, and they'll not slip back into the old ways of service so easily. I'd say the gentry way of life will be all but dead. And good riddance to it.'

They stared at each other for a long time. Brendan looked as if he were weighing something up in his mind. She allowed herself to hope that he would let go of his anger. As she waited, his eyes grew softer and his tone gentler.

'I'll be away back before I lose my place in the queue,' he said, interrupting her thoughts. ''Twas good to see you, Victoria.'

Relief rushed through her. He had used her first name. 'It was good to see you too, Brendan,' she whispered.

With that he was gone. Victoria stood for a moment then looked down at the glum-faced boy who was waiting for her and busied herself with his bandage.

'Ah, 'tis too tight, missus,' he protested.

'Sorry.'

Later that night she lay in bed replaying Brendan's visit over and over in her mind. The dream that she would one day see him again had come true, but it was worse than if he had never come at all. She feared that she had lost him now for a second time. She had wanted to call after him when he left – to ask him where he was staying, to suggest that they meet some time – but she had been paralysed by a mixture of desire and fear. Now she regretted that she had not had courage enough to tell him how she felt.

She closed her eyes and recalled the last night she spent with him in the walled garden at Ennismore – his sad eyes as he had told her about his mother's death, his slender fingers clutching hers as he spoke, the soft feel of his lips when they had kissed. There was no sign of that Brendan today.

He was hidden far below the brash, defiant face he had shown her. The feelings the old Brendan had aroused in her were still there. Would they ever be given a chance to ripen? She buried her head in the pillow, craving sleep. But sleep remained a stranger to her that night and for many nights after.

Ever since her success in placing Rosie at the Gaelic League, Lady Marianne Bellefleur had developed a robust interest in all things nationalist. As she had opined on many visits to Ennismore, the nationalist movement amongst Dublin's Protestant Ascendancy was growing. This development appealed to Lady Marianne's French sensibilities, given France's own glorious revolution and, more importantly, to her desire to be on the cusp of all new and exciting activities indulged in by the most inventive and passionate members of her own class.

She and her companion, Mr Shane Kearney, attended many League events such as charity fund-raisers, speeches, debates, and, of course, musical and cultural evenings. What she enjoyed most, however, was attending the Abbey Theatre. She was already well acquainted with Lady Augusta Gregory, dramatist, and the poet, William Butler Yeats, co-founders of the Abbey, having visited Lady Gregory's Coole Park estate in Galway a number of times. The Abbey had become a venue for nationalist dramas and was popular among League members.

One evening at the end of May, Lady Marianne finally persuaded Victoria to accompany her and

Mr Kearney to a performance of *The Devil's Disciple* by George Bernard Shaw – a play about the American Revolution. At first, Victoria had refused, pleading fatigue, but Lady Marianne had been insistent.

'You must get back out in society, Victoria. You are burying yourself in that hospital to the exclusion of everything else. I applaud you for the good work you are doing there, but you need some respite, my dear. You have been looking rather haggard of late. It's most unattractive.'

Victoria walked behind her aunt and Mr Kearney into the midst of a bustling crowd of theatre-goers. When they had taken their seats she looked around her. The Abbey struck her as more of a village hall than a formal theatre. People in the audience left their seats to chat with friends and milled about moving between the cheap seats in the pits and the grander stalls blithely ignoring the dividing rope between. The atmosphere was exciting and alive. She recognized many of the women who patronized Dr Cullen's clinic. Geraldine Butler was there. As soon as Geraldine caught Victoria's eye she rushed over to greet her.

'Darling Victoria,' she cried, 'how wonderful to see you here.' Geraldine nodded towards Lady Marianne and Mr Kearney. Then she turned back to Victoria. 'I haven't seen you since I accompanied Mama on her last visit to Dr Cullen's clinic.'

Before Victoria could answer, Lady Marianne piped up. 'Victoria is no longer at the clinic, my dear. She is volunteering for the poor at the Union Hospital. Is she not marvellous, Geraldine?'

Geraldine's eyes widened. 'Marvellous indeed. I am so happy to hear it. Although I have heard that it is an awful place.'

Victoria tried to change the subject. She was annoyed with Lady Marianne for publicly announcing her new position – she had not even told her parents she had made the change. Mama, she knew, would be mortified if she found out and would come to Dublin immediately and insist that she return to Ennismore.

'How is Rosie?' she said. 'I have been reading her articles in the *Sword*.'

Geraldine clapped her hands. 'Oh, yes. Isn't she a wonderful writer? She has quite a following now.'

'I imagine her sister, Bridie, is proud of her,' said Victoria.

Geraldine frowned. 'I expect she is. But Rosie is not living with Bridie any more. Haven't you heard?'

Victoria, her aunt, and Shane Kearney all pricked up their ears.

'No, she has moved in with Mr Cathal O'Malley.'

'Who?'

Geraldine shrugged. 'All I know about him is that he is the Catholic son of a doctor from Westport, and has had some military experience. He is in charge of training new recruits to the Irish Volunteers.'

An image of Brendan entered Victoria's mind.

'He's some years older than Rosie,' Geraldine said, frowning slightly, 'some say old enough to be her father.' She paused, then brightening continued, 'He's also very handsome. You'll see him yourself. He has a walk-on part in the play tonight – I believe he plays a revolutionary who fights an English soldier. They've recruited some English soldiers from Dublin garrison to play themselves. Quite apt, wouldn't you say?'

With that Geraldine ran off, called away by a group of young women signalling her from the other side of the room. Victoria gaped at her aunt, while Mr Kearney looked amused. He leaned over to whisper in Lady Marianne's ear.

'Dark horse, our girl, wouldn't you say, dearest?'

Lady Marianne's eyes sparkled. 'Delicious,' she declared.

Victoria was trying to gather her thoughts when a young man appeared out of nowhere.

'Is this seat taken?' he asked, pointing to the empty seat beside her.

Victoria felt an unexpected flush of pleasure rise over her throat and cheeks as she recognized Brendan.

'No,' she said, choking out the word.

She should have told him the seat was reserved, she thought. That would have been the proper thing to do. But his arrival had been such a shock, and her physical reaction to seeing him even more so, that she had not had time to think.

He sat down. He wore his Volunteer uniform and his dark hair, brushed back from his forehead, shone in the golden glow of the globes mounted on the theatre walls. He smelled of fresh air and faintly of tobacco. Victoria stole a look at his profile – his straight nose and strong, sharp chin. She looked away quickly as he turned to her.

'I see you've taken a liking to everything that's Irish.'

'And why wouldn't I – I *am* Irish.'

He chuckled. 'Ah, there's them in your family would hardly agree with you on that.'

'My family's been here for hundreds of years. They're Irish whether they admit it or not. Besides, my aunt is here with me.'

'Well said, Miss Bell – more power to you.'

'My name's Victoria.'

'Aye, so it is,' he said, grinning.

She turned away to look at her aunt. Lady Marianne was in deep conversation with Mr Kearney and had not noticed Brendan's presence.

'I didn't know you liked the theatre,' Victoria said in a low voice.

'Ah, there's a lot you don't know about me. A friend of mine has a walk-on part. He's to play a rebel and fight an English soldier – which wouldn't be too hard for him, I'd say.'

'I heard,' she said. 'A Mr O'Malley.'

Brendan raised an eyebrow. 'The very same.'

'I hear they've arranged for some English soldiers from the garrison to play themselves.'

'Aye. I'd say 'twill be a splendid rehearsal for our own revolution.'

The lights dimmed and they settled back in the darkness to watch the play. Victoria, distracted by Brendan's closeness, found it hard to concentrate. Memories of their times together back at Ennismore flooded her mind, especially their last night in the garden when she had held his hands and kissed him. She wondered if he was remembering it, too.

'There he is now,' he said suddenly, interrupting her thoughts. 'Cathal O'Malley. That's him, the tall feller in the long military coat.'

Victoria stared at the man. Something about him was familiar but she could not place him. He was indeed handsome, and his voice was strong and tempered with a County Mayo accent. No wonder Rosie had fallen for him, she thought. He must remind her of home. But living with him? She chased the thought out of her head. Anyway, who was she to judge?

After the play finished there was a musical finale. Harpists, fiddlers and bagpipers played old Irish airs and the audience sang aloud to the melodies of poet Thomas Moore. Victoria watched Brendan out of the corner of her eye as he clapped and sang along. He became light again, just as when he had played his fiddle in the servants' hall at Ennismore. He reached over and took her hand. She did not pull it away.

When the performance ended, Victoria whispered in her aunt's ear.

'This young man's a friend of mine from the Union. I'm going to walk with him for a while.'

Before Lady Marianne could insist on an introduction, Victoria pulled Brendan up from his seat and, grasping his hand, rushed him out of the building.

'Is it ashamed of me ye are?' he said when they reached the street.

She dropped his hand and turned to him in alarm. 'Heavens, no! I just didn't want to get caught up with my aunt. She would have asked a hundred questions.'

When she saw he was smiling, she smiled back in relief. She took his hand again and they began to walk. It had rained while they were inside and the street lamps reflected on the dark, wet pavement. Crowds milled around them, streaming out of theatres and pubs, hailing horse drawn cabs or running after trams. Snippets of music and laughter spilled out behind them as the pub doors swung open then closed. But despite the crowds Victoria had the feeling that she and Brendan were the only two people in the world.

'What do you think of Dublin?' she said, as they made their way through the throngs.

''Tis a far cry from Ennismore so it is,' he said. 'Every class of people mixed up together. I like that none of these people has any notion who I am, nor cares.'

'The poverty is awful though. You got a taste of it at the Union.'

Brendan squeezed her hand. 'The Union, aye. 'Twas not the place I ever thought I would find yourself.'

Victoria smiled. 'Ah, but you're thinking of the old Victoria – the one who was spoiled and sheltered. The new Victoria is much different.'

'Aye, the old Victoria was nice enough, but I must say I've taken a quare liking to this new one!'

She swung his hand playfully. 'I like her better too. I felt as if I were suffocating at Dr Cullen's clinic. Now at least I am doing something worthwhile for the poor.'

She felt herself swell with sudden pride at her accomplishment. Surely Brendan must be proud of her too.

'Are you sure it's not guilt that's behind it?'

His unexpected words stung. She dropped his hand and moved away from him, looking straight ahead as she walked. He fell into step beside her.

'You're right,' she said at last, 'it *was* guilt that caused me to leave the clinic and volunteer at the Union. But it's not guilt that keeps me there. The work is fulfilling, and I try to do my best. Some of the other nurses think I'm just a dilettante – you know, a person who's not serious–'

'I know what it means,' Brendan cut in gruffly. 'I'm not ignorant, for fuck's sake.'

They walked on in silence, the space between them widening. A tram rumbled by, splattering rain water from the gutters on to the hem of Victoria's skirt. She struggled to hold back tears. Brendan reached over for her hand but she snatched it away. 'I'm sorry for what I said about the guilt just now,' he said, 'it wasn't fair. I can see this work means a lot to you.' He paused. 'And, for the first time in my life,' he went on, 'I have respect for what *I'm* doing now, too. I used to hate myself for working for the very people who killed my granda, waiting on them hand and foot, bowing and scraping. There was no honour in it, I can tell you.'

'That's not fair, Brendan. It wasn't my family who killed him.'

'Aye, but in my mind all the gentry were cut from the same cloth.'

Victoria's fought to control her temper. Why had their conversation suddenly become so cross? 'If you felt that way, then why did you not hate me as well? Why did you arrange meetings with me? Why did you kiss me?'

Brendan halted and reached over, pulling her close to him, ignoring her protests. He stared into her eyes and she could not look away. They stood, unaware of the crowds who parted like a sea around them.

'Because you're not like the rest of them,' he said. 'You never were. There was a compassion and kindness in you that wasn't in the others. You have a beautiful heart, Victoria.' Suddenly he grinned at her, and danced away a little, his features bright under the glow of the street lamp. 'And anyway, much as I wanted to kiss you every time I saw you, it was you, my bold girl, who kissed *me* that night in the garden!'

Victoria blushed and gave him a playful punch. He laughed and pulled her close to him again. They strolled on, arms encircled about each other's waists, smiling at everyone they met. The storm of anger had passed as quickly as it had come. When they reached O'Connell Bridge, the crowds thinned out, replaced by shawlie women clutching skeletal, sad-eyed children, imploring passers-by for money. Brendan reached into the pocket of his uniform and pressed some coins into the children's hands. City lights glimmered on the dark water as a sudden wind picked up, carrying with it the distant stench of fish decaying on the dock.

At length they sat down on a bench, laughing as Victoria's hat threatened to sail off into the water below. She caught it and held it in her lap then laid her head on Brendan's shoulder. She wanted to cling on to this moment for ever but, in spite

299

of her efforts, a distant fear surfaced that she could not dismiss. She sat up and looked at him.

'I'm frightened that the revolution may come,' she blurted out, 'and what changes it will bring. I'm frightened of what might happen to you. To us.'

He hugged her close. 'Ah now, love, there's no need to fret. Won't we be together through it all? And won't we still be together when it's over?'

He reached for her chin, brought her face towards his and gently kissed her on the lips. She returned his kiss, gently at first, but then fiercely, with a passion she could not hold back.

He drew away. 'Jaysus, you're a bold girl all right,' he grinned.

She grinned back. 'Meet the new Victoria.'

The night grew cold and reluctantly they rose and strolled on in silence towards Lady Marianne's house on Fitzwilliam Square. The only sounds now were the echo of their footsteps. As they walked, Victoria gazed up at the lighted windows, catching occasional sight of a family gathered beside a glowing fire. Usually she rushed by them, never stopping to look, but tonight she allowed herself to fantasize, imagining her and Brendan and their children occupying such rooms in a future life. When they reached Lady Marianne's steps they stood clinging to each other, unwilling to let go.

'I'm so glad I found you again,' whispered Brendan, his breath ragged. 'And I'll not be letting you go.'

'I'm not going anywhere,' she said as his lips pressed down on hers.

300

CHAPTER 26

In the autumn of 1915, Victoria returned home one evening from the Union to find her brother standing in the drawing room.

'Valentine!' she exclaimed in surprise, as she rushed towards him. Tears filled her eyes. 'Valentine, I can't believe it.'

She hugged him fiercely and then stood back at arm's length to examine him.

'You're not injured, are you?' she said. 'Tell me that's not why you are home.'

Valentine laughed. 'No, dear sister, I am not injured. I am embarrassed to say I have not seen any action yet. My regiment has been on training exercises in England. We are scheduled to begin shipping out to France soon.' He paused and frowned. 'I hope my turn comes quickly. I joined up to fight the enemy, not to sit around at the barracks here in Dublin.'

Secretly Victoria hoped the war might be over before he had to leave, but she would not dare tell him so. Instead she said, 'Have you been home? Do Mama and Papa know you are back in Ireland? And Sofia? And Julian?'

Valentine shook his head. 'I stopped to see my favourite sister first. I shall go down to Mayo tomorrow. It is so good to see you. I have missed you.'

'And I you, Valentine.'

Valentine took her by the hand and led her to the sofa. They were alone in the room – Lady Marianne and Mr Kearney being away on a visit to the coast. Celine came in and served tea, smiled and left.

'You look well, Victoria. Tired, but well. How are they treating you at that clinic?'

Victoria was momentarily confused. Clinic? Then she realized her brother would have no way of knowing where she worked now. She had not told her parents about the change and had lied to Dr Cullen, telling him she was returning home.

'I no longer work at the clinic,' she said proudly. 'I'm a nursing volunteer at the South Dublin Union. It's a public hospital where they treat the poor and–'

'I know of it, of course,' said Valentine. 'How splendid of you! I had no idea you had it in you.'

Victoria smiled. 'Me, neither.'

They sipped their tea in companionable silence. Then Valentine set down his cup and turned to her, his expression serious. 'There is another reason I have come to Dublin. I must see Rosie. Is she still living with her sister? I plan to visit her this evening.'

'No!' It was out before Victoria could catch herself. Seeing his startled expression, she hurried on. 'I mean, no, she is not living with Bridie any more. I went there to see her myself and Bridie's husband said she had moved. He didn't say where,' she lied.

Valentine studied her face. 'I see. Did he say where she works?'

Victoria's face grew warm. She hated lying to

302

her brother. 'I did enquire, yes, but he said he had no idea. And Bridie wasn't there.'

'Did she go back to Mayo?'

'I don't think so. I should have heard.'

Valentine stood up and began to pace about the room. 'But aren't you worried about her? She was your best friend. Surely you can't just accept that she's lost somewhere in Dublin? What if she's ill, or in trouble? We must find her.' He hesitated for a moment then swung around to face Victoria. 'I will go to Bridie's house tonight. Surely she has some information. She must know where her sister is.'

Victoria swallowed hard. Thoughts crowded her mind. Should she tell her brother what Geraldine Butler had said about Rosie and Cathal O'Malley? What if he went to search for her and discovered that she was living with a man?

Valentine moved towards the door. 'Are you coming with me, or shall I go alone?'

Victoria stood and braced herself. 'No, Valentine, I am not going with you. And I don't think you should go either.' Her tone was as stern as she could make it. 'Sit down. I need to talk to you.'

Valentine was so shocked he sat down immediately on one of Lady Marianne's delicate chairs. His face turned pale.

'Rosie was in love with you, Valentine,' Victoria began, not knowing exactly what she was about to say, but praying that God would guide her. 'She always was, and I think you know that.'

Valentine bowed his head.

'You hurt her badly when you left for America and even more when you married Sofia. Why do you think she ran away from Ennismore without any warning? She was trying to forget you – to forget all of us. And then you had the cheek to show up at the Metropole Hotel and ask her to dance with you. How could you have been so cruel?'

Victoria's voice grew shrill. All the old anger she had felt about how her family had treated Rosie that night came flooding back. 'You *knew* how she felt about you and yet still you trifled with her. You hurt her badly and I will not let you do it again. Stay away from her. She is none of your business any more.'

Valentine stared up at her. He looked as if he was fighting back tears.

'I tried to explain everything to her last time I saw her, but I'm not sure she really understood,' he murmured.

'Explain? There's nothing to explain. You are a married man now, and a father. All the explanations in the world cannot reverse that. Leave her alone, Valentine.'

'But...' Valentine began to speak, but let his words trail off.

Victoria trembled, her heart thumping against her ribcage. Please God let me have convinced him, she thought. Please don't let Rosie suffer any more humiliation. She pictured the look on Rosie's face if Valentine were to go to Moore Street and find her living with Cathal O'Malley. She waited.

'You are right,' he said, looking at her as if suddenly coming to his senses. 'I was being selfish.'

He fiddled with his hat as he spoke, not meeting her eye, like a young boy caught out in some mischief. Victoria felt a rush of pity for him.

'I only wanted her to think well of me,' he went on. 'I didn't stop to think that my presence might open up old wounds best left alone.' He stood and reached into his pocket, took out an envelope and handed it to her. 'If … if I should not come back from the war, will you please give her this? I want to make sure she fully understands why I had to do what I did.'

She looked down at the envelope and then up at her brother with a wan smile. 'But of course you'll come back, Valentine.'

'Just please make sure she gets it in the event… You see, I still want her to think well of me even if I am dead.'

Victoria pulled him to her in a tight hug. 'You're not going to die, Valentine, don't even be thinking that way.'

After he left, she turned the envelope over in her hands. What could Valentine possibly want to tell Rosie that she did not already know? Well, it didn't matter. She would never have to give it to Rosie. Valentine would survive the war. She would not allow herself to think anything different.

Valentine's unexpected visit roused the residents of Ennismore out of their torpor. At the sound of his carriage Lord and Lady Ennis rushed to the front door, followed by Sofia carrying Julian while Lady Louisa brought up the rear. They stood peering out through the sheets of rain that rose and fell in waves across the driveway. Mr Burke emerged carrying a huge umbrella and made his way through the puddles to the door of the carriage.

'Welcome, my lord,' he boomed as Valentine climbed down. 'Welcome home.'

Valentine waved away the umbrella and stood smiling, his head thrown back, the rain drenching his uniform.

'Thank you, Burke. It's good to be home. I have certainly missed it.'

He stood inhaling the familiar rich, damp smells of sodden earth, stacks of cut turf and steaming hides of wet cattle.

'Papa, Papa!' Julian struggled out of his mother's arms and toddled towards Valentine, his dark eyes alight.

Valentine lifted the child and swung him around causing him to squeal. 'Look at you, my darling boy. How big you have grown!'

Carrying Julian, he walked towards his family, who stood arrayed on the front steps. He kissed his mother and aunt on the cheek, shook hands with his father and pulled Sofia to him in a warm embrace. She returned his kiss quickly then took Julian from him. 'My goodness, you are both soaked,' she laughed. 'Come in before you get your death of cold.'

Burke followed them into the hallway, carrying Valentine's bags.

'Put those down, Burke. Where's the footman?'

'We have no footmen left,' said Lady Louisa.

'Then I shall take them up myself,' said Valentine cheerfully, wrestling his bags from an indignant Mr Burke.

Lord Ennis winked. 'Indeed, Burke. You must save your strength for your upcoming nuptials.'

He turned to his son as Mr Burke blushed. 'Mr Burke and Mrs Murphy have become engaged, Valentine. Isn't that wonderful news?'

Valentine grinned. 'It is indeed, Papa. Congratulations, Mr Burke, and to you, Mrs Murphy.'

The housekeeper, who had appeared in the hallway, blushed even more deeply than Mr Burke as she nodded her thanks.

Dinner was a lively affair. Everyone peppered Valentine with questions.

'How long will you be staying?'

'When do you leave for the front?'

'What do you think of young Julian? Hasn't he grown?'

And then the inevitable question from Lady Ennis. 'Have you seen Victoria?'

'Yes, I stopped to see her at Aunt Marianne's yesterday. She is looking very well.'

Lady Ennis shrugged. 'I truly can't understand why she chooses to stay in Dublin.'

'As I recall, dear sister, you are the one who sent her away,' said Lady Louisa.

'I would have thought she had learned her lesson by now and would be begging to come home. But as it is, she hardly even writes, let alone visits.'

'I imagine she is getting along splendidly with Dr Cullen,' put in Lord Ennis. 'She seemed quite excited about the prospect when I left her. I suppose I could contact him to see how she is getting along.'

'I don't think that's necessary, Papa,' said Valentine quickly. 'Victoria may think you're prying. Besides, she seemed very content to me.'

Lord Ennis nodded. 'You make a good point.

Anyway, we shall all be going to the Fairyhouse Racecourse in Dublin this coming Easter for the Irish Grand National. I have a horse running. It would be a capital time for a family reunion.'

Valentine nodded and stood up. 'It's stopped raining, Sofia. Shall we take Julian for a walk in the garden before his bedtime? We can show him the lovely rainbow I can see out there over the lake.'

Everyone turned to look out the window at the hazy arc of luminous colour that had descended from the sky.

'They say it's a sign of good luck,' murmured Lord Ennis. 'God knows we need it.'

While Sofia went to get Julian ready for his walk, Valentine followed his father into the library where they shared a brandy.

'You sound rather glum, Papa. Is everything all right?'

Lord Ennis looked up from his drink with a worried expression. 'I'm afraid things are not all right, Valentine. As you know, cattle and crop prices have been falling for some time. The estate debts are mounting and the banks are not as ready to lend working capital as in the past. And this house is badly in need of repair. The roof is leaking worse than ever and the façade is beginning to crumble.'

'But what can be done, Papa?'

'I've been thinking we might have to sell off some of the land.' He hurried on before Valentine could interrupt. 'The Wyndham Act has been amended to allow the government to offer significant inducements to landlords to sell. John

Killeen has approached me more than once about buying out his tenant farm. He can get a government loan and is offering a fair price. He is a good man and–'

'No, Papa, you can't possibly be serious! You cannot sell Ennis Estates! There must be some other way! I can talk to Sofia – surely she would not want to see Julian's legacy destroyed.'

Lord Ennis set his mouth in a grim line. 'You will stoop to no such thing. I will not embarrass our family by begging for American money.' He paused, then gave Valentine a cold look. 'Perhaps if you'd chosen to stay here rather than enter the army we might have found a way to cope with this together. But as it is I am the one left to bear the brunt of the problem.'

Had Valentine paid more attention, he would have seen a hint of desperation in Lord Ennis's eyes and fatigue in the set of his shoulders. As it was, the young man merely shrugged, his expression telling his father he had heard all this before.

'I'm sorry you think I let you down by joining the army, Papa, but I believe it was my duty.'

His father glared at him. 'And what about your duty to this family?'

Valentine glared back at him. 'Oh, I think I've more than done my duty towards this family.'

Lord Ennis was about to challenge Valentine's words when Julian burst into the library followed by Sofia. Valentine opened his arms and the child leaped into them. 'Let's go see the rainbow, Julian,' he said. 'It's supposed to bring good luck to anyone who makes a wish on it. But you have to believe it will come true. Do you understand?'

The child nodded happily. 'Yes, Papa.'

Below stairs the kitchen staff admired the rainbow from the open door.

'A sign of good luck,' said Mrs O'Leary. 'Young Master Valentine's brought the luck with him.'

'Let's hope so,' said Anthony Walshe, puffing on his pipe. 'We could all do with some of it, the way things are.'

'I'd hoped he was home to say the war's over,' went on Mrs O'Leary, 'but it sounds like it's just really beginning.'

'Aye, and there'll be no help for us here at all,' said Sadie glumly. 'There won't be a lad left within miles looking for work as a footman. They're all away to Dublin either to join up with the army, or to join the Volunteers like Brendan.'

Immelda put down her mending. 'Brendan and the rest of them is fools if they think they can beat the British Army. They're just hotheads, the lot of them.'

'I wouldn't be so sure, Immelda,' said Anthony. 'From what I hear they have some mighty support among some rich Protestants in Dublin – the likes of Mr Yeats and Lady Gregory from Galway among them.'

Immelda scowled. 'Ah sure, aren't they just all the idle rich looking to amuse themselves. When it comes right down to it they'll side with the British just as they've always done. Look at how Victoria treated our Brendan. And even worse, look at how they crucified Rosie when they found out who she was. Blood's always been thicker than water.' She finished stitching the seam and noisily bit off the thread. 'Besides,' she went on, 'I doubt it will make much difference to us if they rise up or not. We're still all going to be stuck here with bloody Ennismore crumbling down around us.'

They sat, each lost in their own thoughts, as the kitchen clock chimed the hour. Outside, the rain began again. Mrs O'Leary drained the last of her tea. 'Well now, there goes the rainbow and the good luck with it.'

CHAPTER 27

One morning, not long after Valentine's visit, Victoria arrived at the Union to the usual suspicious glances of her co-workers. In spite of her hard work, she knew that the other nurses didn't think highly of her. Although she had said nothing about her background, just her accent and bearing set her apart from them – and the fact that she worked without pay. Had she been a married woman of the same class they might have taken it in stride – another rich matron determined to 'do good' – but as a young single woman they were left to assume she was from the wealthy class. She had tried hard to be diligent, keeping longer hours than most, accepting any task no matter how distasteful, showing respect to the other nurses and patients alike, but still they viewed her with suspicion.

This morning was no different. The head nurse gave her a tight-lipped nod and walked away.

Victoria sighed and went about her duties, grateful that the hospital waiting room was, as usual, crowded with patients. If she kept busy she would not worry about Valentine, or find herself daydreaming about Brendan. She was in the midst of taking the temperature of yet another hollow-eyed, feverish, sullen young mother when the head nurse came to find her.

'Miss Bell, I need you to assist in the operating theatre. At once.'

Her voice was crisp. Victoria swallowed hard.

'But I have no experience there, Sister,' she began. 'Surely they need someone with experience.'

The head nurse looked at her sternly. 'Do not question my judgement, Miss Bell. We are short-staffed, and of the nurses available you are the best option. Go now. They are waiting for you.'

Victoria was in a daze as she hurried to the operating theatre. Part of her was thrilled that the head nurse had shown such faith in her – it meant that her work was more than satisfactory – but the other part of her was terrified. She blinked as she opened the doors to the theatre where bright lights shone down on a patient in a bed, surrounded by a group of masked doctors and nurses. She went immediately to a sink to scrub up while another nurse helped her with her surgical mask and gown. The smell of blood mixed with disinfectant nearly made her vomit, but with effort she held it down. She trembled as she edged in beside the nurse who had helped her dress. The nurse turned and smiled at her.

'Don't worry,' she smiled, 'you'll be all right.

Just hand me the instruments as I ask for them.'

Victoria nodded. As the operation progressed her tension eased. She watched with fascination as the surgeon cut through the patient's flesh, examined his organs, and excised what appeared to be a small tumour. Then he deftly sewed up the cut and nodded to the nurses. Victoria was impressed not just by the surgeon's apparent confidence, but by the gentleness with which he examined the patient's body. He had a tall, commanding presence, and though she could not see his face behind his mask, she was sure it was kind. When the operation ended, he walked by her and stopped.

'Well done, young lady,' he said. His voice was warm and genial.

Victoria blushed.

'Thank you, sir.'

He threw his head back and laughed. 'Ah, I've not been knighted yet, miss. Mr O'Malley will suit me just as well.'

Victoria looked up at him. She recognized his County Mayo accent at once. And she recognized his name. Could this be Cathal O'Malley – the man she had seen in the play at the Abbey, the man Rosie was said to be living with? She told herself it was just a coincidence. Wasn't O'Malley a common name? She went about her business of stripping off her mask and gown, and scrubbing her hands. When she walked out into the corridor, however, she stopped dead in her tracks. It *was* him. There was no mistake. He had removed his mask and gown and was chatting with one of the nurses. She recognized the handsome face, broad shoulders and shaggy brown hair. Instinctively, she put her head down and rushed past him and back to the hospital waiting room.

For the next week she could not get Cathal O'Malley out of her mind. At first, she could not understand her obsession with him. Why did she care about this man? He was Rosie's friend, not hers. Her mind should be on Brendan or Valentine – and it was – but every now and then an image of Cathal O'Malley would interrupt her thoughts. As she thought about it, she realized that he represented her only connection with Rosie. She missed her friend dreadfully. All the anger of her last encounter with her had evaporated and she longed to see her, talk to her, share secrets as they had done so many years before. She made up her mind to confront Cathal O'Malley.

She did not have to wait long. One evening, as she exited the Union and walked out under the old archway, he appeared beside her.

'Aren't you the lass assisted us at the operation last week?' he asked.

Victoria nodded. She kept walking without breaking her stride. He kept up with her.

'I never got your name. I'd like to ask for you again next time we're short-staffed. You were far more efficient than most of the girls they send us.'

She looked up at him. 'Victoria Bell,' she said.

She waited to see would her name register with him. Evidently it did not.

'And where do you hail from, Miss Bell?'

'County Mayo,' she said.

He threw his head back and laughed. 'Ah, sure shouldn't I have guessed 'twas a Mayo girl was in it? 'Tis hard to beat them.' He halted and turned to face her. 'Cathal O'Malley, a County Mayo man, at your service, miss.'

Victoria took a deep breath. It was now or never.

'I believe you know a friend of mine from County Mayo. Her name is Rosie Killeen. Well, her name is Roisin, actually, but I've always called her Rosie.'

He blinked at her. 'Rosie? You know Rosie? But I thought she had no friends in Dublin, save for myself, of course, and her sister Bridie.'

Victoria grew bolder. 'We grew up together at Ennismore,' she said. 'You may know the place. Anyway, we were great friends in childhood, but now...' she hesitated, 'well we've fallen out and I haven't seen her in a year. I heard you and she are living together.'

Victoria tried to sound casual, but she knew she had not succeeded. The tension in her voice was evident. Cathal O'Malley took her arm.

'Can we sit down somewhere and talk about this?'

They sat together on a bench not far from the Union. It was twilight, but she could see his face plainly enough. He was indeed a handsome man. No wonder Rosie was drawn to him. At Cathal's urging she told him more details of how she and Rosie had come to know each other. She left out any details she thought might be embarrassing to Rosie.

'And when I came to Dublin, I went to Bridie's house to find her,' she finished up, 'but she wanted nothing to do with me. We had a quarrel and I haven't seen her since. I was hoping you might give her a message from me. Tell her that I miss her and long to see her again.'

Cathal O'Malley had listened to her in silence. Now he leaned back on the bench and gave a long sigh. He took out a cigarette and lit it. He offered her one but she refused. She waited.

'Well isn't Roisin Dubh the dark horse,' he said, sounding bemused.

'Please, Mr O'Malley, I don't want her to be upset with me for telling you all this. I didn't know how much you knew.'

He patted her arm. 'Don't be fretting now, Miss Bell. I'll be as tactful as a diplomat.' He puffed on his cigarette then ground the stub out beneath his boot and stood up. 'I'm glad to have met you, Miss Bell, and I'm glad to know that Rosie has a friend like you in Dublin. I'll do what I can to bring her around. But you know Rosie as well as, if not better, than I do. She can be as stubborn as a donkey on the bog, so she can. Goodnight, now.'

'Goodnight, Mr O'Malley,' she murmured.

She sat on the bench and watched him disappear into the dusk. At length she stood up and dusted off her clothes. Well, it was done. She had left her future with Rosie in Cathal O'Malley's hands. She hoped he could be persuasive. But as he had said, Rosie was stubborn. There seemed no point holding out a lot of hope.

Rosie had moved into Cathal O'Malley's house the day after Micko's assault. She had woken up the morning after she had arrived on his doorstep and gone back to Foley Court for her belongings. Bridie was alone with young Kate. She watched

316

silently as Rosie threw her clothes in a bag along with a few other personal effects. At last Rosie stood before her sister.

'I have to leave, Bridie.'

Bridie nodded. 'I know you do.'

Rosie had said nothing about the incident with Micko, but it was clear to her that Bridie understood. She reached out and took her sister's hands in her own. Bridie had grown gaunt and hollow-eyed. Poverty and circumstance had driven all the spirit out of her. Where was the Bridie who had been such a strong, feisty girl? Rosie choked back tears as she spoke.

'I've left the address where I'll be in case you need it. And I'll get money to you as often as I can.' She sighed. 'I wish I could take you and Kate with me away from this hellhole, but...'

Bridie nodded. 'Ah now, stop that, Rosie. Sure you know as well as I do that Micko would never let us go. If we left here he'd hunt us down and drag us back. And besides, as Ma always said, I've made me bed and I have to lie in it.'

Rosie found herself wishing Micko Delaney dead. If she was a man she would have choked him with her own hands. She bit her lip and nodded. Letting go of her sister's hands she went over and knelt down and enfolded young Kate in her arms.

'You get better now, that's the girl.'

The child looked up at her with wide eyes so like Ma's that it caused Rosie to choke up again. Quickly she got up, lifted her bag and left the room.

When she returned to Cathal O'Malley's house

317

that afternoon she found that he had prepared the third-floor bedroom for her. Clean linens were on the bed, along with fresh towels and a jug of water. The room was swept and the window left open to air it out. And on a small dresser sat a vase of fresh-cut flowers. She sat down on the bed and began to weep.

As the weeks passed they settled into a routine. Each came and went of their own accord. He had usually left by the time she rose in the morning, and often was not home when she returned at night. He had presented her with a key to her bedroom door, and each night she locked it as if locking out the world. Still, she found herself listening for his key in the front door and his tread on the stair before she could settle into sleep.

Sometimes he brought company home with him. Often she heard men's voices rising from the parlour; other times the throaty laughter of a woman drifting up from his bedroom beneath hers. It was the woman who caught her attention, even though she told herself it was none of her business. She lay in bed wondering what the woman looked like and curious about her relationship with Cathal. Was she a prostitute, or a casual acquaintance, or was she someone from his past whom he cared about? The thought that Cathal might have a romantic past that she knew nothing about caused a twinge of jealousy to creep in before she forced it away. Hadn't she been the one who had been insulted when he first invited her to live in his house? Hadn't she readily agreed to their 'rules' of privacy and insisted on locking her door every night? Still, as time passed, she could not deny her growing attraction to Cathal O'Malley.

She knew she had become the main subject of gossip around the *Sword* offices and among members of the Gaelic League. The old Rosie would have been mortified with shame at such speculation, slinking past her colleagues, aware of the abrupt halt in the conversation her appearance brought. But now, she held her head high, smiled and greeted them and, as so often happens when gossip finds nothing to feed on, it dissolved. She went about her work as diligently as always, and found an ever-widening audience for her columns. For now, she was content.

In time she grew so comfortable around Cathal that she often invited him to share a meal she planned to cook. On those evenings he would present himself early at the kitchen table, looking pleased and filled with compliments. After dinner, as they sat by the fire in easy conversation, Rosie had a sensation of contentment mixed with a vague longing. As he talked, she could not help becoming lost in fantasy, imagining the feel of his hair under her fingers, or the touch of his hands on her body, or how it would be to lie naked with him, his long limbs entwined around her own. With difficulty she would bring herself back to the conversation, nodding when appropriate, asking a question here and there.

The feelings took her by surprise. The only fantasies she had ever had involved Valentine. Could they so easily now be transferred to Cathal? And yet she sensed this was different. Her thoughts about Valentine had been ethereal, even childlike, but Cathal was a real flesh and bone man and he was here beside her every day.

She wondered if he was imagining similar things. Certainly she felt she was not mistaken when she noticed how his hands lingered too long on hers when she handed him a dish, or when she turned suddenly and caught him gazing at her. Still, she told herself, they had made a pact, and she would not be the one to break it.

As wide-ranging as their conversations were, they were both careful not to touch on personal matters. Rosie never asked about his past, or how he spent his time during the day. He had never asked these questions of her, either. And that might have continued had it not been for Cathal's chance encounter with Victoria at the Union hospital. It so happened that evening Rosie had cooked a stew and baked soda bread and she had invited Cathal for supper.

'I met a friend of yours today,' he began when they had settled by the fire in the parlour.

Alarm bells sounded in Rosie's head. He may only have been referring to one of the Butler sisters or another League member, but her past was never far behind her.

'Who was that?' she asked as casually as she could.

'Victoria Bell,' he said. 'Lovely girl. She said to tell you that she misses you and would love to be friends again.'

He leaned back in his chair and stretched out his legs before the fire.

Rosie's mind raced. Victoria? Where on earth had he met her? What had she told him about their past? What had she said about Valentine? Had she told him how Rosie had tried to pass herself off in society? Each time a new thought entered her head, her panic grew.

'I met her at the Union hospital. She works there.'

'And what were *you* doing there?' she said, trying to deflect the subject.

'Ah, just some business. Anyway, she's a lovely girl. Brought up at Ennismore.'

Rosie nodded and said nothing. She folded her arms in front of her.

Cathal took a sip of his whiskey. 'She told me the two of you were brought up there.'

'I had lessons with her, that's all.'

He smiled. 'Well, that certainly accounts for your fine way with words, and your gentry manners. I never quite took you for a poor farmer's daughter.'

Rosie shrugged. 'What else was she after telling you?'

'Not much more, other than the two of ye were great friends one time.'

'Aye, well that's all in the past now.'

It was Cathal's turn to shrug. 'I'm only the message boy.'

Later that night Rosie lay awake. Why couldn't they all just leave her alone? That life at Ennismore with Victoria and Valentine was over. She had made a new life for herself here in Dublin. Please, God, let her live it without interference. But this was Ireland, she thought, and the past was never far behind the present.

CHAPTER 28

Rosie gazed from the window down on to snow-covered Moore Street. It was the day after Christmas, St Stephen's Day, and the normally bustling street was almost empty. The gaudy flower and fruit carts were covered by tarpaulins upon which the snow had piled up in pristine drifts. Church bells rang across the silent city as the old mantel clock chimed five times in the parlour. She turned back from the window. Cathal had gone out on an errand and the house was quiet. The evening firelight glowed while lighted red candles cast shadows across the room. The earthy scent of pine cones and the tart smell of holly berries mingled with the lingering aroma of yesterday's roast goose.

Cathal had brought the goose home for Rosie to cook for Christmas dinner. She had prepared and dressed it the way Ma used to do and served it with hearty vegetables, followed by a plum pudding and sherry trifle. Cathal was delighted with the spread. He had invited Padraig Pearse, the teacher and poet who was the leader of the Volunteers, and a number of the young Volunteer recruits who were away from home, to join them. To Rosie's surprise, Brendan Lynch had been among them, and when she got over her shock she welcomed him with the rest. As if by silent agreement, no word of Ennismore was spoken between them.

Later, Rosie brought the leftovers and other gifts to Foley Court. She prepared herself for the encounter with Micko – the first since the night he had assaulted her. She refused to let his presence interfere with her attempt to make Christmas a little brighter for Bridie and Kate. He was sullen and silent, regarding her from beneath lidded eyes. The room was bitterly cold, and ice had formed along the window ledge. Rosie was glad she had brought woollen blankets as well as food. She cried when she returned to Moore Street. Later she decided she would entitle her next article 'A Poor Christmas in Dublin'.

As she thought back to the visit, she found herself thinking about home. On St Stephen's Day the young men of the village dressed up in gaudy costumes and carried a pole with streamers upon which rested a basket containing an effigy of a dead wren. The 'Wren Boys', as they were known, called at each house asking for a 'penny for the wren'. Ma would give out red apples and sweets and Rosie would stand at the door watching them as they danced on their way, colourful birds in the snow.

While Rosie was lost in thought, she was unaware of another richly plumed creature making his way towards her house. Valentine Bell, his scarlet uniform brilliant against the white of the snow-covered pavement, strode purposefully towards Moore Street. When the doorbell rang, loud and insistent, Rosie assumed Cathal had forgotten his key. She smiled and ran down the stairs calling out.

'I'm coming, Cathal. Sure you'd forget your head if it wasn't screwed on!'

When she opened the door she froze in place. Valentine stood scowling down at her. With effort, Rosie gathered her wits about her.

'I thought you were in France,' she said.

'Obviously not.'

His tone matched his scowl. What on earth was wrong with him? she wondered. She had never seen him like this – angry, impatient and arrogant. She scarcely recognized him.

'What do you want?' she said, her tone matching his.

'I must speak to you.'

'I told you before, we have nothing more to say to one other. Please go.'

As Rosie attempted to shut the door he put his foot forward to wedge it open. 'Are you alone?' he said.

Irritated, she nodded.

'Then please let me in, Rosie, there's something you have to know.'

She saw that he was shivering. He wore only his uniform, no overcoat like Cathal always wore. The few passers-by in the street were beginning to stare. She realized she could not have a British soldier lingering on her doorstep. She opened the door and let him in.

'I'll give you five minutes to say whatever you have to say, then you must promise to leave.'

A faint look of regret crossed his face.

'Why aren't you in France?' she said, as he followed her up the stairs.

He shrugged. 'My unit has been slow to ship

out, and I appear to be at the end of the list.'

They entered the parlour. Valentine looked around, taking in the cosy fire and decorations. Rosie did not offer him a chair or refreshment. It hurt her heart to treat him like this, but she knew she must. She stood facing him.

'Now say what you have to say and be quick about it.'

It was a moment before he spoke. Then he stood erect, puffed out his chest, and began.

'Since I've been in Dublin, I've been anxious about your welfare.' Rosie opened her mouth to interrupt but he put up his hand. 'Regardless of what you think, Rosie, I still care about you very much. Victoria said she did not know of your whereabouts, so I made my own enquiries. I discovered you were living in this house with a man named Cathal O'Malley.'

'That's correct and I've no intention of moving out. So you can leave now.'

'You may change your mind when you hear what I have to say. I have made enquiries about this man and have discovered some very disturbing things. He is a dangerous man, Rosie, and you must get away from him at once.'

'He's a soldier training the Irish Volunteers. That hardly makes him dangerous, for God's sake.'

'But being a murderer does.'

His words struck her like an explosion, followed by deafening silence. Rosie stared at him in astonishment. He continued speaking, his words clipped and reproachful.

'I have it on good authority he killed a woman in Westport. He was a trained doctor and after he lost his licence he turned to morphine. He is a murderer and drug fiend and you must get away from him this instant. I want you to pack your things and come with me.'

Rosie was gaping at him when she heard a cough from the doorway. She swung around. There stood Cathal. Valentine followed her gaze.

'Who the hell are *you?*' Cathal's voice betrayed a cold fury.

He strode into the room, his right arm tensed and fist clenched as if ready to set upon the visitor. Sensing the danger, Rosie placed herself directly in front of Valentine.

Valentine stood erect. 'Second Lieutenant Valentine Bell of the Irish Guards. I am here to take Rosie away to safety.'

Cathal's jaw tightened. He looked at Rosie and for a moment she thought he was going to push her out of the way and strike Valentine. He appeared to struggle with himself before backing away and glaring at him.

'Bell, is it? From Ennismore then?' The casualness of the words could still not disguise his anger.

'The same.'

Rosie found her voice. 'Cathal. He is making terrible accusations against you. They can't be true, surely.'

Cathal went to the sideboard, taking time to regain his composure. He poured out a whiskey, took a sip, and turned towards her.

'I am not in the habit of defending myself to British soldiers, but for your sake, Rosie, I will.' He paused and drew a deep breath. 'It is true I killed a woman in Westport.' He ignored Rosie's cry. 'That woman was my wife. She was in a very difficult labour with our child. She needed a caesarean. I insisted on operating on her myself even though I was not sufficiently qualified to do so. They both died on the table.' He spoke with no emotion, as if reading from a report. 'I blamed myself. I started taking morphine – to ease the guilt and dull the memory. And while I never lost my licence, I stopped practising medicine.'

'But why didn't you tell me, Cathal?' Rosie whispered.

'Why would I? I've tried to forget that part of my life.'

Valentine spoke up, scarcely hiding the triumph in his voice. 'You see, I was telling you the truth, Rosie.'

'Yes, he was,' said Cathal. 'And I won't blame you if you want to leave with him.'

Rosie looked from one man to the other. She didn't know who she was angrier with – Cathal for withholding this from her, or Valentine for telling her.

'Was that what you were doing at the Union? Operating?' she said to Cathal.

He nodded. 'Aye, they're badly in need of doctors over there. It took me a while to get back my nerve, but I've not killed anybody on the operating table yet.' He gave a wry laugh.

A sudden fury engulfed Rosie. She pushed Valentine backwards, beating her fists on his chest. 'Get away from here now, Valentine Bell, and never come back. All you Bells have ever done is try to ruin my life. Get away!'

Rosie shoved Valentine towards the door. He

looked at her in alarm, much of his earlier hubris gone. He bowed. 'As you wish, Rosie.'

When Valentine had gone, Rosie and Cathal sat in silence beside the fire listening to the ticking of the mantel clock.

Darkness had fallen that evening when Cathal finally began to speak. He spoke quietly, as if to himself.

'Her name was Emer,' he began.

Rosie awoke from her doze and sat erect in her chair.

'She was the most delightful girl I had ever met. She had a contagious laugh. I was a very serious lad back then, not much for laughing, but I couldn't help myself when she was around. Ah, she loved a joke. She'd play tricks on me and then she'd laugh and laugh. I still can hear the sound of it – like a waterfall.'

He paused and took a drink from the glass of whiskey on the table beside him. 'She had the face of an angel, ah, but she could be a divil when she wanted. She was stubborn and fearless and opinionated. Sure she didn't give a damn what people thought of her.'

He fell silent for a moment, as if remembering some long-ago incident.

Rosie waited.

'I met her in London where I was studying medicine. Her da was one of the professors. She was Irish though, Dublin born. She was like a child when she came back to Ireland with me and saw the west for the first time. I was posted to a rural area miles away from Galway city. I thought she'd be bored, but she was delighted with everything – the mountains, the bogs, the wild Atlantic. I saw everything through new eyes – her eyes.'

Rosie smiled in spite of herself as she imagined this young girl falling in love with the west of Ireland.

'We were very happy in each other's company, but we were overjoyed when we learned we were to have a child.' Cathal stirred and seemed to register Rosie's presence for the first time. 'Did I tell you that despite her fearlessness she had an irrational dread of hospitals? Odd, isn't it, her being a doctor's daughter and a doctor's wife?'

Rosie nodded her head in the dark.

'All went well enough in the beginning. We engaged a midwife and waited for her time to come. But when it did, it was evident something was wrong. She was in labour for a day and a night and still no sign of a child. By then I knew she needed a caesarean but she refused to let me take her to the big hospital in Galway. So I decided to do the operation myself, with the midwife as my nurse.'

He uttered a sudden cry which startled Rosie.

'Ah, why did I think I could do it? Arrogant young eejit – I should have known better. I was a qualified surgeon, but I'd never done a caesarean before. Why didn't I take her to the hospital no matter her protests? Why did I wait so long? I should have acted sooner. I let her stay in labour far too long.'

Rosie fought back tears as she listened. His grief was raw and there was nothing she could say to help him. She wanted to enfold him in her arms. She began to get up, thinking he had

329

finished his story, but he was not done. The worst part was yet to come.

'The child was alive when I took him,' he uttered between sobs. 'I laid him on her chest and she looked up and smiled that beautiful smile of hers. And then she was gone. And ... and within minutes the child was gone too.'

Rosie was crying openly now, along with Cathal. He had finished speaking. He did not have to explain to her about the morphine addiction and how he had lost himself. His guilt had crushed him. She wanted to tell him it was not his fault, that what he had done was out of love for Emer, but it would have done no good. Her forgiveness would not matter – he had to forgive himself.

She stood up and walked to him and sat down on the edge of his chair. She put her arms around him and rocked him as he sobbed, his head buried in her chest. Her thoughts turned to Valentine. How could she ever forgive him for resurrecting Cathal's pain?

CHAPTER 29

At the dawn of 1916 a casual observer in Dublin may still not have noticed the growing unrest that seethed beneath the city's surface. The war, which was supposed to last only six months, dragged on, casualties mounting every day. The Home Rule Bill, which would have given Ireland some measure of self-determination, still lay in limbo.

Nationalist ardour gained traction in Dublin and across the country. Enrolment in military organizations grew – farm boys from rural counties signing up alongside teachers, clerks, poets and scions of the Protestant Ascendancy – all with the same goal of overthrowing English rule. Dubliners, with typical scepticism, dismissed the notion out of hand, calling the Volunteers chancers and dreamers.

Victoria heard all this bantering as she went about her daily business at the Union and was inclined to agree. But for Brendan and his comrades it was a deadly serious proposition. After the night he and Victoria met at the Abbey Theatre, they had become constant companions. They lingered in small, dark pubs or in cafés or, when the weather improved, strolled through Phoenix Park or rode a tram to the beach at Sandycove.

They were a world unto themselves in which their social differences were of no account, where being together and in love was as natural as rain, and where no clouds dimmed the future they dreamed of. Even at night, when she was alone in bed, Victoria refused to let doubt enter her mind. Why should she not be with Brendan? Why should she not support the coming revolution as fiercely as he did? And when it was over, and Ireland was independent, why should she not marry him? Anything was possible in this safe little world they had created.

But as the threat of an uprising grew, Victoria found herself growing more and more torn about Brendan's revolutionary talk. She continued to let him think that she supported him, but when she was alone, grave doubts began to creep into her mind, and she found herself thinking more and more about her family. If the Volunteers and their comrades were successful, would such a revolution give rise to more violence around the country? What would happen to Ennismore? She still loved her home passionately and would not be able to bear it if the old house and her family came to harm.

And then there was Valentine. She had thought him safe while he was delayed in Dublin and had prayed the war might be over before he shipped out to France. But now, with her brother still part of the Dublin garrison, he would also be brought into the conflict. She could not bear the thought that her beloved brother and the man she loved would be enemies. How was she supposed to choose between them?

How could she explain to Brendan that her concern for her family and Ennismore did not mean that she wanted to go back and live there in the way she had in the past? She loved her freedom in Dublin, and she loved Brendan. She would live with him anywhere. But she knew that Brendan saw love and loyalty as the same thing. How was she ever to make him understand?

For the first time, Victoria found herself suspended between two worlds. She thought of Rosie. This was exactly the fate Rosie had suffered. She had never fully understood it until now. Sympathy for her friend swept through her. She wished that she could talk to her. She had heard nothing from Cathal O'Malley, so assumed Rosie still did not want to see her.

At last she could stand it no longer. She had to be honest with Brendan.

'I need to talk to you, Brendan,' she began one evening as they sat in the snug in Toner's – the same private snug where Rosie had once sat with Cathal.

Brendan smiled. 'I thought that's what we were doing, darlin'.'

'This is serious, Brendan.'

He gave her a look of mock alarm and knocked on the partition to signal the barman. 'In that case I think we need another drink.'

'I told you. This is serious. Please.'

He stared at her, his dark eyes alert, reminding her of the way he had first looked at her back in the servants' hall at Ennismore – wary, but with a hint of passion.

'It's about the revolution,' she began. Then the words poured out of her – all the anxieties she had been hoarding up alone at night – her fears for her family, and Ennismore, and Valentine. 'And I don't want to have to choose between all of you. I just can't do that,' she finished up.

Tears filled her eyes as she looked up at him. He said nothing. The barman arrived with two lagers and disappeared. She waited, searching his face for some indication of his reaction. He picked up his glass and took a long slow sip, all the while his eyes never leaving her face. She could not guess what emotions were coursing through him and was suddenly fearful that she had lost him forever. When he finally spoke his voice was cold.

'Well, well. They say the leopard can never change its spots. I should have realized it's the same with the gentry. So, I've let you make a fool of me again, Victoria Bell – first beyond at Ennismore and now in Dublin.'

She began to protest but he put up his hand to silence her.

'You're a very good liar, I must say. You really had me believing you were behind me all the way, that you had left the gentry life, and that you loved me.' He swallowed noisily as if holding back tears. Then he laughed. 'And like an eejit I believed you. I believed you were ready for a life with me when all of this is over. But all the while you were making a fool out of me. All that sweet talk about getting married. It was all shite.'

He fixed his eyes on a point over her shoulder. 'I saw Rosie at Cathal O'Malley's house on Christmas Day last. Now there's a girl knows who she is and where she came from, no matter how much your kind tried to spoil her. She's even joined the Cumann na mBan, the women's auxiliary. She knows where her loyalties belong. She would never stoop to lying about it the way you did.'

'But, Brendan, I *do* love you. And I *have* left the gentry life. I wasn't lying about that part.'

He shoved his chair back from the table and stood up. 'For God's sake, Victoria, no more of this. You've made yourself plain. I'll never belong in your world, nor you in mine. And that's an end of it! Go back to your own kind and leave me alone!'

Before she could answer, Brendan had thrown some money on the table, reached for his jacket, and stalked out, leaving the snug door banging on its hinges. She stared after him, unable to move.

The barman came in, took the money and collected the glasses. He gave her a sympathetic look.

'Take your time, miss,' he said, 'sure there's no rush.'

Eventually, she rose and left the pub. She walked in a daze towards Fitzwilliam Square, turning every word that was said over and over in her mind. She had hoped against hope that Brendan would accept her love without insisting on her loyalty to the revolution. But deep down she had known he would not. He had confused her lack of loyalty with an unwillingness to abandon the gentry way of life. She balled her fists, suddenly angry. Why did he have to be so stubborn? Why did she have to fight to prove herself to him?

The anger fuelled her and she walked faster. But by the time she reached Aunt Marianne's house a heavy, dark blanket had wrapped her in a cocoon of despair from which she would not soon emerge.

CHAPTER 30

Rosie awoke to the sound of sobs coming from the room below. It was the middle of the night and she thought surely she was dreaming. She turned over and pulled the bed covers up to her ears but still the sound persisted. This was no dream, she realized, it was Cathal.

In the days following Valentine's visit, she noticed changes in Cathal's behaviour. His vigorous cheerfulness had ebbed, leaving behind only a faint politeness of manner. He spoke to her as if he didn't know her. Valentine's revelations had become a wall between them. Since that first night when Cathal had explained to her what had happened with Emer, he had not spoken of it again.

Rosie desperately wanted to talk about it in the hope that it might help him, but each time she broached the subject he cut her off. She thought if she told him about her own past, it would open the way for him to reciprocate. But although he listened attentively to her story of life at Ennismore, her humiliation at the hands of Lady Marianne, and Valentine's betrayal, he remained silent.

Around the offices of the *Sword* the whispers began. Cathal appeared to have lost all interest in the Volunteers. He missed meetings, and when he did appear, people said, his moods swung between euphoria about the uprising and dire predictions of defeat. The Volunteers, they said, who practically worshipped Cathal, were confused and dejected by his unpredictability. Such news distressed Rosie. She realized that Valentine's accusations had brought up painful memories for Cathal, and understood why he might have sunk into melancholy. But something more was amiss, she felt it in her bones.

One evening, when he was away from the house, she slipped into his bedroom. She didn't know what she was looking for, but was determined to solve the mystery behind his behaviour. She tried to suppress the guilt that engulfed her as she tiptoed about the room. She was breaking the trust that had underpinned their relationship since she moved in to Moore Street. He had never once set foot in her room, and it was understood that she would never enter his. Each of their rooms represented a sacred covenant of privacy outside which their friendship was free to blossom.

She was shocked when she saw the unmade bed, the pile of dirty clothing on the floor and the row of empty whiskey glasses on the bedside table. The room smelled of stale sweat and alcohol. She was tempted to open the windows to air it out, but she did not dare. Such squalor did not fit the Cathal she knew – the one who always appeared bright and scrubbed, favoured clean, starched linens, and smelled of good soap and tobacco. She opened a cupboard and found a jumbled assortment of bottles, jars and vials. She assumed they were various medicines left over from his days as a practising doctor. She tried to read the labels, but most were in Latin. She picked through them and was about to close the cupboard door when one label caught her eye. There was no mistaking this one. Morphine! Rosie sank down on a nearby chair, holding the vial with trembling fingers. All at once she knew the truth. Pity washed over her as she tried to imagine what desperation had brought him to this abyss.

'Ah, Cathal, no,' she whispered aloud.

From then on she had watched him closely for signs of his addiction. They were all there – euphoria, confusion, distraction, fatigue. How could she have missed it before? For a while she cursed Valentine, but stopped when she realized the futility of such thoughts. She lay awake at night wondering how she could help him. Victoria came immediately to mind. She was a nurse at the Union hospital. Surely she would know what was needed. But the thought left her as soon as it came. How could she throw herself on Victoria's mercy after the harsh words they had exchanged? She also knew that seeking any outside help would betray the unspoken trust between her and Cathal that their private lives would remain private. She finally realized that any help would have to come from her.

She read everything she could find about morphine addiction – perusing files at the newspaper office and at the library. She even went to a doctor under an assumed name and asked for his advice. What she learned frightened her. She began to understand how relentless and crippling the addiction was, and how nearly impossible it was to overcome. If she was going to help him, she thought, she would have to confront him. His response was as she had feared.

'In the name of God where did you get that notion? 'Tis a rich imagination you have, girl.'

'It's not my imagination. I've been reading up on it, and you're showing all the signs.'

'Ah, so you're a doctor now, are you?'

'No, but I know what I see.'

He banged his fist on the table. 'Enough, Rosie!'

'Please, Cathal. I want to help you.'

'No one can help me.'

Her heart ached for him as he stalked out of the room. She had not dared tell him she found the morphine and had all the proof she needed. Well, if he wouldn't listen to her, she would take the bull by the horns and attack the problem at its source. She waited until she heard the front door close behind him and went immediately to his room. This time the morphine was easy to find, and she slipped the two vials in her pocket and left. Later that night she heard him thrashing around in his room followed by the slam of the front door as he left the house. The next morning he said nothing to her, although she suspected he knew she had taken it. She tried not to think how easy it would be for him to get more at the Union. No matter, she thought, I will not give up that easily. She waited a few days and went back to his room and retrieved two more vials. The third time she tried, the door was locked.

How ironic it is, she thought, when you have nowhere else to turn, you turn to God. In recent years she had done nothing but curse God for her troubles, but now she prayed for forgiveness and asked Him to heal Cathal. She cried as, night after night, she lit candles in the cathedral and bowed her head in prayer. At first she noticed Cathal's symptoms growing worse. His twitching became uncontrollable and he had bouts of vomiting accompanied by alternating chills and sweats. Was God laughing at her? If so, she could hardly blame Him, she thought. The cheek of herself asking for a miracle after all she had accused Him of! But after a time she realized that these new symptoms were signs of withdrawal and she got down on her knees and thanked Him.

It was during those terrible days that Rosie finally admitted to herself how much this man meant to her. Her fear of losing him was overwhelming. She realized that she had not just come to rely on his friendship and protection, she had come to love him. Despite her fantasies about making love to him, and her jealousy when he brought women home, this realization took her by surprise. She had thought she knew what love was with Valentine – a sweet, passionate yearning. But this love was different. Apart from the physical attraction which, before his illness, had been growing palpable between them, this love also expressed itself as a steadfast devotion, based on a mutual respect and concern, and a willingness to reach out beyond oneself and put the welfare of another above one's own. She had never imagined she was capable of such selflessness. And as she thought of Cathal's pain she acknowledged that, while her own life had been painful at times, she had never suffered in the way that he had.

Now, as she lay in bed listening to his sobs, she was overwhelmed with a desperate need to comfort him. She must go to him. She didn't care about their covenant of privacy. He needed her. Before she could change her mind, she slipped out of bed and put on her robe. Clutching it to her, she left her room and padded down the stairs. The door to his room was unlocked. She crept in and closed it gently behind her. It took her eyes time to adjust to the dark. She approached the bed on tiptoe and bent over him. He continued to sob, unaware of her presence. Quietly she lay down beside him and gathered him in her arms.

He murmured incoherently as she held him, at times attempting to cling to her with weak hands that gripped her arms briefly before slipping limply away. Rosie held him tighter. She had

340

strength enough for both of them. He drifted in and out of sleep, shouting as he fought off imaginary demons. Each time he quieted she kissed him gently on the brow. She moved her body closer to his, admitting to herself that she had come not only to give comfort but to seek it. She was unaware until now of how lonely she had grown without the old Cathal. They lay together that night, equal in their desire for the warm comfort of another living, breathing human being beside them.

After that first night Rosie went to Cathal's room often. She was always gone by dawn. She came to think of his bed as a secret place of healing and peace. She lay beside him whispering soothing words while he clung to her, then pushed her away, then clung to her again.

During the daytime Cathal said nothing about her night visits. Rosie supposed he thought it was a dream. But as he began to heal, she realized that he had stopped believing it was just a dream. While he still never mentioned it, she could tell by the way he looked at her – curious, tentative, flashes of passion in his eyes. And when he touched her he let his hand linger more than usual before abruptly snatching it away.

Over the next weeks, his health continued to improve. No more sobs came from his room and Rosie ceased her night-time visits. While she was delighted that he was well again, a part of her was sad that he no longer needed her to comfort him. She was sad, too, that she was now denied the comfort such visits had brought to her. She had resigned herself to the loss, when one evening he knocked on her bedroom door. When she opened it he stood before her, smiling, his hands outstretched. Without a word he led her down to his own room.

Her heart leaped in her chest as he drew her to the bed. Without waiting, he took her in his arms. Even though she did not resist, she knew what was about to happen and she was frightened. She had never made love to a man before although she had a general understanding of such matters from books she had read, and from listening to the awkward, crude couplings of Bridie and Micko. But it was not her ignorance that frightened her – it was knowing that her entire life was about to change. After tonight she would no longer be a girl but a woman.

Until now, when she imagined herself making love it was always with Valentine in some idyllic place – in the woods near the fairy fort, on silk sheets in his bed at Ennismore, or stowed away on a ship to America. They were beautiful, childish fantasies. But now, here in this room, here in this bed, with Cathal naked at her side, his breathing ragged and his arms strong around her, this was no fantasy. She chased away an image of her old parish priest lecturing on purity. She was about to leave that state of purity. She was about to give the gift of herself to Cathal.

Her heart pounded as she edged closer to him. She let him slip her nightgown over her head. His gentleness reminded her of the night he cleansed and bandaged the wounds Micko had inflicted. Slowly her fright ebbed away as a warmth filled her body. She began to touch him, tentatively at first, and then with deliberateness. She remembered how often she had secretly stared at his broad shoulders, his muscular arms and long legs and wondered what it would feel like to touch him. Now she caressed him like a greedy child, her hands travelling over his shoulders and down his torso to his hips and thighs. As she did so, Cathal cried out, a fierce whimper, and pulled her so tightly to him she could scarcely breathe.

Random fears tried to push their way into her mind – was she condemning herself to hell for her mortal sin, what would Ma say if she knew, what if she were to become pregnant – but melted in the fierce heat that blazed between her and Cathal. None of those things mattered. She was powerless against what was happening to her body. Her mind thus emptied, she was free to let all of her physical senses totally engage with this man whom she loved and trusted with her life. They both cried out as he entered her. She moved closer, straining to possess him as he possessed her. They moved together, clutching each other in mutual need for intimacy and release.

Afterwards, she lay in his arms, her head on his chest, listening to the rhythmic beating of his heart. She smiled in contentment. She had given Cathal her most precious gift, and she had given it gladly.

From then on all pretence that their relationship was merely friendship disappeared and they fell into the easy intimacy of lovers.

CHAPTER 31

The Easter race card at Fairyhouse Racecourse featured the Irish Grand National and was the highlight of the racing season. Crowds filled the grounds. Lords and ladies moved easily among farmers and labourers. Women in festive hats and silk dresses, men in tailcoats and in rough, wool jackets, English soldiers in uniform, and jockeys wearing riding silks in a rainbow of colours, all strolled about leisurely, admiring one another. Bookmakers stood on platforms barking out odds, their voices carrying above the music and thudding hooves out on the track. Smells of turf and horse-sweat mixed with intoxicating fragrances of perfumed women amid triumphant roars and raucous laughter. And above all the festivity the sun blazed hot as summer.

Victoria made her way through the throngs of people towards her family's box. At any other time she would have been delighted with the spectacle, but a fog of sadness still gripped her. It had been with her ever since Brendan left. She went about her daily work in a daze, her emotions flat like muted notes on a piano. Aunt Marianne tried in vain to coax her out to social events, but eventually gave up in frustration. The only reason Victoria had ventured to the racecourse today was the chance to see her family, particularly her dear papa.

'My dearest Victoria. How good to see you! How well you look.'

Lord Ennis encased his daughter in a hug more enthusiastic than any she remembered. She smiled up into her father's face.

'It's good to see you too, Papa. I have missed you.'

She held back tears as she looked at her father. His frame was thinner than she remembered, his hair greyer, and lines etched his face. He had aged greatly in a year and she feared he might be ill.

'Come on, your mama is waiting.'

Victoria let her father lead her to a private box on the highest level of the pavilion. Her mother, Aunt Louisa and Sofia sat in a row like so many plumed birds in their large, feathered hats and silk and brocade dresses. Sofia stood up to embrace her while her mother and aunt remained seated so that Victoria had to stoop to kiss each of them on the cheek. Her mother patted the chair beside her.

'Sit, Victoria. I want to hear about everything you have been doing.'

Victoria and Sofia exchanged glances and smiled. Lord Ennis excused himself to place a wager on a race.

'The National is coming up later,' he said. 'I have a horse running named after Julian. Wish him luck. There will be competition from a horse owned by an American fellow. We can't let the Americans win, can we? No offence, of course, Sofia.'

He was ebullient as he went off down the steps. A sense of abandonment filled Victoria as she watched her father leave. She looked around for her brother.

'Is Valentine here?' she said.

Sofia's expression went blank, but Lady Ennis spoke up.

'I expect he is here somewhere with his regiment. Although why he fails to seek out his parents – and of course his wife – is beyond me. But at least he has not been reduced to fighting his way out of a mud-filled ditch in France.'

Victoria arranged her face into a smile. 'So, Mama, do tell me all the news from Ennismore. I'm dying to hear everything.'

For the next hour the conversation flowed easily, from accounts of young Julian's antics, to gossip about neighbours and acquaintances, to the plummeting standards of the staff and to Mr Burke and Mrs Murphy's upcoming nuptials. In an effort to postpone her mother's inevitable inquisition, Victoria kept the conversation going by asking as many questions as she could think of. Eventually she ran out of ideas, and her mother pounced.

'You have been lying to us, Victoria. Your father and I met Dr Cullen at breakfast this morning, and he said you have not been working with his clinic for almost a year. Imagine how embarrassing it was for us to be caught on the back foot. Please explain yourself.'

Victoria swallowed hard. 'It's true, Mama. I left his clinic to work at the South Dublin Union Hospital. I find the work there more challenging. I wanted to tell you, but I was afraid it would upset you.' She took a deep breath and continued. 'I'm enjoying it very much and I am learning a

346

great deal about nursing.'

She paused and hoped she had said enough to satisfy her mother. She was certainly not going to tell her that the Union served Dublin's poor, that the working conditions were deplorable, or, that she was exposed daily to any number of infections and diseases.

Her mother drew her lips into a tight line of disapproval. 'I still don't understand why you would leave the safety of Dr Cullen's clinic where you were surrounded by people of our class just to learn more about nursing. What good will it do you? When the war ends you will give it up and return to Ennismore. It's not as if you plan to make a lifetime career out of it.'

Victoria opened her mouth to say she had no intention of returning to Ennismore but her words would have been drowned out by the roar of the crowds around them as the Grand National race was called. Instead, she stood up with Sofia to cheer on the horses. The race covered some three and a half miles and the horses had to jump twenty-five fences along the way. Her father's horse, Julian, ran well, but he was neck and neck with the American-owned horse, named Fifth Avenue. A horse named All Sorts eventually went on to win. Julian beat Fifth Avenue, but neither horse placed. Victoria was disappointed for her father, but was sure he would at least be pleased that he had vanquished the American horse.

That afternoon, a group of English soldiers, emboldened with the effects of alcohol, mounted the steps near where the Bell family sat. Victoria watched them, craning her neck to see if

Valentine was among them. Her ears pricked up when she caught a snippet of their conversation.

'Eleven o'clock this morning,' one soldier said, 'marched into the city bold as brass and took over the General Post Office, That fellow Pearse stood out in front and read a proclamation declaring a free Ireland, and then they took down the British flag and put up an Irish one. It beggars belief.'

'I heard the local people just laughed at them,' said another. 'Pack of fools the lot of them. They'll get no support from Dubliners, mark my words.'

'Bloody nuisance, I'd say,' put in a third soldier. 'They've occupied the Four Courts, the Union and some other buildings as well. Tried to storm Dublin Castle but they were pushed back.' He sighed. 'They've caused enough of a problem, though, that we've all been ordered back to our garrisons. I, for one, am not happy about it.'

The soldiers continued grumbling among themselves but Victoria had stopped listening. Sudden anxiety pierced through the fog of her sadness. The uprising had begun. She must get back to Dublin at once, and find Brendan. She didn't care that they had parted on such bad terms. She loved him and needed to be with him. She prayed he had not been hurt. In a frenzy she looked around her – how was she to get back? Where was Valentine? Lady Ennis, Louisa and Sofia were staring up at her.

'What on earth's the matter with you, Victoria?' said her mother. 'Are you unwell?'

Victoria turned to her mother. 'Unwell? Yes, Mama, yes I am. I feel faint. I have to go home.'

'You will come with us then. I think we are all ready to leave. We will be back at Ennismore in a few hours and you can take a few days of rest.'

'No!' Victoria realized that she had shouted too loudly. People had turned to stare. 'No,' she said again, trying to control her trembling voice, 'not Ennismore. I must get back to Dublin.'

'But why?' persisted Lady Ennis. 'What is so urgent?'

'There's been an uprising! Didn't you hear the soldiers?'

Lady Ennis's face turned pale. 'An uprising?' She stood up. 'Where is Edward? We must leave immediately. You too, Victoria.'

Victoria was about to protest when Valentine appeared beside her. He put his arm around her and turned stiffly to his family. 'Mother,' he said, 'Aunt Louisa, I hope you are both well.' Before they could answer he took Sofia's hand and kissed her on the cheek. 'It is good to see you, Sofia. And Julian is well?'

Sofia nodded while Lady Ennis and Lady Louisa sat in silent expectation, apparently waiting for Valentine to say more.

Victoria broke the silence. 'Valentine. It's so good to see you. Please. I need your help. I must get to Dublin right away. There's been an uprising and I have to find ... there is someone I have to find to make sure he's all right.'

Valentine's face turned pale. He had obviously not yet heard the news. She waited for his confusion to pass and prayed. He looked at his mother and aunt, let his gaze linger for a time on Sofia, and then turned back to her. At last he spoke. 'Of

349

course. Come with me. I have access to an army motor car. I will drive you into the city if we can get through. Are you ready to leave now?'

'Yes,' Victoria said. 'Oh, thank you, Valentine.'

She turned to her mother, aunt and Sofia. 'I'm sorry. I'll explain everything later. Please say goodbye to Papa.'

With that she took Valentine's arm and together they made their way back through the crowds and to the perimeter of the grounds where his car was parked. He settled her into the passenger seat then took the wheel.

'Dublin it is,' he said.

As they drove, Victoria's earlier anxiety reasserted itself. Where was Brendan? Was he part of the uprising? She knew the answer, of course. He was bound to be in the forefront of all of this mayhem. At first she was angry. Why on earth did Brendan and his comrades have to be so stubborn? Did they not realize the odds against them? But her anger ebbed as she pictured Brendan's glowing face when he had talked about the purpose of the revolution – 'A free Ireland, Victoria,' he had said, 'can you imagine what that will mean?' She was being selfish, she realized, worried only what this could mean for her. Brendan might be killed. If the revolution spread, Ennismore might eventually be destroyed and her parents put in grave danger. She shivered with fear and looked over at her brother.

'What are we to do, Valentine?' she said.

Valentine shrugged. 'If it has begun, there is not much we *can* do.'

Suddenly he pounded his fist on the steering

wheel, startling her. 'I curse the army for delaying my deployment. By rights I should be fighting in France by now – fighting a real enemy, not my own countrymen.' He looked at her and she saw tears of frustration in his eyes. 'Tell me, Victoria, how am I supposed to take up arms against other Irishmen?'

Victoria looked at him in alarm. 'Because they'll kill you if you don't.'

The outskirts of the city were eerily quiet. There were no soldiers to be seen on the streets, nor any Metropolitan police. Victoria looked left and right. She flinched when she caught sight of a dead horse lying on the side of the road.

'One of the Lancers,' said Valentine, referring to the British army mounted division. 'There must have been some fighting earlier.'

'Can we drive past the Union?' she said. 'I want to see what's going on there. I have to go there to work in the morning.'

'I'd advise you to stay home until this thing is over,' said Valentine. 'It won't be safe on the streets for anybody.'

'Can we just go and see it please?'

They drove slowly past the Union. The hospital building was quiet, as were the various old work-house buildings that surrounded it. The light was fading, but Victoria could make out men peering from behind the grimy windows. Was one of them Brendan? The news that there had been little fighting buoyed her hopes but she worried what would happen when the army regrouped and began shelling. She began to tremble.

As they drove on into the city centre they saw

the shattered windows of the shops along Sack-ville Street. Broken glass, discarded boxes, old clothes and other debris covered the pavement. Victoria uttered a cry.

'Looters,' said Valentine. 'It's no wonder they took advantage of the situation. There's not a policeman in sight.'

As he spoke, a few stragglers peered at them. A sour-faced girl, wearing several coats, a huge hat with plumes, and carrying two handbags on each arm, made a rude gesture at them as they passed. 'One can hardly blame them,' said Valentine. 'Many of them have next to nothing.'

Victoria thought of Bridie and nodded.

The car crept past the General Post Office where the uprising had begun. Sandbags filled the windows and an Irish flag flew from its roof, but all else was quiet. Copies of the proclamation declaring a free Ireland that the soldier at the race track had mentioned were tacked up on every post and building.

On St Stephen's Green, a group of men, some with only a bandolier over their street clothes for a uniform, guarded the perimeter, rifles cocked. Victoria spied a couple of women among them. She recognized one of them as Nora Butler, Geraldine's sister. She wondered if Rosie was there as well. Suddenly two of the rebels jumped out in front of them, waving rifles and signalling them to pull over. Instead, Valentine revved the engine and pulled around them.

'They want the car for the barricade,' he said, indicating a makeshift barrier of cars and carts that surrounded the Green.

As they sped past the men lowered their rifles. Victoria caught a glimpse of their faces. They were boys, not men, she thought, they couldn't have been more than fourteen or fifteen. Where was Brendan?

There was no sign of the army. It was obvious from what she had heard out at the races that they had all been caught unawares.

As if reading her thoughts, Valentine turned to her, his face grave.

'It's quiet now but mark my words it will be a different story tomorrow or the next day. The army will have called in reinforcements and they'll be bringing out the heavy artillery. Those poor bastards beyond in the GPO and elsewhere won't stand a chance.'

They drove on in silence. When they finally arrived at Fitzwilliam Square he helped her out of the car. She held his arm, not wanting to let go of the comfort of his presence.

He took her hands in his. 'Be careful, Victoria. I shall wait here until you are inside. Please stay there and make sure you lock and bar all the doors.'

Victoria smiled. He was her big brother again, her gallant protector of their youth. 'Be safe, Valentine,' she whispered as she stepped out of the car.

CHAPTER 32

Victoria slept fitfully that night and rose before dawn. As soon as it was light she would leave for the Union. She had to find Brendan. Lady Marianne and Mr Kearney had left Dublin for the holiday weekend before the uprising had begun and only Celine was in the house. The frightened maid stood in front of her to try to prevent her from leaving. But Victoria pushed past her and opened the front door.

'I will be needed at the Union,' she said firmly. 'There are likely to be casualties.'

The streets around Fitzwilliam Square were quiet. The sun was up and promised another warm day. She walked resolutely towards the hospital, her head up, portraying a confidence she did not feel. When she reached the Union everything looked normal on the outside, just as it had the night before when Valentine had dropped her off. As she entered an older nurse ran towards her, wringing her hands.

'Victoria, I'm so glad you've come. The rebels have taken over all the buildings, and a lot of the girls are afraid to come down here. We have almost no nursing staff. And we have only a few doctors – many of them were out of town for the holiday and can't get back through Dublin.' She blessed herself. 'I don't know how we're going to manage when the casualties come in. I can only pray to God this thing is over quick.'

Victoria wanted to look for Brendan but had no chance. She was thrown into work immediately. Uprising or no uprising, Dublin's poor still streamed in looking for care. She worked all morning without a break. At noon she managed to slip out into a side yard. She saw a furtive movement near one of the old workhouse buildings. It was a young man lighting up a cigarette. He wore civilian clothes but Victoria guessed he was with the Volunteers. He had laid a rifle at his feet. Slowly she approached him, her hands held out in front of her in reassurance. She hoped her nursing uniform would lessen his alarm.

'I'm just looking for someone,' she whispered as he bent to retrieve his rifle. 'Brendan Lynch. D'you know him?'

'What are ye after wanting with him?' His country accent almost made her smile. He might have been from Mayo.

'I'm his friend. I heard some of the Volunteers were to be garrisoned here. I just want to see him. To be sure he's all right.'

He was suspicious, she could see. Maybe it was her upper-class accent. She moved closer. 'Please, I just want to know.'

His face softened. 'He was here yesterday all right, but some of the boys were moved out this morning. Reinforcements were needed down at St Stephen's Green and other places. I'm sorry I don't know where they sent him.'

Her heart sank.

The boy's face brightened. 'If I see him, who will I say was asking after him?'

'Victoria,' she whispered.

By late afternoon people were coming into the Union filled with accounts of what was happening in the city. Victoria realized some of it was rumour, but she listened to all they said. The troops were apparently beginning to walk the streets and there'd been some shooting. The rebels were commandeering houses and shooting down on the soldiers from the rooftops. People were scurrying about trying to buy provisions – bread, milk, meat – before the military reinforcements arrived. After that, the fight would begin good and proper, they said. Dublin was still full of looters, they said, and there were still no police to be seen. Victoria could see for herself the spoils of the looting – children wearing coats too big, their mothers in new shoes too small, babies in brand new prams. She wondered if Bridie and Micko had been among them, but somehow she didn't see Bridie stealing, no matter how desperate she was.

By evening she was exhausted. The head nurse told her to go home.

'You'll need all your strength for tomorrow,' she said, 'once the casualties start coming in.'

Victoria nodded. She left the ward and made her way out through the front archway and onto the street. She debated whether to walk by St Stephen's Green. After the incident yesterday, when the rebels tried to commandeer Valentine's car, the thought frightened her. But she had to find Brendan.

'Miss Bell.' A voice startled her. She had almost walked headlong into Cathal O'Malley. She

356

stared up at him. He looked thinner than she remembered, his face drawn, and his back slightly bent.

'A girl like you should be at home where 'tis safe,' he said.

In spite of herself she smiled. 'You sound like my papa.'

Cathal smiled back. 'I suppose I do. But your family will be worried about you. No matter, I'll escort you home now.'

'I'm not going home. I'm going to St Stephen's Green. There's someone I have to find.'

'What? Why?' Cathal studied her, a look of understanding crossing his face. 'Ah, I see the way of it. This boyo you're looking for, Brendan Lynch, is patrolling over there.'

Victoria looked at him in shock. 'How ... how did you know?'

'I know Brendan well. He's talked to me about ... well, about things. He was gutted, poor lad, after the two of you separated.' He put up his hand to stop Victoria's protests. ''Tis none of my business what went on between the two of ye. That's up to yourselves, but you're a foolish girl if you go looking for him now.'

Victoria began to cry. 'I can't help it,' she said, 'I'm still in love with him.'

Cathal's face took on a faraway look. His voice was gentle when he spoke. 'Ah, sure isn't love the most foolish of things, and aren't our hearts just as foolish to follow its lead?'

Victoria smiled and put her hand on his. 'Will you help me find him, Cathal?'

Cathal nodded. 'I will. But not tonight. I have

to be back for a late shift. We have hardly any doctors at all. I will see you here at the Union tomorrow.' He linked her arm in his. 'Now will you walk back to your house with me and promise to go inside and lock the door and stay there for the night?'

'I promise.'

Rosie sat leaning against the chimney on the roof of the Moore Street house holding a rifle on her lap. The weapon belonged to a young Volunteer who had been lying on his stomach on the roof, aiming at British soldiers down on the street below. He had handed it to her when she brought him sandwiches and water and had crawled behind the chimney to take his refreshment. The rebels had taken possession of the rooftops along Moore Street, breaking through walls of adjoining houses to open a clear path from one end of the block to the other, up and down both sides.

Rosie fingered the rifle absent-mindedly as she gazed down at the people scurrying along Moore Street, some dragging children, others carrying bread or baskets of food. They ducked hurriedly in and out of doorways, crossed the street to avoid soldiers and occasionally chanced a glance up at the rooftops where rebels lay in wait. She saw a soldier fall, and watched as his comrades raced to his aid, dragging him into the safety of a nearby doorway. She wondered where Valentine was. She had not thought of him in months but now, as she watched the soldiers, she could not help but see his face. Could she shoot him, she wondered? Maybe, she told herself, but only in self-defence.

All evening the metallic cracking of continuous rifle fire had filled her ears. Now, in the open air, the noise was louder and more urgent. Ambulance sirens blared across the city, mixing with the rumbling thunder of armoured army vehicles. Bricks fell off old chimneys, rattling down to the street. A stray bullet shattered the glass of a nearby window. An old man's head appeared in the opening as he launched a string of curses down on both the rebels and the soldiers. Rosie began to cough. The smoke had locked in her throat and the heavy, humid air had made it hard to breathe. She gave a small shiver. When the weather was like this the memory of the humid night at Foley Court with Micko was never far away.

She handed the rifle back to the young man and crawled around the chimney, carefully making her way over the roof tiles and in through the skylight that led into the attic. A ferocious heat slammed into her as she found the staircase and made her way down to the kitchen. The house was filled with people coming and going – some heading for the rooftop, others gathering in the living room to talk. She recognized leaders of the Volunteers, Citizen Army and the Brotherhood, League members, journalists from the *Sword* – all of them making a great commotion. They talked about the fact that the orders for the uprising were countermanded by one of the Volunteer leaders due to a communication mix-up. As a result, the number of men who showed up was greatly reduced. Cathal's house had become an informal headquarters for the exchange of information.

She was slicing bread for more sandwiches when Cathal appeared beside her. She peered up at him anxiously, as always assessing his health. He looked worn out. She dropped the knife, led him to the table and urged him to sit down.

'Stay there,' she said, 'until I bring you some food.'

Cathal sank down wearily on the chair. 'I can't stay long, darlin',' he said, 'I have to get out and see how the lads are doing. They're taking a lot of fire across the city. 'Tis my duty to go.'

'It's your duty to save lives too, Cathal,' she said. 'You can't be doing both. You haven't the strength for it.'

Since the uprising had begun she worried about Cathal constantly. She tried not to think of the danger he faced every time he went out to check up on the Volunteers. She had almost lost him once, she could not bear the thought of losing him again.

Cathal smiled weakly. 'Ah, sure I'm not for going after the British Army single-handed. But I trained these lads, Rosie, I need to be sure they're doing all right. I'm worried for them. I can't abandon them. I don't want to see harm come to any of them.' He sighed and bit into the sandwich she set before him. 'None of us expected the bloody army to put up such a fight. Sure can't they see these are only young lads...'

'I understand you feel a responsibility for them, Cathal. I do. But you're only one man. And you are a doctor first.'

She did not add, 'And besides, you'll be safer at the hospital.'

'Aye, I *was* a doctor first, but I lost the right to call myself that a long time ago.'

He bowed his head. Rosie bent over and hugged him. 'How many casualties at the Union?' she asked, changing the subject.

'What? Oh, not so many now, but 'twill get worse. I feel it. The army has dug in. They'll be bringing out the heavy artillery before long. And Pearse and Connolly are not for giving up any time soon. They took a gamble, and now they have to live with it. They're brave boys, the lot of them.'

Rosie made no reply. She sat down beside him and sipped a cup of tea. Rosie had joined the Cumann na mBan, the women's auxiliary, some months before, along with the Butler sisters and other women. She had learned how to shoot a rifle and was ready to do what she could for the rebellion. Cathal had taken to calling her his 'darlin' rebel' and she had laughed. But now that the Uprising had begun she was no longer sure what she thought of the gamble the rebel leaders had taken, especially with reduced manpower as a result of the communications blunder. Many of those boys would be killed before it was over. Maybe even Cathal. She sighed. It was one thing to talk about being willing to pay the price, but when it was being paid in front of your eyes in bloodshed and death, you had to question if the end was really worth that price.

'I saw young Victoria today.' Cathal's voice interrupted her thoughts. 'She's beyond at the Union saving lives when she could be barricaded inside her fancy house on Fitzwilliam Square. More power to the wee lass, she's braver than I

361

would have thought.'

Rosie swallowed hard. She was reluctant to praise Victoria out loud, but deep down she felt a tender pride in her old friend.

'She wants me to find Brendan Lynch for her. Says she needs to see him. They had a bad fight. But she says she still loves him.'

Rosie forgot the momentary pride she felt for Victoria and remembered instead the quarrel they had over Brendan. She was convinced then that Victoria had just been using Brendan. So how had things progressed to this?

'Surely Brendan would never have let himself be seduced by her,' she said aloud.

Cathal laughed. 'I would say they seduced each other. Love is a queer thing, Rosie – as you and I both know. Anyway, I plan to find the lad tomorrow night and bring him to her house – the aunt is away with her fancy man, I gather.'

Rosie shot to her feet. 'No! It's too dangerous, Cathal. For all of you. You owe Victoria Bell nothing.'

'She's your friend, Rosie.'

'I won't stand by while she manipulates yet another person to do her bidding.'

'She's bound and determined to find him, regardless of what I do. I'd rather be there to protect the both of them.' Cathal stood and put his hand on Rosie's arm. 'Sure she's only a lass, Roisin Dubh, like you, but she's innocent, she's not a born rebel like yourself.'

Rosie drew her mouth into a tight line. She was angry with him, but she knew he would do what he wanted.

'I just don't understand your priorities, Cathal.'

He looked at her, a trace of sadness in his eyes. 'Ah, Rosie, that's just your stubbornness talking. Love should always be our priority – 'tis the only thing we can ever count on.'

He took her hand. She looked up at him, tears stinging her eyes. 'My priority is you, Cathal O'Malley. It's you I love.'

'Ah, sure I know you do, Rosie. And I love you, darlin'. So let's not begrudge young Victoria her love for Brendan.'

After he left, Rosie sat back down at the table, lost in thought, indifferent to the hubbub of people that continued to stream in and out of the kitchen. She had been mean and selfish and she was ashamed of herself. Maybe Victoria was right when she had told her it was time for her to stop blaming everyone else for her troubles. Perhaps she had been too quick to judge her friend when it came to Brendan. She sighed. She had allowed such pettiness to destroy her friendship with Victoria, but she must not let it destroy her relationship with Cathal. It was time to let such feelings go before they destroyed her as well.

She rose and made another batch of sandwiches and brought them up to the roof where yet another young rebel bravely faced paying the ultimate price for what he believed in – love of his country.

When the sun came up on Wednesday the people of Dublin arose and crept to their windows. What they saw caused relief in some, and fear in others. The British military reinforcements had arrived. A battalion of weary-looking troops, some smooth-faced as schoolboys, tramped up Sackville Street under a hail of bullets from the rooftop rebels. The rebel rifle fire was met with the ricochet of machine guns. By noon, the sound of cannon fire echoed from the River Liffey as a gunboat shelled Liberty Hall where rebels were garrisoned. Machine-gun fire erupted from behind the windows of the stately Shelbourne Hotel, raining down bullets on the rebels dug into trenches on St Stephen's Green.

And yet for many Dubliners the scene resembled more a pageant than a war. Few had taken the threat of an uprising seriously although the Volunteers had been drilling openly on the streets of Dublin for weeks. How could a rag-tag group of poets and teachers and clerks and farm boys transform overnight into citizen soldiers able to stand up to the British Army? It was quixotic at best and deadly at worst. And thus many Dubliners basked in the afternoon sunshine on their front steps or in their gardens and watched the skirmishes as they would a holiday parade. Their relative ease of passage on the streets on Monday and Tuesday had lulled them into a state of denial. Even the occasional sight of the dead body of an unfortunate civilian lying in the street failed to rouse them.

By Wednesday evening, however, the atmosphere became more sinister. Fires broke out throughout the city. Ambulances carrying the wounded screamed on their way to hospitals. The noise of British machine-gun fire and shelling reached a deafening crescendo. Foodstuffs had run short and people scurried furtively through the streets in search of bread and milk, trying to avoid being caught in crossfire. Many were turned back by soldiers attempting to maintain a curfew. The rebels at the General Post Office held their positions from behind sandbagged windows, returning fire for fire with the army.

It was against this growing danger that Victoria hurried arm in arm with Cathal from the Union to Fitzwilliam Square. The hospital was in turmoil throughout most of the day as more and more injured were brought in by the ambulances. Some were soldiers, some rebels, but most were civilians. All of them were badly injured. The few doctors present had to make life and death decisions on whom to operate. They worked feverishly to complete the procedures while the lights flickered with every boom of cannon fire. Victoria was pulled into the operating theater to assist even though she had only scant experience. With the staff shortage, there was no choice. At first she felt she might vomit at the amount of blood she saw and smelled, but took several deep breaths and forced herself to concentrate on the job at hand. No sooner did she allow relief to fill her than another patient was wheeled in. They saved three of them, but lost the last one. She didn't know if he was a soldier, rebel or civilian, but it didn't matter. She wandered out of the operating room in a daze.

It was dark when she left the hospital and stood inhaling the warm evening air. She realized then that she had hardly thought about Brendan or Valentine, except for a hurried inspection of each injured man who was brought in. Now her anxiety flooded back. Would Brendan even agree to see her? As if in answer to her thoughts, Cathal appeared beside her.

'I'm sorry it's so late,' he said, 'but I had an awful time getting Brendan out of St Stephen's Green. The army have locked themselves in at the Shelbourne Hotel and they're raining bullets down on the lads.'

Victoria gasped and put a hand on his arm. He shook it off. 'We're all right,' he said, 'but we don't have much time. Your boy Brendan is below at Fitzwilliam Square. The maid let him in. He's waiting for you. Come on now.'

Relief surged through her. 'Thank God,' she whispered.

The noise of gunfire seared her ears as the two of them came closer to St Stephen's Green. The Shelbourne hotel, which faced the Green, was bright with the flame of bullets. Every now and then a bullet found its mark and a cry pierced the darkness. Victoria flinched and held on tighter to Cathal. He led her around the perimeter piled with cars and carts and pieces of timber, and on down to Fitzwilliam Square. There, the darkened streets were quiet, but no less sinister. Cathal stood to make sure she was in the front door and then disappeared.

Brendan met her in the hallway.

'Brendan,' she whispered. 'Oh, Brendan, thank God you're alive.'

'Aye, so far.'

They stared at each other for a long moment. She watched him wrestle with the anger that he still obviously felt towards her. But as she watched, the hardness in his eyes disappeared, replaced by a soft faraway look. It was the same transformation that happened each time he had taken up his fiddle to play. She let out a sigh of relief and moved closer to him.

'I'm sorry for what I said, Brendan, about the uprising...'

He put his finger on her lips to quiet her. 'No more of that now, darlin'. You only spoke the truth. At the time I took it as a betrayal of me, but after a while I understood. You're afraid for your brother and your family and your home. If I were in your shoes, sure I'd feel the same. I still love you, and as long as you love me that's all that matters.'

'I do, Brendan, I do.'

He buried his lips in her hair. He reeked of sweat and dirt but she didn't care. She pulled him closer. His lips moved over her brow and cheeks and then met her mouth. His kiss was hungry and hard.

She felt a quiver of fear run through her. She had never seen him this intense, not even in the old days at Ennismore when he had resented her as one of the gentry. There was an urgency in his voice she could not ignore. At length she reached out and took his hand.

'Let's go upstairs.'

When she closed the bedroom door behind them, Brendan took her by the shoulders and kissed her so fiercely she eventually had to push him away in order to regain her breath. She was keenly aware, as must he be, that this was the first time they had ever been truly alone. She sat down on the bed and patted the coverlet. 'Sit here,' she said.

He unbuttoned and removed his uniform jacket, loosened the collar of his shirt and rolled the sleeves up to his elbows. She tried to ignore a sudden urge to touch the dark hairs that sprouted on his forearms. He leaned back against the pillow. He put his arm around her as she lay back beside him and began to talk.

'I have to fight, Victoria, do you understand that? 'Tis not even so much for myself as for my family – my granda, my mother, and everybody like them. We need to have a free country where we can all be equal. We need to be able to make our own laws so that everybody, even the poorest of us, can have an equal chance at a decent life. 'Twas never fair that people like your family had all the wealth. All the land they have was stolen from the native Irish and then they made laws against us so that we could never be educated, or own land, or...'

'But things are getting better, Brendan, you must see that.'

He sighed. 'Aye, I do. But do we have to wait another eight hundred years?'

'Surely Home Rule will be implemented as soon as the war's over.'

'Ah, sure I wouldn't trust the British government as far as I could throw them. They've lied to us before and will again.'

Victoria stroked his arm, finally allowing her fingers to caress the tiny hairs that grew there. There was no anger in his voice now. Instead it

368

was tinged with sorrow. Her heart hurt for him. She spoke gently.

'But you have so few fighters and hardly enough arms and ammunition. Do you really expect you can overcome the British Army?'

He smiled. 'Ah, that's the thing about rebels, Victoria, their actions are always based on hope rather than practicality. Deep down I believe none of the lads expect to win this, but they will fight with all their heart just the same. And sure eventually passion and the right cause can overcome any army.' He paused and looked directly into her eyes. 'We might not win this round. But we will have made a start. And there's other boys will follow us. And eventually all the native Irish will be behind us. And one day we will have a free Ireland.'

'And when this is over we shall be together. I shall never go back to live at Ennismore, nor to that way of life. I belong with you.'

They lay down together then. Victoria sighed as his hands caressed her body. They were still as rough and calloused as when she had first touched them and yet they were gentle on her skin. He murmured words in Irish as he slowly removed her clothing and kissed the length of her body. Fiercely she tore at his clothes until he too was naked against her. All the fantasies that had haunted her back at Ennismore flooded back, unleashed, as she urged him on to make love to her. As her body rose and fell, matching his rhythms, she was aware of a bittersweet mixture of ecstasy and sadness. The cloud of danger that hovered over them heightened the urgency of their coupling, but when they finished a deep and profound sadness pervaded her spirit.

That night they slept beside one another, lost in dreams of tomorrow.

CHAPTER 33

For the next two days Dublin burned. Smoke poured from tenement houses on side streets as the British Army tried to burn the rebels from the rooftops. Flames flickered and grew. City fire brigades remained at their stations rather than risk loss of life from bullets still arcing across streets from rifles and machine guns. The unrestrained flames rose and leaped from building to building and street to street. Soon, much of Sackville Street was engulfed, its stately buildings creaking and crackling against the fire's wrath. Dubliners could only shudder and gaze in awe at the terrible spectacle before them.

By Saturday the worst was over. Bricks and plaster from destroyed buildings littered the streets, while gnarled and twisted steel girders hung like skeletons above the debris. Among the latter was the Metropole Hotel where so many grand balls had once swelled with gaiety. Amazingly, the General Post Office, focal point of the uprising, still stood. Columns of smoke poured from it as the rebels hosed down the roof. But by evening, the persistence of the flames overcame their efforts and eventually the building was engulfed and the Irish Republican flag flickered in the flames and fell.

Rosie had watched all of this from the roof-top of the Moore Street house. Cathal had gone out every day and returned weary every night. They hardly spoke – the physical evidence of the fires and smoke and noise made it clear what was happening. Geraldine and Nora Butler sometimes came and sat with her in the big kitchen. The mood was sombre as the sisters brought information about the killed and wounded. The rebels were paying a terrible toll, they said, but many soldiers had been killed or wounded also. It was not all one sided, they said, in a weak attempt at optimism.

On Saturday afternoon, she ventured out onto the streets, despite Cathal's insistence that she stay put. When she arrived at the ruins of the Metropole Hotel she stood rooted to the pavement. She had expected to feel triumph – this place had represented one of the worst humiliations of her life. But as she looked up at the scarred remains she felt as if she was beholding the corpse of an old enemy. There was no triumph in it after all, just a hollow void where feeling should have been. She moved on up Sackville Street, stepping around piles of rotting rubbish, aghast at the sight of half-burned houses, shattered glass and filthy water running in the gutters. There was blood, too, staining the pavements and walls, a mute testimony to the violence that had gripped the city. She prayed that Bridie and Kate were all right. Foley Court was far enough away from the city centre that hopefully they had escaped the worst of it.

As she returned back down Sackville Street that evening she saw a column of rebels, disarmed and dejected, their leader carrying a white flag. They had surrendered. She stood and watched them go by, escorted by the soldiers to Dublin Castle where they would be arrested. A woman next to her sighed. 'Ah, sure you have to feel sorry for them. I wasn't for them in the beginning, but the poor divils fought their hearts out.' Rosie nodded. She recognized some of the young lads who had fought on the roof. Behind her, the General Post Office continued to burn while tatters of the Irish Republican Tricolour sailed past her on the breeze.

She was within sight of Cathal's house when she saw a commotion outside. Without knowing why, she began to run. Something was terribly wrong. She knew it in her bones. As she arrived at the house a clutch of people parted and let her through. There stood Valentine, his red jacket darkened with the stain of fresh blood. His face was distorted with emotion. She looked down. There on the ground lay Cathal, blood seeping from a wound in his chest. She knelt down beside him. He was barely breathing. A voice not her own began to shout.

'Help me get him inside. For God's sake. Would you have the man die on his own doorstep?' There was a shuffle of feet and outstretched hands as Cathal was raised up and carried inside and up the stairs to the parlour. They laid him out on a sofa and stood uneasily waiting for Rosie to tell them what to do next. She screamed at them all to get

out, and they left quickly. Only Valentine remained, silent and distraught. She had not seen
him follow the men inside. She began to tell him
to bring water and bandages but she knew it
would be useless. He looked as if he were in shock.
Instead she ran to Cathal's medicine cabinet and
took out what she needed. As she attended to his
wound, she had a vague image of the night he had
dressed her own wounds after Micko had attacked
her. How gentle and caring he had been. The
touch of his fingers had lingered on her skin for a
long time afterwards. She turned to Valentine.

'Why did you shoot him?' she screamed. 'For
God's sake, Valentine, why did you do this?'

Valentine shook his head as if waking up from
a dream. 'It wasn't me, Rosie,' he cried, 'I tried to
save him.'

He paused, swallowing hard. 'I was patrolling
with my captain when Cathal came running out
of the General Post Office. We both called to him
to halt, and he stopped and raised his hands. But
... but as he turned to face us the captain raised
his rifle. I knew what he was going to do so I
grabbed his arm to stop him, but it was too late.
He had already got off his shot.' Tears flowed
down Valentine's face. 'I grabbed the rifle before
he could fire again and knocked the bastard
down. Then I dragged Cathal away.'

He looked at Rosie, his eyes pleading with her.
'Please, Rosie, please believe me. There was
nothing more I could have done.'

Rosie took in only part of what Valentine was
saying. Cathal began to moan. 'He should be in a
hospital,' she cried. 'Why didn't you take him?'

'I tried but he wouldn't go. He insisted I bring him home, to you.'

'He needs a doctor. I know nothing about medicine. He needs a doctor.'

Valentine looked at her, wild-eyed. 'I'll try to find one,' he said, 'but I'll go for Victoria first. She will know what to do.'

With that he disappeared. Rosie brought brandy and tried to insert a drop between Cathal's lips. He was ghostly white, and when he did open his eyes they were glassy and unresponsive. He groaned again in pain. She thought of the morphine that she had hidden in her room during his addiction. She raced up the stairs and, returning with the vial, administered a tiny drop.

She knelt beside him and cradled his head in her arms. 'Cathal, please don't leave me,' she whispered.

Darkness had fallen when someone tapped her on the shoulder. Rosie started. She must have fallen asleep. At length the woman bending over her came into focus.

'Victoria?' she whispered. 'Help me.'

Victoria nodded, pushed Rosie gently aside and went to work on Cathal's wound. Rosie watched her as she examined and cleaned it, packed it with gauze and replaced the bandages.

'We must keep pressure on the wound,' she said to Rosie. 'He needs to be in hospital. Valentine was searching for a doctor, but I told him to bring an ambulance. Cathal needs surgery as soon as possible.'

When she had done what she could she went and sat in a chair by the fireplace. She lit two lamps, but the fire was out, and the room was dim. She sat in silence while Rosie cradled Cathal again, keeping her hand on the wound as Victoria had advised. At length, the ambulance siren screeched outside and feet pounded up the stairs. This time there was no fight left in Cathal. He did not resist as they lifted him onto a stretcher.

'Wait,' he said, as they began to move him. He looked up at Rosie. She bent her ear close to his lips.

'We put up a good fight, didn't we, Roisin Dubh?' he whispered.

She nodded, tears flowing freely. 'Aye, so we did, Cathal.'

His breath grew ragged as he filled his lungs to say more. 'Move on from this, darlin'. Don't let anger and stubbornness harden your heart. Open it up to love again – 'tis all that matters in this life'

Rosie bit her lip and nodded through tears.

'I love you, Roisin Dubh.'

Victoria stayed the night with Rosie. They dozed off occasionally, but sleep eluded them. No words were exchanged between them. Instead they sat in silence in the way old friends provide comfort to one another, each acutely aware of the other's presence. As dawn broke, the house began to fill up. Nora and Geraldine Butler made tea while others brought news of the prisoners. The leaders were taken to Kilmainham Gaol – fifteen of them, including Padraig Pearse and James Connolly, leaders of the Volunteers and the Irish Citizen Army. The rest were still at Dublin Castle, but would be sent to jails in England and Wales. One man chuckled as he told of Constance Markievicz, the activist countess from Sligo, who had kissed her revolver before handing it over to a British Army officer. She was one of about two hundred women who had joined in the armed conflict.

Casualty reports were pouring in and, while the numbers were not yet certain, it was clear that they had been heaviest among civilians – two hundred and fifty dead, and over two thousand wounded – most as a result of indiscriminate army machine-gun fire and shelling. Other reports counted rebel dead at sixty-four and army dead at one hundred and sixteen, with an unknown number of wounded on both sides. Rosie paid scant attention to the reports. The only casualty that mattered to her at that moment was Cathal.

At dawn, Victoria left to go to the Union where Cathal had been brought. She arrived back swiftly. Her expression told Rosie all she needed to know. Cathal was gone. Rosie began to shiver, and Victoria wrapped her in a shawl and gave her tea. The other visitors crept around her, rendering her chair a small, isolated island in the middle of the room.

'Sure if the poor cratur hadn't died by a bullet,' whispered one man, 'he'd be awaiting execution beyond in Kilmainham with the rest of them.'

'Ah, he was a fine man, so he was,' said another.

By noon, Victoria left to go home to Fitzwilliam Square and change. She was due back at the Union at one o'clock. She had pressed the crowd at Rosie's house for information on the casualties. Had Brendan survived? If he had, where was he?

At the last minute she decided to go to Dublin barracks instead of the Union and find Valentine.

His first question was about Cathal. Victoria shook her head.

'Poor Rosie,' he whispered.

'I did what I could for him,' she said, 'but even when the ambulance came I knew it was too late. Only a miracle would have saved him.'

They stood in silence for a moment, heads bowed in sorrow.

At length, Victoria spoke. 'Valentine, can you get a list of the prisoners at Dublin Castle?'

He looked at her in surprise. 'Yes, I suppose so. Why?'

'I need to find out if Brendan is on it.'

'Ah, of course. I'm so sorry, I should have realized you'd be worried about him, but with all that's been happening...'

'Please. I just need to know.'

Valentine left her and disappeared through a door. Victoria fidgeted as she waited. Part of her wanted to hear that Brendan was in prison rather than among the casualties. She wanted to know he was alive. But alive, and in prison? What consolation was that?

Valentine returned quickly, a smile lighting up his pale face. 'Good news. He's being held at the Castle.' His smile faded. 'He'll be found guilty of treason, of course, but I doubt that they'll execute him. He'll be sent to a prison on the mainland, most likely in Wales.'

'Is there any chance I can see him?'

Valentine shook his head. 'No, alas I have no power to arrange that. But I promise you I will find out where he has been sent and you can write to him.'

Victoria bowed her head. 'Thank you,' she said.

Valentine moved closer and gave her a kiss on the cheek. 'I'm sorry I can't do more. I know how much he means to you.'

'I love him, Valentine.'

'I'm sure he knows that.'

As she turned to leave, Valentine put his hand on her arm, his expression serious. 'Victoria, there are some things happening here at the barracks that I should warn you about. I cannot predict the outcome at the moment, but I want to be able to count on your support when the time comes. You are the only one of our family who was actually here during the uprising – who saw how things were...'

He bowed his head.

'What is it, Valentine?'

She waited while he appeared to wrestle with a decision. When he looked back up at her, he was smiling. 'It's nothing. I should not have brought it up. You have had enough turmoil of your own this week. My news will keep.'

She left the barracks and walked slowly towards the Union. Her thoughts tumbled over one another. She was curious about Valentine's news, but soon thoughts of Brendan intruded. She should be grateful that he had been spared. But prison? He could be sent away for years – possibly for a lifetime. What was she to do without him?

CHAPTER 34

In early May the fifteen leaders of the Uprising were lined up in Kilmainham Gaol in Dublin and executed. Hundreds more who had surrendered were sent to prisons across England and Wales. As the coffins of the leaders were paraded through the streets of Dublin, public opinion began to shift almost imperceptibly, their earlier ridicule turning slowly to outrage. The swift and stern punishment meted out by the English government had transformed the poets and dreamers of Easter Monday into martyrs.

Victoria went about her work in a daze. Lady Marianne had observed her niece's pallid face and hunched shoulders and insisted she stay in bed and rest. But Victoria ignored her advice. The only concession she allowed was to let Celine escort her to and from the Union each day. On those walks they spoke not one word but Victoria welcomed the support of Celine's steadying hand under her elbow. Numbly, she went through the motions each day – bandaging a wound here, checking for fever there – her hands moving automatically from one patient to another. Her mind, however, was locked in a faraway place, a dim jail cell in Wales where Brendan Lynch stood looking out from behind the bars.

A new virus was making its way through the Dublin slums. More and more patients were presenting with fever and vomiting. Victoria and the other nurses comforted them as best they could. Doctors worried about how quickly the virus was spreading and warned the nurses to maintain the highest standards of hygiene. Even though deaths began to occur, the danger hardly registered with Victoria. And she was numb to the sadness she would otherwise have felt when she covered the face of a mother or infant with a white sheet.

Likewise, she registered no surprise when Bridie, holding her young daughter, staggered into the waiting room and collapsed on a chair. At first she did not recognize her. Nothing distinguished Bridie from the other gaunt-faced mothers cradling infants who had become a common sight each morning. But as she checked her for fever, something about the woman's eyes looked familiar.

'Bridie? Is that you?'

The woman nodded wearily. She betrayed no recognition of Victoria.

'Look after the child first, miss,' she said. 'Don't worry about me.'

Victoria frowned. She could see that both the mother and child were equally ill. They both needed to be admitted. The problem was that the wards were already full. But this was Rosie's sister. The thought pierced through the fog of Victoria's mind. I have to get them help. I can't let Rosie's sister die.

But even the best efforts of the doctors could not save Bridie. In the end they had to prise the child from her grip before covering her with a sheet. Word was sent to her husband on Foley

Court but he was nowhere to be found. The child remained in the hospital.

That evening, Victoria made her way to Moore Street and to Rosie. The front door was open and she crept in, cradling the news she brought to her breast like a sick infant. She found Rosie alone, sitting in a chair in the parlour by the unlit fire, her eyes focused on some faraway image. She did not move as Victoria took a seat in the chair opposite her. Silence enveloped them. Memories of the past few weeks filled Victoria's mind – Cathal lying wounded in this room, his burial days later in Dublin's Glasnevin Cemetery in a plot reserved for rebel leaders, Rosie's pale and stoic face as she dropped a white lily on his coffin. She waited for her friend to acknowledge her.

'Victoria?' Rosie's voice was no more than a whisper as she finally shifted her gaze. 'I didn't hear you come in.'

Victoria smiled. 'I didn't want to disturb you. You appeared lost in thought.'

Rosie nodded. 'It's where I live these days. In my mind. In memories.'

'I know.'

'Let me make you some tea.' Rosie made to stand up.

'No, let me.'

Victoria was glad of the chance to delay her news. She busied herself in the kitchen and, when she could linger there no longer, returned to the parlour. Some colour returned to Rosie's cheeks as she drank and she became more alert.

'I'm glad you came.' She waved her hand. 'I've had so many visitors. Cathal had more friends than I ever realized. But it's grand to have one of my own friends come – my best friend.'

Victoria swallowed hard. The fact that Rosie had finally acknowledged her as her best friend would at any other time have filled her heart with joy. But today Rosie's best friend was here to bring her the most dreadful news. She put down her cup and knelt down before Rosie, holding both of her hands.

'Rosie, I would have given anything not to be the one to bring you this news. But yet I know it should not come from anyone but me. Poor Bridie has died. She caught the fever that's been raging in the city. We did all we could to save her, but she hadn't the strength to fight it.'

She felt Rosie's hands stiffen in hers.

'Little Kate has survived,' Victoria rushed on. 'They are keeping her at the hospital. Micko is nowhere to be found.'

There was nothing more to say. She waited for Rosie to speak. Instead her friend stood up, walked to the window and stared down on Moore Street.

'Cathal left this house to me,' she said, her voice flat, 'and I was going tomorrow to fetch Bridie and Kate and bring them here. I wasn't going to let Micko stand in the way any more.'

Silence fell between them again. At length Rosie turned back from the window. 'Where is she now?' she said.

Victoria started. 'Kate? She's still at the hospital.'

'Bridie.'

'Bridie? Ah, she's at the hospital too.'

'She needs to go home.'

'Yes, of course. My aunt has offered to have her sent by train to Mayo.'

Rosie nodded. 'Aye. She would want to be buried there.'

Two days later a young nurse escorted Victoria home from the Union after she had collapsed exhausted on the floor.

Lady Marianne telephoned her sister-in-law at Ennismore. 'We must arrange for her to be brought home immediately, Thea,' she said. 'I cannot be responsible for her. She is very ill.'

Victoria held onto Celine's hand as she lay on the daybed listening to her aunt. 'I cannot go back there, Celine,' she whispered. 'I promised Brendan. And besides, I must stay here to be close to Rosie. She will need me now.'

Celine frowned. 'Yes, of course,' she said, as she patted Victoria's hand.

The next morning a motor car drew up in front of the house on Fitzwilliam Square. Victoria's heart sank. Had her mother arrived so soon? She pulled together what strength she had, prepared to resist. But it was not her mother who came into the downstairs hall. She heard a man's voice talking to her aunt, then a rustle of activity as Celine came into her bedroom.

'D'accord. Your aunt has arranged a car to take you home. I must pack a few things. I am to accompany you.'

'But I told you, I cannot go back there. Please, Celine.'

The maid, ignoring Victoria's pleas, began pulling items of clothing from drawers and cupboards and hurriedly thrusting them into a suitcase. When she finished she turned back to Victoria and saw that she was in tears. She came closer and knelt down before her and took her hands.

'Don't you realize how sick you are, *mademoiselle?* You must go where you can be cared for. You need only stay at Ennismore until you are well again. Please, come!'

She stood and pulled Victoria up to her feet, then led her downstairs and into the hallway. Lady Marianne stood at the drawing room door. She hugged her niece, tears hovering on her eyelashes. 'I wish you a safe journey.'

All protest left Victoria.

'Goodbye, Aunt Marianne,' she said. 'Thank you for everything.'

Celine helped her down the front steps to where the car waited. The driver reached for the suitcases and put them in the boot. As Victoria stood waiting for him to open the rear car door she realized someone sat in the front seat. She held her breath as the door opened and Rosie got out, handing her young niece to Celine. She came towards Victoria, her arms outstretched, a smile on her face. Without a word, Victoria moved forward into Rosie's embrace.

'We're going back to Ennismore, Rosie,' she whispered.

'Aye, we're going home.'

PART FIVE

HOMECOMING

CHAPTER 35

Rosie gazed out of the car window while Victoria slept beside her. As the noise and grime of Dublin slipped away, so did her harsh memories of the last four years, replaced by long-buried, gentler reflections. With every passing mile she drank in the changing scenery like a wanderer sating his thirst. Every sight filled her with pleasure – yellow gorse spreading its cloak over the fields and hillsides, budding fuchsia preparing to dress the hedgerows in scarlet, delicate white starflowers waving from the bogs.

Farther west, farmers guided their carts to the side of rutted lanes to let them pass, tipping their caps, smiles on their weathered faces. Rosie's heart ached as she thought of her da. He and she were a part of this place and these people. This was their home – this place so full of hardship that the conqueror Oliver Cromwell likened it to hell, this place with land so poor farmers fertilized it with seaweed, and which suffered more than any other during the famine. She was sad that she had ever abandoned her home and family.

Victoria moaned softly in her sleep and leaned her head against Rosie's shoulder. Rosie tucked the blanket Celine had brought more tightly around her friend. They rode in the back of the car together while Celine sat beside the driver in the front, little Kate sleeping in her lap. No one had spoken since they left Dublin. Rosie studied the back of the driver's head. The proud set of it and the way the breeze rustled his thick brown hair reminded her of Cathal. She pictured him that first night on O'Connell Bridge chasing away the taunting prostitutes. Even then she had known he would be someone special in her life.

She didn't want to think about Cathal because it was too painful. But his image kept appearing before her, his eyes searching her face. She recalled the first night she cradled him in her arms as he sobbed. When they awoke the next morning they both knew an unspoken bond had formed between them that could never be severed. He was flawed, yes, and still she had loved him without judgement. She had never thought herself capable of such loyalty. Certainly she had not felt this way about Valentine – judging *him* harshly at every turn, ridiculing his loyalty to family, duty and traditions. Cathal had taught her that people did not always have a choice where their loyalties lay – his was to the uprising and the young Volunteers, willing to risk everything, including their relationship, for it. She'd seen, too, how the young Volunteers would sacrifice their lives for loyalty to the cause they believed in. She sighed. She accepted now that life, people, and she herself were far more complicated than she had ever allowed.

It was evening when they arrived at Ennismore. There was no warning of their arrival, so no one stood on the steps to greet them. Rosie took a deep breath as she recalled her early years there. How grand it had all once seemed. Now, as she gazed at the crumbling stone and ragged grasses beside the front steps, she realized the house no longer had any hold over her. Instead, Ennismore looked like a forlorn, neglected old woman whose beauty was long past.

At the sound of the car, a curious Mr Burke opened the door. The driver alighted and helped Celine out of the front seat, taking the child in his arms. Rosie gently woke Victoria and with Celine's help slid her out of the car, supporting her as she stood unsteadily on the gravel driveway. Mr Burke's face registered alarm when he saw Victoria. He rushed towards her and putting his arm around her waist, led her up the steps. Mrs Murphy appeared and looked around in confusion.

'Ah, Mrs Murphy,' said Rosie, 'this is Celine, Victoria's maid who has come with her from Dublin. As you can see, Victoria is not well. She collapsed a day ago from the fever, and her aunt asked me to bring her home.'

Mrs Murphy looked from Rosie to Celine and the child. 'This is Bridie's child, Mrs Murphy,' Rosie said. 'I'm bringing her home to Ma.'

Rosie could not bring herself to talk about Bridie's fate. They would all know soon enough. Not wanting to linger, she hurried back into the car with Kate and the driver and rode away.

The driver parked on the grassy apron at the gate of the Killeen farm. Rosie took Kate in her arms and thanked him as he handed out her suitcase and drove away. She walked up to the cottage and, as she approached, she expected to see their old dog, Rory, coming to greet her. Then she realized Rory would have died long ago. She felt her throat tighten. As she drew closer to the front door where Ma waited, she was crushed to see the deep sorrow in her mother's eyes. Wordlessly, she handed little Kate over to her. Ma took the child in her arms and clung to her, then turned and walked back into the cottage. Rosie stiffened. The black wreath hanging on the front door told her that Bridie's coffin already lay inside the house. Fighting back her tears she followed her ma through the door.

The sky was bright and the wind blustery on the day of Bridie's funeral. An overnight rain had washed the landscape, leaving the grasses a brilliant green and the wildflowers a dazzling profusion of colour. Six pallbearers – Rosie's da and three brothers, stiff in coarse new suits, and her two red-faced uncles – carried the coffin from the cottage. A small procession of mourners, family and neighbours, walked behind it down to the main road and out towards Crossmolina and the church. Along the roadside people stopped and bowed their heads, blessing themselves as the cortège passed. Ma held young Kate by the hand, while Rosie held tight to Ma's arm, aware of how small and fragile it felt in her grasp.

St Brigid's church was full when they entered. Rosie recognized farmers and shop owners, girls and boys she had played with years ago, now fully grown, and a group of elderly, black-scarved women who were fixtures at every mass she had ever attended. As she walked towards the altar she saw Mrs O'Leary, head bent and sobbing quietly, kneeling beside Mrs Murphy and the rest of the Ennismore staff. She looked at the pew in front of them, expecting to see some of the Bell family, but the only one there was Sofia who knelt, deep in prayer, her head in her hands.

Rosie was relieved when the mass was over. The organ music swelled as the men bore the coffin back down the aisle towards the door. She looked straight ahead as she walked behind it, still gripping her mother's arm, while the mourners shuffled out of the pews. She had been in this church many times. She was baptized here, made her first Holy Communion and Confirmation here, attended christenings and weddings and funerals here, as well as mass on Sundays and holy days. Yet now she felt like a stranger. She mourned the innocent girl she was but would never be again.

St Brigid's Cemetery sat in the shadow of a soft green hillside on which cows grazed freely. A statue of St Brigid, Ireland's best known female saint, stood in the centre of the graveyard. Beside it was a holy well where pilgrims came to pray for healing miracles. A small hawthorn tree stood to one side, covered in colourful ribbons, bird feathers and dried flowers – all offerings to the saint. Rosie had a vague memory, of watching Ma tying a strip of bright red velvet to a branch while praying for her oldest daughter, Nora, sick with pneumonia, who later died. She turned and walked to the open grave where Nora lay, and where Bridie would now join her.

The priest read prayers aloud, the pages of his missal flapping in the breeze. When he finished he threw a shovel full of dirt on the lowered coffin. Little Kate, guided by Ma, tottered forward and dropped a lush, red rose into the grave. Her simple action moved the mourners to tears as each came forward to toss in more flowers while a lone bagpiper's music filled the air. One by one the Ennismore staff came up to pay respects to the Killeen family. Mr Burke bowed solemnly while Mrs Murphy wept and muttered how fond she had been of Bridie. Anthony Walshe shook hands with Da. Thelma blushed and said little, while Immelda muttered a few words. Sadie nodded while casting sidelong glances at Celine who hugged Ma and kissed little Kate, murmuring in French.

When the funeral ended, everyone was invited back to the Killeen cottage for food and drink, as was the custom. Rosie turned Ma over to Da and stood back while the mourners streamed out through the cemetery gate.

'Excuse me, Rosie?'

Rosie swung around. Sofia stood beside her, her hand outstretched.

'I wanted to give you my condolences,' she began, sounding rather formal. 'I'm sorry I'm the only one of the Bell family here, but they are so greatly concerned about Victoria's health they did not want to leave her.'

Rosie nodded. 'It's all right, I understand. How is she?'

Sofia frowned. 'There is no change. We have had the doctor in daily since she came home. All we can do is follow his instructions and keep watching her. Celine, er, Lady Marianne's maid, has not left her side except to attend the funeral today. The girl seems very devoted to her.'

The women looked at each other as if they had much left to say, but neither of them wanted to say it. Rosie felt a vague discomfort.

'Well, thank you for coming,' she said, unsure how to address Valentine's wife, 'it was thoughtful of you. Will you come down to the cottage?'

Rosie was relieved when Sofia shook her head. 'You are very kind, but I must be getting back. My son Julian will be looking for me. We always have lunch together.'

'Of course.'

An uneasy silence fell between them once more. Turning, Sofia walked away briskly down the road. Rosie waited until she was far ahead of her before making her way back to the Killeen cottage.

Later that evening the staff of Ennismore filed into the servants' hall.

'Put on the kettle for a cup of tea, Thelma, there's a good lass.'

Mrs O'Leary sighed as she limped in, sat down and removed her hat, and bent over to massage her tiny feet. 'Funerals are all right for auld ones the likes of ourselves, 'tis only the natural way of things. But when you have to watch them bury a young one like our Bridie...' She let her words hang in the air.

The rest of the staff took their usual places at the table. Mrs O'Leary sighed again.

'And to watch that poor wee dote Kate drop that rose on the coffin. It would scald your heart to see it.'

No one answered her as they sat, each lost in their own thoughts. Thelma came in and served tea. Always stout, Thelma had gained more weight in the last year so that her white fingers now resembled fat rolls of dough wrapped around the handle of the teapot. When she finished serving, she sat down, her bovine eyes wide and dreamy.

'Weren't Rosie's brothers so handsome, all dressed up?'

Mrs O'Leary glared at her. 'Arrah, will you whisht with your foolishness, Thelma. Sure weren't we all there to pay our respects to Bridie's family, not to be mooning about over handsome men?'

Thelma looked defiantly at the cook. 'Well you couldn't help noticing. Besides, I saw Sadie looking at them as well.'

'I was not,' said Sadie, tossing her copper curls. 'I passed no remarks on them at all. Anyway, I was more interested in that French one Victoria's after bringing home with her. A bit above herself for my liking. Imagine insisting on eating with Victoria instead of down here with us?' She sipped her tea. 'Things won't be the same here any more. I should have gone to America along with my cousins when I had the chance. I could have been living in luxury by now.'

'Or you could be lying drowned at the bottom of the ocean,' snapped Mrs O'Leary.

As silence fell once more upon the small group, Anthony Walshe stoked his pipe and took a long draw of tobacco. ''Tis many's the change we've seen in the last few years,' he said. 'Master Thomas dead and buried, Master Valentine away in the

394

army and Miss Victoria sent away to Dublin only to come back sick with the fever. And down here, poor Bridie and poor Seaneen gone, and Brendan in prison. Not to mention the Rising in Dublin.'

'Ah, sure nothing stays the same, Mr Walshe,' put in Mrs Murphy.

'And it will get worse before it gets better, mark my words.' Immelda suddenly spoke up. 'The Easter Uprising was just the beginning of it. There'll be trouble across the length and breadth of Ireland and the likes of the Bell family will be rousted out and sent back across the water with their tails between their legs, so they will.'

There was a collective gasp around the table at Immelda's words.

'On my oath I'd say Immelda's right,' said Anthony at last. 'The tide's been turning against the English ever since they executed the leaders of the Rising. Now that the ordinary Irishmen have had a taste of revolution they won't be too anxious to let it go.'

The staff looked towards Mr Burke, waiting for his rebuke, but this time it did not come. Instead, he stared wearily down at his teacup and said nothing.

Mrs O'Leary stood up and reached for a clean apron from the cupboard. 'Revolution, or no revolution,' she said, 'they'll still be wanting their dinner.'

The rest of the staff drained their tea mugs and rose from the table.

'Did you see the cut of the Rosie one?' said Sadie. 'I'd say life was good to her in Dublin. Did you see the dress she wore? Her ma said she'd been writing articles for a newspaper up there, but I'd say there's more to it than that. I heard a rumour she'd been living up there with a man.'

'That's enough gossip, Sadie,' said Mrs Murphy.

'I suppose you'd like to see her back here down scrubbing on her hands and knees,' said Immelda, glaring at Sadie. 'Why shouldn't a poor, country girl like her do well for herself? She certainly did better than the Victoria one who had to come crawling back home the minute she took sick. I always said the Bell family was weak. And she proves me right.'

'That's enough!' said Mrs Murphy.

But Immelda wasn't finished. 'Just because the likes of ye haven't the gumption to make a better life for yourselves, you begrudge anyone that does. Well, as Anthony says, things are changing, and when the gentry are gone from this country where will that leave the rest of you? All you know is how to go down on your knees and lick the boots of them you think are better than you.'

'I said that's enough, Miss Fox,' said Mrs Murphy again. 'How dare you insult us in that manner? You will apologize this minute.'

'Ah, I'd say she's just poisoned with jealousy,' said Sadie. 'She wishes she'd been born into the gentry herself. Why else would she hate them so much?'

'Brendan hated them too!' said Immelda, her face red.

'Not all of them,' Sadie retorted. 'He was very thick with one of them. For all we know he took up with her again in Dublin.'

'Will ye whisht. There's work to be done.' Mrs

396

O'Leary turned around, her hands on her hips. 'I for one am not ashamed of the work I do for the Bell family, and the rest of you shouldn't be either. There's dignity in a hard day's work, no matter what it is. And as for you, miss,' she turned and glared down at Immelda, 'you'd better watch yourself. If Lady Ennis ever heard your talk she'd throw you out on your arse. And then where would you go? I doubt they'd even take you back at the convent, except maybe as a skivvy.'

Mr Burke finally rose to his feet. 'Well said, Mrs O'Leary.' He turned to Immelda. 'I will try to overlook your outburst, Miss Fox. We are none of us ourselves today after witnessing such a sad occasion. But if you so much as utter one more criticism of the Bell family in my presence I will see to it that you are dismissed without so much as a warning and any wages owed will be forfeited. Is that understood?'

Immelda glared back at Mr Burke with an almost imperceptible jerk of her head.

'I think we're going to be in for some great craic,' Sadie whispered to Thelma as she and the others followed Mrs O'Leary into the kitchen.

CHAPTER 36

By late June, Victoria's fever had passed and the doctor pronounced her well enough to leave her bed and venture outside into the garden for a couple of hours a day. At those times she sent word to Rosie and together they spent pleasant afternoons enjoying the sunshine and the brilliant colours of the garden.

'It's just like old times, isn't it, Rosie?' said Victoria, clutching Rosie's hand as they sat together on their favourite bench.

'Aye, there's many's a memory in this place. But it all seems a lifetime ago.'

Rosie looked around the garden. Despite the blooming flowers, it showed the same sad neglect as the crumbling stone and untrimmed grasses at the front of the house. The borders of the flower beds, once straight and precise as a diagram in a geometry book, now ran crooked and ragged. The boxwood hedges were uneven, and unrestrained weeds climbed mutinously up the stone walls around the perimeter, smothering the roses.

'It's the war,' said Victoria, reading Rosie's thoughts. 'Almost all of the gardeners left to join up.'

Rosie nodded. 'Aye, the war has changed everything.'

They lapsed into silence. Victoria allowed herself to picture Brendan sitting beside her in this garden and as he had looked the last night he kissed her in Dublin. She tried not to picture him lying alone in a cold, dark prison cell.

'I'm sorry about Brendan,' Rosie said.

'He fought for what he believed in,' said Victoria, looking out towards Mount Nephin which towered strong and dark above the lake. She turned to look at Rosie. 'I know you didn't much care for him, nor did my family or any of the staff, but none of you knew him the way I did. Beneath all of his roughness, he's a gentle soul.'

Tears welled in her eyes and Rosie gently stroked her hand. 'You still love him, don't you?'

Victoria nodded. 'Cathal once told me that it's your heart not your head that will always decide who you love – and it will not be told different, no matter how much you argue with it.'

A tiny wren flew down and hopped on a stone urn beside them and Victoria smiled as she watched its antics. She stole a look at her friend. They had neither of them mentioned the agonizing week they had spent together in Dublin during the uprising. What mattered was that her friend was here again with her at Ennismore. Celine arrived to help Victoria inside. Victoria rose heavily, kissed Rosie on the cheek and left, leaning on Celine for support. Although her fever had passed, her energy had deserted her, and she needed help doing everything. The doctor had tut-tutted when she told him about her days and nights spent at the Union hospital, particularly during Easter week. It was no wonder, he said, that she was worn out.

By the beginning of July, however, while her energy had returned, Victoria began to suspect something else was wrong. She was ill almost every morning, and could hardly keep any food down, the smell of it alone sending her stomach churning. She implored Celine not to say anything to her family.

'But if you are ill, *mademoiselle*, the doctor must be fetched *tout de suite*.'

'Let's not alarm them yet, Celine. I'm sure it will pass.'

As the summer days slipped by, however, Victoria finally admitted to herself that her earlier fever had nothing to do with her present condition. She was pregnant. Her emotions swung between feelings of dread and joy. She fretted constantly, asking herself the same questions over and over. What if the fever had harmed her unborn child? What would her family say? What would become of her in this condition? Who could she turn to for help? At other times she was thrilled at the thought of having part of Brendan to hold and love, imagining gazing into a tiny face so much like his.

Celine was as good as her word, betraying nothing even in the face of persistent questioning from Sadie.

'Is Miss Victoria sick? She didn't touch her breakfast again this morning. And when I brought the fish course in for lunch she raced out of the room as if the divil himself was after her. And when she came back in she was pale as a corpse.'

Celine simply shrugged and pretended not to understand.

Sadie Canavan was less circumspect than Celine, however, since it was not in her nature to ignore such a shocking development. She waited until the staff had finished dinner one evening and pounced, announcing the news dramatically to enhance the effect.

'Miss Victoria is in the family way.'

She sat back and waited for the inevitable gasps and signs of the cross that followed. Thelma's eyes widened as she stood, her plump white fingers frozen on a pitcher of water. Mrs Murphy

400

put her hand to her mouth, while Mr Burke gulped on his glass of wine. Mrs O'Leary's face turned scarlet and Anthony Walshe dropped his pipe. They all looked at Sadie in astonishment.

'May God forgive you,' said Mrs O'Leary, when she could find her voice. 'You've said some choice things in the past about this family, Sadie Canavan, but I can't believe even you would stoop to such lies. I might have expected it from Immelda here, knowing how much she seems to resent Miss Victoria, but you ... you...' She halted, at a loss for words.

'Don't be bringing me into it,' said Immelda.

Thelma found her voice. 'How would you know, Sadie? Sure I thought expectant girls had big fat bellies, and Miss Victoria's thin as a rail.'

Sadie smirked. 'She won't be for long, mark my words.' She looked around at the others. 'Don't be blaming me, I'm just telling you what I've seen. She's not touched her breakfast in weeks and she's forever running out of the room to vomit. I'm surprised her ma or Lady Louisa haven't caught on. I tried talking to that French one, but she pretends she doesn't understand me.'

'Where's the husband?' said Thelma, setting down her pitcher of water and giving Sadie her full attention.

Sadie shook her head. 'Arrah, Thelma, did your ma teach you nothing? Sure a girl doesn't need a husband to get pregnant. Any man will do.'

Thelma gasped and turned scarlet. 'But that ... that would be a ... a mortal sin, so.'

'I'd say I could take a good guess whose child it is,' said Immelda.

401

'You'll keep your guesses to yourself, Immelda,' said Mrs O'Leary. 'Sure we could all guess till the cows come home and be none the wiser. If Sadie is right, and I'm not saying she is, only Miss Victoria knows for sure. And anyway, 'tis none of our business.'

Mr Burke finally stood up, his shoulders slouched from weariness. 'I hardly know where to begin,' he said. 'I never thought I would live to witness such impertinence on the part of household staff members. I doubt there is any other house in Ireland with staff as undisciplined as some of you. Your behaviour causes me great shame.' He looked at Sadie, Thelma and Immelda in turn. 'If it were not for the alarming shortage of available staff, I would sack all of you this very minute. All I can do is implore you to keep this conversation to yourselves and not let it go beyond these walls.'

He nodded toward Mrs Murphy and together they walked out of the servants' hall. Anthony watched them go. 'Ye have all the fight knocked out of that poor man with your shenanigans. Ye should be ashamed of yourselves.'

Thelma blushed and slunk away into the kitchen while Sadie shrugged and headed towards the back stairs. Mrs O'Leary bustled out of the room, leaving Anthony and Immelda alone.

'Well, colleen,' Anthony said to her, 'you've your wish now surely. You always wanted to see young Victoria get her comeuppance and now she has.'

Immelda set her mouth in a prim line. 'I've no idea what you're after talking about, Anthony.'

402

Victoria knew it was only a matter of time until her secret would become apparent to everyone. She had not yet begun to show and told herself she would be able to hide her condition for another three months. Once she had plucked up the courage she would confide in Rosie and together they would devise a plan for her future. The thought consoled her. But things did not proceed in the orderly way she had planned.

Her mother and Aunt Louisa approached her one afternoon as she sat alone in the garden. The grim set of their faces told her all she needed to know. Resolutely, she stood and waited for the onslaught.

'Walk, Victoria,' commanded her mother as she and Lady Louisa fell into step on either side of her, each carrying a colourful parasol. 'For the benefit of the servants who are no doubt watching us you will smile as if we are having a pleasant exchange.'

Victoria did not attempt to speak. What would be the point? There was no denying the fact that she was pregnant. She should have realized secrets did not stay hidden for long at Ennismore.

'My maid, Fox, has come to me with very disturbing news,' began Lady Ennis, her fingers digging into the flesh of Victoria's arm as they walked. 'I told her of course that her allegations were preposterous. But now I hear that Louisa's maid has told *her* the same thing. Can they both be wrong, Victoria? Deny it now and we can put an end to this nonsense.'

Victoria felt the blood rush from her face. She

wished fervently that Rosie was there but she had gone with her mother on an errand into Cross-molina. If Immelda and Sadie were talking about her, then surely Rosie must have heard the gossip as well and everyone else in the house besides. Shame began to rise within her but she tamped it down. No, she would not let shame define what she and Brendan had created. They had conceived a child out of love – a child she must now protect and defend. She looked from her mother to Aunt Louisa.

'It is true,' she said.

Lady Louisa uttered an audible gasp while Lady Ennis's hand tightened in a death grip on Victoria's arm.

'I hope I did not hear you correctly,' Lady Ennis said, her voice trembling.

'I said, it's true, Mama. I am pregnant.'

Lady Ennis let go of her daughter and collapsed on the nearest bench, fanning herself furiously. She looked at her sister. 'Fetch me a glass of water, Louisa. I fear I may faint.'

Lady Louisa merely grunted and sat down beside her. 'I'm not leaving until we get to the bottom of this.'

Victoria stood looking down at the two women. For a moment she saw them only as two pathetic creatures clinging desperately to a way of life that was rapidly dying, and pitied them. But the feeling passed as she braced herself for what was to come.

'And the father?' Her mother's voice was high and cracked as if bordering on hysteria.

'Brendan Lynch.'

Lady Ennis stared at her daughter, open-mouthed. Victoria wondered if her mother had expected her to deny it, to make up some story about a British officer whom she had married in secret and who was killed in the uprising. And indeed Victoria had, in moments of panic, conjured up such a lie to tell when the time came. She had told herself the lie would serve as a protection for her family as well as herself. But now – now she realized such a lie would be traitorous not only to Brendan but to herself and her child.

Lady Louisa glared up at her, all pretence of pleasant conversation for the sake of the servants gone.

'You hussy,' she said. 'You are no better than a common whore.' She turned to her sister. 'I told you she would come to a bad end. Who knows what she and that peasant girl were up to in Dublin?'

Lady Ennis dabbed her eyes with her handkerchief. 'That Killeen girl,' she said, 'always that Killeen girl. We were all cursed from the day she came to Ennismore.'

'Rosie has nothing to do with this,' said Victoria, her temper rising. 'I hardly saw her in Dublin. She didn't even know about Brendan and me.'

'A footman! How could you sink to that level, Victoria? And how could you shame us so?'

'Where is he?' said Lady Louisa. 'Does he plan to make an honest woman of you?'

'He's in prison. He was arrested after the uprising.'

'Thank God,' said Lady Ennis. 'He will undoubtedly be there for life. He will not be coming around to claim his offspring.'

405

The fact of Brendan's imprisonment seemed to revive Lady Ennis. 'In that case we have time to devise a plan – a story that will save us all from embarrassment. We will not be the first family to have to do so. But we must hurry. This news will not stay confined to Ennismore for very much longer.'

Before Victoria could answer, Lady Louisa shot to her feet. 'You can't possibly be thinking of letting her stay on here, Althea?'

'What else do you propose we do, Louisa? We could send her to the Continent, but that would be too obvious. No, I think a story of a young woman, an officer's wife perhaps, widowed by this awful war, will be much more plausible.'

Lady Louisa, red-faced with anger, spoke up. 'And what of me, Althea? Am I to stay here at Ennismore and become governess to young Julian and this one's bastard? Well, I shall not do it. I shall not.'

As Louisa flounced away, Lady Ennis uttered a sharp laugh. 'Poor Louisa,' she said. 'Where else is she to go?'

Victoria watched her mother gather up her fan and parasol and prepare to leave the garden. Suddenly she grabbed her mother's arm, swinging her around to face her.

'How dare you, Mama?' she began. 'How dare you expect me to lie about my child and deny this baby's father? I won't do it. I refuse to make up some ridiculous story just so you can save face. I am not ashamed of what I have done and will not act as if I am.'

Lady Ennis recovered herself from the shock of

Victoria's onslaught. 'I am doing this to save *your* reputation, not mine, you foolish, ungrateful girl.'

Victoria shook her head. 'No, Mama. Everything you do is for *your* sake. You don't care who you hurt or embarrass as long as it suits your purposes. I have seen it too often, and this time is no different.'

Lady Ennis stepped closer to her daughter and fixed her with a glare. But as Victoria looked into her mother's eyes she saw not anger, as she had expected, but panic – the sort of frenzied alarm one might see in the eyes of a rabbit caught in a trap.

'But what will people say? How shall I face them?' Her mother's voice grew high-pitched.

'I really don't care, Mama,' said Victoria as she walked away, leaving her mother staring after her.

Later that evening Victoria stood at her bedroom window listening to the gulls calling from the lake. Tonight their cries sounded plaintive. She wondered how she would endure the endless procession of long, light evenings still to come.

CHAPTER 37

One September afternoon Victoria sat alone in the garden enjoying the dwindling rays of summer sun. Without warning, a fierce rain squall whipped through the trees, sending leaves scattering and flattening flower heads against the ground. She closed her book, gathered her skirts and stood up.

Her first instinct was to run to the house for shelter, but instead she found herself standing with her face turned up to the sky, letting the rain drench her face and hair. She laughed aloud, remembering how Rosie and she had danced in the rain as children, ignoring commands from Lady Louisa to go inside. She wanted to dance now, but the thought of servants' prying eyes stopped her.

By the time she reached her bedroom she was drenched, water dripping from her clothes and leaving puddles on the carpet.

'Celine?' she called. 'Can you fetch some towels? I am soaked.'

A noise in the adjoining dressing room sent her in that direction. 'Celine, can you...'

Victoria's mouth dropped open. 'Miss Fox, what are you doing?'

Immelda Fox, clad in one of Victoria's gowns, swung around from a mirror, where she had been gazing at herself. Hurriedly she unhooked the back, pushing the dress roughly down over her hips and stepping out of it. Without looking at Victoria she lifted the garment and began to smooth it. Victoria saw that her hands were trembling.

'What are you doing?' she asked again.

Immelda turned and looked at her, her eyes blazing with defiance.

'I was just seeing if it could be let out,' she said, looking pointedly at Victoria's stomach. 'Your mother suggested it. She knows I'm good with a needle.'

Victoria looked at the daybed where a pile of her dresses lay. 'Nonsense. My mother suggested no such thing. Besides, these are my summer gowns. I shall not be wearing them again until after my child is born. There would be no need to alter them.' She paused. 'Where is Celine?'

'The French one? She's below in the kitchen drinking tea where she always is. Good-for-nothing foreigner.'

Victoria's nerves had been on edge for some time. Her usually calm demeanour disappeared and an unfamiliar agitation had taken hold. Now fury seized her. 'How dare you speak of Celine that way? Apologize at once!'

Immelda muttered something under her breath and made to leave, pushing her way past her. But Victoria put out a hand to stop her.

'You will stay here until you have explained yourself.'

She crossed to the bedroom door and locked it. 'You will not leave this room until you do. Sit!'

Her anger shocked Immelda into sitting down on a chair.

Victoria's racing heartbeat began to slow as she observed Immelda. She had long been suspicious of her mother's maid. She could feel her hatred every time their eyes met. Brendan had said she despised all the Bell family, but Victoria always sensed that most of it was directed at her. Now, as she looked at the woman's dark, angry eyes, her pale gaunt face, she noticed for the first time how much she had aged. She must be past thirty, she thought. Gradually, her anger began to subside.

A sudden clap of thunder startled them and they both turned towards the window. Heavy, black clouds hung in the sky as if the afternoon had suddenly become night. Immelda made the sign of the cross.

'"Tis God's judgment upon us,' she muttered.

'Why do you hate me so, Immelda?' said Victoria.

Immelda did not answer.

'You needn't deny it.' Victoria's voice was calmer now. 'I should like to know what I've done to you.'

Again, Immelda was silent.

Victoria sighed. 'If it's my dresses you want you are welcome to them. I doubt I shall be wearing such finery in the future. You need only have asked me. There was no need to try and steal them.'

'I wasn't–' Immelda began.

'You *were*, Immelda. Let's not have any more lies.'

Immelda bowed her head. Then she looked up at Victoria, her normally pale face suffused with crimson.

'I was only trying them on to see how they'd look on me,' she said, her voice rising. 'By rights they should be mine. Whatever you have, I should be entitled to the same thing. I'm just as good as you are.'

'I'm sure you are, Immelda,' said Victoria gently, 'but God arranged for us to be born into very different circumstances.'

'Leave God out of this!'

'I realize it's not fair. None of us should be judged by the families we were born into. But that is the way of the world. And the poor stealing from the rich is not the way to fix the unfairness.'

'The rich steal from the poor every day of the week.'

'Yes, and those who do so are wrong. But it still does not excuse you. Rosie was born poor as well, but as far as I know she never stole from me, and she never envied me.'

As she said the words, Victoria realized that Rosie had indeed envied her often. She hurried on. 'And Brendan had every reason in the world to hate us – to hate me – and yet he loves me. I doubt that your reasons for such hostility could be any greater than his.'

Without warning Immelda began to sob, her thin shoulders heaving up and down. A wave of pity overtook Victoria and she went over to where the girl sat and placed her hand on her shoulder. Immelda flinched and shrank away as if unused to human touch.

'It's all right, Immelda. I understand why you would want some pretty dresses to wear. And you can have any of them that you wish. The rose and the blue would look lovely on you. And we will keep this between ourselves. No one need know of it.'

Immelda looked up at Victoria, her eyes wide, and let out a deep sigh. 'Ah, 'tis not the dresses I want,' she said. ''Twas never about the dresses.'

'Then what was it, Immelda?'

''Twas about seeing you grow up doted on by your family, especially your da. You were the apple of his eye. His one and only daughter.'

Immelda looked up at her, tears filling her eyes. She seemed to be struggling to say something. Victoria waited.

'But you're not the only daughter. Don't you see? I'm his daughter too.'

Before Victoria could speak, Immelda rushed on. 'He took advantage of my ma when she was a maid here. Then he sent her off without so much as a penny. She thought it was all her fault. She spent the rest of her life punishing herself, and me, for her sin. Well it wasn't just her sin, 'twas his as well.'

'What?' Victoria turned pale and sat down on the bed. 'Please don't be like this, Immelda. I have given you what you want.'

Immelda composed herself. 'Only your da can give me what I want. He can admit that I'm his daughter. That's all I've ever wanted.'

All that night Victoria tossed and turned. She tried to tell herself the maid had lied just to hurt her, which would certainly fit with her pattern of deceit. But something deep down convinced her the maid told the truth. She tried to recall Immelda's face in detail. Did it bear any similarity to her own? She could think of no resemblance between them in structure, colouring or expression. In an odd way she was disappointed. How often she had yearned for a sister when she was very young. Later, Rosie had more than filled that role, but still – a sister of her own would have brought such joy.

As the night crept on, however, such benign thoughts left her and her initial shock at Immelda's story returned. She thought of her father. Men like him frequently had their way with servant girls and took mistresses – Victoria was not naive enough to believe otherwise. But to bring his illegitimate daughter to live in the same house, under the very noses of his family – how could he? She tried to recall if there were ever any hints of a secret relationship between her father and Immelda but she could remember none. In fact, her father had treated Immelda the way he did all the staff, as if she were invisible. Was it possible he had not even recognized her? Had their fates been reversed, would he have ignored *her* in the same way he did Immelda?

By morning she had made up her mind to confront her father. But her mother struck first.

'Immelda Fox tells me you accused her of stealing,' said Lady Ennis as soon as Victoria entered the room. 'That woman has been in my employ for years and I trust her implicitly. She is as close to a saint as anyone in this house.'

Victoria was speechless. Her mother's attack had knocked her completely off balance. She stood gaping at her in disbelief.

'The poor woman is most overwrought,' her mother went on. 'She is afraid she will be dismissed. Well, I will not allow it, Victoria. You will apologize to her immediately.'

Victoria could not move. She looked from her mother to her father, his head buried, as usual, in his newspaper. Lady Louisa put down her fork and regarded her scornfully while Sofia continued eating as if everything were normal. Victoria had long since recovered from her morning sickness, but now the smell of bacon and kippers made her feel ill. She fought to keep down the bile that rose in her throat. Instead of taking her seat at the table she turned to Sadie Canavan who was laying out dishes on the sideboard.

'You will leave us now, Miss Canavan, and close the door behind you. Do not return until you are summoned.'

Sadie stared at Victoria.

'Now, Miss Canavan!'

Sadie dropped a plate of scones onto the sideboard and hurried out of the room as Lady Ennis glared at her daughter.

'What on earth...' she began.

Victoria took a deep breath. She had not meant to confront her father in front of everyone, but her mother had left her no choice. 'The matter of the dresses is insignificant, Mama. Immelda told me something last evening that I found shocking. At first I did not believe her, but upon consideration I am convinced she was telling the truth.' She turned and looked directly at her father. 'She told me that you seduced her mother who was a maid here. She claims that you, Papa, are her father, that she and I are sisters.'

A stranger entering the breakfast room at that moment might have supposed he had come upon a wax tableau, the figures sitting around the dining table frozen in the act of eating – forks suspended in the air, rigid fingers gripping teacups, mouths agape. Only the blonde young woman standing in the middle of the room showed any signs of life, perspiration covering her forehead, her chest rising and falling rapidly, her hands clenched in fists at her side.

Lady Ennis recovered first, rising to her feet in such a fury that she set the china rattling on the

414

table. 'This is preposterous, Victoria! Your condition has brought you to the verge of madness. First you accuse Fox of stealing, and now this. How dare you? Take it back this minute!'

Victoria steadied her breathing and stood her ground.

'I may be pregnant, Mama, but there is nothing wrong with my mind. I know what I heard.'

Lady Louisa looked pointedly from Lord Ennis to her sister. 'Then why not hear it from the horse's mouth? Why don't we fetch Fox? Ring for her at once, Althea.'

Victoria looked at her father, who glared back at her with a face like thunder. She had never seen him so enraged, looking as if he might strike her. For a moment she wondered if she had misunderstood what Immelda had said, or had imagined the whole thing. But the look of fury on his face told her she had not.

Immelda Fox came into the room and curtsied in front of Lady Ennis.

'You wanted to see me, my lady?' she said, her face expressionless.

Lady Ennis made an effort to collect herself. 'My daughter has told us of a conversation she had with you last evening, Fox.'

'About the dresses, my lady?' Immelda's tone was innocent, but she glanced slyly at Victoria as she spoke.

Lady Ennis waved her arms in exasperation. 'No, not the dresses.' She paused and drew in a deep breath. 'She tells us you accused Lord Ennis of being your father. Something about a liaison with your mother when she was a maid

415

here. Oh, it is all too distressing.' Lady Ennis, unable to go on, sat down.

Immelda looked from Lady Ennis to Victoria and made the sign of the cross. 'May God forgive you, Miss Victoria, for telling such awful lies!' She looked around at the others with a pained expression. 'I am a poor girl who spent much of her life in the convent. My da died before I was born.' She paused to wipe away tears. 'Please don't dismiss me over such lies, my lady.'

As Immelda spoke Victoria watched her father. He stared hard at the maid as if seeing her for the first time.

When Immelda left, Victoria turned to her mother. 'She is lying, Mama. I know what she told me.'

Before her mother could answer, Lord Ennis rose to his feet and roared at Victoria. 'Get out of my sight now! Have you not caused enough pain and embarrassment in this house?'

Victoria fled from the room, fighting to hold back her tears. Her father had never before spoken to her in that manner. Sofia excused herself and hurried out behind her. Lady Ennis turned to her sister.

'What have I done wrong, Louisa? What has changed my sweet, obedient daughter into such a monster? Why is she punishing me so? If I believed any of the ridiculous sayings of the native Irish, I would say a devil has taken possession of her.'

Lady Louisa gave Lord Ennis a suspicious look. 'Perhaps Victoria is not lying. How else would such a story have entered her head? There's another old saying, Thea: where there's smoke there's fire.

Lord Ennis waited until Louisa had left the room. 'Dismiss that maid immediately, Althea,' he said. 'No doubt the other servants will soon hear the accusations – nothing much ever seems to get past them. I will not tolerate being the object of their vile speculation. The sooner she goes the sooner this will be forgotten. Do not oppose me in this, Althea.'

Anthony Walshe came into the kitchen, poured himself a cup of tea and sat down at the table.

'Well, that's her away then.'

Mrs O'Leary closed the oven door and wiped her hands on her apron. She brought a cup of tea over and sat down next to him.

'How did she seem? Did she say anything?'

Anthony shook his head. 'Not a word. Sat up in the cart beside me, still as a statue. She didn't even so much as look at me until we got to Crossmolina. Then she had me leave her off in the middle of the square.'

'But where was she going from there?'

Anthony shrugged. 'I told you, she never said a word to me. I hated to leave the girl alone like that, looking like a lost sheep. But she waved me on. What was I to do?'

'Arrah, poor Immelda,' said Mrs O'Leary. 'You have to feel sorry for her all the same. She has no family that I know of. Maybe that convent will take her back.'

'And maybe they won't. In that case I'd say she'd be for the workhouse.'

Mrs O'Leary shook her head. 'I wouldn't wish that on a dog, Anthony. 'Tis true I never warmed to the girl, but I wouldn't wish that on her.' She paused and sipped her tea. 'Ah, maybe she'll get work somewhere. She has plenty of experience, and she's very handy with a needle.'

'She'll get no work without a letter of reference, and I'd say that's the last thing his lordship will be giving her.'

The house was quiet as the two sat alone in the kitchen.

'I wouldn't say this in front of Sadie,' Mrs O'Leary said, leaning over towards Anthony, 'or it would be all over the village, but I lay in bed last night thinking back over the years, and you know I believe I remember Immelda's ma.'

Anthony raised an eyebrow.

'Aye, there was a young girl working here named Mary Fox. Would have been thirty or more years ago now. Lovely looking little colleen she was. I remember she was sent away in disgrace after only a few months. When Immelda came to work here I never passed any remarks. Fox is such a common name in these parts.'

''Tis indeed,' said Anthony.

'But if that girl *was* her mother, why on earth would his lordship have taken on Immelda?'

Anthony lit his pipe. 'No mystery there, Mrs O. Sure himself probably never even knew the mother's name. You know the way of things with the likes of them – one night's toss in the hay and then 'tis on to the next one.'

'You're right there. God save us. Mary Fox wouldn't be the first girl to be sent away on account of a master, and she won't be the last. And 'tis the innocent babies that suffer. Ah, poor Immelda. I wish I'd been better to her.'

Mrs O'Leary drained her tea and stood up. 'I'd best be seeing to the supper. Although after all that's happened here – first Miss Victoria falling into the family way, and now this terrible business with Immelda – you'd think none of them would have any appetite left.'

Anthony stood and tamped out his pipe with his finger. ''Tis powerful bad days that's in it altogether. They say these things come in threes. On my oath there'll be more trouble before 'tis over.'

Mrs O'Leary sighed. 'May God save us all, Anthony.'

CHAPTER 38

The seeds of discord sown throughout the summer ripened and spread to every corner of Ennismore. Suspicion, anger and resentment permeated every conversation. Food spoiled and milk turned sour at alarming rates. Even the birds seemed to cease their chatter. And while the weather was mild, a chill that would not lift clung to the house. Lady Ennis took to locking her bedroom door, leaving her husband to sleep in his study. Lady Louisa, having lately perceived a sliver of weakness in the Reverend Watson's reluctance to marry her, had begun to press her advantage robustly by making more and more frequent visits to the local rectory. Sofia spent most of her time in the nursery with young Julian, while Lord Ennis found as many excuses as possible to absent himself to London. Victoria spent long, lonely days in her room, asking Celine to bring meals to her rather than face her family in the dining room. Any pretence of normality among the Bell family frayed like an old cloth until it was finally discarded.

It was into this atmosphere that Valentine Bell innocently blundered one late September afternoon when he appeared at the kitchen door unexpected and unannounced.

'Lord Valentine,' cried Mr Burke, rushing toward him. 'I fear I did not hear the doorbell. Forgive me.'

Valentine shrugged. 'Nothing to forgive, Mr Burke. I didn't want to make a fuss, so I came around to the kitchen.'

Mrs O'Leary and the other servants joined Mr Burke. They stared at Valentine, assessing him for injury. What else could have brought him home from the army so soon with the war still raging? And where was his uniform?

'Are you on leave, Master Valentine?' said Mrs O'Leary, addressing him as she had always done since he was a child. 'Ah, what a grand surprise this will be for your family. 'Twill lift all of their spirits.'

Valentine shook his head. 'No, not leave, Mrs O'Leary. I am home for good.'

They stared at him in anticipation, but no explanation came. Valentine picked up his kit bag. 'It is good to see all of you again,' he said briskly. 'Now I must go and find Papa.'

Burke recovered himself. 'Lord Ennis is away, Lord Valentine, but is expected home in a few days. Your mama is resting in her room as is Miss Victoria, and Lady Louisa is off visiting.' He scratched his head as if he had forgotten something.

'And my wife and son?' asked Valentine.

Burke's face flushed. 'Oh, yes, of course. They have gone out for a walk.'

The butler turned and hurried into the hallway. 'We were not expecting you. I'm afraid your room is a little damp. I shall have Miss Canavan set a fire. Can I get you something to eat?'

'No, thank you, Burke. I suppose I should have sent word of my arrival. I think I will go and see my sister first.'

Mr Burke gave him a look of alarm. 'She's resting, sir. I'm not sure it's a good idea to disturb her.'

'Nonsense,' said Valentine as he bounded up the stairs.

Victoria blanched when she saw her brother. He crashed through the door with no warning and she had no time to reach for her robe. She stood instead in her day dress, aware of her bulging stomach swelling beneath it. Automatically, her hand flew to her belly.

'Valentine! Oh my goodness, Valentine! Where did you come from? We had no word. No one was expecting you.'

Valentine stared at her stomach, his eyes wide. Nervous, disconnected thoughts raced through Victoria's head. She had not prepared for this moment, expecting that her child would be born

421

long before Valentine arrived home. She walked towards him and was about to kiss him on the cheek when she saw a wariness in his eyes. She drew back.

'Sit down, Valentine,' she said gently, 'I will explain everything.'

He waved his hand at her. 'No need for explanations. Brendan's?'

Victoria nodded, relieved. 'You can imagine how the news shocked the family.'

Valentine sank into a chair beside the window and sighed. 'And now I'm afraid they must prepare themselves for yet another shock.'

Victoria waited. What could her brother mean? She sat down opposite him, steeling herself for what was to come. He took some time before he spoke.

'Do you remember the last time I saw you in Dublin I warned you I might need your support in the future? Remember I said we were the only two of our family who actually lived through the uprising and understood how things were?' He paused, as if gathering his thoughts. His face turned grim as he continued. 'I have been dishonourably discharged from the army. There, I've said it.'

He stared at Victoria as if challenging her to respond. Her hand flew to her mouth.

'Dear God, Valentine,' she managed to say. 'Why?'

He relaxed his stare and his body seemed to sag in relief. Compassion filled her. How difficult this must have been for him to confess. How he must have tormented himself, worrying about her reaction. Poor Valentine. Did he not realize how much she loved him?

'Tell me about it,' she whispered gently.

He leaned forward and put his head in his hands. His voice was so low she had to strain to hear him.

'I never wanted to be in Dublin,' he began. 'I wanted to be on the Front fighting England's real enemies, not here at home fighting my own countrymen. I did my best to follow orders, Victoria. Believe me I tried. But when I saw those young Volunteers with their rusty old rifles and ragged uniforms, I could not raise my gun and shoot them.' He looked up at her, tears filling his eyes. 'They were just boys up against a well-trained army. They had no hope of winning and yet ... yet they were so brave. Anyway, I did my best to have my shots go astray.'

He chuckled. 'I hoped my comrades would think I was just a really bad shot.'

His laugh faded as he went on. 'But it appears they were growing suspicious of me anyway. One of them saw me visiting Cathal O'Malley's house on the day after Christmas.' He looked up at Victoria. 'Did I tell you about that ill-fated visit? I went to find Rosie and acted like a pompous fool. She put me in my place, of course, but the soldier who saw me knew that house belonged to Cathal O'Malley, and that Cathal trained the Volunteers. From then on they watched me like hawks.'

Victoria held her breath. The sky outside the window dimmed and the room darkened but she dared not move to light a lamp. Valentine was soon in shadow and she could not see his face

423

but the sound of his voice betrayed all of his emotion.

'The worst of it came the day Cathal died. The rebels had surrendered. Their leaders gave the word and they came out of their strongholds carrying white flags and marched up Sackville Street to Dublin Castle. It was clear to all of us that the uprising was over. We were supposed to lay down our arms. I was patrolling with my captain, a mean wretch with a surly temper, outside the General Post Office where the last of the rebels were trapped by fire. Suddenly Cathal came running out past us. He stopped and raised his hands when we called to him to halt. But as he turned to face us the captain raised his rifle and cocked it. I knew then what he was going to do. I grabbed his arm but it was too late. He had already fired and Cathal lay on the ground. He was about to fire again when I lunged at him. I tore the rifle from his hands and struck him hard. He cursed me as he fell and lay reeling on the pavement as I dragged Cathal away.'

He took a deep breath, gathering the energy to finish his story. 'After that they confined me to barracks while I was under investigation. It took some time since they were so busy processing the rebels who had surrendered, and the civilians they had arrested. I didn't hear another thing from them until late summer. I was charged with interfering with and assaulting a superior officer, failure to discharge my duties, and – ah, Papa will love this one – cowardice in the face of the enemy. I suppose I was lucky to escape prison. Perhaps it was Papa's rank that saved me – although I don't believe he knew what was going on.' He sighed. 'He will know it all soon enough.'

Victoria rose and turned up the lamps. 'What will you do now?' she said.

He ran his hands through his hair and gave her an ironic grin. 'Who knows?' he said. 'They'll hardly roast a fatted calf for me.'

Before he left, Victoria reached into a drawer and withdrew the envelope Valentine had given her for Rosie. She handed it to him, smiling wanly. 'Here, now you can give Rosie this yourself. No matter what has happened, I am happy to return it to you, because it means you are still alive.'

She reached over then and kissed her brother gently on the cheek.

Two nights after Valentine's arrival, Lady Ennis left the seclusion of her bedroom to join her family for dinner. She could barely hide her anticipation of witnessing her husband's reaction to their son's shocking news. She would have known nothing of it had not Sadie Canavan, who was eavesdropping outside Victoria's room as Valentine confided his secret, gone straight to Lady Louisa with the news. Lady Louisa, in turn, brought Lady Ennis the dreadful details that same evening – news she delivered with undisguised glee. And, while Valentine's behaviour caused great embarrassment to Lady Ennis, she knew it would be nothing less than calamitous for a member of the House of Lords to have a coward for a son.

Ever since she learned the truth about Immelda, all of Lady Ennis's stored-up resentments toward her husband swelled into an explosion of fury.

425

How dare he humiliate her by bringing his bastard daughter into her house? She shuddered to think of how many intimacies she had shared with that woman, and all the while the trollop was laughing at her behind her back. Who knew what details she had shared with the other servants? Yes, Edward deserved this disgrace.

No sooner had Lady Ennis and the family taken their seats in the dining room than, without notice as usual, Lady Marianne Bellefleur and Mr Shane Kearney swept in, bringing a current of cold air with them. Lady Marianne was dressed stylishly in a royal blue two-piece costume, trimmed with fur, while Mr Kearney sported a three-piece suit of a rather loud russet and grey striped material with a white stand-up collar and a russet silk tie. Lady Ennis greeted them with a withering look. The irritating woman and her friend had a knack of always showing up at the most inopportune time. Now they would be made privy to Valentine's news also. Lady Ennis shrugged. No matter, their presence would just add to Edward's humiliation.

It had grown dark outside and the gas lights cast a golden hue upon the room. Lady Marianne looked around.

'Why, dear Edward, yours must be the only house left in Ireland without electricity!'

Mr Kearney smiled as he escorted her to her chair. 'You must admit the gas is rather picturesque, my dear.'

Lord Ennis, ignoring his sister's comments, looked directly at his son. 'So what is it that has brought you home from Dublin, Valentine? When I arrived this afternoon and Burke mentioned

426

you were here I assumed you were on leave, but Burke assured me you are home for good.'

His question lingered in the air as everyone stopped talking at once. Victoria reached underneath the table and squeezed her brother's hand.

Valentine returned his father's look. 'Why don't we enjoy our meal first, Papa, and then I will tell you everything.'

'Very well,' Lord Ennis said, his tone neutral but his eyes wary.

Mr Burke and Mrs Murphy who, at the request of Lady Ennis, had been pressed into service instead of Sadie, hurried to serve the main course. Mr Burke poured the wine and the family began to eat and drink, idle chatter masking an undercurrent of uneasiness.

Lady Marianne turned her attention to Victoria. 'I must say you are blooming, my dear. Your condition appears to agree with you, wouldn't you say so Thea?'

Lady Ennis pursed her lips and made no answer as Lady Marianne continued. 'I believed she was at death's door when she left my house. I must say I was greatly relieved when Edward told me the real cause of her illness. Inconvenient, perhaps, but hardly fatal.'

Sofia, who had observed the previous exchanges in silence, moved to turn the subject away from the family towards a safer topic. 'How are things in Dublin, Lady Marianne? Victoria has told me how awful it was during the week of the uprising. I hope it is more peaceful now.'

Mr Kearney lifted his wine glass with manicured, bejeweled fingers and nodded towards

Sofia. 'Yes, simply dreadful business. Fortunately, Lady Marianne and I missed most of the trouble that week. We were away visiting friends on the coast. No one you would know, I daresay.' He leaned closer into the table in a conspiratorial fashion. 'Did you know that some of our own class actually took part in the rebellion?'

Lady Ennis gave him a pointed look. '*Your* class may well have done, Mr Kearney, but I know of none of our set who did so.' She paused for a moment, then went on irritably, 'I think we have heard enough about that awful affair, Marianne. It was a pathetic attempt by the rabble to destroy our way of life. Thank God the army squashed them like ants. They will never drive us out!'

Valentine spoke up. 'I wouldn't be so sure, Mama. The army prevailed in Dublin, yes, but it is not over. Support for the Volunteers and their cause has spread all over the country. There are even Volunteer units training out here in the west.'

Lord Ennis frowned. 'That's enough, Valentine. No need to upset your mother. Besides, we at Ennismore have no reason to be concerned. That sort of thing is confined to the cities.'

'Not from what I hear, Papa. A manor house like this one was set on fire in the countryside in County Cork. We are the symbol of everything the rebels despise. You and your neighbouring landlords would be well advised to be on your guard!'

Lady Ennis glared at her son. 'Nonsense, Valentine. We have no enemies on our estates. Look at how our servants have remained loyal to us – a testament to how much they respect us. Is that not so, Mr Burke?'

'Indeed, my lady,' murmured Mr Burke, his head bowed.

'This detestable event in Dublin almost turned you children against us,' continued Lady Ennis, 'but thank God you chose to leave it and come home where you belong. You will see eventually that our way of life is the right path and how fruitless it is to struggle against it.'

By now everyone had stopped eating, and even the hurried ministrations of Mr Burke and Mrs Murphy could not break the pall which hung over the gathering.

But Valentine was not finished. 'That is your opinion, Mama, and I am sure you believe every word you have said. But you were not in Dublin during the uprising and you have no idea of how things were. Victoria here did not 'choose' to come home. Instead she stayed and nursed casualties until she dropped from exhaustion. Any other mother would be proud of her, but not you. You were annoyed that she did not come running home at the first sign of danger and hide out here at Ennismore.'

Lord Edward grunted. 'Maybe she should not have come home at all. She has done nothing but bring disgrace and sow discord among us.'

Suddenly Valentine jumped up and, amid gasps around the table, physically dragged his father out of his chair so that they were standing face to face.

'Apologize to Victoria this instant, Papa,' he shouted.

Lord Ennis stared at his son in disbelief. Mr Burke and Mrs Murphy froze where they stood while Lady Marianne and Mr Kearney looked up in awe. Lady Ennis turned to Lady Louisa in alarm, gripping her wrist. Lady Louisa gave her sister a look of disgust and wrenched her arm free. Sofia got up and tried to pull Valentine back to his chair, but he had not finished.

'I said apologize. How dare you say such a thing to your own daughter?' Valentine's fury grew as he pushed his face closer to his father's. 'You are nothing but a hypocrite. Victoria has told me all about you bringing your own illegitimate daughter into this house.'

Lord Ennis attempted to recover himself. 'That will be quite enough, Valentine!'

'No, Papa, it's not enough. Do you want to know why I am back? I have been dishonourably discharged. Yes, Papa, the army charged me with cowardice.' Valentine laughed scornfully. 'You always said I was a coward and a failure, didn't you? Well, I will tell you now this was not cowardice. I refused to kill my countrymen. I found the courage of my convictions, and I refuse to allow you to brand me as a weak imitation of my brother Thomas any longer!'

Lord Ennis lunged forward and took a swipe at Valentine, but his son was quicker, blocking his father's punch. He swung his fist, catching his father on the jaw, sending him stumbling, gripping his chair lest he fall to the floor. Valentine stood glaring at him, his breathing ragged, then turned and marched out of the room, banging the door behind him as his family looked on in astonishment.

No one moved for several minutes. Even the servants stood motionless, uncertain what to do. Eventually, Lord Ennis let go of the back of the chair and slumped onto its seat, rubbing his jaw. Sofia let out a cry, reached for Victoria's arm, and together they rushed towards the front door, calling out Valentine's name. The servants took their cue and, after quickly clearing the remaining dishes, scurried down to the sanctity of the kitchen. Lady Marianne rose and poured a brandy for Lord Ennis, who gulped it down.

'Come, dear Mr Kearney,' she said as she poured brandies for herself and her companion, 'time to retire, although I doubt if I shall sleep after such excitement.'

'Yes, this was all most unnerving.' Mr Kearney sighed.

Lady Louisa, shaking her head in disgust, rose and followed the pair up the stairs, leaving Lord and Lady Ennis regarding each other sullenly across the table.

Late that night, Lady Ennis lay in bed contemplating the events of the evening. She had hoped the emphasis would be on Edward's humiliation at Valentine's dishonourable discharge, but things had not turned out quite as she had anticipated. She had scarcely expected her husband and son to come to blows in front of the servants. And it provoked her that her sister-in-law and that horrid companion of hers were so obviously entertained. Still, Edward had received his comeuppance and that was all she could have wished for.

CHAPTER 39

Rosie sat lost in thought while young Kate held the attention of her family with her antics. They were all crowded into the kitchen. Her three brothers, all grown tall and broad-shouldered, laughed and joked with one another, enjoying a rare night at home together, while her parents, grown small and shrivelled by contrast, sat together on the old settle bed. The turf fire burned brightly in the hearth, warming them against the night-time chill.

It was a tranquil, familiar and safe place and yet Rosie felt somehow apart from it. Much as she wanted to slide back into her old life she knew she never again would. Too much had happened since she had last felt comfortable here. She had told her parents all about Cathal and, while she sensed they disapproved of her living with a man not her husband, they had passed no judgement. Still, she knew they now viewed her differently than before and, as she thought back over the years, she realized that her sense of displacement had begun long before she had left for Dublin. It had begun the first day she went up to the Big House to attend school with Victoria.

A loud pounding on the cottage door interrupted her thoughts. Ma went to answer it. Rosie paid little attention. Neighbours and friends often dropped in of an evening to share news and a cup of tea, or something stronger. Suddenly Ma came up behind her and shook her on the shoulder.

'You're wanted at the door, love.'

'Who is it?'

'Go and see,' said Ma.

Rosie got up and went to the open door. No one stood there, so she stepped outside and looked around. A bright, full moon and the shaft of light from the open cottage door lit up the front yard, but still she could not see the visitor. She walked on farther. 'Who is it?' she called.

And then she saw him. He stood with his back to her but she would have known him anywhere. Her heart jumped and then fell as a tide of emotions passed over her – surprise, elation, fear. She wanted to turn and run back into the safety of the cottage, but by then Ma had closed the door behind her. Slowly she composed herself, inhaling deeply and calming her trembling hands.

'Valentine?' she said, her voice steady. 'Valentine, is that you?'

He turned around. His head was bowed and she could not see his face, but she could tell by his ragged breaths that something was wrong. She stood, waiting for him to speak.

'Yes, Rosie, it's me. Will you walk with me please? There are things I need to tell you.'

She remembered the last time he had asked her to walk with him, but back then it had been a command, not a plea as it was now. It was New Year's Eve, a lifetime ago, when he had found her crouched against the wall of the Big House and escorted her to the garden where they embraced and pledged their love. Without understanding how she knew, she was certain their walk tonight would not end as sweetly. She stiffened, preparing herself for whatever was to come.

They fell into step side by side in silence. She stumbled once or twice over rough stones but shrugged off his arm when he tried to steady her. She needed to keep her distance because being here in this place with him brought back old memories and old hurts and they made her wary. When they reached the farm gate, Valentine stopped and leaned against it. The moon shone brightly on his face and what she saw there alarmed her. In his eyes anger warred with desperation. What on earth could be wrong with him?

'I have been dishonourably discharged from the army,' he said at last.

His stare challenged her to react. Rosie winced but she knew better than to launch into a tirade of questions. Instead, she waited. When he realized she was not about to immediately condemn him, he continued with his story. It was only when he came to the part about Cathal's shooting that she broke her silence. A wave of anger overtook her.

'If you're saying that you tried to save Cathal's life to please me, and that it's my fault you're in this predicament, well save your breath.'

Valentine shook his head vehemently. 'No!' he cried. 'You have it wrong. That's not what I'm saying at all. How could you even think such a thing?'

Tears filled his eyes and he reminded her of a young boy pleading his case after being wrongly accused. 'I would have done the same for anyone,' he said, 'it just happened that it was Cathal.' He paused and went on, as if speaking to himself. 'But I'm glad it *was* him. The fact that he didn't die there – it gave you the chance to say goodbye to one another. I'm truly glad for that, Rosie.'

Without warning she began to weep and Valentine pulled her to him and held her close. They stood together for a time until he began to walk, his arm still around her. This time she did not pull away.

'What did your family say?' she asked.

He shrugged. 'Papa and I came to blows,' he said, his tone bitter. 'He made an inexcusable remark about Victoria and everything I'd been holding in just exploded. He was such a hypocrite, particularly in light of the Immelda business.' He paused. 'You heard about that, didn't you?'

Rosie nodded. Victoria had shared the story with her.

Valentine continued. 'I lost control completely. I struck him. After that, telling him of my discharge seemed almost anticlimactic. I'm not proud of my behaviour. No son should ever lift his hand to his father, no matter what the provocation.'

He stopped and turned to face Rosie. 'Everyone stared at me, and all I could think was that I had to get out of there and find you. I can't truly explain it but I knew that you were the only person in this world who could help me make sense of things. I ran all the way here.'

Rosie squeezed his hand. In a strange way she knew exactly what he meant. She wanted to tell him she felt the same, but held back the words. They began to walk again, moving past the main gate of the Ennis Estate and down the road that ran along the estate's perimeter. Valentine was quiet for a time, then suddenly something inside him seemed to come loose and a torrent of words poured out.

'I wanted to tell you again that I love you, Rosie. I'm afraid that I might not be able to stay at Ennismore and I might never see you again.' He pulled an envelope out of his pocket. 'And I wanted to give you this letter. I wrote it after we parted in Dublin and I thought I was going to France. I wanted to make sure you really understood why I had to do what I did.'

Rosie thrust the envelope back into his hands. Her voice was weary as she spoke. 'We've been through all this before. That letter will not tell me anything I did not already know. The truth is that your duty to Sofia and your family was more important than your love for me. You married Sofia and I stayed in Dublin and fell in love with Cathal. There is nothing more to say.'

Valentine seized her and pulled her close. 'But it doesn't have to end here for us, Rosie. I've finally made up my mind to ask Sofia for a divorce. After all, neither of us is happy tied together like this. This way, she can have a new life too – and a chance at love.'

How sweet these words would have been to Rosie's ears had he uttered them in the past – at the Metropole Ball in Dublin, or when he came to Foley Court and waited for her on the doorstep. But too much had happened since then. She had fallen in love with Cathal. And even though Cathal was gone, she would still honour his memory.

'No!' she said. 'No, it would not be right to build a life based on the destruction of someone else's. You owe it to Sofia and Julian to stay here at Ennismore and honour your marriage vows.' She paused, choking slightly on her words. 'And besides, I gave my heart to Cathal.'

'But...' Valentine whispered, 'Cathal is gone, Rosie. You still have a life to live.'

Rosie put her fingers on his lips. 'I loved you once, Valentine, and I believe that you love me now, but we must leave it there.'

'I'm sorry I ruined your life, Rosie.'

Rosie smiled. 'You didn't ruin my life, Valentine, in a way you saved it. I was hurt, of course, and I ran away. But without my time in Dublin I would never have met and loved Cathal, nor found my talent as a writer, nor grown from a naive young girl into a clear-minded, practical woman. It has all been for the best.'

They clung to each other and kissed – a tender, sad, loving and passionate kiss – and bid each other goodbye.

As she made her way home, the moon slid behind a bank of clouds, and darkness enveloped her. At first she wept for herself and for Cathal and the love they had shared. She wept too for Valentine and the dream that had almost been theirs. As she walked she fancied she saw Cathal's face in the dark and she remembered his last words to her: 'Don't let anger and stubbornness harden your heart. Open it up to love again – 'tis all that matters in this life.'

CHAPTER 40

The leaves on the trees around Ennismore made little effort at any display of autumn colour that year and by winter only bare, lifeless branches remained. Even the intermittent daylight was gloomy and drab. Day after day, Victoria watched the leaden clouds gather outside her bedroom window and wondered if the sun would ever shine again. It was as if nature were reflecting the sense of foreboding that engulfed Ennismore.

She took as many meals in her room as she could, but occasionally boredom forced her downstairs to dine with her family. Each time she entered the dining room she felt she might crumple under the weight of the tension that hung there. Even the servants crept silently about as they served meals, carefully holding each plate as if it might crack and splinter into pieces at any moment.

Lord Ennis left Ennismore immediately after the confrontation with Valentine and, on the rare occasions he returned, he and his wife barely acknowledged, much less spoke, to one another. Sofia and Valentine ate together every day in silence. Had it not been for Lady Louisa, who had finally brought Reverend Watson to heel, constantly gushing about her upcoming nuptials, Victoria would not have been able to bear being there. As it was she clung with gratitude to the lifeline of Lady Louisa's news of wedding plans and rectory refurbishments, encouraging more details on even the most insignificant of matters.

Such malaise was not confined to the inhabitants of Ennismore and its surrounds. A sense of foreboding engulfed all of Ireland. Far from being quashed by the British victory of Easter week, as Lady Ennis had so confidently declared, the Irish Volunteer Movement was growing in numbers and was no longer confined to Dublin.

'There's more boys joining every day,' said Anthony Walshe. 'Sure didn't I myself see them drilling out in the open in the middle of Castlebar a week ago.'

Mrs O'Leary grunted. 'Dreamers, just like the boyos in Dublin. Don't they realize what they're up against? Didn't they learn anything from so many young lads dying?'

Anthony shook his head. 'Those fellers in Dublin might have failed but when the English made martyrs of them they woke a sleeping giant. 'Tis only a matter of time till they try again. There'll be new leaders coming up to take their place.'

'At the minute they're just a crowd of eejits playing soldier,' said Sadie Canavan as she came into the kitchen. 'They've no discipline at all. I hear some of them are running around down in Cork burning down manor houses like this one and chasing everybody out in their night clothes.'

'Sure that's just oul' rumours Sadie,' said Mrs O'Leary, 'they'd never dare do such a thing.'

'Sure didn't I hear it from Lady Louisa with my own ears?'

Thelma looked up from stirring a pot of soup.

439

'They wouldn't come *here*, would they, Anthony?'

Anthony looked at Thelma's worried face. 'Who's to say what they'll do, Thelma? Stranger things have happened.'

'Arrah now, Anthony, don't be frightening the girl,' said Mrs O'Leary.

Sadie Canavan got up and flounced out of the kitchen. 'Well if they come, it won't bother me at all,' she called over her shoulder. 'I won't be here. I'll be living beyond in Castlebar with herself and the vicar. I'd say we'd be safe there. 'Tis the landlords they're after. 'Tis about time they paid for the sins of the famine.'

'You sound like Immelda,' said Mrs O'Leary. She paused. 'Now that I mention her, has anyone seen the girl?'

Sadie and Thelma shrugged. Mrs O'Leary looked at Anthony who had begun to speak but stopped.

'Anthony?'

Anthony fussed with his pipe. 'I heard tell she had a job on the late shift at Biddy Gillespie's tea room. I saw her through the window one night serving a crowd of young fellers just in from the pub. I have to say she looked as sour as ever.'

'That filthy oul' place? Tea room, me arse! You'd never catch me drinking tea in the likes of it,' said Mrs O'Leary.

'Beggars can't be choosers, Mrs O.'

'I suppose so. Did you go near her?'

'I did not!'

Mrs O'Leary shook her head. 'She was always a strange one, God help her. I hope she's found some peace.'

The family made no plans for a Christmas celebration that year, nor for a visit to Westport House,
as had been their habit in the past. On Christmas
Eve they dined together in near silence. Only
young Julian was effusive, excited by the prospect
of Christmas morning when he would open the
gaily wrapped presents that waited for him under
the tree in the library. Had it not been for Julian,
Victoria thought, there might have been no
acknowledgement of Christmas at all.

She was relieved when dinner was over. Her
mother and aunt retired to their rooms and Sofia
and Valentine guided a reluctant Julian up to the
nursery.

Her father went alone to the library as he did
every night when he was at home. She was about
to climb the stairs to her own room when she
hesitated. She turned back, walked to the library
door and lingered there. She pictured her father
sitting alone in the big room sipping his brandy
and staring into the fire. Her heart ached as she
thought of other happy Christmas Eves when the
whole family would gather in there around the
Christmas tree, dear Thomas playing carols on
the piano, and everyone singing merrily.

She leaned against the library door and let her
tears flow freely. True, she missed her family as
they had been in happier times, but what she
missed most, she realized, was her Papa's affec-
tion. For as long as she could remember she had
always claimed a special place in his heart. She
smiled as she recalled the time she begged him to

let Rosie be her friend – how kind his eyes had been as he smiled down at her, how filled with love. That love was still in his eyes when he left her in Dublin to work for Doctor Cullen, and again when he embraced her at the Fairyhouse Racecourse on Easter Monday. Now when he looked at her, if he did so at all, it was from the hollowed-out void that love had left behind.

Before she could stop herself, she tapped on the door and opened it. At first her father did not seem to hear her. He sat, as she had imagined him, in his old leather armchair staring into the glowing fire.

She crept towards him and stood at his side.

'Papa?' she whispered. 'May I join you?'

He started, as if coming out of a trance, and turned to look at her. A smile creased his face as if he had momentarily forgotten his anger, but it quickly hardened into a stern mask. He looked away from her and back at the fire.

'As you wish,' he said.

She reached for a taper from the mantel shelf, thrust it into the flames, and walked over to the Christmas tree in the corner where she re-lit one of the candles that had gone out. She stood back smiling, admiring the glittering silver ornaments, inhaling the fresh, evergreen smell of Christmas and the smoky tang of the burning candles.

'I always loved this time of year,' she said.

Her father made no answer.

She turned back and sat down in a chair opposite him. She had not dared to look directly at him in some time, and now when she did she was shocked by how frail he had become. His shirt, the buttons of which used to strain against his chest, hung loosely on him, his usually ruddy face had a grey pallor even in the firelight, and his once thick hair had grown sparse. She leaned forward, her hands clasped together.

'Please, Papa, can we put all this behind us? Can we go back to the way things were?'

'You brought it all on yourself, Victoria.' Lord Ennis's voice was cold. 'You have brought shame on this household, for which you have refused to show any remorse. In fact, you have been blatant in your refusal to admit any wrongdoing.'

The hairs stood up on the back of Victoria's neck. She clenched her fists in an effort to control her anger. 'That's because I don't believe I have done anything wrong, Papa,' she said as calmly as she could manage. 'I love Brendan, and he loves me. After our baby is born I intend to bring the child to visit his father in prison, and eventually Brendan and I will be married. Our child will grow up with a mother and father who love him. What can possibly be wrong with that?'

Lord Ennis sat up in his chair. 'For God's sake, Victoria, you know what's wrong with it. You are going against all you have been brought up to believe.'

Victoria felt her temper rising in spite of herself. 'You mean I am going against all the rules you and society have set down for me? In that case I plead guilty. But would you rather I had married someone "suitable" who did not love me nor I him, and lived together in an indifferent tolerance of one another like you and Mama?'

She could have bitten her tongue when those

443

last words slipped out. They had been unfair. She began to apologize, but her father was already on the edge of his chair, his cheeks florid with anger.

'How dare you? If you were my son I would strike you.'

Victoria's urge to apologize vanished. The last thing she had intended was to fight with her father, but now it was too late. 'You know it's true, Papa. Oh, maybe in the beginning you loved each other, but I saw little evidence of it when I was growing up. Perhaps Mama turned against you when you began your trysts with house servants the likes of Immelda's mother. How many others were there, Papa that I don't know of?'

Her father appeared to struggle for words. 'You are making me out to be a scoundrel. I can assure you I was not as profligate as many of my acquaintances...'

Victoria laughed scornfully. 'Not as profligate? That's a good one, Papa. In other words you were following the rules of your society. Men were expected to cheat on their wives. No wrongdoing there!' She paused for a moment. 'Tell me, Papa,' she continued in a calmer voice, 'if Brendan had been a member of our society, an officer in the army perhaps, or the son of another landowner, would you have shut me out in the way you are doing now?'

'That's beside the point, Victoria!'

'No, Papa, it's exactly the point. I am accused of wrongdoing because I dared to fall in love with a man who is not of our class.'

Lord Ennis leaned back in his chair, sighing as if all his energy had been spent. 'What is it you

444

want from me, Victoria?'

Victoria, her anger exhausted, came forward and, kneeling down awkwardly in front of her father, took his hands in hers. 'I want you to be happy for me. I want you to welcome your new grandchild. Papa, don't you see that your old society, your old way of life, is dying? If you insist on standing in the way of such changes you will continue to be disappointed.'

Lord Ennis shook his head wearily. 'You may be right, child. But I am an old man. I don't have the strength to change. I will leave that to you and Valentine.' He gave her a weak smile. 'I just don't understand any of the things that are happening anymore. Maybe you children will protect me from the worst of it.'

Victoria laid her head in his lap. 'Papa, don't you know that we love you?' she whispered. 'We will not let you come to any harm.'

As Victoria knelt she sensed her father's hand hovering over her head. Was he going to stroke her hair as he had done when she was a child? She held her breath and prayed that he would. And then it came, the lovely soft touch that she remembered.

'You have disappointed me, child,' he murmured, 'but I have never stopped loving you.'

Tears pricked the edges of her eyes. 'I know, Papa,' she whispered.

They remained there for some time, neither one moving, while the candles on the Christmas tree flickered in the firelight.

On New Year's Eve, 1916, Victoria took a deep

breath and pushed through the door of Biddy Gillespie's tearoom, Rosie close behind her. It was late evening, but the rickety, wooden tables and chairs which lined the stained floor were empty. The place would not fill up until the pubs closed and the men of the village came in for tea and bread and plates of greasy chips before shuffling off home.

Victoria looked around uneasily. On a wall shelf, in a nod to the season, sprigs of holly adorned two white ceramic cats with orange faces and bright eyes glinting in the lamplight. The cats were flanked by dusty bric-a-brac and faded photographs. A real cat, its white fur tinged grey with dirt, sidled up to her ankle and she jumped back with a shudder.

'Welcome, ladies.'

A dark, heavy-set woman with rouged cheeks and watchful, owl-like eyes, approached and gave them an appraising look. Victoria had seen women like her in Dublin – proprietresses who measured strangers at a glance, judging them as to the potential value of their custom. A cold shiver ran down her back. The woman led them to a table which she dusted off with the hem of her apron.

'What can I be getting ye?'

'Two teas, please. And I would like to speak to Miss Fox. Is she here?'

Biddy Gillespie's eyes narrowed. 'She's here all right, but she's busy in the kitchen. Can I give her a message?'

Victoria shook her head. 'No, I must speak to her in person.'

Biddy leaned in close to her. 'Five minutes

446

only. I don't pay her for doing nothing.'

Victoria did not answer, concentrating instead on quelling the bile rising in her throat from the smells of sour milk and grease mixed with Biddy Gillespie's cheap perfume. The sounds of a whistling tea kettle and the rough sawing of a knife through bread came from the kitchen. Victoria hoped they would drown out the loud drum of her heartbeat. She smiled weakly at Rosie, then bowed her head and waited.

She had been planning the outing for days. Since Christmas, when she had sought out her father and made peace with him, she was haunted by the fact that her half-sister was out somewhere on the cold streets with no family to protect her. She tried to put the thought out of her head but her heart refused to let her. Eventually, she found out from Anthony where Immelda was working, then approached her father who agreed to sign a letter of reference. He handed the letter back to her along with some banknotes.

'Look out for her, Victoria,' he said, 'make sure she gets settled.'

Victoria started as two tea mugs were slammed roughly down on the table. She looked up. Immelda Fox glowered down at her.

'What is it you're wanting? Have ye not finished with me yet?' Immelda's tone was surly and her eyes filled with suspicion.

Victoria had expected a hostile reaction but still the words hurt her. She took a deep breath. 'Please sit down, Immelda. I want to talk to you.'

Immelda glanced over her shoulder where Biddy Gillespie stood watching. 'I'll stand. I don't have all night.'

Victoria gathered herself and began to speak. 'Papa has admitted your story is true, Immelda, and he asks your forgiveness. He is not a well man and–'

Immelda shrugged. 'What's that to me?'

Victoria reached tentatively for her hand, but she pulled it away. 'I want you to know that I accept you as my sister...' She broke off. The words were not coming out right at all.

'*Accept* me, is it?' Immelda gave an ugly laugh. 'So you're going to take me back to Ennismore and treat me like one of the family? You're going to have the servants wait on me and you'll introduce me to your friends as Lady Immelda Bell?' She looked off in the distance as if addressing a stranger. 'Sure I can see it now – ah, this is me sister Immelda, she's me da's bastard, but we're taking her in just the same.' She looked back at Victoria. 'You expect me to believe that shite?'

Then she turned to Rosie. 'You know I'm right, don't you? Look how they treated you. We're not that different.'

Rosie blushed but said nothing. Victoria jumped in quickly, desperate to make Immelda understand. 'You know what you suggest is not possible. But I do want to help you.' She reached into her reticule and produced an envelope which she held out to Immelda, her hand trembling. 'This is a letter of reference signed by Papa. You should be able to get work at a respectable house. And ... and there's some money in there too. It's not charity,' she added quickly, 'it's your last three months' wages plus the Christmas bonus you'd have earned if Papa had not sent you away.'

Immelda stared down at the envelope but made no move.

'Take it, Immelda,' said Rosie. 'Don't let your pride stand in the way.'

Immelda looked from one to the other then snatched the envelope from Victoria's hand and thrust it into her pocket. No one spoke. The three women studied one another in silence. The spell was interrupted only when Biddy Gillespie appeared at their table and cleared her throat loudly.

'Everything all right, ladies? I need Immelda back in the kitchen if you have finished with her. There'll be a rush of customers soon,' she went on, looking at the clock, ''tis near closing time at the pubs.'

She returned to the kitchen and Victoria and Rosie stood up, but Immelda did not move. She appeared to be turning something over in her mind. When she finally spoke, all anger had left her voice.

'You'd better be getting back to Ennismore. There's some local boyos planning to burn it down tonight.'

Immelda's tone was so soft that Victoria did not think she had heard her properly. She was about to ask her to repeat herself when Rosie spoke.

'How do you know?'

'T'was meself sent them.'

Rosie eyed her with suspicion. 'And why would they listen to *you?*'

Immelda rolled her eyes. 'Sure they weren't that hard to convince. They'd heard of some boyos in Cork burning down landlords' houses, and they wanted to do the same around these parts. So I told them they may as well go to Ennismore. All it took was a few stories about how I'd been turned out on the street over a lie, and how they'd sacked Brendan after the daughter of the family seduced him.' She paused and looked accusingly at Victoria. 'And besides, there's plenty around here resents the Bell family for all their wealth when themselves have hardly a shilling between them.'

Rosie grabbed Immelda by the shoulders and shook her. 'Can't you stop them?' she cried. 'For God's sake, Immelda!'

Immelda smiled, her eyes bright as a zealot's. 'If you'd come after me sooner I would have stopped them, but you came too late. 'Tis in God's hands now,' she said, crossing herself.

Victoria found her voice. 'We have to warn them, Rosie,' she cried. 'Oh, God, we have to go. Maybe we can still get there in time.'

She rushed to the door, pushing past a group of men in cloth caps who had just arrived, ignoring their drunken calls of 'Hold your horses, darlin'.' Rosie ran out after her.

Immelda watched them go, not moving from where she stood until Biddy Gillespie came up beside her and stood, hands on hips.

'Bejaysus,' she cried, 'they've left without paying. Feckin' gentry.' She turned to Immelda. 'This is coming out of your wages, my girl. Now get back to work.'

Outside, Rosie caught up with Victoria. 'We have to wait for Anthony to bring the pony and cart back,' she said. 'You can't go all that way on foot in your condition.'

But Victoria wrenched free and ran on down the dark road. She ran until she choked on her breath, gasping for air. She clutched her belly as her knees began to buckle beneath her. Rosie caught her as she fell and eased her down onto a large stone at the side of the road.

'Stay here,' she said, taking off her coat and putting it around her friend's shoulders. 'I'll go ahead and send Anthony back for you.'

When Victoria began to protest, Rosie's tone was sharp. 'You're to stay here, I said, unless you want to risk losing your child.'

Victoria bowed her head and nodded.

As Rosie raced towards Ennismore, the urgency of Immelda's words began to sink in. At first she tried to dismiss the threat as fantasy, the rantings of a crazy woman, but something told her they were more than that. Immelda might be mad, she thought, but she was also vengeful. Now she saw that in an unexpected way the Dublin fight had come home. She had been reluctant to take sides in Dublin, but now she had no hesitation – she must save Ennismore. Rosie had finally realized that, for good or ill, the years spent there had shaped her life. Ennismore was as much her home as was the Killeen cottage. She would not see it destroyed.

When she arrived at the estate gates all looked normal except that the gates were swinging wide open. She paused and bent over to catch her breath which came in short, painful stabs. Straightening up, she walked on through, thanking God that a bright moon lit her way. There was no sign of smoke or fire as she came in sight of the house. Lights flickered from the upstairs windows and the library, otherwise everything was still. As she moved to the side of the house she heard strains of music coming from the servants' quarters where their New Year's Eve party was in progress. Normally, she would have smiled, picturing the gaiety within, but her gut told her something was not right.

As she neared the archway that led around the side of the house to the kitchen and stables she heard another sound. She stopped and listened. It sounded like a car engine idling. She crept forward. She was right – a car, its headlamps out, sat facing her. Holding her breath, she moved closer. A young man sat behind the wheel, a rifle on the seat beside him. He appeared to be asleep. Silently and swiftly she leaned in, snatched the rifle and trained it on him.

'Where are they?' she demanded.

He awoke, blinking and confused. She recognized him as one of her youngest brother's friends, a boy named Paddy. It was obvious he had been drinking. He put up his hands. 'They're up beyond at the back of the house, Rosie ... Miss Killeen. Please, I've done nothing wrong...'

'Except steal this feckin' car!'

'No – no, 'tis belonging to Tommy Boylan's da's boss. T'was Tommy himself took it. I-I'm just keeping it running for them.'

'Well stop idling and drive away now if you know what's good for you.'

'But, what about me pals?'

'I'll take care of them. Go now while you still have the chance, or so help me...'

She cocked the rifle, confident of the feel of it in her hands. The boy's eyes widened and he gunned the engine and sped off, swerving erratically towards the estate gates. As the car left, the music from the servants' party swelled. She crept around to the back of the house, crouching close to the wall. She could see them clearly in the moonlight. Four young men were raking their fingers through the soil in an urn which stood beside the back door. Then one of them held a key aloft.

'I have it now,' he laughed. 'For a minute I thought Immelda was having us on.'

As Rosie watched from the shadows a flame of anger erupted inside her. Images of Cathal and Brendan flashed before her, along with the young Volunteers on the Moore Street rooftop who died fighting the British Army. These young men at the back door, whom she recognized from the village, were nothing but hooligans and chancers, good-for-nothings out for sport, jumped up Wren boys egged on by Immelda. She could hardly contain her contempt.

By now the first man had opened the back door and begun splashing paraffin into the hallway. A second man took out a box of matches. Rosie straightened up and stepped out into the moonlight, her rifle cocked and trained on him. In that moment all pretext of ladylike behaviour was gone. She was Roisin Dubh, Irish warrior, defending herself and her land.

'Light that match, John Joe O'Hanlon,' she roared, 'and I'll blow your fecking head off.'

453

The man turned around, stunned, while the first man dropped the paraffin can and made to run.

'You're going nowhere!' she said. 'Your boy Paddy is away without you.'

'For fuck's sake,' he muttered.

'I know all your names,' said Rosie. 'Mother of God, was being Wren boys too tame for you? You think youse are heroes burning down other people's property and maybe them with it? You're a disgrace to every man and woman who fought in the uprising.'

'But Immelda said we'd be greeted as heroes...'

'Immelda! You let a fecking mad woman talk you into doing this? Youse are bigger fools than I thought.'

Meanwhile, Anthony Walshe, who had emerged to go and fetch Rosie and Victoria back from the tea room, heard the disturbance and came to investigate. A sudden noise behind her made Rosie swing around. Anthony was running towards them, brandishing a shovel over his head. 'Get away from here now, ye *amadans*, before I smash your heads in!'

By the time Rosie turned back, John Joe O'Hanlon had lit the match and thrown it into the paraffin-spattered hallway and taken off running with the others around the far side of the house. Rosie swore under her breath. She fired in the air after them, but they had already disappeared.

'Never mind them, Rosie,' cried Anthony. 'We know rightly who they are. Go and wake the house. I'll go for the others. We'll bring water.'

Anthony slammed the back door shut to

prevent the air from feeding the fire and ran towards the kitchen. Rosie dropped the rifle to her side and raced around to the front door. It opened as she was about to pound on it and Valentine and Lord Ennis appeared.

'We heard rifle fire, what is–' Valentine began.

But Rosie interrupted him. 'There's a fire!' she shouted. 'Get everybody out! Anthony's gone for help.'

Valentine turned and bounded past his dazed father and up the front staircase two at a time. As he did so, smoke began billowing from the back hallway. One by one the bewildered family emerged and made their way, coughing and spluttering, outside onto the front lawn, Lord Ennis behind them. By now smoke was curling through the entrance foyer and up the front staircase, and creeping under the doors of the library, dining and drawing rooms. Rosie stood mesmerized as she watched bursts of flame beginning to lick the old wall hangings, carpet and wood panelling in the back hallway. Suddenly she came to her senses and rushed into the smoke-filled library where she ripped down a pair of heavy curtains. She ran to the back hallway and threw them down, stamping on them in an attempt to smother the flames. Suddenly Valentine was alongside her, pulling down tapestries, grabbing what he could to help staunch the fire.

Rosie swore under her breath as the flames kept reigniting. Without thinking she began to beat at them with her bare hands, oblivious to the pain. Suddenly she let out a cry as she watched the remaining flames gather and, as if in slow motion,

455

merge together into a funnel of fire which rolled towards them down the narrow hallway. She stood rooted, unable to make her legs move, until Valentine seized her by the arm and pulled her with him into the foyer and out the front door.

At that moment Anthony appeared with the servants and grooms, all carrying water buckets. Rosie and Valentine joined in as they attacked the fire from both the back and the front hallways, feverishly passing buckets of water along a line. They doused the flames over and over with water. As the fire died, thick smoke filled the first floor rooms, depositing a black film over everything in its path.

At last the fire was out and Rosie finally stumbled out through the front door and into the moonlight. When she saw Victoria standing in front of her, looking dazed, her hand flew to her mouth. In all the commotion she had forgotten to send someone to fetch her from the side of the road. She must have made her way back on her own. She ran to where her friend stood and put her arms around her. 'It's all right, everybody's safe.'

As she let go of Victoria, she turned to see Valentine gazing at her, smiling through tears. He came towards her, his arms outstretched. Rosie noticed that his hands were blackened from the fire. When she looked down at her own she realized they were burned as well.

'My dear brave girl,' he whispered, 'my brave Roisin Dove. Thank you for saving us.'

'On my oath she did that all right,' put in Anthony, who had come up beside them. 'If it wasn't for this girleen threatening them boyos they'd have emptied the whole canister of paraffin into the hall and there'd have been no putting the fire out at all. She's as brave a warrior as any in Ireland!'

Rosie blushed and sank into Valentine's outstretched arms. There was no need for more words. She realized then that her love for Valentine had never left her. As she held him she saw Sofia approaching, but she did not let him go. Sofia stopped short of them and Rosie and she exchanged a long look before she turned away and disappeared into the shadows.

Lord Ennis's funeral took place on a freezing morning in mid-January, 1917. Fresh snow coated the ancient stones in the small, family graveyard, blurring their hard edges and rendering the scene at once beautiful and macabre. Victoria wept as the Reverend Watson threw the last shovel of dirt upon her father's coffin. The stress of the fire had brought on a heart attack from which he was unable to recover. She was thankful she'd had the chance to make peace with him and tell him she loved him. She was glad, too, that Valentine had been able to spend the final days at his father's bedside.

Her mother and Aunt Louisa clung to each other as they threaded their way out of the cemetery gate and down towards the house. Victoria pitied them as she watched them go. She wished they could have shown the understanding that her father had shown in his last days, but she knew such a thing was beyond them. She understood their desperate need to hold on tight to what vestiges of their old lives and values remained to them.

She looked around at the rest of the mourners gathered like black crows on the snow-covered hilltop. Lady Marianne remained, along with her escort Mr Kearney, despite the cold rebuff they had received from Lady Ennis and Lady Louisa. Valentine and Sofia stood close together, Sofia dry-eyed while Valentine wept quietly. Mr Burke and Mrs Murphy stood arm in arm, the rest of the staff clustered around them. Victoria wondered what was going through their minds. She knew they had respected her father and would feel his loss deeply, but suspected they felt even more deeply the uncertainty which they now faced.

She caught Rosie's eye and they nodded to one another. Rosie stood with her family and a number of tenant farmers and neighbours, many of whom Victoria had never met. They had paraded one by one past the graveside to pay their respects to the family and remark on what a fine gentleman her father was. They too, she thought, were facing an uncertain future. It was as if all of Ireland were restless.

Victoria cradled her belly. The child was restless too, thrashing about in recent weeks as if impatient to join the world. He represented the future, not the past. She thought about her beloved Brendan in the far-off Welsh prison. She could not wait to visit him and introduce his son to him. She smiled. She knew it would be a boy. She never questioned it. She had already decided on his name – Thomas Pearse – Thomas, after her dear brother, and Pearse, after Padraig Pearse, leader of the Volunteers, whom Brendan had so admired.

From this distance Ennismore, sheathed in winter white, appeared unblemished. Victoria tried to fix the image in her mind. She wanted to remember the great house this way – as beautiful and magical as it had seemed to her in childhood. She realized then that, like so many others that day, she too was mourning not only the death of her father, but a way of life that would be no more.

Thanks to Rosie, Ennismore still stood, its structure preserved. The ground floor, including the library and dining room, had suffered heavy smoke and water damage, but the rest of the house was relatively unscathed. As Anthony had said, had Rosie not raced there to sound the warning, and interrupted the arsonists at their work, Immelda's revenge might have destroyed the entire house.

Mrs O'Leary took the opportunity to retire, leaving a hapless Thelma to cook the meals, which family members were now obliged to take in the kitchen instead of the smoke-singed dining room. Perhaps it was this final indignity, Victoria thought, that caused Lady Ennis to announce her plans to leave Ennismore for good and repair to her father's estate in England.

'If I never hear another Irish accent again,' she said, 'it will be too soon. Oliver Cromwell spoke the truth – living in Mayo is like living in hell. I will not spend every day terrified that more peasants will come and try to burn me out. I will not give them the satisfaction.'

Victoria watched her mother go. She made no plea to her to stay. She knew how unhappy her mother was and, with her husband gone and her sister about to be married to the Reverend Watson, lonely, as well. She refused her mother's half-hearted offer to follow her to England after the baby was born, knowing she had made it solely out of duty and with the belief that Victoria would never agree.

One evening, soon after Lady Ennis's departure, Sofia took Valentine's arm after supper and asked him to walk with her.

'But it's freezing out,' said Valentine. 'You'll catch your death.'

'For God's sake, Valentine, I'm not made of porcelain. I survived worse weather growing up in New York. Anyway, I need to clear my head. I cannot think in this place.'

They walked together across the frost-covered lawns and down the avenue towards the main gate of the estate, Valentine holding Sofia's elbow. When they reached the gate she shook free of him and turned to face him. As if on cue the moon slid out from behind the clouds and they could see each other's faces clearly. Sofia took a deep breath.

'I have decided to take Julian back to New York.'

Valentine nodded. 'I see. After the war is over that is probably a good idea, Sofia. Things will be a mess here until we have restored the house. And it will give Julian time to get to know his other grandfather,' he paused, 'particularly since he just lost Papa.'

'You don't understand, Valentine. I mean to return immediately to America and to stay for good.'

'What? Why? You can't leave and take our son. It's far too dangerous.'

'He is *my* son, Valentine. Besides, I shall take an American ship. America is not in the war yet.'

Valentine swallowed hard. 'But we had an agreement, Sofia.'

Sofia put her hand gently on his arm. 'Yes we did, Valentine. And I want you to know I will be eternally grateful for what you did for me – and for Julian.' She put her fingers to his lips as he started to protest. 'But we did not love each other – and we never will. I know you love Julian, but it is not enough. We are each other's prisoners. It's time to free ourselves while we are still young enough to make a happy life.' She paused and looked away from him, staring up at the moon instead. 'The night after your fight with your father the person you ran to was Rosie. If I ever had doubts about the strength of the love you two shared, they began to dissolve that night. And when I saw you together the night of the fire I finally accepted that you and she belong together.'

'Sofia–' Valentine began.

But she continued before he could speak. 'I will give you a divorce, Valentine. With my father's contacts in New York I believe it will be approved quickly. But, I have some conditions.' Without waiting for an answer she went on. 'You continue to protect the truth about Julian's father, and agree that he, and not any of your own sons, shall

461

inherit Ennis Estates when the time comes.'

'If there's anything left to inherit.'

'I'm serious, Valentine. I will set up a trust in Julian's name to provide funds to help with the refurbishment of the house. The management of the estates will of course be your responsibility. I understand that given the current unrest in this country none of us can predict the future, but I would ask you to promise me you will do your best to preserve something of Thomas's legacy for my son. It is only fair.'

Valentine nodded. 'You are right, Sofia. Ennismore and the estates are rightfully his. After all, Thomas was the first-born son, and as *his* son, Julian inherits his legacy. I would never take that away from him. All I want is to live out my life here in peace.'

'With Rosie.' Sofia's tone was gentle.

He smiled. 'Aye, with Rosie – if she'll have me.'

Sofia linked her arm in his as they walked back up towards the house. 'She'll have you, Valentine, don't worry.'

CHAPTER 41

On a June morning in 1917 Rosie Killeen left the warm comfort of her family's cottage for the last time. Smiling to herself, she walked down through the green fields to the narrow road that divided the Killeen farm from the Ennis Estates. She wore a simple dress of white cotton edged

with lace and on her black hair a wreath of wildflowers. She was on her way to her wedding.

She pushed through the heavy iron gates that
led to the Estates and thought of the anxious
eight-year-old girl who had made this same
journey seventeen years earlier. Today, no ghosts
leered at her from behind the trees that lined the
twisting avenue. Today, instead of hanging her
head in fear, she raised her eyes and gazed boldly
around her, taking pleasure in everything she saw
– the verdant green of the open pasture, trees
abundant with fresh, shiny leaves, and Ennismore, newly dressed in a pink limewash, glowing
in the sunshine.

She walked closer to the house, enjoying the
tickle of damp grass between her bare toes and
the warm caress of the sun on her face. Birds
sang from the trees as if in welcome while wildfowl called from above Lough Conn and cattle
lowed from a distant pasture. She was glad she
had insisted on making this walk alone. She
wanted to savour every moment of this journey
from her past to her future. As she walked,
flashes of memory came and went – her years in
the schoolroom with Victoria, her shame as she
scrubbed the front steps for the first time, her
shock when she heard of Valentine's marriage to
Sofia. Such old memories seemed distant and
faded now, and though they would always be part
of her, paled in the face of the new memories
waiting to be born.

That previous evening she had knelt and confessed her sins to the new young curate from St
Brigid's church. She held no details back about

her relationship with Cathal. When finished she waited as if for God's judgement, but instead she received absolution. She felt Cathal at her side as she left the confessional.

Bridie's child, Kate, suddenly appeared, running down the steps of Ennismore and calling out to her. Rosie rushed towards her, picking her up in her arms and kissing her. Kate wriggled out of her arms. 'Granny says I'm not to ruin my dress,' she said.

Rosie set her down. The child wore a dress identical to her own, both made by Ma, and on her head a wreath of daisies. She had Rosie's same dark curls and hazel eyes. Another Roisin Dubh, Rosie often thought when she looked at her. Now she took the girl's hand and walked on towards the house. From the garden she could hear music. She recognized the tune as 'Haste to the Wedding', a lively traditional jig. She was tempted to slip over and spy on the garden where the ceremony was to be held, but just then Victoria appeared on the front steps. She wore a pale blue dress that reminded Rosie of the one she wore the first day they met, and on her blonde hair a wreath of cornflowers. She raced down to hug Rosie.

'She's not wearing any shoes,' said Kate, tugging at Victoria's dress and pointing to Rosie's bare feet.

Rosie quickly pulled on the pair of white slippers she carried and walked up the steps with Kate and Victoria on either side of her. Her father met her at the door. He wore a new grey suit and beamed as he offered her his arm. Rosie's heart swelled at the sight of him.

'Come on, daughter,' he said, 'your bride-groom's waiting.'

John Killeen led his daughter around the house towards the garden. They waited outside the gate as Kate entered first, carrying a basket of rose petals which she tossed vigorously on the path as she walked. Victoria followed, slender and regal, the sun glinting on her blonde hair. The musicians began to play 'Give Me Your Hand', a haunting, slow traditional air.

As the music swelled Rosie entered through the gate and walked with her father towards the stone grotto at the edge of the garden where the ceremony was to take place. She could hear the rustling and whispers of the guests who sat on chairs on either side of the path, but as she drew closer to the grotto all sound seemed to cease. There stood Valentine, the sun glinting on his blond hair. Rosie's eyes fixed on Valentine's face and his on hers. For a moment they held one another's gaze as if no one else in the world existed. Then Rosie's father withdrew and Valentine offered her his hand.

The reception was a lively affair. Anthony Walshe entertained with tunes on the accordion, accompanied by Mrs Murphy on the tin whistle, and Rosie's youngest brother on the fiddle. A wooden deck was laid down for dancing. Mrs O'Leary returned from retirement to cook the wedding lunch, assisted by Thelma. The food was served buffet-style with small tables set up throughout the gardens where guests were free to eat, drink and mingle. Rosie smiled at the thought of Lady

Ennis's scandalized reaction to such informality had she been there.

As it was, neither Lady Ennis nor Lady Louisa and her new husband attended, although Rosie was amused when she saw that despite this Sadie Canavan had somehow managed to come. Reverend Watson had declined to perform the ceremony but Lady Marianne Bellefleur produced an eminent judge to serve in his stead. The good lady and her ever-present escort, Mr Kearney, had arrived, as always, with great fanfare.

When lunch finished Mr Burke and Mrs Murphy carried an exquisite three-tiered wedding cake into the garden and set it down on a table in the centre. Mrs O'Leary beamed as she accepted the applause of the guests. The cake was her wedding gift to Rosie and Valentine. For the first time since the ceremony, Rosie let go of Valentine's hand and walked about amongst the guests. She smiled and thanked them for coming, enjoying the grip of gnarled hands on her own, the prayers and proverbs uttered for her future good fortune, and the pride in Ma's moist eyes. Young Kate took Thomas Pearse on her lap, fussing over the bright, inquisitive infant. Rosie stood for a moment watching Victoria smiling down at her son, then went up to her and took her arm.

'Would you like to go for a walk?'

Victoria nodded.

The afternoon grew chilly as they strolled together by the lake.

'Do you remember the first time we met here?' asked Rosie.

Victoria laughed. 'How could I forget it? I was

466

standing here crying over my toy boat when this strange, wild, black-haired girl appeared out of nowhere, stripped down to her petticoat and dived into the water. I was fascinated from the minute I saw you.'

'Aye. There were times since when I wished I'd just let your boat sink. Then you'd never have dragged me up to your schoolroom and your Aunt Louisa.'

'Ah, you don't mean that, Rosie. If we'd never been friends, you would never have met Valentine.'

Rosie grinned. 'I suppose it was worth it, so,' she said.

They sat down on an upturned boat on the lake shore, looking out over the water – two old friends talking easily about old times and future plans.

'Do you intend to stay in Dublin?' said Rosie.

Victoria nodded. 'I do. I've found paid work as a nurse in a fine hospital and it suits me. I still volunteer at the Union though. I like helping other people, feeling needed. And, thanks to you, I have a comfortable apartment in Cathal's house. And dear Celine looks after Thomas as if he is her own son. I don't know how I'd manage without her.'

Victoria laughed suddenly. 'Aunt Marianne wanted to keep paying Celine's wages as a christening present for Thomas Pearse, but I told her I was perfectly capable of paying Celine's wages myself.' She shook her head. 'I know she meant well, but the old attitudes die hard. She still has not absorbed the idea that I intend to be self-sufficient from now on.'

'Do you have any social life at all?'

'Of course I do. I am very active in the Gaelic

467

League. The nationalist movement is still very much alive, you know. The Easter Rising was only the beginning. I intend to do what I can to help bring about the independence that Brendan fought for.' She turned and smiled at her friend, taking both of her hands. 'And, please don't say anything, but there's a chance the British will release the prisoners of the Rising soon. Brendan might be coming home!'

Rosie almost wept at Victoria's evident joy.

They sat in silence for a while, each staring out over the still waters of the lough, lost in their own thoughts. At length Rosie stood up. 'I should be getting back. My guests will be wondering where the bride has got to – as will my new husband.'

The word 'husband' felt sweet on her lips and she smiled.

'The duties of the lady of the manor are never done, Lady Ennis,' said Victoria smiling back.

Rosie reddened. 'As far as I'm concerned, I'm just a farmer's daughter who has married a local farmer, as would be expected of me. I've already told Valentine I'm not for sitting up beyond on me arse expecting to be waited on hand and foot. I intend to get my hands dirty and work alongside him on the estate. And I can keep my own house and cook my own meals, thank you very much.' She paused for breath. 'Mr Burke and Mrs Murphy will stay on. They're to be married next month. And we'll keep Thelma. Poor creature has nowhere else to go, so she says. And Anthony will stay on to do the odd jobs. But that's all the staff we'll need.'

Victoria stood up and took Rosie's hand. They

began to walk back towards the house. 'You may still have to give some formal dinner parties, though. After all, Valentine will take Papa's place in the Lords.'

'Well, you'll just have to come down from Dublin and show me what to do.'

'Or you can always ask Aunt Marianne to come. There again, she doesn't usually wait to be asked, does she?'

They both giggled as they hurried back towards Ennismore.

Later that evening, when the guests and staff had gone – some to the Killeen cottage to continue the celebration, others back to their homes – Valentine and Rosie were at last alone in the house. Valentine lifted her up in his arms and carried her over the threshold of his bedroom, set her down and kissed her.

'I love you, Roisin Dove,' he said. 'I will love you forever.'

Sometime after midnight, Rosie awoke to the light of the moon shining through the bedroom window. She glanced at Valentine sleeping peacefully beside her and slipped out of bed. She walked to the window and stood looking out over the darkened fields towards the lough which glinted silver in the distance. As she stood, a peace she had never known before filled her. Here with Valentine at Ennismore she had finally found her place in the world. She was home.

ACKNOWLEDGEMENTS

My thanks to my US agents, Denise Marcil and Anne-Marie O'Farrell, of the Marcil-O'Farrell Literary Agency in New York. I value their support, guidance and steadfast faith in me more than I can say. Thanks also to my UK agent, Anna Carmichael, of the Abner Stein Agency in London, for her diligent efforts in placing this book with Corvus. I also want to thank Louise Cullen at Corvus, as well as Sara O'Keeffe, for their insightful editing, and all of the Corvus staff for the attention and care they have given to this book.

I would like to acknowledge Susan Kellett and her son, D.J., owners of Enniscoe House in County Mayo, Ireland, who threw open the doors of their magnificent home and answered my many questions, which aided me greatly in my research. My stay there was made even more pleasant by the staff at the County Mayo Heritage Centre and adjacent cafe, as well as by modern day raconteur, Anthony Walsh, and old childhood acquaintance, P.J. Lynn, who regaled me with colourful stories of the 'old' days.

In addition, I would like to acknowledge my Aunt Nan, who lived in the cottage across the road from the 'Big House' and where I spent many childhood summers, and her daughters, Beatrice, Nancy and Rosie, all of whom worked at the 'Big House' at one time or another. Their stories were the main inspiration for this book.

And, as always, I would like to acknowledge the love and support of my dear sister, Connie Mathers, of Meigh, County Armagh, who keeps the spirit of Ireland alive and well in me.

Lastly, in this 100th Anniversary year of the 1916 Easter Uprising, I would like to humbly acknowledge the bravery and sacrifice of the men and women who fought for Irish Freedom.

Patricia Falvey
Dallas, Texas
August 2016

The publishers hope that this book has given you enjoyable reading. Large Print Books are especially designed to be as easy to see and hold as possible. If you wish a complete list of our books please ask at your local library or write directly to:

Magna Large Print Books
Magna House, Long Preston,
Skipton, North Yorkshire.
BD23 4ND

This Large Print Book for the partially sighted, who cannot read normal print, is published under the auspices of

THE ULVERSCROFT FOUNDATION